★附隨堂評量

大考英文句型 GO

呂香瑩　編著

三民書局

國家圖書館出版品預行編目資料

大考英文句型GO／呂香瑩編著.——初版四刷.——
臺北市：三民，2022
　　　面；　公分.——(文法咕嚕Grammar Guru系列)

　　ISBN 978-957-14-6277-6　(平裝)
　　1. 英語 2. 句法

805.169　　　　　　　　　　　　　　106002356

大考英文句型 GO

編 著 者	呂香瑩
發 行 人	劉振強
出 版 者	三民書局股份有限公司
地　　址	臺北市復興北路 386 號 (復北門市) 臺北市重慶南路一段 61 號 (重南門市)
電　　話	(02)25006600
網　　址	三民網路書店 https://www.sanmin.com.tw
出版日期	初版一刷 2017 年 3 月 初版四刷 2022 年 2 月
書籍編號	S800690
I S B N	978-957-14-6277-6

http://www.sanmin.com.tw　三民網路書店

序

如果說，單字是英文的血肉，文法就是英文的骨架。想要打好英文基礎，兩者實應相輔相成，缺一不可。

只是，單字可以死背，文法卻不然。

學習文法，如果沒有良師諄諄善誘，沒有好書細細剖析，只落得個見樹不見林，徒然勞心費力，實在可惜。

Guru 原義指的是精通於某領域的「達人」，因此，這一套「文法Guru」系列叢書，本著 Guru「導師」的精神，要告訴你：親愛的，我把英文文法變簡單了！

「文法 Guru」系列，適用對象廣泛，從初習英文的超級新鮮人、被文法糾纏得寢食難安的中學生，到鎮日把玩英文的專業行家，都能在這一套系列叢書中找到最適合自己的夥伴。

深願「文法 Guru」系列，能成為你最好的學習夥伴，伴你一同輕鬆悠遊英文學習的美妙世界。

有了「文法 Guru」，文法輕鬆上路！

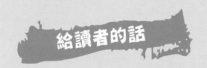

給讀者的話

　　在高中學習英文的過程中，有些人可能背了很多單字、學了不少文法卻只能寫出 S + V 或 S + V + O 的簡單句；有些人在面對段考或大考題目時，對於綜合測驗的文法題感到不知所措，對於閱讀測驗中的複雜句心生畏懼，對於翻譯與寫作題毫無下筆的頭緒。這些挫折可能都是高中英文學習路途上的絆腳石。

　　有鑑於此，本書整合大考及常見的句型與用法，收納 100 個句型，適用於普高一到三年級瞄準大考的學生，以及技高一到三年級希望加強英文學習的讀者。在編寫上有以下特點：

系統化呈現：依據各句型的意義和功能分類，共有 16 個章節，每單元均以循序漸進的方式有系統地建立概念。

豐富的例句：每單元有多則範例供參照學習，以期讀者在接收大量資訊後能高效率地轉成正確的產出。每則例句均以粗體與底線標示出架構與用法要點，讓讀者快速掌握關鍵。

詳盡的解說：每單元提供詳細說明，以螺旋方式由簡單逐漸深入到複雜概念，視句型特色以圖形呈現用法或歸納成表格，讓重點一目瞭然。

學習補給與秘訣：將較艱深或延伸的用法在學習補給站中補充，並以 tip 提供快速記憶方法，讓讀者輕鬆學習。

與大考連結：提供近十多年來曾出現於學測等大考的實例，並將部分改寫成練習題，讓高一、高二的讀者提前與大考連結，鎖定大考方向，讓高三的讀者準確切入重點，熟悉出現於大考的句型與文句，快速培養實戰能力。

充足的練習：每個單元後的練習與附贈的題本讓讀者可即時檢視所學，藉由充足的練習強化學習效果。選擇題幫助讀者釐清觀念，翻譯題讓讀者發展大考翻譯與寫作的能力，利用所學的句型寫出活潑有變化的文句。

　　語言的可貴之處在於富有變化性，可隨說話者的情緒與意願作各種表達。要將英文學得精、用得巧，除了單字、文法二項元素，還需搭配句型的輔助，才能正確理解文意，完整表達想法。讀者若能善用本書，確實閱讀與演練習題，必能將大考常用的 100 個句型融會貫通、突破閱讀複雜句的障礙、寫出生動優美的文句，並有效整合中學三年所學句型，瞄準大考方向，輕鬆迎戰。

Table of Contents

大考
英文句型 GO

略語表

略語	中英文名稱	略語	中英文名稱	略語	中英文名稱
adj.	adjective (形容詞)	adv.	adverb (副詞)	conj.	conjunction (連接詞)
etc.	et cetera (等等)	N	noun (名詞)	O	object (受詞)
S	subject (主詞)	V	verb (動詞)	V-ed	past tense (過去式)
aux.	auxiliary (助動詞)	prep.	preposition (介系詞)	sb	somebody (某人)
p.p.	past participle (過去分詞)	V-ing	gerund (動名詞); present participle (現在分詞)	OC	object complement (受詞補語)

1–1

of + N = adj.
with + N = adv.

句型範例

- The manager decided to give Andrew a pay rise, for he was a man **of diligence**.

  經理決定幫 Andrew 加薪，因為他是個勤勞的人。

- In chemistry class, the students conducted the experiment **with care**.

  在化學課，學生們小心地做實驗。

☆ The principal of this school is a man **of** exceptional **generosity**.

這所學校的校長是個非常慷慨的人。 (105 學測)

☆ If you mistreat your body by keeping bad habits, neglecting symptoms of illness, and ignoring common health rules, even the best medicine can be **of little use**. 若你因為養成壞習慣、不理會病徵並忽略一般的健康規則而不善待自己的身體，即使是最好的藥也沒多大的用處。 (95 學測)

用法詳解

1. 「of + 抽象名詞」表示「⋯的」，作用同形容詞 (請見下表)，置於修飾的名詞或 be 動詞後，形成 N + of + 抽象名詞 或 be + of + 抽象名詞的結構，並可在名詞前加 much、great、little 等字表示程度。本句型的反意表達法為 **of + no + 抽象名詞**。

of patience = patient	of passion = passionate	of intelligence = intelligent
of talent = talented	of wisdom = wise	of no use = useless
of ability = able	of responsibility = responsible	of no help = not helpful
of value = valuable	of importance = important	

- Calculators are **of great use** for solving math problems. 計算機對數學解題很有用。
- Eric is a man **of no passion**; he is not interested in anything.

  Eric 是個沒有熱情的人；他對任何事情都沒興趣。

2. 「with + 抽象名詞」表示「⋯地」，作用同副詞 (請見下表)，用於修飾動詞，可在名詞前加 much、great、little 等字表示程度。本句型的反意表達法為 **without + 抽象名詞**。

with delight = delightedly	with joy = joyfully	without care = carelessly
with ease = easily	with care = carefully	with attention = attentively
with caution = cautiously		

- Seeing their idol at the airport, these die-hard fans screamed **with delight** (= delightedly). 在機場看見他們的偶像，這些死忠的影迷開心地尖叫。
- The magic show was so amazing that all the kids watched it **with attention** (= attentively). 這場魔術表演如此精彩，以致於孩子們全都聚精會神地觀賞。

學習補給站

有些表情緒的抽象名詞會搭配 in 形成副詞，如 in fear (恐懼地)、in fright (驚嚇地)、in terror (害怕地)、in horror (驚恐地)、in anger (生氣地)、in astonishment (驚訝地)、in amazement (驚愕地)。

句型練習

一、選擇

( ) 1. A compass would be _____ much help when you go mountain climbing.
　　(A) at 　　　　　(B) with 　　　　　(C) of 　　　　　(D) about

( ) 2. The road is slippery after the rain; motorists must proceed _____ caution.
　　(A) under 　　　　(B) in 　　　　　(C) with 　　　　　(D) of

( ) 3. The club members finally elected _____ to be their president.
　　(A) an experience man 　　　　　(B) a man of experience
　　(C) a man for experience 　　　　　(D) an experiencing man

二、句子改寫 (以本單元的句型改寫下列各句底線部分)

1. The students have learned very valuable lessons from Aesop's Fables.

　_____

2. The basketball coach taught the players very patiently.

　_____

三、翻譯

1. Jeremy 是個負責的人，所以他被派到公司總部。

　Jeremy is a man _____ _____ , so he was assigned to the headquarters.

2. 每個人對於這聰明的男孩輕易地解開謎題都感到很驚訝。

　Everyone was surprised that the smart boy solved the riddles _____ _____ .

3. 沒人可否認互信對友誼非常重要。

　No one can deny that mutual trust _____ _____ _____ _____ to friendship.

4. 這道菜很燙，所以服務生必須非常小心地上菜。

　_____

1-2

from N to N
from one N to another

句型範例

- The salesman went **from door to door** to sell vacuum cleaners.

  這銷售員挨家挨戶地推銷吸塵器。

- Mr. Wall traveled **from one country to another** on business. Wall 先生到各國洽公。

 ☆ E-mail is different. It is instant, traveling **from point to point**.

大考
實例 電子郵件不一樣。它很即時，從一端點傳到另一端點。 (95 指考)

用法詳解

1. from N to N 的句型意為「從…到…」，二個名詞須為相同字，且均為單數形，亦不加冠詞 (a、the) 或指示形容詞 (this、that)。

2. from one N to another 亦表示「從…到…」。注意，another 之後不需要再接名詞。

挨家挨戶	from door to door	from one door to another
從一國到另一國	from country to country	from one country to another
每個文化	from culture to culture	from one culture to another
從一地到另一地	from place to place	from one place to another
每人；各人	from person to person	from one person to another

- The anxious mother went **from house to house** to ask if anyone had seen her son.

➡ The anxious mother went **from one house to another** to ask if anyone had seen her son. 這焦慮的母親挨家挨戶地詢問是否有人看見她的兒子。

- Thanks to folk artists, glove puppetry has been passed down **from one generation to another**.

➡ Thanks to folk artists, glove puppetry has been passed down **from generation to generation**. 幸虧有民俗藝術家，布袋戲才能世代相傳。

句型練習

一、選擇

( ) 1. On the other hand, plants cannot move from _____ to _____ and do not need to learn to avoid certain things, so this sensation would be unnecessary. (94 學測)

(A) a place; a place　　　　　　　(B) places; places

(C) place; place　　　　　　　　　(D) one place; the other place

( ) 2. Handwritten or typed, letters travel in envelopes through actual space and take time getting from ＿＿＿＿ to ＿＿＿＿ . (95 指考)

(A) places; another　　　　　　　(B) one place; another

(C) one place; the other　　　　　(D) a place; others

( ) 3. We saw a monkey in the tree; it swung ＿＿＿＿ .

(A) from branch to another branch　　(B) from one branch to another

(C) from branches to branches　　　　(D) from a branch to others

二、翻譯

1. 對肢體語言的解讀可能因文化而異。

The interpretations of body language may differ ＿＿＿＿ ＿＿＿＿ ＿＿＿＿ ＿＿＿＿ .

2. 印度人會左右傾頭 (tilt) 表示非常同意他人。

＿＿＿＿＿＿＿＿＿＿＿＿＿＿＿＿＿＿＿＿＿＿＿＿＿＿ to mean that they strongly agree with someone.

3. 這個傳染性的疾病可能會在短時間內在眾人間散佈。

＿＿＿＿＿＿＿＿＿＿＿＿＿＿＿＿＿＿＿＿＿＿＿＿＿＿＿＿＿＿＿＿＿＿

1–3

to + sb's + 情緒名詞, S + V . . .

句型範例

● **To Melissa's delight**, she won a scholarship to a renowned university.

令 Melissa 高興的是，她獲得著名大學的獎學金。

● **To the relief of the chairman of this airline**, the flight attendant strike has ended.

令航空公司董事長鬆口氣的是，空服員罷工已經結束了。

☆ **To the delight of the Empress**, the egg opened to a golden yolk.

讓皇后高興的是，釉蛋裏頭有個金蛋黃。 (104 指考)

☆ **To no one's surprise**, it (the film version) has enjoyed similar popularity.

不令人意外的是，電影版本也一樣受歡迎。 (100 學測)

用法詳解

1. 「to + sb's + 情緒名詞」意為「令某人覺得…的是，…」。注意，本句型中必須使用所有格與表示情緒的名詞。常見的情緒名詞有：

高興	joy、delight	遺憾	regret
驚訝	surprise、amazement、astonishment	滿意	satisfaction
放心	relief	沮喪	dismay
傷心	sorrow、grief	失望	disappointment

● **To Carol's joy**, she passed the road test and got the driver's license.

令 Carol 高興的是，她通過了路考並取得駕照。

2. 若描述的對象字詞比較長時，也可改為「to + the 情緒名詞 + of sb」。例如：

● **To the satisfaction of** our history teacher, there were no late homework submissions. 令我們歷史老師滿意的是，沒有人遲交作業。

3. 若要加強語氣，可用「much + to sb's 情緒名詞」或「to sb's + great + 情緒名詞」表示。

● **Much** to our surprise, many ordinary people have achieved fame overnight in talent shows.

➡ To our **great** surprise, many ordinary people have achieved fame overnight in talent shows. 令我們大感驚訝的是，不少素人在選秀節目中一夕成名。

句型練習

一、選擇

( ) 1. _____ Cindy's relief, her son has made a full recovery from the serious disease.

    (A) For   (B) As   (C) At   (D) To

( ) 2. _____ , the popular basketball player just announced his retirement.

    (A) What made us sad   (B) To everyone's regret

    (C) We felt surprised   (D) To their amazed

( ) 3. _____ , the celebrity died of lung cancer last week.

    (A) We were dismayed   (B) Great to our dismay

    (C) Much to our dismay   (D) Very dismayed

二、翻譯

1. 令大家傷心的是，這場水災奪去多條人命，也讓數百人無家可歸。

_____ _____ _____ , the flood claimed many lives and made hundreds of people homeless.

2. 讓導演滿意的是，這部電影成為賣座片。

_____ , this movie became a box-office hit.

3. 令新娘非常失望的是，她的閨蜜未能參加她的婚禮。

_____

1-4

some . . . others . . .
some . . . the others . . .

句型範例

● **Some** people like extreme sports, while **others** don't.

有些人喜歡極限運動，其他人不喜歡。

● **Some** of my friends are phubbers, but **the others** aren't.

我有些朋友是低頭族，其他則否。

 ☆ Another discovery about fish sounds is that not all fish are equally "talkative." **Some** species talk a lot, while **others** don't. (102 指考)

另一個與魚聲有關的發現是並非所有的魚類都同樣「愛說話」。有些魚類很健談，其他則否。

用法詳解

1. 這二個句型用於將人、事、物概分為二部分時。二者差別在於 some . . . others . . . 意為「有些⋯，另一些⋯」，用於指**無特定範圍**的人或事物，通常泛指一般的人、事、物；而 some . . . the others . . . 意為「有些⋯，其他⋯」，則用於指**有特定範圍**的人或事物，此用法的句中或上下文通常會標明某群體或某範圍。如下圖所示：

(A) some⋯ others⋯ 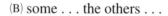 (B) some . . . the others . . .

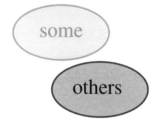

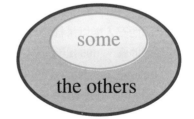

● People have different tastes for music. **Some** enjoy classical music; **others** love pop music. 人們對音樂有不同的品味。有些人喜歡古典樂，也有些人喜歡流行樂。

① 泛指世界上的一般人，無特定範圍。

● This shop sells various hats. **Some** of them are women's, while **the others** are men's. 這間店銷售各種帽子。有些是女士帽，而其他的為男士帽。

① 特別指這間店的帽子，有特定範圍。

2. others (= other + N) 與 the others (= the other + N) 為代名詞，其後不可再接名詞。

● **Some** gestures are universal, while **others** (= other gestures) are not.

有些手勢是通用的,其他的則不是。① 泛指一般的手勢,無特定範圍。

● **Some** actors in this film speak with a British accent, while **the others** (= the other actors) speak with an American accent.

這部影片裡的有些演員說話有英國腔調,其他的則是美國腔調。

句型練習

一、選擇

(　) 1. Some families have a tradition of passing down the father's first name to the first born son. In _____ families, a surname is included in the selection of a child's given name to keep a family surname going. (103 學測)

(A) another　　(B) other　　(C) some　　(D) the other

(　) 2. Some borderlines were drawn that split same groups into different colonies. _____ borders threw different groups together. (97 指考)

(A) The other　　(B) Another　　(C) Others　　(D) Other

(　) 3. _____ prefer outdoor activities, while _____ like indoor ones better.

(A) Some of the people; other people　　(B) Some people; the others

(C) Some people; others　　(D) Some of the people; another people

(　) 4. _____ of the physicians in this hospital reside within a certain distance from the hospital, but _____ don't.

(A) Some; the others　　(B) Some; others

(C) Most; other physicians　　(D) Many; the others

二、翻譯

1. 有些人認為納茲卡印地安人能以某種方式飛翔,也許是搭氣球。其他人則說這些線圖是外星人太空船的降落地區。 (95 指考)

_____ _____ believe the Nazca Indians were somehow able to fly, perhaps in balloons. _____ say the lines were landing areas for alien spaceships.

2. 上週有大批人群湧進港口。有些人來看黃色小鴨,其他人是來此放鬆。

Crowds of people swarmed to the harbor last weekend. _____ _____ _____ came to see the giant Rubber Duck, while _____ _____ came for relaxation.

3. 這植物園的遊客可以看到多種植物。有些植物來自熱帶地區,其他來自亞熱帶地區。

Visitors to the botanic garden can see various types of plants. _____

_____

2-1

It + be + adj. + *to V/that-clause*
It + V + O + that-clause

句型範例

- **It** is not easy to learn a new language. 學習一個新語言並不容易。
- **It** is probable that the auto manufacturer will recall the new vans soon.
  這家汽車製造商可能很快會召回新上市的貨車。
- **It** shocked many people that a sky lantern should have caused a massive fire.
  天燈竟然引起了大火讓很多人感到驚訝。

用法詳解

1. 當主詞太長時，會造成句子頭重腳輕的情形。為了方便閱讀，可用 **it** 當虛主詞，並將真主詞 (通常為 to V 或 that 子句) 移至句尾。

   - To go rock climbing without any equipment is dangerous.
   - ➡ **It** is dangerous to go rock climbing without any equipment.
     沒帶任何工具攀岩很危險。
   - That Patricia will get married next June is true.
   - ➡ **It** is true that Patricia will get married next June. Patricia 明年六月會結婚是真的。
   - **It** annoys Tessa to hear people answering calls in the middle of a movie.
     聽到人們在看電影過程中講手機讓 Tessa 感到很惱火。
   - **It** worries Brad that his grandmother hasn't come home yet.
     奶奶還未回家，這讓 Brad 很擔心。

2. 注意虛主詞的疑問句用法。

   - Is **it** likely that global warming will get worse in the future?
     未來全球暖化可能加劇嗎？
   - How long does **it** usually take you to tidy up your room?
     你通常花多少時間整理房間？

學習補給站

1. It + be + adj. + to V 的句型還可搭配 for sb 或 of sb 來表示其他意思。用法請見 2-2。
2. 在 It + be + adj. + that-clause 的句型中，若形容詞為表「必須、義務、重要」等意思時 (如 necessary、crucial、important)，可省略 that 子句中的 should，故動詞必須為原形。用法請見 4-6。

3. 轉述、報導、預測等句子中也常見 it 做虛主詞的用法，常見動詞有 say、report、expect、predict 等。句型為：it + be + *said/believed/reported/etc.* + that-clause，用法請見 2–5。

句型練習

一、選擇

( ) 1. It is impossible _____ Paris without its cafés. (97 指考)

    (A) imagine   (B) to imagine   (C) imagined   (D) imagination

( ) 2. In Japan, it is acceptable _____ slurping sounds when eating soup.

    (A) making   (B) made   (C) make   (D) to make

二、翻譯

1. 好友要搬到別的城市，這讓 Grace 很沮喪。

    _____ upsets Grace _____ her best friend is moving to a different city.

2. 於網路上散播他人的謠言在法律上與道德上都是錯誤的舉動。 (103 學測)

    _____ to spread rumors

    about other people on the Internet.

3. 世界糧食短缺的問題有可能在十年內解決嗎？

    _____

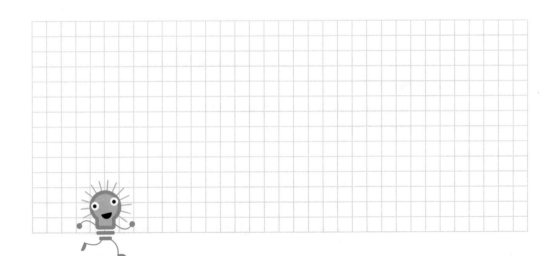

2-2

$$It + be + adj. + \begin{Bmatrix} for \\ of \end{Bmatrix} + somebody + to\ V$$

句型範例

- It is difficult **for** most foreigners to learn written Chinese.

  對大部分的外國人而言,學寫中文字很困難。

- It is nice **of** Melvin to lend me his electronic dictionary.

  Melvin 真好心,他借我電子字典。

☆ However, it is not unusual **for** them to come up with a decision before they have the time to do so.

然而,他們通常在有時間仔細考慮之前就做出決定。(103 學測)

用法詳解

1. 本單元的句型亦屬於虛主詞的用法,以**虛主詞 it** 代替真主詞 to V,須由形容詞判斷介系詞用 for 或 of。

   a. It + be + **adj.** + for sb + to V 表示「對某人而言,做某事是…的」。在此用法中,使用修飾事情的形容詞常見的有 difficult、convenient、possible、acceptable、natural、dangerous、important、necessary 等。

   - It is dangerous **for** fishermen to go fishing on stormy days. 對漁夫而言,在暴風雨天裡捕魚很危險。⓵ dangerous 用於修飾事情,故使用 for。
   - It is essential **for** parents to communicate with their teenage children. 對父母而言,和青少年期的孩子溝通很必要。⓵ essential 用於修飾事情,故使用 for。

   b. It + be + **adj.** + of sb + to V 描述某人因某個舉動展現了特質。在此用法中,使用描述人的特質的形容詞,常見的有 kind、nice、cruel、friendly、generous、stingy、stupid、foolish、brave、honest 等。

   - It is generous **of** the lady to donate part of her salary to the orphanage every month. 這女士很慷慨,她每個月捐出部分薪資給孤兒院。

     ⓵ generous 表示人的特質,故使用 of。

   - It was cruel **of** the man to chain and abuse stray dogs.

     這男人真殘忍,他把流浪狗綁起來虐待。⓵ cruel 表示人的特質,故使用 of。

2. 有些可修飾人與事物的形容詞,如 good、bad、foolish 等,則必須由句意判斷是修飾事情或人以決定搭配 for 或 of。

● It is good **for** Nick to do yoga regularly.

　規律地做瑜珈對 Nick 有益。ⓘ good 形容做瑜珈這件事情，故使用 for。

● It is good **of** Kelly to buy suspended coffee for those who can't afford a cup.

　Kelly 真善良，她購買待用咖啡給買不起的人。ⓘ good 形容 Kelly，故使用 of。

句型練習

一、選擇

(　) 1. It was customary in those days _____ a widow to dress in black for a short time after the death of her husband. (91 指考)

    (A) for   (B) of   (C) that   (D) to

(　) 2. It is difficult _____ most of us to imagine what life is like in countries where diamonds are the source of so much chaos and suffering. (96 指考)

    (A) with   (B) about   (C) of   (D) for

(　) 3. It was rude _____ Ian to shout at his mother and slam the door.

    (A) for   (B) of   (C) that   (D) on

(　) 4. _____ think up a brilliant idea to solve the problem.

    (A) Britney was smart of   (B) It was wise for Britney

    (C) It was clever of Britney to   (D) It was intelligent that Britney

(　) 5. It was foolish _____ such a ridiculous story.

    (A) that Cindy believes   (B) to Cindy to believe

    (C) for Cindy to believe   (D) of Cindy to believe

二、翻譯

1. 你有必要澄清這個論點。 (91 學測)

　_____ _____ necessary _____ you to clarify this point.

2. 現在男人戴耳環是可以被接受的。

　Nowadays, _____ _____ acceptable _____ men _____ _____ earrings.

3. 這男孩很自私，他喝光了果汁並吃光了披薩。

　_____ to drink up all the juice and eat up the whole pizza.

4. 這學生真好心，他在捷運上讓座給孕婦。

　_____

2-3

$$S + think/make/find + it + \begin{Bmatrix} adj. \\ N \end{Bmatrix} + \begin{Bmatrix} to\ V \\ that\text{-}clause \end{Bmatrix}$$

句型範例

● The new students think **it** difficult to fit in at his new school.

這位新來的學生覺得很難適應新學校。

● Fiona thinks **it** a pity that she has lost contact with her childhood friends.

Fiona 認為與童年朋友失聯很可惜。

☆ Wealthy British thought **it** awkward to use their hands to eat.

英國的富人認為用手進食很笨拙。(101 學測)

☆ The scientist modified his speech to make **it** easier for children to understand the threat of global warming.

這科學家修改了他的演講，讓孩子們可容易了解全球暖化的威脅。(98 指考)

用法詳解

1. 本單元介紹 it 作**虛受詞**的用法。與虛主詞的概念相同，太長的受詞會影響閱讀。為了增加閱讀的便利性，將真受詞移至句末，並在原位置補上 it。真受詞多半為不定詞，其次為 that-clause。此句型通常使用形容詞或名詞當受詞補語。

● Richard thinks **it** convenient to do online shopping.　Richard 認為線上購物很方便。

　　　虛受詞　　　　　　　　真受詞　　　　① 形容詞 convenient 為受詞補語。

● Experts find **it** true that adequate sleep is essential to our health.

　　　虛受詞　　　　真受詞

專家們發現充足的睡眠對健康的確是必要的。① 形容詞 true 為受詞補語。

● Justin makes **it** a habit to drink milk before sleep every night.

Justin 習慣每晚睡前喝牛奶。① 名詞 a habit 為受詞補語。make it a habit to 意為「習慣⋯」。

2. 本句型常搭配表「認為、使⋯成為」等意思的動詞，其他常見還有：consider、feel 等。

● Scientists have **made** it possible to bring back some extinct species.

科學家讓某些絕種物種復活成為可能。

● Many singers **feel** it a great honor to receive a Golden Melody Award.

許多歌手感覺獲得金曲獎是莫大的榮耀。

3. 當真受詞為 to V 時，可在前面加上 for sb 表示其動作執行者。

● Quite a few parents **consider** it important for their children to develop their talents. 相當多的父母認為讓孩子發展天分很重要。

句型練習

一、選擇

( ) 1. Rapid advancement in motor engineering makes _____ technically possible to build a flying car in the near future. (98 學測)

　　(A) that　　　　(B) which　　　　(C) it　　　　　(D) this

( ) 2. What made it _____ to build a road through the Glacier National Park? (97 學測)

　　(A) necessary　　(B) necessarily　　(C) to be necessary　(D) that is necessary

( ) 3. Walt finds it worthwhile _____.

　　(A) read this novel　　　　　　(B) to visit a museum

　　(C) does some exercise　　　　(D) watched this movie

( ) 4. Researchers believe it threatening to our environment _____ global warming keeps worsening.

　　(A) for　　　　(B) which　　　　(C) while　　　　(D) that

二、改寫或合併句子

1. It is romantic to dine by candlelight. (用 Shannon thinks . . . 改寫)

　_____

2. { Some people eat hot pot on scorching hot days.
　{ Victor considers it unbelievable.

　_____

三、翻譯

1. John 和老師之間的衝突讓老師很難客觀地評斷他的表現。 (92 學測)

　The conflicts between John and his teacher made _____ _____ for the teacher _____ _____ his performance objectively.

2. 這些裝置讓門能自動開啟，讓酒神奇地從雕像的口中流出。 (92 學測)

　These devices _____ _____ _____ for doors to open by themselves and wine _____ _____ magically out of statues' mouths.

3. Allen 認為打線上遊戲很浪費時間。

　_____

4. 我有些外國朋友認為吃皮蛋 (millennium egg) 很怪異。

　_____

2–4

It + *seems/seemed* + that-clause
S + *seem/seemed* + to *be/V/have p.p.* . . .

句型範例

- **It seems that** food safety has become a primary public concern in Taiwan recently.
- ➡ Food safety **seems to** have become a primary public concern in Taiwan recently.
  食安問題似乎近來在台灣已經成為大眾主要關切的事情。

☆ **It seems** the snake is able to endure certain degrees of dehydration in between rains. 黃腹海蛇似乎能在雨季間承受某種程度的脫水。(105 學測)

☆ Today the car **seems to** make periodic leaps in progress.
現今，車輛在發展上似乎有週期性的躍進。(103 學測)

用法詳解

1. 本單元的句型用於對事情的推論，意為「似乎」。

2. 根據時間順序，須留意是否使用完成式。

   a. V 與 seem 發生的時間點相同。

      - It **seems** that most of the employees in this office commute from the suburbs.
      - ➡ Most of the employees in this office **seem to** commute from the suburbs.
        這公司的大部分員工似乎都從郊區通勤而來。

   b. 推論某事似乎已經發生或已持續一段時間。

      - It **seems** that Keri forgot to pay the phone bill.
      - ➡ Keri **seems to** have forgotten to pay the phone bill. Keri 似乎忘記繳電話帳單。
      - It **seems** that the students in this class have developed good reading habits.
      - ➡ The students in this class **seem to** have developed good reading habits.
        這個班的學生們似乎已經養成良好的閱讀習慣。

   c. 推論過去的事情，have p.p. 的時間點早於 seem。

      - It **seems** that Alison had a serious fight with her husband last night.
      - ➡ Alison **seems to** have had a serious fight with her husband last night.
        Alison 昨晚似乎和丈夫有激烈的爭吵。
      - It **seemed** that Joseph had finished his new book.
      - ➡ Joseph **seemed to** have finished his new book.
        看樣子，Joseph 老早就完成他的新書。

3. seem to + V 也可與 there be 連用，形成 there seem(s) to be + N 的結構，意為「似乎有…」，seem 的單複數形由 N 的單複數決定。

- **There seems to be** <u>a spelling mistake</u> in this passage. 這篇短文似乎有個拼字錯誤。
- **There seem to be** <u>many celebrities</u> living in this neighborhood.
  似乎有許多名人住在這區。

學習補給站

當 seem to be + 名詞或形容詞時，可省略 to be，將形容詞或名詞變成主詞補語。

- Having played all day, the boys **seem** <u>tired</u>. 玩了一整天，男孩們似乎累了。

句型練習

一、選擇

(　) 1. Selling fried chicken at the night market doesn't ＿＿＿＿ a decent business, but it is actually quite profitable. (95 學測)
　　(A) seem that　　　(B) seem be　　　(C) seem being　　　(D) seem to be

(　) 2. ＿＿＿＿ "Schweizer Offizier Messer" was too difficult for people to say, so they just called it the Swiss army knife.
　　(A) It seems that　　　　　　　(B) It seems to be
　　(C) There seems to be　　　　　(D) It had seemed that

(　) 3. ＿＿＿＿ prefer coffee to tea.
　　(A) It seems that Terry　　　　(B) Terry seems that
　　(C) Terry seems to　　　　　　(D) It seemed that Terry

二、翻譯

1. 這些海豚似乎能夠透過模仿哨音來叫喚熟識的同伴。 (104 指考)
　＿＿＿＿ ＿＿＿＿ ＿＿＿＿ dolphins can call those they know by mimicking their distinct whistles.

2. Agnes 似乎有吸引人的性格。幾乎每個初次見到她的人都會被她吸引。 (101 指考)
　Agnes ＿＿＿＿ ＿＿＿＿ ＿＿＿＿ a magnetic personality. Almost everyone is immediately attracted to her when they first see her.

3. Daniel 上週似乎一時衝動下 (on an impulse) 買了三台平板電腦。
　＿＿＿＿＿＿＿＿＿＿＿＿＿＿＿＿＿＿＿＿＿＿＿＿＿＿＿＿＿＿＿＿＿＿＿

2–5

It + be + *said/believed/reported* (+ that) + S + *be/V/V-ed*
. . .
S + be + *said/believed/reported* + to *be/V/have p.p.* . . .

句型範例

● **It is believed that** vitamin C offers many health benefits.

➡ Vitamin C **is believed to** offer many health benefits.

　　據相信，維他命 C 對健康有很多好處。

☆ **It is said that** in ancient times a man would place a drop of blood between his wife's eyes to seal their marriage. 據說，在古代男人會在妻子的兩眼之間滴一滴血，用以封住他們的婚姻。　(102 學測)

☆ A country **is said to** have a comparative advantage over another when it can produce a commodity more cheaply. 據說，當一個國家能夠低價生產某商品時，它就相對比他國有優勢。　(105 學測)

用法詳解

1. 此類句型用來表示「人們說」、「據說」、「據相信」、「據認為」、「據估計」、「據報導」、「據傳聞」等意。常用的動詞有：say、believe、think、estimate、report、rumor 等。

2. 除了上述句型外，還可使用 *People/They* + *say/believe* + that-clause 表示：

被動	It + be + *said/believed/reported* (+ that) + S + *be/V/V-ed* . . .	It 當虛主詞時，使用被動，「據說」等內容以 that-子句當真主詞的結構呈現。
	S + be + *said/believed/reported* + to *be/V/have p.p.* . . .	人或事物當主詞時，使用被動，「據說」等內容以不定詞的結構呈現。
主動	*People/They* + *say/believe* + that-clause	People 或 They 當主詞時，使用主動，「據說」等內容以 that 子句當受詞的結構呈現。

● *It is said/They say* **that** well-organized people are highly productive.

➡ Well-organized people **are said to** be highly productive.

　　據說做事有條理的人很有成效。

● *It is thought/People think* **that** generation gap is a major problem between parents and children.

➡ Generation gap **is thought to** be a major problem between parents and children.

　　一般人相信，代溝是親子間主要的問題。

3. 在 S + be *said/believed/reported* . . . to + V 的句型中，必須注意動詞的時態。

　　a. 要表示不定詞後的動作已發生，以 **to + have p.p.** 表示。

　　　● The flood **is estimated to have caused** hundreds of deaths.

　　　　據估計，這場水災已經造成數百人喪生。

　　b. 要表示不定詞後的動作較早發生，以 **to + have p.p.** 表示。

　　　● The famous speaker **is said to have been** a stutter when she was little.

　　　　據說這有名的演說家小時說話會結巴。

　　　① was a stutter 的時態比 is said to 早，故用 to have been。

學習補給站

若要表示「根據傳說」或「根據謠傳」，還可使用 Legend has it that + S + V (根據傳說)
與 Rumor has it that + S + V (根據謠傳)。

● **Legend has it that** the city of Troy was destroyed because of a wooden horse.

　根據傳說，特洛伊城因為木馬被攻陷。

句型練習

一、選擇

(　) 1. The French were also slow to accept forks, for using them ＿＿＿＿ awkward.

　　　(A) thought to be　　　　　　　　(B) was thought to be

　　　(C) was thought that　　　　　　 (D) thought that it was　(101 學測)

(　) 2. ＿＿＿＿ young visitors get more out of a visit (to a museum) if they focus on no

　　　more than nine objects.　(95 指考)

　　　(A) They are reported that　　　　(B) It is reported that

　　　(C) People are reported to　　　　(D) It is reported to

(　) 3. The disabled man is said ＿＿＿＿ an athlete when he was young.

　　　(A) to be　　　　(B) that he was　　　(C) to have been　　　(D) that was

二、翻譯

1. 在日本，普遍相信人的血型會決定他 / 她的脾氣與性格。　(105 學測)

　In Japan, a person's blood type ＿＿＿＿ popularly ＿＿＿＿ ＿＿＿＿ decide his/her
　temperament and personality.

2. 一般人相信，希臘眾神看起來像人，也擁有人類的情緒。

　＿＿＿＿＿＿＿＿＿＿＿＿＿＿＿＿＿＿＿＿＿＿＿＿＿＿＿＿＿＿＿＿＿＿＿＿

2-6

It occurs to + somebody + *to V/that-clause*
It strikes + somebody + that-clause
something *occur to/strike* somebody

句型範例

- **It occurred to** Jacob **to** reply his email messages.

  Jacob 突然想到要回電子郵件訊息。

- **It struck** Liz **that** she still owes her friend for the musical tickets.

  Liz 突然想到還欠她朋友音樂劇門票的錢。

 ☆ One day, an idea **occurred to** Art Fry.

某天，Art Fry 突然想到一個主意。 (98 學測)

用法詳解

1. 本句型意為「突然想到…」，以 it 為虛主詞，真主詞可用 to V 或 that 子句表示。

   - **It occurs to** Luke **to** watch the soccer championship on TV.

     Luke 突然想起要看電視上的足球冠軍賽。

   - **It strikes** Catherine **that** she needs to buy some sugar.

     Catherine 突然想到，她需要買一些糖。

2. 本句型可有疑問形、否定形、過去式與完成式等的結構。

   - **Did it occur to** you to visit Naoko when you went to Japan?

     妳去日本時，有想過要拜訪 Naoko 嗎？

   - It **didn't strike** Peter that he should close the window when taking a shower.

     當 Peter 洗澡時，他沒想到應該關窗戶。

   - It **had** never **occurred to** Nicholas that he could win Fiona's heart.

     Nicholas 從未想過他能贏得 Fiona 的心。

3. 可直接用名詞當主詞。

   - When the creative team were wondering what to do, a good plan *struck/occurred to* Ray. 當創意團隊正考慮該怎麼做時，Ray 想到一個好計畫。

4. 下列用法也可表示「突然想到…」。請注意主詞的差別。

   $\begin{cases} \text{sb + hit } on/upon \text{ sth = sb + come up with sth} \\ \text{sth + } come \text{ } into/flash \text{ } through/cross \text{ sb's mind} \end{cases}$

● Martin **hit upon** a brilliant idea.

➡ A brilliant idea **came into** Martin's mind.　Martin 想到一個很好的主意。

學習補給站

與本句型類似的用法尚有 It + dawns on + sb + that-clause，表示「某人突然明白⋯」。

● It **dawned on** Angela **that** what she said had hurt her friend's feelings.

Angela 突然明白，她說的話傷害了朋友的感情。

句型練習

一、選擇

(　) 1. ＿＿＿＿＿ occurred to Nick to take the garbage out.

　　　(A) That　　　　　(B) It　　　　　(C) Idea　　　　　(D) Thought

(　) 2. ＿＿＿＿＿ the student that she should hand in a report next week.

　　　(A) It hit upon　　(B) It happened to　　(C) It occurred　　(D) It struck

(　) 3. It occurred to Mr. Dickens ＿＿＿＿＿.

　　　(A) forget to lock the back door　　　(B) he should do the laundry

　　　(C) that left his coat in the office　　　(D) that he had to return some calls

(　) 4. When Elle was wondering what to do, a good plan ＿＿＿＿＿ her.

　　　(A) occurred to　　(B) came up with　　(C) crossed　　(D) hit upon

二、句子合併

1. ⎰ Something occurred to Phoebe.
　 ⎱ She should charge the cell phone battery.　　(以 It occurred to . . . to 合併)

＿＿＿＿＿＿＿＿＿＿＿＿＿＿＿＿＿＿＿＿＿＿＿＿＿＿＿＿＿＿＿＿

2. ⎰ Something struck my father.
　 ⎱ We had run out of salt.　　(以 It struck . . . that 合併)

＿＿＿＿＿＿＿＿＿＿＿＿＿＿＿＿＿＿＿＿＿＿＿＿＿＿＿＿＿＿＿＿

三、翻譯

1. 我突然想到要聯絡我的兒時玩伴。

＿＿＿＿ ＿＿＿＿ ＿＿＿＿ ＿＿＿＿ to contact my childhood playmate.

2. Cunningham 先生突然想起他必須繳電費。

＿＿＿＿＿＿＿＿＿＿＿＿＿＿＿＿＿＿＿＿＿＿＿＿ that he had to pay

the electricity bill.

3. Claire 從沒想到購物前應該列一張購物清單。

＿＿＿＿＿＿＿＿＿＿＿＿＿＿＿＿＿＿＿＿＿＿＿＿＿＿＿＿＿＿＿＿

2-7

It + be + *N/phrase/clause* + that . . .

句型範例

- **It was** chocolate **that** Sebastian gave Belle on Valentine's Day.

  Sebastian 在情人節送給 Belle 的禮物就是巧克力。

- **It is** in spring **that** we can enjoy beautiful cherry blossoms.

  就是在春天我們能欣賞到盛開的櫻花。

☆ Many times nowadays, **it is** the children **who** teach the songs to their parents. 現在通常是孩子們教家長這些歌。 (104 學測)

☆ **It was** in the 19th century **that** the magician Robert Houdin came along and changed people's views and attitudes about magic. (92 學測)

就是在 19 世紀，魔術師 Robert Houdin 出現，改變人們對魔術的看法和態度。

用法詳解

1. 本單元介紹分裂句句型，目的在利用句型強調**主詞**、**受詞**、**副詞** (地方副詞、時間副詞、副詞片語) 等。

2. 形成分裂句的步驟為：(1) 先找出原句中要強調的部分，置於 It is 與 that 之間。

   (2) 再將原句中剩餘的部分移至 that 之後。

- Emily will have dinner with Willy in a fancy restaurant this Sunday.

  主詞　　　　　　　　受詞　　地方副詞　　　時間副詞

  這週日 Emily 將要和 Willy 在一家精緻的餐廳吃晚餐。

  ➡ **It is** Emily **that** will have dinner with Willy in a fancy restaurant this Sunday.

  ➡ **It is** Willy **that** Emily will have dinner with in a fancy restaurant this Sunday.

  ➡ **It is** in a fancy restaurant **that** Emily will have dinner with Willy this Sunday.

  ➡ **It is** this Sunday **that** Emily will have dinner with Willy in a fancy restaurant.

3. 當強調人的時候，that 可以代換為 who；強調事物時，that 可代換為 which。

- **It was** the doctor **who** suggested Amy to do regular exercise.

  是醫生建議 Amy 做規律運動。

- **It was** the antique vase **which** Becky broke accidentally.

  Becky 不小心打破的是個古董花瓶。

學習補給站

分辨其他的強調用法：

1. 強調動詞：用 do、does、did。
   - Oliver **does** cook well. Oliver 真的很會做菜。
2. 強調名詞：用 the very。
   - Dr. Lee is **the very** man that Shelly admires. 李博士正是 Shelly 崇拜的人。

句型練習

一、選擇

( ) 1. It is the fans _____ support the kingdoms of the recording companies. (91 指考)
   (A) which   (B) where   (C) that   (D) when

( ) 2. Secondly, _____ by participating in any IMO (International Mathematical Olympiad) contest that young mathematicians of all countries can foster friendly relations. (91 指考)
   (A) it is   (B) that is   (C) this is   (D) they are

( ) 3. More importantly, _____, why not put our energy there rather than on the size of our body? (94 學測)
   (A) if we want is happiness   (B) if it's we that happiness wants
   (C) if it's happiness that we want   (D) if happiness that we want

( ) 4. It was Mr. Chao _____ was awarded the best leading actor.
   (A) when   (B) who   (C) where   (D) which

二、句子改寫

1. Children go trick-or-treating on Halloween. (強調 on Halloween)

   _____

2. Elaine usually drinks coffee in the morning. (強調 coffee)

   _____

三、翻譯

1. 也是因為 Robert Houdin，許多魔術師才能夠在名字前面加上 Dr. 或 MD。 (92 學測)

   _____ _____ also because of Robert Houdin _____ many magicians were able to add Dr. or MD to their names.

2. 真正有影響的不完全是孩子吃的東西，而是它停留在口中的時間有多少。 (96 學測)

   _____ _____ _____ exactly what a child eats _____ truly matters, but how much time it stays in his mouth.

3. Iris 常用來和她祖母交談的是客家話 (Hakka)。

   _____

2-8

It + is + useless + to V
It + is + (of) no use + V-ing
There + is + no use + V-ing

句型範例

- **It is useless** to ask the stingy man to donate his wealth to charities.
  要求那個小氣鬼捐錢給慈善機構是沒有用的。
- **It is (of) no use** crying over spilt milk. 【諺】覆水難收。
- **There is no use** overprotecting a child. 過度保護孩子是沒有用的。

用法詳解

1. 本單元的句型意為「…是沒有用的」。

2. 注意不同句型中所使用的動詞形態不同：

   a. It is useless + to V：

   - **It is useless** to argue with that unreasonable man.
   ➡ **It is no use** arguing with that unreasonable man.
     和那個不講理的男人爭論是沒用的。

   b. It is (of) no use + V-ing：

   - **It is no use** worrying about your exam results without studying hard.
   ➡ **It is useless** to worry about your exam results without studying hard.
     一味的擔心你的考試成績而不努力讀書是沒有用的。

   c. There is no use + V-ing：

   - **There is no use** persuading smart customers into buying what they don't need. 要說服聰明的顧客買他們不需要的東西是沒有用的。

   > **TIP**
   > 可以記為 no use 之後的動詞都是用 V-ing。

句型練習

一、選擇

( ) 1. It is useless just _____ iced tea to cool down on such a scorching hot day.
(A) drink　　(B) to drink　　(C) drinking　　(D) drunk

( ) 2. It is no use _____ the little girl to keep off sweet or fried food.
(A) asked　　(B) asks　　(C) to ask　　(D) asking

(   ) 3. There is no use ＿＿＿＿＿ about this matter.

      (A) to complain   (B) complained   (C) complaining   (D) to complaining

二、翻譯

1. 要那個自私的男孩在乎別人的感受是沒有用的。

＿＿＿＿＿ ＿＿＿＿＿ ＿＿＿＿＿ ＿＿＿＿＿ tell the selfish boy to care about other people's

feelings.

2. 如果你不認真準備工作面試，光是緊張是沒有用的。

＿＿＿＿＿ ＿＿＿＿＿ ＿＿＿＿＿ ＿＿＿＿＿ feeling nervous if you don't prepare yourself for the

job interview.

3. 當我們面對挫折時，自我憐憫是沒有用的。

There ＿＿＿＿＿＿＿＿＿＿＿＿＿＿＿＿＿＿＿＿＿＿＿＿＿＿＿＿＿＿＿ self-pity when

we are faced with frustrations.

4. 為已經發生的事情後悔是沒有用的。

＿＿

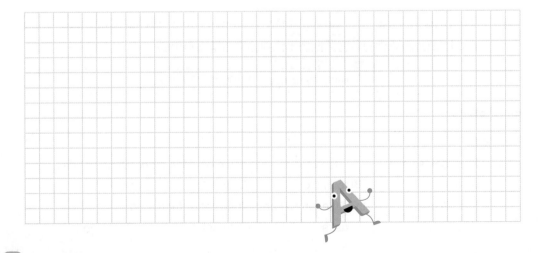

2-9

There's no + V-ing

句型範例

- **There's no** denying that hard work brings success. 不可否認，努力就會成功。
- **There's no** telling when poverty will disappear from the world.

  不知道何時貧窮才會從世上消失。

用法詳解

本句型表示「…是不可能的」。注意，There's no 之後接動名詞 V-ing。

- **There's no** knowing when this damaged village will be reconstructed.

  不知道這個受創的村莊何時才會被重建。

- **There's no** expecting that the government will subsidize all elderly people.

  要期望政府給所有的年長者津貼是不可能的。

- **There's no** accounting for tastes. 【諺】人各有所好。

學習補給站

下列用法也可用來表示「…是不可能；…發生的可能性很低」：

1. It is *impossible/unlikely* + to V

2. It is out of the question + to V

3. There is no question of + *N/V-ing*

4. There is no possibility of + V-ing

- **It is *impossible/unlikely/out of the question*** to predict when this volcano will erupt.

➡ There is no *question/possibility* of predicting when this volcano will erupt.

  預測這座火山何時會爆發是不可能的。

句型練習

一、選擇

( ) 1. _____ knowing when the continuous rain will stop.

　　(A) It is not　　(B) There's no　　(C) There are not　　(D) It's no

( ) 2. There is no possibility of _____ back to the past.

　　(A) go　　(B) went　　(C) going　　(D) goes

( ) 3. _____ predicting which team this famous basketball player will join.

  (A) It's no

  (B) There's no

  (C) It is out of the question

  (D) There is not possible

( ) 4. _____ that laughter is the best medicine.

  (A) There's no arguing

  (B) It is out of the question of denying

  (C) There's no question to know

  (D) It is no possibility to explain

二、翻譯

1. 不可否認，科技讓我們的生活更加便利。

_____ _____ _____ that technology has made our lives more convenient.

2. 這些受害者看到自己的家被摧毀很傷心是不容爭辯的事實。

_____ these victims were

sad to see their homes destroyed.

3. 不知道這個有天分的魔術師會呈現什麼魔術給觀眾。

_____

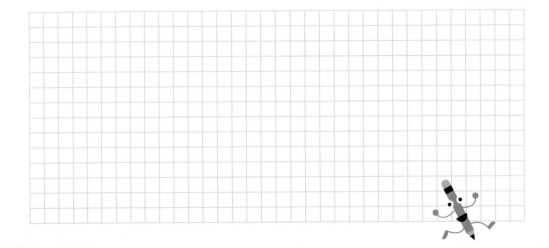

2-10

There be + N + *V-ing/p.p.*

句型範例

● **There are** some people **flying** kites in the park.

公園裡有些人在放風箏。

● It is said that **there is** some treasure **hidden** on this island.

據說，在這個島上藏有一些寶藏。

☆ It is estimated that **there are** currently over 500,000 pieces of man-made trash **orbiting** the Earth at speeds of up to 17,500 miles per hour. (102 學測)

根據估計，目前有超過五十萬塊人造垃圾，以高達 17500 哩的時速繞著地球運行。

☆ **There are** still a lot of questions **unanswered**, but three main causes have been identified. (102 學測)

許多問題尚未獲得解答，但有三個主要的原因已獲得確認。

用法詳解

1. 本單元為表示存在的句型。There be 結構中已含有 be 動詞，其後再出現動詞時，必須將它改為分詞，以免同一句子中出現兩個主要動詞。若 There be 後的名詞與動詞間為**主動關係**時，使用**現在分詞 (V-ing)**，若是**被動關係**，則使用**過去分詞 (p.p.)**。

● **There are** many fans **waiting** for the award-winning singer at the airport.

有許多歌迷在機場等待迎接那位得獎歌手。

ⓘ fans 與 wait 為主動關係，使用現在分詞 waiting。

● In the car accident, **there are** several pedestrians **injured**. 有多位行人在此次車禍中受傷。ⓘ pedestrians 與 injure 為被動關係，使用過去分詞 injured。

● The people in the party ate to their hearts' content, but **there was** much food **left** on the table. 派對裡的人們都吃得心滿意足，但仍有許多食物留在桌上。

2. 有些字常使用主動語態，在本句型中須以現在分詞形呈現；而有些字雖為主動意義，但常以過去分詞的形式出現，這類的字常已轉化成形容詞。注意分辨下列各字的用法：

常用**主動語態**的動詞	mean (意指)、represent (代表)、symbolize (象徵)、sit (位於)、lie (位於)、stand (位於)
常用**被動語態**表示主動意義的字	dressed (穿好衣服的)、seated (就座的)、aged (…歲的)、located (位於)、situated (位於)

- **There is** an old church **sitting** on the hill. 有一座老教堂座落在山丘上。
- In spring, **there are** always <u>many people</u> **seated** on the grass to admire cherry blossoms. 在春天時，總是有很多人坐在草地上欣賞櫻花。

句型練習

一、選擇

(   ) 1. It is sunny today. There are several kids _____ bicycles in the park.
    (A) riding   (B) to ride   (C) rode   (D) ridden

(   ) 2. There will be a special meal _____ tonight to celebrate my sister's 20th birthday.
    (A) to be prepared   (B) prepares   (C) preparing   (D) prepared

(   ) 3. On weekends, there are often many teenagers _____ in this square to practice dancing.
    (A) gather   (B) gathering   (C) gathered   (D) gathers

(   ) 4. Do you know there is a sign _____ peace?
    (A) said   (B) means   (C) represented   (D) symbolizing

(   ) 5. On Dragon Boat Festival, there are many activities _____ to celebrate this day.
    (A) occurred   (B) happened   (C) held   (D) take place

二、句子合併

1. { There is an annoying man in the movie theater.
    { The man is talking loudly on the phone.

_____

2. { There is a new design school.
    { The school is situated in the city center.

_____

三、翻譯

1. 上週五有一個音樂會被舉辦來紀念已故的流行歌手 Michael Jackson。
_____ _____ a concert _____ last Friday in memory of the late pop singer Michael Jackson.

2. 它的網站一次公布 (post) 14 位藝人的作品。 (102 指考)
_____ _____ works of fourteen artists _____ at a time on its website.

3. 今年將會有超過四億人玩樂高積木。 (97 指考)
_____ with Lego bricks this year.

4. 在化妝舞會 (masquerade) 裡，有很多舞者穿著奇怪的服裝。

_____

3-1

not only A but also B

句型範例

- Air-sign people are often considered **not only** friendly **but also** communicative.
  風向星座的人通常被認為友善而且善於溝通。

- Mr. Deng is **not only** an inventor **but also** a designer. 鄧先生是發明家，也是設計師。

- Chimpanzees can **not only** use tools **but also** communicate through bodily gestures. 猩猩不只會使用工具還會透過身體姿勢來溝通。

 ☆ After years of hard work, Kareem has **not only** realized his dream **but also** transformed a piece of deserted property into a beautiful forest. (105 學測)
經多年努力，Kareem 不但實現他的夢想，還將一塊廢地改造成一片美麗森林。

☆ The book is **not only** informative **but also** entertaining, making me laugh and feel relaxed while reading it. (102 學測)
這本書不只有教育性，也深具娛樂性，讓我閱讀時大笑並很放鬆。

用法詳解

1. not only A but also B 為對等連接詞句型，表示「不只 A 還有 B」。使用時必須連接相同詞性或文法結構相等的字詞，A、B 可為形容詞、名詞、動詞 (片語) 或副詞，其中 also 可省略。

   - Extreme sports like bungee jumping are **not only** exciting **but also** dangerous.
     像高空彈跳這樣的極限運動不但刺激也很危險。① 連接形容詞。

   - To ask for his girlfriend's hand, Ted bought **not only** a diamond ring **but also** 99 roses. 為了向女友求婚，Ted 不只買了鑽戒，也買了 99 朵玫瑰。① 連接名詞。

   - The careless mother **not only** forgot to lock the door **but also** left her kid at home. 這粗心的母親不只忘記鎖門，也把孩子留在家裡。① 連接動詞片語。

   - The secretary works **not only** diligently **but also** efficiently.
     這秘書不只工作很認真，也很有效率。① 連接副詞。

2. not only A but also B 連接二個主詞時，**動詞與最接近的主詞一致**。因本句型常用直述句，可直接記憶為動詞由**主詞 B** 決定。

   - **Not only** this country's culture **but also** its people have made a good impression on these tourists. 不只這國家的文化還有國民都讓這些旅客留下好印象。

句型練習

一、選擇

( ) 1. They (scientists) _____ want it (the Great Sphinx of Giza) to look like it did when it was first built _____ are looking for ways to keep it from deteriorating more than it has. (105 指考)

(A) not only; but also   (B) neither; or

(C) both; and   (D) either; nor

( ) 2. Advertising can be persuasive communication _____ about a product _____ an idea or a person. (101 指考)

(A) both; or   (B) either; and

(C) not only; but also   (D) not; and

( ) 3. In this sense, bullying affects not only the bullied _____ his friends and classmates and the whole society. (100 指考)

(A) also   (B) but   (C) and   (D) or

( ) 4. A recent study suggests the marine mammals not only produce their own unique "signature whistles," _____ they also recognize and mimic whistles of other dolphins they are close to and want to see again. (104 指考)

(A) and   (B) while   (C) but   (D) so

( ) 5. Not only the illustrations but also the story of this book _____ to kids.

(A) attracts   (B) attract   (C) appeal   (D) appeals

二、翻譯

1. 在古典希臘時期，捲髮不只是一種流行，也代表了生活的態度。 (98 指考)

In the classical Greek period, curly hair was _____ _____ the fashion, _____ it _____ represented an attitude towards life.

2. 太極拳不只是身體的也是心靈的運動。

Tai Chi Chuan is _____ exercise.

3. 不只是演員還有電影裡的特效都吸引了觀眾。

_____

3-2

either A or B
neither A nor B

句型範例

- To give flavor to this dish, you can add **either** some herbs **or** some spice.
  為了為這道菜增添風味，你可以加點香草或調味料。

- *SpongeBob SquarePants* is an animated series that people **either** love **or** hate.
  海綿寶寶卡通系列不是讓人喜歡就是讓人討厭。

- This old clock is **neither** broken **nor** inaccurate. 這座老鐘既沒壞掉也沒不準確。

 ☆ The 14th typhoon in 2003 can be labeled **either** as Typhoon 0314 **or** (as) Typhoon 200314. (101 學測)
   2003 年發生的第 14 個颱風可被標示為「0314 號颱風」或「200314 號颱風」。

 ☆ Winning international fame, however, was **neither** the original intention **nor** the main reason why Camake founded the group in 2006. (104 學測)
   然而，贏得國際名聲不是查馬克在 2006 年創立傳唱隊的初衷或原因。

用法詳解

1. either A or B 表示「非 A 即 B」，neither A nor B 表示「非 A 也非 B」，兩者都是對等連接詞的句型，連接動詞 (片語)、名詞、形容詞、副詞，注意 **A 與 B 的詞性須相同**。

   - The detective's frown showed that he was **either** pessimistic **or** dissatisfied with the results of the investigation.
     偵探皺了一下眉頭，表示他不是對調查結果感到悲觀就是不滿意。① 連接形容詞。

   - According to the weather forecast, the continuous heavy rain will stop **either** this Friday **or** Saturday. 根據氣象預報，連續大雨將在這週五或週六停。① 連接副詞。

   - The seriously ill patient swore that he would **neither** smoke **nor** drink again.
     這個重症病患發誓他再也不會抽煙或喝酒了。① 連接動詞。

2. either A or B 與 neither A nor B 連接二個主詞時，**動詞與最接近的主詞一致**。此二個句型常用於直述句，故可記憶為動詞由**主詞 B** 決定。

   - **Either** James **or** his parents are travelling with us.
     不是 James 就是他的父母會和我們一起旅行。① 動詞最接近 his parents，故用複數形。

- **Neither** drinks **nor** food is allowed in the library.

  飲料或食物都不能帶進圖書館。① 動詞最接近 food，故用單數形。

3. either A or B 用於否定句時，則表示全部否定，等於 neither A nor B。

- The young man **can't** play **either** the guitar **or** the ukulele.
- ➡ The young man can play **neither** the guitar **nor** the ukulele.

  這年輕人不會彈吉他或烏克麗麗。

句型練習

一、選擇

( ) 1. In most cases, backpackers are _____ adventurous _____ independent travelers.

    (A) not; and   (B) not; but   (C) neither; nor   (D) either; or

( ) 2. This thick book is too difficult; it is _____ interesting _____ useful to such young children.

    (A) neither; nor   (B) either; or   (C) both; and   (D) not only; but also

( ) 3. In the story of *the Phantom of the Opera*, Christine turned town the Phantom, because she didn't like _____ his heart _____ his looks.

    (A) both; or   (B) not only; and   (C) either; or   (D) neither; nor

( ) 4. Neither the evidence nor the witnesses _____ make the murderer admit his guilt.

    (A) is able to   (B) are able to   (C) is likely to   (D) are possible to

二、句子合併

1. ⎰ Getting tired of her job, Edith will probably take a long vacation.
   ⎱ It is also likely that Edith will quit her job to study abroad.

   Getting tired of her job, _____

2. ⎰ Mike will buy an iPad for his wife.
   ⎱ It is also likely that Mike will buy a smartphone for her.

   _____

三、翻譯

1. 教師們將志工工作結合教室作業，或讓服務工作成為必修課程。 (98 指考)

   Teachers _____ with

   classroom lessons _____

   a requirement.

2. 學生們上課不該打瞌睡或用手機。 (. . . neither . . . nor . . .)

   _____

3-3

not A but B

句型範例

- Snakes are **not** warm-blooded **but** cold-blooded. 蛇不是溫血而是冷血動物。
- Some squirrels are **not** herbivores **but** carnivores.

  有些松鼠不是草食性動物而是肉食性動物。
- Jasmine got the job as a flight attendant **not** because she had attractive appearance **but** because she had a sweet smile.

  Jasmine 得到空服員的工作，不是因為她迷人的外表，而是因為她有甜美的笑容。

用法詳解

1. 對等連接詞句型 not A but B 意為「不是 A 而是 B」，使用時必須連接文法結構相同的字詞，即 **A 與 B 的詞性必須一樣**。

   - The task the teacher assigned was **not** easy **but** challenging.

     老師指定的任務不簡單，而是很有挑戰性。① 連接形容詞。
   - The place where Lucas had his first date was **not** a fancy restaurant **but** a local zoo. Lucas 第一次約會的地點不是精緻的餐廳而是當地的動物園。① 連接名詞。
   - It matters **not** how a man dies, **but** how he lives. (—Samuel Johnson)

     【名言】一個人如何死去並不重要，重要的在於他如何活著。① 連接片語。
   - Joshua and Hank met in the coffee shop **not** because they wanted to enjoy afternoon tea **but** because they had something important to discuss.

     Joshua 和 Hank 約在咖啡店見面，不是因為要享用下午茶，而是要討論重要的事情。

     ① 連接子句。

2. 在含一般動詞的否定句或在被動語態的句子中，not 必須前移與助動詞或 be 動詞結合以形成否定結構。

   - The new employee **didn't** work efficiently **but** slowly.

     新進員工工作沒有效率，而是緩慢。①⑴ 連接副詞。⑵ not 前移與 did 形成否定 didn't。
   - This expensive leather purse was **not** made in Japan **but** in Italy.

     這個昂貴的皮包並非日本製，而是義大利製。

     ①⑴ 連接副詞片語。⑵ not 前移與 was 形成否定 was not。

3. not A but B 連接二個主詞時，**動詞須與最接近的主詞一致**。本句型常用於直述句，故可記憶為動詞由**主詞 B** 決定。

- **Not** Greg **but** his parents have to make the decision.

  不是 Greg 而是他父母必須做出決定。

- **Not** the students **but** the teacher was late to the classroom.

  不是學生而是老師晚進教室。

句型練習

一、選擇

( ) 1. Whales are not fish _____ mammals, because they, unlike fish, breathe air directly.

    (A) and   (B) but   (C) or   (D) nor

( ) 2. Fortunately, the earthquake that took place last night was not devastating but _____ ; only slight damage was caused.

    (A) mild   (B) seriously   (C) fierceness   (D) disastrous

( ) 3. You need not feel guilty. It was not _____ but _____ .

    (A) yours; Aaron's fault   (B) you; Jacob

    (C) your fault; Vincent's   (D) your fault; Peter

( ) 4. _____ the water _____ the pollen causes Olivia's allergy. Whenever she smells it, she gets an allergic reaction.

    (A) Neither; nor   (B) Either; or   (C) Both; and   (D) Not; but

( ) 5. It's not the irresponsible coach but the enthusiastic basketball players that _____ the championship.

    (A) deserving   (B) deserved   (C) deserves   (D) deserve

二、句子改寫

1. The protagonist in this popular TV series is not heroic. Instead, he is timid.

_____

2. What this old man needs is not money. What he needs is care and company.

_____

三、翻譯

1. 他們將不會由膚色被評斷，而是他們品格的內涵。(—Dr. Martin Luther King, Jr.)

They will _____ be judged _____ the color of their skin _____ _____ the content of their character.

2. 這座有歷史意義的教堂不是由木材而是石材建成。

The historic church _____

3. Teresa 決定要出國唸書不是因為她想要加強語言技能，而是因為她想拓展視野。

_____

3-4

whether . . . or . . . , S + V
whether . . . or not, S + V

句型範例

- **Whether** Logan <u>walks</u> **or** <u>dines</u> with his friends, he keeps swiping the screen of his smartphone. 不論 Logan 走路或和朋友吃飯,他都一直滑手機。

- **Whether** the students like it **or not**, they have to submit their assignments before the deadline. 不論學生是否喜歡,他們都必須在期限之前交作業。

☆ **Whether** simple **or** lavish, proms have always been more or less traumatic events for adolescents who worry about self-image and fitting in with their peers. 無論簡單或豪奢,對於擔心自我形象與憂慮難融入同儕的青少年而言,舞會或多或少都是一種痛苦的活動。 (99 學測)

☆ It doesn't make a difference **whether** you fix your eyes on *him/her* **or not**. 不論你是否直視某人都沒關係。 (100 學測)

用法詳解

1. whether 為連接詞,常與 or 連用,引導表示讓步的副詞子句,表示「不論…或…」。whether A or B 用於連接**相同詞性**或**對等結構**的字詞。

   - **Whether** <u>in summer</u> **or** <u>in winter</u>, this young man always wears short-sleeved T-shirts. 不論在夏天或冬天,這年輕人總是穿短袖 T 恤。① 連接副詞片語。

   - **Whether** people <u>visit a museum</u> **or** <u>go to a gallery</u>, they should not wear slippers. 不論人們參觀博物館或畫廊,他們都不應該穿拖鞋。① 連接動詞片語。

2. whether 亦常與 or not 連用,whether . . . or not 表示「不論是否…」。當引導的子句過長時,可將 whether 與 or not 寫在一起,以利閱讀。

   - **Whether** you believe it **or not**, waste coffee grounds can be used to make fabrics. 不論你相信與否,廢棄的咖啡渣可被用來製成布料。

   - **Whether or not** many extinct species will be brought back from the grave, we must deal with this issue carefully.
   不論是否許多滅絕的物種將被復活,我們都要謹慎處理這個議題。

句型練習

一、選擇

( ) 1. When people encounter a complex issue and form an opinion, how thoroughly have they examined all the important factors involved before they make their decisions? The answer is: not very thoroughly, _____ they are executives, specialized experts, or ordinary people in the street. (103 學測)

(A) either　　　　(B) neither　　　　(C) no matter who　　(D) whether

( ) 2. _____ a dog feels excited _____ wants to show friendliness, it wags its tail.

(A) What; and　　(B) Whether; or　　(C) Which; but　　(D) Either; or

( ) 3. _____ Darren decides to take a gap year, he has to save some money first.

(A) Whatever　　(B) No matter　　(C) Whether or not　　(D) It doesn't matter

二、翻譯

1. 不論天氣是晴天或雨天，派報生都必須送報。

_____

2. 不論人們喜歡與否，政府都要調漲燃油價。

_____

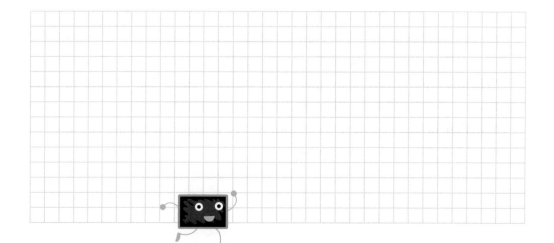

3-5

祈使句, $\begin{Bmatrix} and \\ or \end{Bmatrix}$ + S + aux. + V

句型範例

- **Read** the instructions carefully, **and** you will know how to operate the machine.
  仔細閱讀說明,那麼你就會知道如何操作機器。
- **Put** the medicine on the shelf, **or** the children may reach them.
  把藥放在櫃子上,否則孩子們可能會拿到。

☆ **Agree** to use each other's cars, **and** you can save bucks on car rentals, too.
   同意使用彼此的車,那麼你也能省下租車的錢。 (99 學測)

☆ Industrial waste must be carefully handled, **or** it will contaminate the public water supply. (102 指考)
   工業廢料必須小心處理,否則會污染公共用水的供應。

用法詳解

1. 本單元介紹祈使句搭配連接詞 and 及 or 的用法。
   a. 表示「祈使對方做某事,那麼另一事就會發生」時,連接詞用 **and**。
   b. 表示「祈使對方做某事,否則另一事就會發生」時,連接詞用 **or**。
   - Follow the doctor's advice, **and** you will get well sooner.
     聽醫生的建議,那麼你會早一點好起來。
   - Complete your pre-swim stretching routine before jumping into the pool, **or** your muscles will go into spasm.
     跳入泳池前要做完例行的伸展運動,否則你會抽筋。

2. 本句型中的 or 可代換成 otherwise,但 otherwise 為副詞,沒有連接詞功能,在正式用法中,前面必須使用分號以分隔二句。
   - Fasten your seat belt; **otherwise**, you may be injured when there's a vehicle accident. 繫緊安全帶,否則當有車禍時,你可能會受傷。

句型練習

一、選擇

( ) 1. ＿＿＿＿ a camera with you, and you can capture every precious moment.
   (A) Taking　　(B) To take　　(C) Take　　(D) Taken

( ) 2. Avoid drinking too much water before sleep, _____ you can't sleep well.

    (A) so that   (B) otherwise   (C) and   (D) or

( ) 3. Always look on the bright side, _____ you can lead a happy life.

    (A) and   (B) or   (C) then   (D) but

二、翻譯

1. 戴上太陽眼鏡,那麼你可以保護眼睛不受太陽傷害。

    _____ on your sunglasses, _____ you can protect your eyes from the sun.

2. 保持環境乾爽,否則蟑螂會猖獗。

    _____ environments dry and clean, _____ cockroaches will thrive.

3. 喝點鹽水,那麼你就能舒緩喉嚨痛。

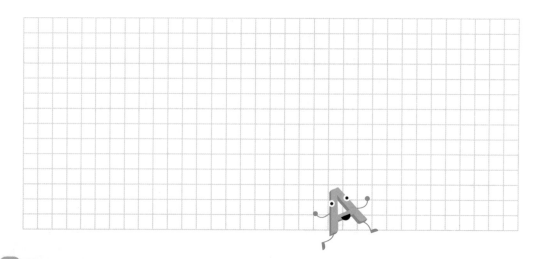

4-1

$$S + \textit{must/may/can/might/could} + \begin{cases} V \\ \text{have p.p.} \end{cases}$$

句型範例

- This company has had a steady growth in sales. They **must** have good marketing strategies. 這間公司的銷售有穩定成長。他們一定有很好的行銷策略。
- Joseph didn't take the bus. He **might** have walked home.
  Joseph 沒搭公車。他有可能走路回家。

 ☆ While the twins knew that genetics **might** have played a role in their condition, they recognized that their eating habits **might** have also contributed to their heart problems. 這對雙胞胎知道基因可能在他們的情況中扮演重要的角色，他們也意識到飲食習慣可能讓他們罹患心臟病。 (93 學測)

用法詳解

1. 本單元介紹以情態助動詞表示推測的用法，可分為對現在與過去事情的推測。
   情態助動詞代表的可能性由高至低為：must (一定) > *can/may* (可能) > *could/might* (較低的可能性 / 委婉的猜測)。

2. 對現在事情的推測：以「助動詞 + 原形動詞」表示。

<table>
<tr><td rowspan="4">肯定</td><td colspan="2">用法</td><td>意思</td><td rowspan="4">否定</td><td>用法</td><td>意思</td></tr>
<tr><td colspan="2">must + V</td><td>一定</td><td>*can't/cannot* + V</td><td>絕不可能</td></tr>
<tr><td colspan="2">can + V</td><td>可能</td><td rowspan="1">may + not + V</td><td rowspan="1">可能不會</td></tr>
<tr><td colspan="2">may + V</td><td>可能</td><td rowspan="1">*could/might* + not + V</td><td rowspan="1">不太可能</td></tr>
</table>

肯定	用法	意思	否定	用法	意思
	must + V	一定		*can't/cannot* + V	絕不可能
	can + V	可能		may + not + V	可能不會
	may + V	可能		*could/might* + not + V	不太可能
	could/might + V	也許			

- The baby is crying loudly. Her diaper **must** be wet.
  這寶寶正大聲哭。她的尿布一定濕了。
- Elaine is late. She **may** be stuck in traffic.
  Elaine 遲到了。她很有可能遇到塞車。
- Nick **can't** be home. I just met him in the bank.
  Nick 不可能在家。我剛剛才在銀行遇到他。

3. 對過去事情的推測：以「**助動詞 + have p.p.**」表示。

	用法	意思		用法	意思
肯定	must + have p.p.	一定	否定	*can't/cannot* + have p.p.	絕不可能
	may + have p.p.	可能		may + not + have p.p.	可能不會
	could/might + have p.p.	或許		*could/might* + not + have p.p.	不太可能

- The ground is wet. It **must** have <u>rained</u> last night. 地上是濕的。昨晚一定下過雨。
- Aaron didn't show up yesterday. He ***could/might*** have <u>forgotten</u> about our date. Aaron 昨晚沒有出現。他可能忘了我們的約會。
- I **may not** have <u>arrived</u> home earlier even if I had finished my work earlier. The traffic was too busy. 即使我早點做完工作也不可能早點到家。路上太塞了。

學習補給站

1. 注意，must 表示推測時，其否定用法為 can't。must + not 是表示強烈禁止的意思。
   - We **must not** talk back to our parents. 我們不該向父母頂嘴。
2. 情態助動詞 *would/could/might/should* + have p.p. 可搭配假設語氣表示「過去會 / 能夠 / 可能 / 應該發生，但實際上卻未發生的事」。用法請見 10–6。

句型練習

選擇

( ) 1. Branden is willing to do everything for Mica. It ＿＿＿＿ love.
  (A) must be　　　　　　　　　(B) can't have been
  (C) could have been　　　　　(D) might not have been

( ) 2. Teddy lives an extravagant life. He ＿＿＿＿ born with a silver spoon in his mouth.
  (A) must not be　　　　　　　(B) could have been
  (C) can't be　　　　　　　　(D) should have been

( ) 3. Noah looks pale; he ＿＿＿＿ under the weather.
  (A) can't be　　　　　　　　(B) may be
  (C) must have been　　　　　(D) might not have been

( ) 4. Teresa couldn't find her keys. She ＿＿＿＿ them on the taxi.
  (A) must not have left　　　　(B) may leave
  (C) could have left　　　　　(D) can't leave

( ) 5. Through observing chimpanzees' learning process, researchers hope to gain insight into what the development of our earliest ancestors ＿＿＿＿ like. (103 指考)
  (A) is to be　　　　(B) was to be　　　　(C) might have been (D) will have been

4–2

S + had better (+ not) + V

句型範例

- You **had better** preview the lesson before class. 你最好在課前預習功課。
- Ken **had better not** wake up the sleeping baby. Ken 最好不要把熟睡的嬰兒吵醒。

用法詳解

1. had better 的意思為「最好…」，用於建議某人去做某事，其後加**原形動詞**。使用時，不論主詞的人稱與時態為何，均**不須改變 had** 的形態。had 可與主詞縮寫成 S'd。
   - You **had better** turn down the radio; it's too loud.
     你最好把收音機音量轉小，它太大聲了。
   - Sleepless people **had better** drink some milk before going to bed.
     失眠的人最好在睡前喝些牛奶。
   - They**'d better** set off before it gets dark. 他們最好在天黑前出發。
2. had better 的否定形為 **had better + not + V**。
   - Parents **had better not** spoil their children. 父母親最好不要寵壞小孩。
3. had better 的附加問句為「hadn't + S?」，had better not 的附加問句為「had + S?」。
   - Passengers on the plane **had better** fasten their seat belts, **hadn't they**?
     飛機上的乘客最好繫緊安全帶，不是嗎？
   - These students **had better not** speak ill of others behind their backs, **had they**?
     這些學生最好不要在背後說別人是非，對吧？

句型練習

一、選擇

( ) 1. These basketball players ＿＿＿＿ warm up before the game.
 (A) are better (B) have better (C) had better (D) has better

( ) 2. Students had better ＿＿＿＿ attentive in class; otherwise, they can't learn well.
 (A) to be (B) be (C) are (D) being

( ) 3. The marathon runner had better do some training every day, ＿＿＿＿?
 (A) hadn't he (B) had he (C) does he (D) doesn't he

(　　) 4. Drivers ＿＿＿＿＿ before they drive. Drunk driving is dangerous and drivers will be punished.

    (A) had better to drink   (B) had better drink

    (C) had not better drink   (D) had better not drink

二、句子改寫

1. If the patient doesn't take the doctor's advice, he can't recover soon.

   (以 had better 改寫)

   ＿＿＿＿＿＿＿＿＿＿＿＿＿＿＿＿＿＿＿＿＿＿＿＿＿＿＿＿＿＿ ; otherwise, he can't

  recover soon.

2. If the woman eats any seafood, she will have an allergic reaction.

   (以 had better not 改寫)

   ＿＿＿＿＿＿＿＿＿＿＿＿＿＿＿＿＿＿＿＿＿＿＿＿＿＿＿＿＿＿ ; otherwise, she will

  have an allergic reaction.

三、翻譯

1. 在洗完頭髮後，你最好立刻擦乾它。

   After you wash your hair, you ＿＿＿＿＿ ＿＿＿＿＿ ＿＿＿＿＿ it at once.

2. 這小孩最好把玩具收拾好，不是嗎？否則他的媽媽會生氣。

   The child ＿＿＿＿＿ ＿＿＿＿＿ put away his toys, ＿＿＿＿＿ ＿＿＿＿＿ ? Otherwise, his mother

  will get angry.

3. 在西方國家用餐時，我們最好不要忘記給服務生小費。

   When we dine in Western countries, ＿＿＿＿＿＿＿＿＿＿＿＿＿＿＿＿＿＿＿＿＿＿

   ＿＿＿＿＿＿＿＿＿＿

4. 你最好不要相信 Julia 說的話，因為她總是說謊。

   ＿＿＿＿＿＿＿＿＿＿＿＿＿＿＿＿＿＿＿＿＿＿＿＿＿＿＿＿＿＿＿＿＿＿＿＿＿＿

4–3

S + used to + V
Did + S + use to + V?
S + didn't + use to + V

句型範例

- Teresa **used to** visit the doctor regularly, but now she doesn't have to.
  Teresa 以前曾定期看醫生，但是現在不用了。
- Eric likes heavy metal, but he **used to** listen to classical music.
  Eric 喜歡重金屬樂，但他以前聽古典樂。

 ☆ Abdul Kareem, who **used to** be an airline ticketing agent, has a great love for the woods. 曾是機票銷售員的 Abdul Kareem 對森林懷有狂熱。 (105 學測)

用法詳解

1. 本句型表示過去的習慣或狀態：以前常常…；以前曾經…。used to 之後要接**原形動詞**。
   - The boy **used to** mess up his room, but now he puts things away after using them. 這男孩以前常把房間弄亂，但如今他在使用東西後會收好。
   - Paul Potts **used to** be a cell phone salesman, but now he is a well-known singer.
     保羅‧帕茲曾是個手機業務員，但現在他是家喻戶曉的歌手。
2. used to 的疑問句與否定句均以助動詞 did 來改，並須將 used 改為原形 use，句型為：
   [疑問] Did + S + use to + V?
   [否定] S + didn't + use to + V
   - This deserted building used to be a restaurant. 這棟廢棄的建築物以前曾是家餐廳。
   [疑] **Did** this deserted building **use to** be a restaurant?
   [否] This deserted building **didn't use to** be a restaurant.
3. used to 可與 there be 連用，成為 **there used to be**，意為「曾經有」。
   - **There used to be** a slide in the park, but now it's gone.
     公園裡以前曾經有座溜滑梯，但是現在它不見了。

學習補給站

注意下列用法意義與所接動詞形與本句型不同：

1. be used to + V：被用來…
2. be *used/accustomed* to + *N/V-ing*：習慣於… (to 為介系詞，故接 V-ing)

- Roses **are used to** decorate this coffee shop. 玫瑰被用來裝飾這間咖啡店。
- Miriam **is used to** smelling the fragrance of roses whenever she comes home. Miriam 回到家後習慣聞到玫瑰的香味。

句型練習

一、選擇

( ) 1. Besides, I remember telling you I _____ have two part-time jobs when I was in college just to make ends meet. (95 學測)

    (A) am used to   (B) get used to   (C) used to   (D) use to

( ) 2. I _____ carry a fresh suit to work with me so I could change if my clothes got wrinkled. (91 學測)

    (A) was used to   (B) used to   (C) didn't use to   (D) got used to

( ) 3. Beepers, or pagers, _____ widely-used devices for personal communication.

    (A) are used to   (B) are used to being

    (C) used to being   (D) used to be

( ) 4. They (the howler monkeys) _____ the weather there. (97 學測)

    (A) were not used to (B) used to   (C) didn't use to   (D) were using

二、句子改寫

1. Nicky used to take delight in reading science fictions. (改為疑問句)

_____

2. My brother used to be allergic to nuts and pollen. (改為否定句)

_____

三、翻譯

1. 以前教學在一面黑板及少數的破舊教科書下進行。 (102 指考)

Teaching _____ _____ be conducted with a blackboard and a handful of tattered textbooks.

2. 被稱為搖滾之王，Michael Jackson 以前曾經吸引全世界的注意。

Known as the "King of Pop," Michael Jackson _____

3. 因為 Michael 的父親很嚴格，他曾有個悲慘的童年。

Since Michael's father was very strict, _____

_____

4-4

S + would rather + V₁ (+ than + V₂)

句型範例

● I **would rather** see a movie in the theater **than** watch TV at home.
我寧願去電影院看電影，也不要在家看電視。

● The soldiers **would rather** die **than** surrender. 這些軍人寧死不屈。

☆ While one person enjoys playing seventy-two holes of golf a week, another **would rather** play three sweaty, competitive games of tennis. (95 學測)
有的人喜歡一週打 72 洞的高爾夫球，有些人則寧願打三場會出汗而且有競爭性的網球。

用法詳解

1. 本句型表示「寧願…(也不要…)」。因位於助動詞 would 之後，V₁ 與 V₂ 都須使用原形。

● Jeremy **would rather** do anything to keep healthy **than** lose health to make a fortune. Jeremy 寧願做任何事來保持健康，也不要因為賺大錢而失去健康。

● Debby **would rather** memorize English vocabulary **than** do math exercises.
Debby 寧願背英文單字也不要做數學練習。

2. 本句型亦可寫為 would + V₁ + rather than + V₂。此外，would 可以和主詞縮寫。

● The little boy **would rather** starve **than** eat green peppers and carrots.

➡ The little boy **would** starve **rather than** eat green peppers and carrots.
這小男孩寧願挨餓也不吃青椒和紅蘿蔔。

3. 在下列情形中，可有省略的寫法。

a. 當強調重點在 V₁ 時，可只保留 V₁，省略 than + V₂。

● It's freezing cold outside. I **would rather** warm myself by the heater.
外面好冷。我寧願在暖氣旁邊取暖。

b. would rather + V₁ + than + V₂ 的句型中，若 V₁ 與 V₂ 指同件事，可省略 V₂。

● My mother **would rather** do the shopping in the supermarket **than** (do the shopping) in a traditional market. 我媽媽寧願在超級市場購物，也不要去傳統市場。

學習補給站

表示「偏好 A 勝於 B」，也可用 prefer (比較喜歡)。prefer 常與 to 連用，其用法如下：

1. prefer *to V/V-ing*：較喜歡…
   - David **prefers** to wear jeans. ➡ David **prefers** wearing jeans.

   David 比較喜歡穿牛仔褲。

2. prefer N_1/V_1-*ing* to N_2/V_2-*ing*：喜歡 N_1/V_1-*ing* 勝於 N_2/V_2-*ing*
   - Bob **prefers** reading novels **to** playing computer games.

   Bob 喜歡讀小說勝於打電動。

3. prefer to V_1 rather than V_2：喜歡 V_1 勝於 V_2
   - The children **prefer to** play Frisbee in the park **rather than** study at home.

   孩子們喜歡在公園玩飛盤勝於在家唸書。

句型練習

一、選擇

( ) 1. The newlywed couple _____ buy a house _____ rent an apartment.

    (A) would rather; to   (B) prefer; to

    (C) prefer; than   (D) would rather; than

( ) 2. Mr. Wang would rather _____ out a loan than _____ down his factory.

    (A) taking; shut   (B) to take; to shut   (C) take; shut   (D) taking; shutting

( ) 3. The researchers were therefore unable to answer their research questions of whether cattle prefer _____ north or south, and whether that differs in the northern and southern hemispheres. (98 學測)

    (A) to look   (B) look   (C) to looking   (D) than look

( ) 4. Baseball, on the other hand, seems more mental, like chess, and attracts those fans that _____ a quieter, more complicated game. (95 學測)

    (A) would like   (B) prefer   (C) like more   (D) rather

二、句子合併與改寫

{ Hank stayed up to do the report.

{ Hank didn't want to miss the deadline.   (would rather. . .than. . .)

_____

三、翻譯

1. 有些父母寧願讓他們的女兒留在家也不願讓她們在其他地方過夜。

Some parents _____ have their daughters stay at home _____ stay somewhere overnight.

2. 這個小孩寧願被處罰也不要寫作業。

The child _____

3. 那個年輕人寧願辭職也不要失去他的夢想。

_____

4-5

S₁ + *command/demand/beg/ask/order/require/suggest/advise/insist* + that + S₂ (+ should) + *be/V* . . .

句型範例

- Experts **suggest** that overweight people (should) change their diet patterns to lose weight. 專家建議過重的人應該改變飲食型態來減重。
- The teacher **asked** that her students read the article before class.
  老師要求學生們課前要讀這篇文章。

 ☆ If a member country suffers great damage from a certain typhoon, it can **request** that the name of the typhoon be deleted from the list at the annual committee meeting. 如果會員國受到某颱風的嚴重災害,它可在每年的委員會議中要求從名單中刪除這個颱風的名字。 (101 學測)

用法詳解

1. 本句型與表示「建議」、「堅持」、「要求」、「命令」等動詞連用。其所接 that 子句中常搭配 **should**,且可以**省略**,省略 should 後,動詞保持原形。常用於本句型的動詞有:

建議	suggest、advise、propose、recommend	要求	ask、beg、request、require、demand
堅持	insist	命令	order、command

- The police **commanded** that this car (should) be towed away.
  警察命令這輛車被拖走。① 省略 should 之後使用原形動詞 be。
- Ann's mother **advises** that she (should) manage her time well.
  Ann 的媽媽建議她應該要好好管理時間。① 省略 should 之後使用原形動詞 manage。
- The general manager **asked** that the employees **not** be late for work.
  總經理要求員工上班不能遲到。
- The doctor **insisted** that the patient **not** consume too much fat and salt.
  醫生堅持這個病人不能食入太多脂肪和鹽。

2. 當這類動詞轉成名詞,其後使用 that 引導的名詞子句當同位語修飾時,that 子句亦保有可省略 should 的用法。常見的名詞有:

建議	suggestion、proposal、recommendation	要求	request、requirement、demand
堅持	insistence	命令	order、command

- The chairman repeated his **request** that the meeting (should) be postponed.
  主席重申會議應該延期的要求。
- The authorities concerned have made a **suggestion** that houses (should) not be built on this hill. 有關當局建議房屋不要建在這個山丘上。

學習補給站

有些表示「建議」、「要求」、「命令」的動詞後也可直接使用 S + V + O + to V 的結構。

☆ Hotels and corporate offices now **require** guests **to present** a photo ID at check-ins and entrances. (92 指考)
旅館與公司辦公室現在要求客人在櫃台和入口出示附有照片的身分證。

句型練習

一、選擇

( ) 1. The fitness coach suggests that Raymond _____ exercise to strengthen his muscles.
　　(A) will do　　　(B) has to do　　　(C) should do　　　(D) might do

( ) 2. When it was time for the bill, he told the manager he had no money and suggested that he _____ him arrested. (91 指考)
　　(A) to have　　　(B) have　　　(C) has　　　(D) had

( ) 3. Geocaching (地理藏寶) requires that items _____ among its participants. (93 指考)
　　(A) to exchange　　(B) exchanged　　(C) exchange　　(D) be exchanged

( ) 4. It would require that no checked bag _____ on a plane if its owner doesn't board the flight. (92 指考)
　　(A) transport　　(B) be transported　(C) should transport　(D) can transport

二、翻譯

1. 因此醫生建議我們每年持續施打流感疫苗以常保健康。 (104 指考)
Therefore, doctors _____ that we _____ to get our annual flu shots in order to stay healthy.

2. 房屋交換網站建議換屋者要事先討論這類的問題。 (99 學測)
Exchange sites _____ that swappers _____ such matters ahead of time.

3. Helen 的醫生建議她接受心臟手術。 (102 指考)
Helen's doctor _____

4. 那個顧客要求商店老闆給她一些折扣。

_____

4-6

It + be + *necessary*/*advisable*/*important*/*critical*/*essential*/ *etc.* + that + S (+ should) + *be*/V . . .

句型範例

● It is **important** that we (should) be optimistic about everything in our lives.
對我們而言，對生活中的一切保持樂觀很重要。

● It is **necessary** that bicyclists and motorcyclists (should) wear helmets.
單車騎士與機車騎士都應該戴安全帽。

 ☆ Therefore, if a child is suspected of AD/HD, it is very **important** that he or she be evaluated by a professional. 因此，如果孩子疑似患有注意力缺失障礙或過動障礙，讓他或她接受專家的評估是很重要的。 (96 指考)

用法詳解

1. 本句型用於表達 「重要」、「必要」、「急切」 等意思，後方的 that 子句中常會使用 **should**，並且可以將 should 省略，省略 should 後，動詞必須保持原形。

2. 常用於本句型的形容詞有：

　a. 重要：important、vital

　b. 必要：necessary、essential、imperative (迫切的)、urgent

　c. 期望：advisable、desirable　　d. 其他：natural

● It is **important** that you (should) be careful about what you consume every day.
你注意每天所吃的食物很重要。

● It is **essential** that parents (should) keep medicine out of their children's reach.
父母必須將藥品放在孩子們拿不到的地方。

● It is **critical** that dog owners **not** forget to brush their teeth on a regular basis.
狗主人不要忘記定期幫牠們刷牙，這很重要。

● It is **advisable** that the old temple **not** be torn down.
不拆除這座古廟是很明智的做法。

3. 當此類的形容詞轉成名詞，其後使用 that 引導的名詞子句當同位語修飾時，that 子句亦保有可省略 should 的用法。

● It is of great **importance** that people (should) have adequate amounts of sleep every day. 人們每天有充足的睡眠量很重要。

● It is of **necessity** that everyone (should) be aware of environment-related issues.
每個人都應該知道與環境有關的議題。

學習補給站

本句型也可以代換成 It is + adj. + for sb + to V。

● In Western countries, it is vital **that** customers (should) tip waiters.
➡ In Western countries, it is vital **for** customers to tip waiters.
在西方國家，顧客必須給服務生小費。

句型練習

一、選擇

(　) 1. It is _____ that Ruth send out her application form for the scholarship before the deadline.
(A) nature　　　(B) needed　　　(C) essential　　　(D) desired

(　) 2. It is necessary for you _____ this point. We simply cannot understand it.
(A) to clarify　　(B) clarifying　　(C) clarified　　(D) clarify. (91 學測)

(　) 3. It is vital that Edith _____ her manager's phone call as soon as possible.
(A) to return　　(B) returns　　(C) return　　(D) returned

(　) 4. It is of importance that these interviewees _____ for their interviews.
(A) to prepare themselves　　　(B) prepare
(C) preparing　　　(D) be prepared

二、句子合併與改寫

1. ┌ People infected with H1N1 flu should wear masks.
　└ This is essential.　　(以 It is + adj. + that-clause 合併)

_____

2. We advised Karl to have his broken battered car fixed.
(以 It is + adj. + that-clause 改寫)

_____

三、翻譯

1. 理所當然，當一個人生氣時，他的臉會變紅。
_____ _____ _____ that a man's face _____ red when he gets angry.

2. 馬上寄出這封重要的信，這件事很緊急。
_____ _____ _____ that this important mail _____ _____ at once.

3. 班長有責任感是很重要的。

_____

5–1

$S_1 + be/V + \text{as adj.} (+ N) \text{ as} + S_2 \ldots$
$S_1 + V + \text{as adv. as} + S_2 \ldots$

句型範例

- The tablet computer is **as thin as** a book. 這平板電腦像書一樣薄。
- Melissa speaks English **as fluently as** a native speaker.

  Melissa 說英文像以英語為母語的人一樣流利。

 ☆ The remedy is **as simple as** standing up and taking activity breaks.

妙方很簡單，就是不時站起來走動走動。 (104 學測)

用法詳解

1. 本句型為原級比較，表示兩者有相同的特質。as . . . as 之間可使用形容詞或副詞。

   - This department store is **as large as** a shopping mall.

     這間百貨像購物中心一樣大。

   - The amateur pitcher pitches **as well as** a professional one.

     那業餘投手投得跟專業投手一樣好。

2. 注意，兩個比較的對象必須為同類型。

   - [正] My hair is **as long as** Janet's. 我的頭髮和 Janet 的一樣長。

     [誤] My hair is as long as Janet. ① hair 須與 hair 比較，須使用 Janet's (= Janet's hair)

   - [正] Sandy's room is **as large as** mine. Sandy 的房間和我的一樣大。

     [誤] Sandy's room is as large as I.

     ① room 須與 room 比較，故須使用 mine (= my room)

3. 否定型為 not + so/as + adj./adv. + as ➡ less + adj./adv. + than。

   - Patrick is **not** *so/as* clever as Marvin. ➡ Patrick is **less clever than** Marvin.

     Patrick 不像 Marvin 一樣聰明。

   - Max **doesn't** work *so/as* efficiently as Alice.

   ➡ Max works **less efficiently than** Alice. Max 工作起來不像 Alice 一樣有效率。

4. 亦可加入名詞，成為 as + *many/much* + N + as。

   - Mrs. Weiss makes **as much money as** her husband (does).

     Weiss 太太賺的錢和她丈夫一樣多。① 此為較正式用法，較為口語用法可省略 does。

5. 本句型也可當成比喻用法，讓描述更生動。常用的用法有：

as busy as a bee	非常忙碌	as stubborn as a mule	非常固執
as proud as a peacock	非常驕傲	as poor as a church mouse	非常貧窮
as happy as a lark	非常快樂	as blind as a bat	非常盲目
as *sly/cunning* as a fox	非常狡猾	as easy as ABC	非常容易

● The responsible secretary is **as busy as a bee**. 這負責任的秘書非常忙碌。

學習補給站

as . . . as 搭配某些字時，有不同的意思。下列為固定用法：

as well as (和)、as soon as (一…就…)、as long as (只要)。

句型練習

一、選擇

( ) 1. The artists gathered at the café may not be _____ those of the past, but faces worth watching are just the same. (97 指考)

　　(A) as greatly as　　(B) so greatly as　　(C) as great as　　(D) as great so

( ) 2. We should also show boys that becoming a child care provider is _____ a choice _____ becoming a police officer or CEO. (98 指考)

　　(A) as acceptable; as　　　　(B) as acceptably; as

　　(C) such acceptable; as　　　(D) so acceptably; as

( ) 3. This child prodigy plays the piano _____ a professional pianist.

　　(A) as better as　　(B) as worse as　　(C) so well as　　(D) as well as

二、句子合併與改寫

1. { This sports car cost six million dollars.

　 { This three-story house cost six million dollars, too.　(以 as adj. as 合併)

　 This sports car _____

2. Gary has read five novels, and Hugh has also read five novels.

　 (用 as + many N + as 改寫)

　 Gary _____

三、翻譯

1. 小說可能像最令人難以置信的童話故事一樣荒謬。　(91 指考)

　 Fiction can _____ _____ fantastic _____ the most unbelievable fairy tale.

2. 對我而言，學習英文像玩遊戲一樣有趣。

　 _____

3. 你的外套和她的一樣貴，而我的不像你們的那麼貴。

　 _____

5-2

$$\left.\begin{array}{l}\text{adj.-er} \\ \text{adv.-er}\end{array}\right\} + \text{and} + \left\{\begin{array}{l}\text{adj.-er} \\ \text{adv.-er}\end{array}\right.$$

句型範例

- As spring approaches, the weather gets **warmer and warmer**.
  隨著春天的到來，天氣變得越來越暖和。

- After getting used to her work, the secretary works **more and more efficiently**.
  在習慣了她的工作之後，這個秘書工作越來越有效率。

 ☆ **More and more** new cars can reverse-park, read traffic signs, maintain a safe distance in steady traffic and brake automatically to avoid crashes.
越來越多新車可以倒車停靠、讀取交通號誌、在穩定的交通路況下保持安全距離與自動剎車，以避免車禍。 (103 學測)

用法詳解

1. 本句型利用形容詞或副詞的比較級來表示「越來越…」。

   - After having been on a diet for a month, Selina gets **thinner and thinner**.
     在節食一個月後，Selina 變得越來越瘦。

   - With the advance of technology, our lives have become **more and more convenient**. 隨著科技發展，我們的生活變得越來越便利。

2. 注意下列形容詞的比較級變化及用法：

原級	比較級	原級	比較級
few	fewer (+ 可數名詞)	good	better
		bad	worse
little	less (+ 不可數名詞 / 抽象形容詞)	much	more

3. 表示劣等的比較級有 **fewer** 和 **less**，注意區分兩者的差別。

   $$\left\{\begin{array}{l}\text{fewer and fewer + 可數複數名詞 (越來越少)} \\ \text{less and less + 不可數名詞 (越來越少)}\end{array}\right.$$

   - In modern times, **fewer and fewer** people communicate through written letters.
     在現代，越來越少人以手寫的信件通訊。

   - As the man lives a luxurious life, he has **less and less** money left in his bank account. 因為這男人過著奢侈的生活，他銀行戶頭裡剩的錢越來越少。

句型練習

( ) 1. After having learned painting for a year, Angelina has become _____ at it.

    (A) more and more   (B) good and good

    (C) well and well   (D) more and more skillful

( ) 2. To pay off his credit card debt, this credit card abuser has to work _____.

    (A) much and much   (B) more and more hardly

    (C) harder and harder   (D) hardly and hardly

( ) 3. The students are learning under pressure, so they seem _____ in class activities.

    (A) less and less active   (B) fewer and fewer energetic

    (C) more and more diligently   (D) badly and badly

1. 越來越多公司允許他們的員工穿便裝上班。 (91 學測)

_____ _____ _____ companies are allowing their office workers to wear casual clothes to work.

2. 在強颱過後，菜價漲得越來越高。

After the severe typhoon, the vegetable prices soared _____ _____ _____.

3. 因為天色越來越黑，工人們決定結束一天的工作。

_____, the workers decided to call it a day.

4. 由於經紀公司 (entertainment agency) 成功的訓練計劃，這搖滾樂團的表現越來越好。

_____

5. 這個病人拒絕任何治療，所以他的健康狀況變得越來越糟。

_____

5-3

*The more (+ N)/adj.-er/adv.-er + S₁+ be/V₁...,
the more (+ N)/adj.-er/adv.-er + S₂ + be/V₂...*

句型範例

- **The sooner** (it is), **the better** (it is). 越快越好。
- **The more optimistic** you are, **the happier** you will be. 你越樂觀就會越快樂。
- **The more saturated fat** a food product contains, **the less healthy** it is.
  含有越多飽和脂肪的食物就越不健康。

☆ **The more** bright students stay at universities, **the better** it is for academics. 越多優秀的學生留在大學裡，就越有助於學術發展。 (100 指考)

☆ **The longer** the food stays in the mouth, **the more likely** cavities will develop. 食物在嘴裡停留得越久，就越可能發生蛀牙。 (96 學測)

用法詳解

1. 本句型利用形容詞或副詞的比較級來表示「越…就越…」。後方的主詞與動詞不必倒裝。
   - **The older** we grow, **the more emotionally stable** we are.
     我們年紀越大，情緒就越穩定。
   - **The more cautiously** people drive, **the less likely** accidents are to happen.
     人們越小心，就越不可能有意外發生。

2. 使用名詞當受詞時，置於比較級形容詞之後。
   - **The fewer** books one reads, **the less** knowledgeable he or she becomes.
     一個人讀的書越少，他 / 她懂得就越少。
   - **The more** profits the factory owner makes, **the more** money he donates to charitable causes. 這工廠老闆的獲利越多，捐給慈善機構的錢就越多。

3. 注意，若使用只能修飾事物的形容詞時，不可用人當主詞，必須以 **it is for + sb + to V** 的結構表示。常用的這類形容詞有：difficult、probable、easy、convenient 等。
   - **The more** junk food you eat, **the more** difficult it is for you to keep healthy.
   - [誤] The more junk food you eat, the more difficult you are to keep healthy.
     你吃越多垃圾食物，就越難保持健康。① difficult 不可修飾人。
   - **The less** rest the patient takes, **the less** probable it is for him to recover quickly.
   - [誤] The less rest the patient takes, the less probable he is to recover quickly.
     這病人越少休息，就越不可能很快康復。① probable 不可修飾人。

學習補給站

當配合「普通名詞 + be 動詞」使用時，可省略 be 動詞。若 S + V 是 it is，也可省略 it is。

- **The greater** the chance of winning (is), **the more** prudent you must be.

  獲勝的機會越大，你就必須越謹慎。

- **The more** (it is), **the better** (it is). 越多越好。

句型練習

一、選擇

( ) 1. _____ a speaker wants to please the audience, _____ likely he will succeed.

    (A) More; more   (B) The much; the much

    (C) The more; the more   (D) The most; the most (94 指考)

( ) 2. _____, causing more severe pain. (97 學測)

    (A) The pause is long, the heat pulse will be strong

    (B) The pause is longer, the heat pulse will be stronger

    (C) Longer the pause, stronger the heat pulse

    (D) The longer the pause, the stronger the heat pulse will be

( ) 3. The _____ the students read, the _____ they are to write good compositions.

    (A) more; more possible   (B) ×; less possible

    (C) less; less likely   (D) fewer; less likely

二、句子改寫

1. If a mall has more sales promotions, it will attract more customers.

    The more _____

2. As the man waited longer, he got less patient.

    _____

三、翻譯

1. 一枚錢幣越稀有，其價值就越高。 (102 學測)

    _____ _____ a coin is, _____ _____ it is worth.

2. 父母越少與子女溝通，他們就越難瞭解彼此。

    _____ _____ parents communicate with their children, _____

    _____ to understand each other.

3. 這些籃球員越常練習，就打得越好。

    _____

5-4

S_1 + be/V_1 + half/twice/three times/etc. + as + adj. (+ N)/
adv. + as + S_2 (+ be/V_2)

S_1 + be/V_1 + three/four/etc. + times + more (+ N)/adj.-er/
adv.-er + than + S_2 (+ be/V_2)

S_1 + be/V + half/twice/three times/etc. + the N of + S_2

句型範例

● Vera's watch is twice **as cheap as** mine.　Vera 的手錶比我的便宜二倍。
● The wealthy man's mansion is five times **larger than** the poor man's house.
　這有錢人的豪宅是那窮人房子的五倍大。
● Mrs. Jenkins is four times **the age of** her son.　Jenkins 太太的年紀是她兒子的四倍。

用法詳解

1. 本句型利用倍數詞配合原級比較 (as *adj./adv.* as) 及比較級比較 (*adj.-er/adv.-er* than)
   來表達兩者差異。常用的倍數詞有：half (一半)、twice (兩倍)、three times (三倍)、
   four times (四倍)…等。注意，**half** 與 **twice** 只和**原級比較**連用。
   ● The library is half **as large as** the museum.　這個圖書館是博物館的一半大。
   ● The encyclopedia is two times **thicker than** the dictionary.
   ➡ The encyclopedia is twice **as thick as** the dictionary.
   　這百科全書是這字典的兩倍厚。

2. 利用名詞當受詞時，必須置於比較級形容詞之後。
   ● Roger ate three times **more** food than Amy. Roger 吃的食物是 Amy 的三倍。
   ● Gina has four times **more** comic books than her brother.
   　Gina 擁有的漫畫書比她弟弟多四倍。

3. 表示倍數也可使用**倍數 + the N of** 的結構，N 為與形容詞相關的名詞。例如：
   ● This river is **four times the length of** that one. 這條河是那條的四倍長。
   ● This skyscraper is **several times the height of** that office building.
   　這幢摩天大樓是那間辦公大樓的好幾倍高。

4. 本句型中的用法可互相代換。常見相互代換的形容詞與名詞列舉如下：

large → size	old → age	heavy → weight	much → amount
long → length	wide → width	deep → depth	many → number
high/tall → height	expensive → price		

句型練習

一、選擇

( ) 1. The laptop is twice _____ the cell phone.

    (A) as many as   (B) as expensive as

    (C) more expensive than   (D) a price of

( ) 2. Angela is three times _____ her daughter.

    (A) older than   (B) as older as   (C) the old of   (D) the age like

( ) 3. This handbag costs half _____ that leather suitcase.

    (A) as expensive as   (B) more expensive than

    (C) the money of   (D) as much money as

( ) 4. My room is _____.

    (A) as twice the size as my brother   (B) five times larger as my brother's

    (C) three times the size of my brother's   (D) four times larger than my brother

二、句子合併與改寫

1. ⎰ The T-shirt is NT$250.   (以 as + adj.+ as 合併)
  ⎱ The jacket is NT$500.

  The jacket _____

2. ⎰ The little girl's grandfather is 80 years old.   (以 adj.-er . . . than 合併)
  ⎱ The little girl is 10 years old.

  The little girl's grandfather _____

三、翻譯

1. 這個國家比它的鄰國大四倍。

  This country is _____ _____ _____ _____ its neighboring country.

2. 這條金項鍊的價錢是那條銀項鍊的兩倍。

  This gold necklace costs _____

  that silver one.

3. 我們英文老師的年紀是我們的三倍大。

  _____

4. 這個老作家的作品是那個年輕作家的五倍。

  _____

5-5

$$as + \begin{cases} adj.\ (+ N) \\ adv. \end{cases} + as + \begin{cases} somebody\ can \\ possible \end{cases}$$

句型範例

- The thirsty man drank **as much water as he could**. 那個口渴的男人儘量喝很多水。
- The police drove **as fast as possible** to catch the robber.
  警察盡可能開快車去捉搶匪。

☆ The kidnappers finally handed over the boy and $250 to the banker and fled town **as quickly as they could**. (105 學測)
綁匪們最後把男孩交出去並付給銀行家 250 美元，然後盡快逃離鎮上。

☆ Living in a highly competitive society, you definitely have to arm yourself with **as much knowledge as possible**. (92 學測)
生活在高度競爭的社會中，你絕對必須盡量讓自己具備大量的知識。

用法詳解

1. 本句型以「原級比較 (as . . . as) + *one can/possible*」的結構表示「盡可能」或「儘量」，as 與 as 之間可用形容詞或副詞。
   - Computer manufacturers are endeavoring to make their tablet computers **as thin as possible**.
   - ➡ Computer manufacturers are endeavoring to make their tablet computers **as thin as they can**. 電腦製造商正努力讓他們的平板電腦越薄越好。
   - In order get to the airport on time, the businessman left **as early as possible**.
   - ➡ In order get to the airport on time, the businessman left **as early as he could**.
     為了準時抵達機場，這商人盡早出門。
2. 使用名詞當動詞的受詞時，必須將名詞置於形容詞後，形成 as + adj. + N + as 的結構。
   - The student read **as <u>many books</u> as she could** to collect enough information for her report. 這學生為了收集足夠資料做報告而盡可能讀很多書。

句型練習

一、選擇

(　) 1. The child jumped _____ possible to reach the shelf, but in vain.
　　(A) higher than　　(B) as higher as　　(C) as highly as　　(D) as high as

( ) 2. Lily studies as _____ as she can to win a scholarship.

    (A) possible   (B) possibly   (C) hard   (D) hardly

( ) 3. The optimistic young man always makes himself as happy as _____ .

    (A) could be   (B) he can   (C) can be possible   (D) he possible can

( ) 4. In order to recover from his illness, the patient should exercise _____ .

    (A) as regular as possible   (B) as regular as possibly

    (C) as much as possible   (D) as possible as much

( ) 5. Many kind-hearted people donated _____ they could to help the survivors of the flood.

    (A) as much food as   (B) as more food as

    (C) food as much as   (D) much more food as

二、翻譯

1. 這個落後的馬拉松選手盡可能試著追上其他的人。

This marathon runner, who had lagged behind, tried _____ _____ _____ _____ to catch up with others.

2. 在上完夜班後，Lisa 跳上自行車盡快地騎過又黑又窄的街道趕回家。　(105 指考)

Lisa hopped on her bicycle and pedaled _____

_____ through the dark narrow backstreets to get home after working the night shift.

3. Jessica 盡可能地維持飲食均衡以保持健康。

_____

4. 你應該盡可能常練習講英文，才能將英文說得很流利。

_____

5-6

$$\text{No other N}_1 + \begin{Bmatrix} \text{be} \\ \text{V} \end{Bmatrix} + \begin{Bmatrix} \text{as} + adj./adv. + \text{as} \\ adj.\text{-}er/adv.\text{-}er + \text{than} \end{Bmatrix} + \text{N}_2$$

句型範例

- In a mother's eyes, **no other** child is **as lovely as** her own child.
  在母親的眼中，她的孩子是最可愛的。
- To me, **no other** subject is **more interesting than** English.
  對我而言，英文是最有趣的科目。

用法詳解

1. 本句型以 「no other . . . + 比較級」 來表達最高級的意義 ， 可使用原級比較 as + *adj./adv.* + as 或比較級 *adj.-er/adv.-er* than 的結構。no other 後方可接單數或複數名詞，但動詞須配合名詞單複數作變化。

   - In my opinion, **no other** fruit is **as smelly as** durians.
   - ➡ In my opinion, **no other** fruit is **smellier than** durians.
     在我看來，榴槤是最臭的水果。
   - As far as we know, **no other** land animal runs **as fast as** cheetahs.
   - ➡ As far as we know, **no other** land animal runs **faster than** cheetahs.
     就我們所知，印度豹是跑最快的陸上動物。

2. 若以「事物」作為最高級比較對象時，no other + 單數名詞可寫成 nothing (else)。若以「人」為最高級比較對象時，可用 no one 或 nobody 作主詞。

   - Mrs. Hanks believes **nothing (else)** in the world is **as important as** health.
     Hanks 太太相信健康是世界上最重要的東西。
   - Greg said *no one/nobody* on the planet is **more beautiful than** his wife.
     Greg 說世界上沒人比他太太更漂亮。

句型練習

一、選擇

( ) 1. _____ larger than whale sharks.

    (A) Any other fishes are   (B) No other fish is

    (C) All the other fishes are   (D) Every other fish is

( ) 2. As far as most people are concerned, _____ is more precious than health.

    (A) all other things   (B) everything   (C) no other things   (D) nothing

( ) 3. _____ better than chocolate to this girl.
   (A) No other food tastes   (B) Any other foods taste
   (C) None of the foods are   (D) No another food is

( ) 4. No other place is _____ one's home.
   (A) so sweeter as   (B) as sweetest as   (C) as sweet as   (D) sweet like

( ) 5. In Vera's view, no other singer _____ Sarah Brightman.
   (A) sings better like   (B) sings as well as   (C) is as well as   (D) sings as good as

二、翻譯

1. 在炎熱的夏日，冰可樂是最清涼的飲料。

   On hot summer days, _____ _____ _____ is _____ refreshing _____ iced coke.

2. Betty 認為最重要的節日是情人節。

   Betty thinks that _____ holiday is _____ _____ _____ Valentine's Day.

3. 對這個鋼琴家而言，彈鋼琴是最重要的事。

   To this pianist, _____

4. 說到打棒球，Luke 班上的男生沒有一個比他厲害。

   When it comes to playing baseball, _____

5. 世上行進最快的物質是光。

   _____

6-1

. . . N + *who/which/that/whom/whose* . . .
. . . N, + *who/which/that/whom/whose* . . .

句型範例

- The man **who** has a mustache is the general manager of this company.
  留著小鬍子的男人是這間公司的總經理。
- Alan Turing**, who** invented the Turing machine, was considered the father of computer science. 艾倫‧圖靈發明了圖靈機,被認為是電腦科學之父。

☆ The *Nina* is not the only traveling museum **that** provides such field trips.
妮娜號不是唯一提供這類校外教學的巡迴博物館。 (105 指考)

☆ Abdul Kareem**, who** used to be an airline ticketing agent, has a great love for the woods. Abdul Kareem 曾是機票銷售員,熱愛林木。 (105 學測)

用法詳解

1. 本單元介紹關係子句當形容詞子句的用法。關係子句由關係詞 (who/which/that/whom/whose) 引導,置於要修飾的名詞 (即先行詞) 之後。

2. 依據功能與先行詞不同,關係代名詞有下列用法:

先行詞\格	人		動物或事物		人 + 動物 / 人 + 事物
主格	who	that	which	that	that
受格	whom	that	which	that	that
所有格	whose		of *which*/*whose*		

- The lady **who** had a flat tire didn't know what to do.
  車子爆胎的女士不知道該怎麼辦。
- Karen lost the necklace **which** her husband bought for her.
  Karen 遺失她丈夫買給她的項鍊。
- The man **whose** wig was blown away felt embarrassed.
  假髮被吹走的男人感覺很尷尬。

3. 關係子句可分為限定與非限定用法:

限定用法	意義:先行詞**不明確**或**有多個對象**,需以關係子句形容,限定對象。 用法:關係代名詞之前**不加逗號**。

	● Danny often goes to the gym with his friend **who is an athlete**. Danny 常和當運動員的朋友去健身房。
非限定用法	意義：先行詞為**唯一對象**或**專有名詞**，關係子句當補充說明用。 用法：關係代名詞之前必須加逗號，**不可為 that**，亦不可省略。 ● Belle used to live in London**, which is the most populous city of the UK**. Belle 曾住在倫敦，它是英國人口最稠密的城市。

學習補給站

1. 當先行詞有以下的修飾詞時，關係代名詞常為 that：最高級形容詞、序數、all、any、the only、the very、the same 等。

2. 在下列情形中，關係代名詞不可為 that：關係代名詞前有**介系詞**或**逗號**。

3. 關係代名詞 which 亦可指**前面整句**或**整件事情**，此用法必須**加逗號**。

   ● The factory dumped poisonous waste into the river, **which** killed all the fish.
   工廠排放有毒廢料到河裡，讓所有的魚都死了。

句型練習

一、選擇

( ) 1. The smartphones _____ have an exploding battery problem are recalled by the mobile phone company.

  (A) whom　　　　(B) which　　　　(C) who　　　　(D) whose

( ) 2. We met the girl _____ Michael has a crush on.

  (A) which　　　　(B) whom　　　　(C) whose　　　　(D) , who

( ) 3. The most famous example was Isaac Singer _____ created franchises to distribute his sewing machines to larger areas. (105 指考)

  (A) that　　　　(B) , that　　　　(C) , who　　　　(D) who

( ) 4. Before the man was rescued, the only thing _____ he drank was rainwater.

  (A) that　　　　(B) who　　　　(C) whom　　　　(D) whose

二、翻譯

1. 大部分他的照片都是描述每天發生的事情。 (104 學測)
   Most of his photos described things _____

2. George 的父母是農夫，每天都很早起。
   George's parents _____ rise very early every day.

3. 幸運地，被困在大雪中的男人和他的狗被救出來了。

   _____

4. Sheila 沒通過全民英檢考試 (the GEPT test)，這件事讓她心情很不好。

   _____

6-2

. . . *a person/anyone/those/people* who + *be/V* . . .

句型範例

● **People who** are tired of their work should take some days off for a short trip.
凡是厭倦於工作的人應該休息幾天去做短程旅行。

● God helps **those who** help themselves. 【諺】天助自助者。

 ☆ Audiences of these shows tend to be **people who** are interested in food and enjoy watching people cook rather than **those who** want to do the cooking themselves. (105 指考)
這些節目的觀眾大多是對食物有興趣並喜歡看人做菜而非想自己下廚的人。

用法詳解

1. 本句型以關係子句表示「凡是…的人」。關係代名詞可用 that，然而 who 較為常見。

   ● **People who** are affected by disconnect anxiety tend to feel anxious or depressed when they can't use their smartphones.
   受離線焦慮症影響的人在無法使用手機時會感到焦慮與沮喪。

   ● **Those who** have no friends usually feel isolated and lonely.
   沒有朋友的人通常會感到孤立與寂寞。

2. 本句型可以用下列結構代換，注意各用法中動詞的單複數形：

those/people who	+ 複數 V
one/he who (較正式)	
a person who	+ 單數 V
anyone *who/that*	
whoever	

   ● *Those/People* who spend much time watching TV are likely to become nearsighted.

   ➡ *One/Anyone/He* who spends much time watching TV is likely to become nearsighted.

   ➡ **Whoever** spends much time watching TV is likely to become nearsighted.
   凡是花很多時間看電視的人容易近視。

- *Those/People* **who** often look on the bright side can live a happier life.
- *One/A person* **who** often looks on the bright side can live a happier life.
- **Whoever** often looks on the bright side can live a happier life.

  凡是常看光明面的人能過著較快樂的生活。

句型練習

一、選擇

( ) 1. People _____ commute by car will gain hours each day to work, rest, or read a newspaper. (103 學測)

    (A) they   (B) what   (C) which   (D) who

( ) 2. Prom night can be a dreadful experience for socially awkward teens or for _____ do not secure dates. (99 學測)

    (A) anyone who   (B) he who   (C) those who   (D) whoever

( ) 3. They can use their sense of vision and smell to tell the difference between _____ who pose a threat and _____ who do not. (100 學測)

    (A) they; he   (B) one; anyone   (C) those; one   (D) people; those

( ) 4. _____ has seen this award-winning film must have been moved to tears.

    (A) They who   (B) Whoever   (C) People who   (D) Anyone

( ) 5. Only _____ the language test are qualified to apply to this renowned university.

    (A) those who have passed   (B) those people have passed

    (C) one who has passed   (D) whoever has passed

二、翻譯

1. 對於那些未必有宗教信仰但喜愛大自然的人，他們很喜歡與美麗事物有關的名字。

   For _____ _____ _____ not necessarily religious but are fond of nature, names involving things of beauty are often favored. (103 學測)

2. 使用迎合式幽默的人愛說笑話，而且通常會使人心情變好。 (101 指考)

   _____ _____ _____ bonding humor tell jokes and generally lighten the mood.

3. 雖然陳先生很富有，但他是個很吝嗇的人，而且從不願意花錢幫助窮困的人。 (101 學測)

   Although Mr. Chen is rich, he is a very stingy person and is never willing to spend any money to help _____

4. 凡是規律運動的人比較可能有年輕的面容。

   _____

5. 亂倒垃圾的人會被罰款。

   _____

6-3

S + V₁ + N, *one/part/some/many/most/both/all/none/etc.*
+ of + *which/whom* + be/V₂...

句型範例

- On the basketball court, there are ten basketball players, **some of whom** are tall like giants. 籃球場上有十個籃球員，有些高得像巨人。
- Meg planted a lot of flowers in her garden, **most of which** are roses.
  Meg 在花園種了很多花，其中大部分是玫瑰。

☆ Sometimes a test leads you down a path to more and more testing, **some of which** may be invasive, or to treatment for things that should be left alone.
有時候做完一項檢查後還有更多的檢查，其中有些可能是侵入性的，或是接著被安排不必要的治療。 (104 學測)

用法詳解

1. 本句型由關係子句變化而來。關係代名詞具有連接詞的功能，連接兩個子句，可在前面加上**數量詞 + of** 表示數量。注意，of 後必須使用**關代的受格** (*whom/which*)。
   - Eric has two brothers, **both of whom** are married. Eric 有兩個哥哥，他們都已婚。
   - There are several books on the shelf, **many of which** are science fiction novels.
     書架上有好幾本書，其中很多是科幻小說。

2. of 之後是使用代名詞或關係代名詞，須從句子是否有**連接詞**來判斷。請見下列句子：
   - There are fifty teachers in this elementary school, **and half of them** are female.
     ① 兩句之間有 and 連接，第二句為完整子句，故 of 之後使用由主詞 they 變化的受格 them。
   - There are fifty teachers in this elementary school, **half of whom** are female.
     ① 兩句之間沒有連接詞，故 of 之後必須使用關係代名詞 whom 連接。
     這間小學有五十個老師，其中半數是女老師。
   - [正] The little boy got many Christmas presents, one of **which** was a robot.
     ➡ The little boy got many Christmas presents, **and** one of **them** was a robot.
       這小男孩在收到很多耶誕禮物，其中一個禮物是機器人。
   - [誤] The little boy got many presents on Christmas, one of them was a robot.
       ① 兩句之間缺少連接詞，故本句錯誤，應加上 and，或將 them 改成 which。

3. 常用數量詞有：half、each、both、some、part、many、most、much、all、few、little、one、two 等。此句型中，關係子句的動詞單複數須視主詞 (即數量詞) 決定。

- There is a pear on the table, **half of which** is rotten.

    桌上有個梨子，有一半爛掉了。① half 指的是一半的梨子，故關係子句中使用單數動詞 is。

- There are a dozen pears on the table, **half of which** are rotten.

    桌上有一打梨子，有一半爛掉了。

    ① half 指的是一打梨子的半數，為 6 個，故關係子句中使用複數動詞 are。

句型練習

一、選擇

( ) 1. There are thirty applicants for this job, many of _____ have a master's degree.

    (A) which   (B) who   (C) whom   (D) them

( ) 2. Gabriel showed us his photos, most of _____ were taken in Korea.

    (A) these   (B) whom   (C) them   (D) which

( ) 3. The drunkard bought some wine, all of which _____ drunk up in ten minutes.

    (A) is   (B) was   (C) are   (D) were

( ) 4. Shannon has twin daughters, _____ of whom love singing and dancing.

    (A) each   (B) two   (C) all   (D) both

二、句子合併與改寫

1. { Sheila invited twenty friends to her birthday party.
   { Many of them brought partners. (以關係詞合併)

   _____

2. The pupils see a lot of animals in the zoo; some of them are herbivores. (以關係詞改寫)

   _____

三、翻譯

1. 基日島被約 5,000 座島嶼環繞，其中有些只是突出地面的大岩石。 (101 學測)

   It (Kizhi) is surrounded by about 5,000 other islands, _____ _____ _____ are just rocks sticking out of the ground.

2. 上個月我看了五部電影，它們全是熱門影片。

   Last month, I watched five movies, _____

   _____ blockbusters.

3. 數學老師問我們十個問題，其中有半數很困難。

   _____

4. 我的鄰居養了兩隻狗，它們都會對陌生人吠叫。

   _____

6-4

. . . N + *why*/*where*/*when*-clause

- Mrs. Robinson can't forget the day **when** her husband proposed to her.
  Robinson 太太無法忘記她丈夫求婚的那天。
- Mr. and Mrs. Craig will celebrate their wedding anniversary in the restaurant **where** they first met. Craig 夫婦將會在他們初次見面的餐廳慶祝結婚週年。
- Red symbolizes good luck. That's the reason **why** people wear red for celebrations.
  紅色象徵好運。那就是人們在慶祝時穿紅色衣服的原因。

　☆ Even these people may look at the calendar to pick a lucky day **when** they make their choice. (103 學測)
即使是這些人也會查看月曆，挑個良辰吉日來取名字。

　☆ They (coral reefs) are stony structures full of dark hideaways **where** fish and sea animals can lay their eggs and escape from predators. (102 學測)
珊瑚礁是石頭般的構造，充滿著黑暗的藏身處，魚與海洋生物可在此產卵與逃離掠食者。

1. 關係副詞兼有**副詞**與**連接詞**的功能，相當於「介系詞 + 關係代名詞」，相對應的介系詞視先行詞決定。當先行詞為表**時間**的名詞時，關係副詞用 **when**；當先行詞為表**地點**的名詞時，關係副詞用 **where**；當先行詞為表**原因**的名詞時，關係副詞用 **why**。

先行詞 　用法	關係副詞	介系詞 + 關代
表時間	when	*at*/*in*/*on* + which
表地方	where	*at*/*in*/*on* + which
表原因	why	for + which

- The earthquake victims will never forget the day **when** (= on which) the tragedy happened. 地震受害者永遠不會忘記這悲劇災難發生的一天。
- The superstar's die-hard fans gathered in front of the hotel **where** (= in which) he stayed. 這位巨星的死忠粉絲聚集在他下榻的旅館前。

2. 若上下文的語意清楚，關係副詞的先行詞可以省略。

☆ Space is (the place) **where** our future is. 我們的未來在外太空。 (102 學測)

學習補給站

關係副詞亦有非限定的用法。當先行詞為**唯一**的對象或為**專有名詞**時，使用**非限定用法**，需在關係副詞前加**逗點**。

☆ Most of the area is covered by <u>woods</u>, **where** bird species are so numerous that it is a paradise for birdwatchers. (105 學測)

這個地域的大部分土地有樹林覆蓋，在此有許多鳥類棲息而成為賞鳥客的天堂。

句型練習

一、選擇

( ) 1. This is the market _____ I bought the beautiful bracelet.

(A) when (B) where (C) which (D) on which

( ) 2. Seeing this, Brahma, the chief god, decided to take their divinity away from them and hide it _____ it could never be found. (101 學測)

(A) which (B) where (C) how (D) when

( ) 3. One Saint Nicholas Day morning _____ the baker was just ready for business, the door of his shop flew open. (102 指考)

(A) that (B) which (C) when (D) , when

( ) 4. Angela told me the reason _____ she decided to keep a dog.

(A) where (B) when (C) why (D) how

二、句子合併

1. { Wyatt told me the reason.
   { He quit his job for that reason.　(以關係副詞合併)

   _____

2. { These football players will always remember the day.
   { They won the World Cup on the day.　(以關係副詞合併)

   _____

三、翻譯

1. 總統的演講將會同時在電視和廣播播出，以便更多人可以在發表的時間聽到。 (97 指考)

   The president's speech will be broadcast simultaneously on television and radio so that more people can listen to it at the time _____ _____ _____ _____.

2. 這個小鎮就是我渡過快樂童年的地方。

   This is the town _____

3. 拍攝這些電影的地點也成為熱門的觀光景點。 (101 學測)

   _____

6-5

what + *be*/*V*
what + S + *be*/*V*

句型範例

- Everyone wonders **what** is inside the magician's box.
  每個人都想知道魔術師的箱子裡有什麼東西。
- **What** the naughty child did annoyed his mother.
  這頑皮孩子所做的事情惹惱了他的媽媽。

☆ By the time he (Turing) was 23, he had already come up with the idea of **what** would become the modern computer—the Turing machine. (105 指考)
他 (圖靈) 在 23 歲時就想出日後會成為現代電腦的概念,即是圖靈機。

☆ **What** she (Morrison) wrote in her novels are true stories of African Americans. 她 (莫里森) 在小說中所描寫的是非裔美國人的真實故事。 (103 學測)

用法詳解

1. 本句型為 what 當關係詞引導名詞子句的用法。 在此用法中 , what = the thing (先行詞) + which/that (關係代名詞),表示「…的東西 / 事情」。

2. what 在名詞子句中可當作**主詞**或**受詞**。當作主詞用時,視為單數,搭配**單數動詞**。

   a. what 當主詞:

   - **What** lies behind the story means a lot to people in that country.
     在故事背後的意義對那國家的人民來說非常重大。
     ① what 當名詞子句的主詞,其後接單數動詞 lies,等於 The thing that lies . . .。

   - **What** matters most to the teacher is not how many scores his students have gotten but how much they have learned in class.
     對這老師而言,最重要的不是學生拿幾分,而是他們在課堂上學到多少。
     ① what 當名詞子句的主詞,其後接單數動詞 matters,等於 The thing that matters。

   b. what 當受詞:

   - Never put off till tomorrow **what** you can do today. 【諺】今日事,今日畢。
     ① what 當名詞子句中 do 的受詞,等於 the things that you can do。

   - Nobody believes **what** the dishonest man said. 無人相信這不老實的人所言。
     ① what 當名詞子句中 said 的受詞,等於 the thing(s) that the dishonest man said。

3. 注意，what 具有「先行詞 + 關係代名詞」功能，故 **what** 之前不可以再使用先行詞。

☆ It is not exactly **what** a child eats that truly matters, but how much time it stays in his mouth. (96 學測)

真正有關係的不完全是孩子所吃的東西，而是它停留在口中的時間有多少。

句型練習

一、選擇

( ) 1. If you want to know _____ your dreams mean, now there are websites you can visit to help you interpret them. (101 學測)

    (A) what   (B) which   (C) that   (D) when

( ) 2. The drummer needs to pay attention to what _____ going on in the plot and follow the rhythm of the characters. (101 指考)

    (A) are   (B) is   (C) have been   (D) has been

( ) 3. In other words, the scarcity of goods is _____ causes humans to attribute value.

    (A) what   (B) which   (C) why   (D) how   (100 學測)

( ) 4. So when a grown man speaks to a girl in _____ is a normal voice, she may hear it as yelling. (96 學測)

    (A) the things what he thinks   (B) he who thinks

    (C) what thinks   (D) what he thinks

二、句子改寫

1. Fashion is the thing which these models always talk about.

_____

2. The rumor which was written in the tabloid about the superstar proved true.

_____

三、翻譯

1. 他理解到只有合作，他才能盡他的力量讓社會變成應該有的樣子。 (99 學測)

He realizes that only by cooperating can he do his share in making society _____

_____ _____ _____ .

2. 科學家正努力找出導致這場災難的原因。 (102 學測)

Scientists are working hard to find out _____ _____ _____ this destruction.

3. 機長被迫幫助航空公司找出飛機的問題。 (101 指考)

He (The captain) was made to help the Airlines find out _____

_____

4. Paul 不確定他這週末要做什麼事。

_____

6-6

whatever . . .、whoever . . .、whomever . . .、whichever . . .

句型範例

- **Whoever** follows a heart-healthy diet can reduce the risk of heart disease.
  任何採取有益心臟健康飲食的人可以減少心臟病的風險。

- Phoebe's parents welcome **whomever** she invites to her birthday party.
  Phoebe 的父母歡迎任何她邀請來參加她生日派對的人。

 ☆ Grab a paintbrush, a trash bag, or **whatever** you need to help your community. 找支油漆刷、垃圾袋，或任何你需要的東西來幫助社區。 (98 指考)

用法詳解

1. whoever、whatever、whichever、whomever 屬於「複合關係代名詞」，表示「任何的…」，代替先行詞 (*anyone/anything*) + 關係代名詞 (*who/whom/that*)，用於引導名詞子句，可當名詞子句的主詞 (S) 或受詞 (O)。

whoever	= anyone who	任何…的人	當名詞子句的 S
whomever	= anyone whom	任何…的人	當名詞子句的 O
whatever	= anything that	任何…的事 / 物	當名詞子句的 S/O
whichever	= *any/either* one of them that	任何一個…	當名詞子句的 S/O

2. 判斷複合關係代名詞為主詞或受詞時，須從它**在名詞子句中的功能**判斷，而非由在句子裡的位置。若句中有插入語 (如 I think, you find 等)，不影響複合關係代名詞的格。

   a. 複合關係代名詞為名詞子句的主詞時，視為單數名詞，後面須接**單數動詞。**

   - **Whoever** treats others with respect is respected. 任何尊重他人的人都會被尊重。

     名詞子句

   - **Whatever** interests you is worth doing. 任何讓你感興趣的事情都值得去做。

     ① whatever 當名詞子句的主詞，視為單數名詞，故接單數動詞 interests。

   - The extroverted boy likes to make friends with **whoever** he thinks is outgoing. 這外向的男孩喜歡和任何他認為活潑的人交朋友。

     ① whoever 為名詞子句主詞，不受插入語影響。

   b. 複合關係代名詞為名詞子句的受詞時。

   - Tina is a gossip, who told her best friend's secrets to **whomever** she knows.

Tina 很八卦，她把好友的秘密告訴任何她認識的人。

① whomever 當名詞子句中 know 的受詞。

● **Whatever** the suspect said couldn't convince people of his innocence.

這嫌疑犯說的任何話都無法讓大家相信他是無辜的。① whatever 當 said 的受詞。

● I bought five cupcakes of different flavors. You can take **whichever** you like.

我買了五個不同口味的杯子蛋糕。你可以拿任何你喜歡的。

① whichever 當名詞子句中 like 的受詞。

句型練習

一、選擇

( ) 1. For this purpose, the parents gave ＿＿＿ they could to their daughter, which consequently went to the groom's family. (98 指考)

　　(A) whoever　　(B) whenever　　(C) whatever　　(D) whichever

( ) 2. ＿＿＿ the rude man spoke to gets mad with his attitude.

　　(A) Who　　(B) Whatever　　(C) Whoever　　(D) Whomever

( ) 3. After the election, the newly-elected mayor thanked ＿＿＿ supported him.

　　(A) everyone　　(B) anyone　　(C) whoever　　(D) whomever

( ) 4. ＿＿＿ the manager thinks is capable can take up this position.

　　(A) Whomever　　(B) Whoever　　(C) Whichever　　(D) Whatever

( ) 5. Father bought me several English novels. You may borrow ＿＿＿ you think is interesting.

　　(A) whoever　　(B) whatever　　(C) whichever　　(D) whomever

二、句子改寫 (以複合關係代名詞改寫)

1. The demanding mother always seems dissatisfied with anything that her son does.

＿＿＿＿＿＿＿＿＿＿＿＿＿＿＿＿＿＿＿＿＿＿＿＿＿＿＿＿＿＿＿＿＿

2. Legend has it that anyone who gazed directly upon Medusa would be turned into stone.

＿＿＿＿＿＿＿＿＿＿＿＿＿＿＿＿＿＿＿＿＿＿＿＿＿＿＿＿＿＿＿＿＿

三、翻譯

1. 這門徒說他會做任何他導師要他做的事。 (97 學測)

The disciple said he would do ＿＿＿ his guru asked him to do.

2. 任何闖紅燈的人都會被罰款。

＿＿＿＿＿＿＿＿＿＿＿＿＿＿＿＿＿＿＿＿＿＿＿＿＿ will be fined.

3. 這個小心眼的女人總是抱怨任何和她共事的人。

＿＿＿＿＿＿＿＿＿＿＿＿＿＿＿＿＿＿＿＿＿＿＿＿＿＿＿＿＿＿＿＿＿

7–1

$$S + have + \begin{cases} \textit{difficulty/problems/trouble/etc.} \\ \textit{fun/a good time} \end{cases} (+ in) + V\text{-ing}$$

句型範例

- This shy boy **has difficulty** making friends with girls.

  這個害羞的男孩和女生交朋友有困難。

- This foreigner **has no trouble** making himself understood in Mandarin.

  這個外國人毫無困難地用中文讓別人瞭解他的意思。

☆ Occasionally, however, they differ greatly in opinion and **have a hard time** making decisions.

  然而，他們偶爾也會意見相當分歧，難以做出決定。 (105 學測)

☆ So he **has little difficulty in** adjusting himself to his role in family life and in the business world, and to his duties as a citizen. (99 學測)

  所以他不太有困難調整自己在家庭生活、業界與市民責任之間的角色。

用法詳解

1. 本句型表示「做…有困難」或「做…很愉快，有趣」。使用時將 in 省略，故之後必須接 **V-ing**。注意本句型中表示「困難」、「問題」或「愉快」的名詞形，如：difficulty、trouble 與 fun (不可數名詞)、problems (複數形)、a good time 與 a hard time (單數形)。

   - The lazy student **has trouble** passing all the exams.

     這個懶惰的學生很難通過所有的考試。

   - The stubborn old man **has problems** communicating with his children.

     這個頑固的老人很難和他的孩子們溝通。

   - These girls **have a good time** doing shopping in the department store.

     這些女孩在百貨公司購物很愉快。

2. 可在名詞前加入 no、little、some、much、great 等字修飾。

   - This exchange student **has no difficulty** fitting in at his new school.

     這位交換學生毫無困難地融入新學校。

   - The young police officer **had little trouble** handling car accidents.

     這年輕的警員處理車禍問題有點困難。

學習補給站

以下句型有類似用法，省略 in 後加 V-ing。

S + spend + *money/time* + (in) + V-ing 花錢 / 時間做…

S + waste + *money/time* + (in) + V-ing 浪費錢 / 時間做…

S + be + busy + (in) + V-ing 忙著…

● Greg is a big baseball fan, who has **spent much money** buying baseball cards.

Greg 是個狂熱的棒球迷，他已經花許多錢買球員卡。

句型練習

一、選擇

( ) 1. Tim often mentions the _____ he had in making ends meet when he was young.

(A) hard times   (B) problem   (C) difficulty   (D) troubles

( ) 2. Inattentive children have difficulty _____ on completing a task or learning something new. (96 指考)

(A) focuses   (B) focused   (C) to focus   (D) focusing

( ) 3. The man with a poor sense of direction has a hard time _____ remembering directions.

(A) at   (B) in   (C) about   (D) with

( ) 4. My aunt, who is nearsighted, has _____ without glasses.

(A) problems driving   (B) difficulties to drive

(C) a trouble in driving   (D) hard times driving

二、句子合併與改寫

1. { Parrots can imitate human sounds.
   { They can do so without difficulty. (以 no difficulty 合併)

_____

2. The young lady thinks it difficult to get rid of her bad habits. (以 a hard time 改寫)

_____

三、翻譯

1. 大部分的其他五歲小孩都無法搆到浴室水槽。 (105 學測)

Many other five-year-olds _____ _____ _____ the bathroom sink.

2. 受時差之苦的旅客在調整生理時鐘方面有困難。 (94 學測)

A traveler who suffers from jet lag _____

_____ his biological clock.

3. 這些童子軍是新手，所以生火有困難。

_____

7-2

S + *keep/finish/mind/enjoy/practice/avoid/etc.* + V-ing

句型範例

● In a conversation, it is necessary that we **avoid** using offensive gestures.

在與人交談時，我們必須避免使用有冒犯之意的手勢。

● By the end of the semester, the students will have **finished** reading two novels.

在學期末之前，學生們將會讀完二本小說。

☆ But he simply ignored them and **kept** working on the soil and planting trees there. 但他不理會他們，繼續翻土和種植樹木。 (105 學測)

☆ Everyone in our company **enjoys** working with Jason. He's got all the qualities that make a desirable partner. (100 學測)

我們公司裡的人都喜歡和 Jason 共事。他擁有所有成為好伙伴的特質。

☆ If people **keep** polluting the rivers, no fish there will survive in the long run. 如果人們繼續污染河川，最後河裡將沒有魚能夠存活下來。 (93 學測)

☆ Ann **enjoyed** going to the flower market. She believed that the fragrance of flowers refreshed her mind. (97 學測)

Ann 喜歡去花市。她相信花的香味可以讓她提振精神。

用法詳解

1. 動名詞具有名詞特質，可當主詞或受詞。本單元介紹有些動詞固定接動名詞當受詞的用法。常用的此類動詞有：

keep、finish、mind、enjoy、practice、avoid、imagine、quit、give up、consider、postpone (延緩 = put off)、suggest、propose、recommend、deny、admit、mention、risk、resent、regret 等。

2. 要表示動名詞的否定意義，在動名詞前加上 no、not 或 never，即 *no/not/never* + V-ing。

● The wounded soldier could hardly imagine **never** being able to walk again.

這受傷的軍人很難想像永遠無法行走。

● The young man regretted **not** thinking twice before he made the decision.

這年輕人後悔沒多加考慮再下決定。

學習補給站

動名詞的執行者與主詞不同時，較正式用法為「**所有格 (one's) + 動名詞**」，表示動名詞的

執行者。因動名詞有名詞的特性，故在前面加上所有格以表示動名詞的所屬對象。近年，「受詞＋動名詞」的用法也變得常見。比較句子：

● Do you **mind closing** the door? 你介意關上門嗎？① 主詞與動名詞的執行者相同，都是 you。

● Do you **mind** *my/me* **closing** the door? 你介意我關上門嗎？

① 主詞與動名詞的執行者不同，主詞為 you，但動名詞的執行者是 I，故用 *my/me* 表示執行關門動作者。

句型練習

一、選擇

( ) 1. To preserve them (truffles), gourmet experts suggest _____ them in closed glass jars in a refrigerator. (100 指考)

  (A) putting (B) to put (C) put (D) to putting

( ) 2. This newlywed couple can hardly imagine _____ each other for one day.

  (A) seeing not (B) not seeing (C) not to see (D) to not see

( ) 3. To avoid _____ by news reports, we should learn to distinguish between facts and opinions. (95 指考)

  (A) misleading (B) being misled (C) leading (D) been misled

( ) 4. Do you mind _____ something first? I am starving to death!

  (A) to eat (B) your eating (C) I eating (D) my eating

二、句子合併

1. { These teenagers practiced skateboarding for their upcoming game.
   { They just finished it.

   _____

2. { Many people communicate with their friends through social networking websites.
   { They enjoy it.

   _____

三、翻譯

1. 即使非常成功，這三兄弟仍然繼續努力 (move forward)。 (103 學測)

   They (the three brothers) _____ _____ forward even after a big success.

2. 雕刻者在寒冷的環境中必須快速工作以避免感冒。

   The carver must work fast in a cold environment to _____

   _____

3. 很多喜歡 (enjoy) 在台灣生活的外國人考慮 (consider) 在這裡定居下來。

   _____

4. 凡是希望享有健康的人應該避免熬夜並戒掉吃高脂 (high-fat) 的食物。

   _____

7-3

S + be worth + *V-ing*/*N*

句型範例

- Having a complete collection of famous paintings and sculptures, Louvre Museum **is** definitely **worth** a visit. 羅浮宮完整收藏了名畫與雕刻品，絕對值得一遊。

- Whatever is **worth** doing at all is **worth** doing well. 凡是值得做的事情就值得做好。

 ☆ The American authorities do not think mice and rats **are worth** counting and, as these are the most common laboratory animals. (100 指考)
美國當局不認為老鼠值得算進去，因為它們是最常見的實驗動物。

用法詳解

1. 本句型表示「值得…」。be worth 後必須加動名詞 (V-ing) 或名詞。注意，在本句型中，以動名詞 (V-ing) 來表示被動意義。

- Nothing in this tabloid **is worth reading**. 這小報裡沒有值得一讀的內容。

  ① 本句不可寫為 Nothing . . . is worth being read，因為 be worth + V-ing 即表示被動意義。

- The origins of these traditional holidays **are worth remembering** forever.
  這些傳統節日的起源值得被永遠記得。

  ① 本句不可寫為 . . . are worth being remembered，因為 be worth + V-ing 即表示被動意義。

2. 若要加強語氣，可以在 worth 前加上 **well**。

- This fashion magazine is **well** worth reading for models.
  這本流行雜誌值得模特兒閱讀。

3. 下列句型亦表示「值得…」之意：

   a. S + be worthy of + *N*/*being p.p.*
   此句型不以 V-ing 表示被動。要表達**被動**意義時，必須使用 be worthy of + being p.p.。比較下列句子：

   - To many foreigners, the night markets in Taiwan **are worthy of a visit**.
   ➡ To many foreigners, the night markets in Taiwan **are worthy of being visited**.
   ➡ To many foreigners, the night markets in Taiwan **are worth visiting**.
     對許多外國人而言，台灣的夜市值得一遊。

   b. It is worthwhile + for sb + to V ➡ It is worth one's while + *to V*/*V-ing*

- **It is worthwhile** for elderly people to spend some time learning new things.

➡ **It is worth elderly people's while** *to spend/spending* some time learning new things. 對年長者而言，花一些時間學新的事物是值得的。

學習補給站

1. 有些 be worthy of + N 的結構有相對應的形容詞，如：be worthy of note = noteworthy (值得注意)、be worthy of trust = trustworthy (值得信任)。
2. be worth it 很值得

句型練習

一、選擇

( ) 1. The artists gathered at the café may not be as great as those of the past, but faces worth _____ are just the same. (97 指考)

　　(A) being watched　　(B) watching　　(C) to be watched　　(D) of being watched

( ) 2. Karen's plan seems risky, but it _____.

　　(A) is worth a try　　　　　　　　(B) is worthy a try

　　(C) is worthy a trying　　　　　　(D) is worth being tried

( ) 3. These volunteers' good deeds _____.

　　(A) are worth being praised　　　　(B) are worth of praise

　　(C) are worth praising　　　　　　(D) are worthy of praised

( ) 4. This is especially _____ when one considers that public television stations must often survive on very limited budgets, on viewers' donations, and on private foundations and some governmental funding. (96 學測)

　　(A) worthy one's note　　　　　　(B) worthy being noted

　　(C) worth noted　　　　　　　　(D) noteworthy

二、翻譯

1. 我也會更注意寫作風格，嘗試以有趣且值得閱讀的方式書寫。 (95 指考)

　　I will also take more care with my style, trying to write in a way that is interesting and

　　_____ _____.

2. 出生率下降的問題非常值得政府的注意。

　　The birth rate decline problem _____

3. 毫無疑問地，我們的言論自由值得捍衛。

　　_____

4. 這受爭論的福利改革議題值得辯論。

　　_____

7–4

can't help + V-ing

句型範例

- Finding that her car has been towed away, the lady **can't help** frowning.
  發現她的車已經被拖走了，這女士忍不住皺眉頭。

- Hearing the hilarious joke, all the students **can't help** roaring with laughter.
  聽到這個令人捧腹的笑話，所有的學生忍不住哄堂大笑。

用法詳解

1. 本句型表示「不得不…」或「忍不住…」。使用時，必須注意其後接動名詞。

   - The exhausted marathon runner **can't help** gulping for air after reaching the finish line. 那個疲倦的馬拉松跑者在抵達終點線後忍不住大口吸氣。

   - The nervous girl **can't help** biting her nails. 這緊張的女孩忍不住咬指甲。

2. can't help 後也可接名詞。

   - The old man tried not to think about the past, but he just **couldn't help** it.
     這老人試著不要回想過去，但他就是忍不住。

學習補給站

1. 表示「不得不」、「忍不住」的句型尚有：

   a. can't but + V：

   - Since a fierce typhoon is approaching, the singer **can't but** consider postponing his concert. 因為強颱接近，這個歌手不得不考慮將演唱會延期。

   b. can't help but + V：

   - The hungry backpacker **couldn't help but** eat up the whole pizza.
     這個飢餓的背包客忍不住把整個披薩都吃光了。

   - The child was so badly behaved that his mother **couldn't help but** scold him.
     這孩子的舉止太粗魯了，他媽媽忍不住斥責他。

2. have no choice but + to V 表示「別無選擇只好…」，注意其與本單元句型的差別：

   - As it is getting dark, all the boys in the park **have no choice but** to go home.
     因為天色暗了，公園裡所有的男孩別無選擇只好回家。

句型練習

一、選擇

( ) 1. Having stayed up for several nights to prepare for the mid-term exam, the student ＿＿＿＿ feeling tired.

    (A) can't help   (B) can't but help

    (C) can't but   (D) has no choice but

( ) 2. The soldier's wound hurt so much that he couldn't help but ＿＿＿＿ out a cry of pain.

    (A) to let   (B) let   (C) letting   (D) to letting

( ) 3. Afraid of being punished by his mother, the little child ＿＿＿＿ crying.

    (A) couldn't help   (B) couldn't but

    (C) couldn't help but   (D) had no choice but to

( ) 4. Having hurt his ankle, the tennis player had no choice but ＿＿＿＿ up the game.

    (A) give   (B) giving   (C) gave   (D) to give

二、句子合併

1. ⎰ The weather was very hot.
   ⎱ Irene drank up two bottles of juice.   (加入 couldn't help)

   The weather was so hot that ＿＿＿＿＿＿＿＿＿＿＿＿＿＿＿＿＿＿＿＿＿＿＿＿＿

2. ⎰ Keith knew that he had passed the final exam.
   ⎱ He gave a sigh of relief.   (加入 couldn't help but)

   After knowing that he had passed the final exam, ＿＿＿＿＿＿＿＿＿＿＿＿＿＿＿

   ＿＿＿＿＿＿＿＿＿＿＿＿＿＿＿

三、翻譯

1. Elsa 是個優雅的女士，所以很多男子忍不住愛上她。

   Elsa is such an elegant lady that many men ＿＿＿＿ ＿＿＿＿ ＿＿＿＿ in love with her.

2. 等著考試結果，學生們忍不住覺得緊張。

   Waiting for the test results, ＿＿＿＿＿＿＿＿＿＿＿＿＿＿＿＿＿＿＿＿＿＿＿＿＿

3. 這個父親到處都找不到兒子，他別無選擇只好報警幫忙。

   This father could not find his son anywhere, so ＿＿＿＿＿＿＿＿＿＿＿＿＿＿＿＿

   ＿＿＿＿＿＿＿＿＿＿＿＿＿＿＿

4. 這個演講者不得不咳嗽來清喉嚨。

   ＿＿＿＿＿＿＿＿＿＿＿＿＿＿＿＿＿＿＿＿＿＿＿＿＿＿＿＿＿＿＿＿＿＿＿＿＿

7-5

. . . to + *V-ing*/*N*

句型範例

- Ariel **is used to** drinking black coffee to refresh herself. Ariel 習慣喝黑咖啡來提神。
- Out of her love for children, the writer **is devoted to** writing children's storybooks.
  出於對孩童的愛,這作家致力於寫兒童故事書。

- ☆ This poses a serious problem **when it comes to** getting enough water to drink. 當提到獲取足夠的水飲用時,這會產生嚴重的問題。 (105 學測)
- ☆ When I asked if she was angry about what she had lost, she **admitted to** being frustrated occasionally. 當我問她是否對所失去的一切感到憤怒,她承認偶爾會覺得很挫敗。 (101 學測)

用法詳解

有些用法中的 to 為介系詞,其後必須加名詞或動名詞 (V-ing)。 常見的此類用法有：*be*/*get used*/*accustomed* to (習慣於)、be *devoted*/*dedicated*/*committed* to (致力於)、be addicted to (沈溺於)、 look forward to (期待)、 object to = be opposed to (反對)、 admit to (承認)、adjust to (適應於)、in addition to (除了)、when it comes to (當談到⋯的時候) 等。

- Living in the woods alone, the old man had **gotten accustomed to** living without electricity. 獨自住在樹林裡,這老人已經習慣於過著沒有電的生活。
- The doctor **devotes himself to** finding the cure for the contagious disease.
  這個醫生致力於找尋這個傳染病的療法。
- I haven't heard from Victor for ages, so I am **looking forward to** seeing him.
  我好久沒聽到 Victor 的消息了,所以我很期待見到他。
- **When it comes to** playing the guitar, Teddy is second to none.
  當談到彈吉他時,Teddy 是最棒的。

學習補給站

比較下列三組用法：used to + 原形動詞 (過去常⋯,曾經⋯)、be used to + 原形動詞 (被用來)、be used to + V-ing (習慣於⋯)。

- ☆ I **used to** carry a fresh suit to work with me so I could change if my clothes got wrinkled. 我以前帶著乾淨的衣服去上班,便於在衣服皺了時替換。 (91 學測)

● Red roses **are used to** <u>decorate</u> the new room. 紅玫瑰被用來裝飾這個新房間。

● Mr. Brown **is used to** <u>taking</u> a stroll with his wife after dinner.

Brown 先生習慣於在晚餐後和他太太一起散步。

句型練習

一、選擇

( ) 1. He _____ the replacement of wooden bridges with stronger iron ones and earned a fortune. (96 指考)

   (A) devoted himself to   (B) was devoted himself to

   (C) devoted for   (D) was devoted with

( ) 2. All the children are looking forward to _____ on a picnic this weekend.

   (A) go   (B) have gone   (C) going   (D) having gone

( ) 3. _____, these students are not interested at all.

   (A) In spite of studying science   (B) In spite of to study science

   (C) When it comes to study science   (D) When it comes to studying science

( ) 4. Choose the WRONG sentence.

   (A) The Virtual Patient can also be used to explore various medical situations.

      (98 指考)

   (B) They were not used to live in the places where the weather was chilly all the time.

   (C) Teaching used to be conducted with a blackboard and a handful of tattered textbooks. (102 指考)

   (D) Each nest used to have but one queen, but now many mounds are often found with multiple queens. (94 學測)

二、翻譯

1. 我們完全致力於幫助狗享有充實和活躍的生活。 (96 學測)

We _____ completely _____ _____ _____ dogs enjoy a full and active life.

2. Sean 是手機控，習慣每小時就查看一次手機。

Sean, who _____ his

smartphone, _____

3. 除了和老朋友開心談天，Sandra 在同學會也盡情地享用美食。

_____, Sandra also ate to

her heart's content in the reunion party.

7-6

S + *keep/stop/save/prevent/protect/etc*. from + *V-ing/N*

句型範例

- The government has created nature reserves to **protect** animals **from** poaching.
  政府創立了自然保留區以保護動物不受盜獵。
- One of the park keeper's duties is to **stop** visitors **from** littering.
  公園管理員的職責一就是阻止遊客亂丟垃圾。

- ☆ Scientists are also worried about how to **keep** the Sphinx **from** falling apart again. 科學家也擔心如何才能使獅身人面像不要再碎裂。 (105 指考)
- ☆ Ongoing conflicts across the Middle East have **prevented** more than 13 million children **from** attending school. (105 學測)
  中東境內持續不斷的衝突已經使超過一千三百萬位孩童無法上學。

用法詳解

1. 本單元介紹一些動詞常與介系詞 from 搭配的用法。在此用法中的 from 有「使免於…」的意思，其後接動名詞 (V-ing) 或名詞。常見的動詞有：keep、stop、refrain (抑制)、ban (禁止)、prohibit (禁止)、prevent、protect、save。

   - The teacher **banned** the students **from** using cell phones in class.
     老師禁止學生們在課堂上用手機。
   - Everyone has the responsibility to **prevent** environmental pollution **from** getting worse. 每個人都有責任預防環境污染繼續惡化。
   - Instead of using a hair dryer, Matilda usually air-dries her hair in order to **protect** it **from** damage.
     Matilda 不使用吹風機，而是讓頭髮自然吹乾以保護它不受損害。

2. 注意，本句型改成被動用法時，必須保留介系詞 from。

   [主動] The lifeguard **saved** the little child **from** drowning.
   [被動] The little child **was saved from** drowning by the lifeguard.
   　　　救生員拯救這小孩，使他免於溺水。

3. 本句型中的此類動詞轉成名詞形時，亦常搭配 from 使用。

   ☆ Normal winter boots and outfits offer little **protection from** the cold.
   　　一般的冬靴及冬裝只提供些微的禦寒效果。 (102 指考)

句型練習

一、選擇

( ) 1. They have talked about constructing a wall around the Sphinx to protect it
_____ the wind and sand. (105 指考)

    (A) by   (B) for   (C) about   (D) from

( ) 2. The space suit provides necessary oxygen supply and _____ the astronauts
_____ feeling the extreme heat or cold outside the shuttle. (95 學測)

    (A) makes; not   (B) lets; not   (C) keeps; from   (D) protects; by

( ) 3. This bark can be pretty thick, well over two feet in the more mature trees. It gives
the older trees a certain kind of protection _____ insects. (100 學測)

    (A) about   (B) for   (C) with   (D) from

( ) 4. The father drives his children to school every day, as he wants to protect them
_____ .

    (A) about being kidnapped   (B) from kidnapping

    (C) for kidnapping   (D) to be kidnapped

二、句子合併與改寫

1. { The woman applies cream to her face every day.
   The woman doesn't want her face to get wrinkled.   (以 prevent . . . from 合併)

_____

2. The boy walked slowly on the wet floor so that he wouldn't slip.
(以 keep . . . from 改寫)

_____

三、翻譯

1. 頂部的岩石是其結構最堅硬的部分，保護下方較柔軟的岩石不被風化。 (104 指考)
The top stone is the hardest part of each formation and _____ the softer rock
underneath _____ erosion.

2. 藉著這麼做，人們希望日本政府會拯救日漸沈重的退休金制度，使它免於破產。
By so doing, it is hoped that Japan's government will _____ its increasingly
burdened pension system _____ _____ _____ . (96 指考)

3. 房客們還得學會如何在極地睡袋裡快速暖身，以及如何防止眼鏡結凍。 (102 指考)
The guests also learn how to warm up quickly in their arctic sleeping bags and _____

_____

4. 如果你想保護電腦不受新病毒的攻擊，你必須經常更新並且升級防毒軟體。 (96 指考)

_____

7–7

$S + V + N_1 + \text{instead of} + \textit{V-ing}/N_2$
$\text{Instead of} + \text{V-ing}, S + V$

句型範例

● Many young kids like to eat hamburgers **instead of** rice.
很多小孩喜歡吃漢堡而不喜歡吃飯。

● **Instead of** drinking bubble milk tea, I ate a cupcake after dinner.
晚餐後，我吃了杯子蛋糕而非喝珍珠奶茶。

 ☆ **Instead of** being hailed as one of the crucial figures in defeating the Nazis,
Turing was convicted of "gross indecency." (105 指考)
圖靈沒被認為是打敗納粹的重要人物，反而被控猥褻。

用法詳解

1. instead of 是介系詞片語，意為「而不是；而非」，用於語意前後相反時，後面接名詞或動名詞。

● Aaron ordered spaghetti **instead of** a pizza. Aaron 點了一份義大利麵而不是披薩。

● **Instead of** going on with their work, these workers would like to take a rest.
這些工人們想要休息一下，而不是繼續工作。

2. 注意比較 instead 與 instead of 的用法：

	詞性	意思	用法
instead	副詞	反而…	置於句首或句尾
instead of	介系詞	而不是	後面接動名詞

☆ **Instead of** treating the homeless man as a shame of the society, Mrs. Wang
provided him with food and water. (91 指考)

➡ Mrs. Wang **didn't** treat the homeless man as a shame of the society; **instead**,
she provided him with food and water.
王太太沒把這個流浪漢當成社會的恥辱，反而提供他食物和水。

學習補給站

與 instead of 同義的有 **rather than**。其用法如下：

a. 當介系詞：後面接名詞或動名詞。

● The baker made some cookies with butter **rather than** margarine.
麵包師傅用牛油而非人造奶油做了一些餅乾。

☆ **Rather than** running away as they did with the smell, the elephants acted aggressively toward the red clothing. (100 學測)

大象對紅色衣服表現出攻擊性，但不會像聞到氣味時會逃跑。

b. 當對等連接詞：後面的動詞形式必須**與前面對等的動詞**一致。

● The obese woman enjoys eating snacks at home **rather than** going out to exercise. 這個肥胖的婦人喜歡在家吃點心而不是出去運動。

☆ Elephants tend to attack **rather than** escape when in danger. (100 學測)

遇到危險時，大象通常會攻擊而非逃跑。

句型練習

一、選擇

( ) 1. Today, the Paralympics are sports events for athletes from six different disability groups. They emphasize the participants' athletic achievements _____ their physical disability. (98 學測)

　(A) in terms of　　(B) at the risk of　　(C) instead of　　(D) at the cost of

( ) 2. The diligent student often turns to books for information _____ going online.

　(A) instead of　　(B) rather than　　(C) not instead　　(D) regardless of

( ) 3. Our English teacher always emphasizes the importance of learning new words in context rather than _____ each of them individually. (93 指考)

　(A) learns　　(B) to learn　　(C) learned　　(D) learning

二、句子改寫

1. The student decided to take a gap year instead of finishing his studies first.

(用rather than 改寫)

2. I cannot alter my father's inability to express his feelings. Instead, I must accept myself. (97 指考)

Instead of _____

三、翻譯

1. 沒有花時間瞭解和尊重彼此，我們反而變成苛求、憤恨、武斷的和偏執。 (94 學測)

_____ _____ taking time to understand and respect each other, we become demanding, resentful, judgmental, and intolerant.

2. 他討厭施捨；反而，他用錢幫助他人自助。 (96 指考)

He abhorred charity; _____

8-1

. . . who/whom/which (+ N)/how/what/etc. + to V . . .

句型範例

- The missing child couldn't find his parents. He didn't know **what to do**.
  這走失的孩子找不到父母。他不知道該怎麼辦。

- The teacher asked a difficult question; many students didn't know **how to answer**
  it. 老師問了一個困難的問題；很多學生不知道該如何回答。

- ☆ Why do we not know **how to sing** these ballads?
  我們為什麼不知道怎麼唱這些古謠？ (104 學測)

- ☆ They (Blasters) decide **what explosives to use**, **where to position** them in
  the building, and **how to time** their explosions. 爆破團隊決定要使用何種炸
  藥、在建物中何處安置這些炸藥，並安排何時爆破。 (101 指考)

用法詳解

1. 本單元介紹將「**疑問詞 + S *can/should* + V**」簡化成「**疑問詞 + to + V**」的用法。
   步驟如下：(1) 省略疑問詞後的主詞。
   　　　　　 (2) 刪除助動詞 can 或 should，改為 to。

   - There are too many books in the library. I am not sure where I can find the novel
     I want.

   ➡ There are too many books in the library. I am not sure **where to find** the novel
     I want. 圖書館裡有太多書了。我不確定哪裡可以找到我要的小說。

   - The lazy student doesn't care when he should hand in his assignment.

   ➡ The lazy student doesn't care **when to hand** in his assignment.
     這個懶惰的學生不在乎何時應繳交作業。

2. 注意，本句型只適用於句子前後的兩個**主詞相同**時。

   - The outstanding student has received offers from many colleges. She wonders
     which college she should choose.

   ➡ The outstanding student has received offers from many colleges. She wonders
     which college to choose.
     這個優秀的學生收到許多大學的入學許可。她在考慮應該選擇哪所。

句型練習

一、選擇

( ) 1. After she graduates, Deborah plans to use her knowledge to educate people _____ care of their bodies. (100 學測)

    (A) how to best take   (B) how can they best take

    (C) what they could best take   (D) what to best take

( ) 2. By the way, if you can, please send this letter back to us. We can erase and reuse it. Just tie it to Maggie's leg and she'll know _____ it. (98 學測)

    (A) where has she taken   (B) where did she take

    (C) where she took   (D) where to take

( ) 3. The keepers at the sanctuary use recorded howls to teach the monkeys _____ the loudest cries to scare people away. (97 學測)

    (A) where the keepers could make   (B) where should the monkeys make

    (C) how to make   (D) what to make

二、句子改寫 (以本單元句型改寫)

1. The shy boy doesn't know what he can talk about with girls.

    _____

2. The earthquake victims wonder whether they should leave or stay in their village.

    _____

三、翻譯

1. 因為僅有冒險精神不足以讓人在冰雕旅館中捱過兩個小時，所以旅館員工會簡要地告知住客該穿什麼、該怎麼做 (behave)。 (102 指考)

    Since an adventurous spirit alone is not enough to withstand more than two hours at the icy hotel, the staff briefs guests on _____ _____ _____ and _____ _____ _____.

2. 在衣索比亞，在教師不在場的情形下，孩子們獨自學用平板電腦與學英文字母。

    In Ethiopia, in the absence of teachers, children figured out _____ _____ and learned the English ABCs. (102 指考)

3. 住客也要學會如何在極地睡袋裡迅速暖身，與如何防止眼鏡結凍。 (102 指考)

    The guests also learn _____ quickly in their arctic sleeping bags and _____ eyeglasses from freezing.

4. 迷路時，指南針可以告訴我們該選擇哪一條路。

    _____

8-2

$$S + \begin{Bmatrix} \text{be + adj.} \\ V_1 + \text{adv.} \end{Bmatrix} + \text{enough + to } V_2$$

句型範例

- The poor man was **fortunate enough to** win the lottery. 這個窮人贏得彩券，很幸運。
- The umpire explained the rule **clearly enough** for the players **to** understand.
  裁判將規則解釋得夠清楚，讓選手們可以瞭解。

☆ One former prime minister considered it **important enough to** reveal in his official profile that he was a type A, while his opposition rival was type B. (105 學測)

某日本前首相認為在官方資料中公佈他是 A 型很重要，而他的競選對手是 B 型。

☆ It (The kilt) should be **long enough to** cover the wearer's knees. (101 學測)
蘇格蘭裙穿起來的長度應該要能覆蓋穿著者的膝蓋。

用法詳解

1. 本句型表示「夠…而能…」，以 enough 置於形容詞或副詞之後做修飾。
   - The eighty-year-old man is **healthy enough to** do Tai Chi every day.
     這個八十歲老翁很健康能每天打太極拳。
   - The deliveryman worked **efficiently enough to** deliver all the goods in four hours. 這位送貨員工作夠有效率，他在四小時內送完了所有貨品。

2. 本句型常會與 S + be/V + too + *adj./adv.* + to V 做比較，詳細介紹請見 14-2。請留意句中 too 與 enough 的位置：
   - The patient is not strong **enough** to walk on his own. 病人不夠強壯，無法自己走。
     ① *adj./adv.* + enough，enough 置於 adj. 或 adv. 的後面做修飾。
   - The patient is **too** weak to walk on his own. 這病人太虛弱而無法自己行走。
     ① too + *adj./adv.*，too 置於 adj. 或 adv. 的前面做修飾。

句型練習

一、選擇

( ) 1. But unfortunately, even the high resolution of Google Earth is not _____ to tell which end of the cow is its head, and which its tail. (98 學測)
(A) powerful enough (B) enough powerful (C) too powerful (D) that powerful

( ) 2. It often demands even greater effort in adjustment since we are not _____ catch up with the new time schedule. (94 學測)

    (A) so quick that we can't   (B) too quick to

    (C) enough quick to   (D) quick enough to

( ) 3. The speaker was knowledgeable enough _____ all the questions the audience raised.

    (A) answering   (B) to answer   (C) about answering (D) by answering

( ) 4. Matthew studied _____ to get good grades on the college entrance examination.

    (A) enough hard   (B) hard enough   (C) enough hardly   (D) hardly enough

二、句子合併 (以本單元句型合併)

1. 　{ The ambulance ran very fast.
　　 It sent the injured man to the hospital in time.

2. 　{ The engineer was very smart.
　　 He solved the complicated problem in 10 minutes.

三、翻譯

1. 台灣的夜市早已被認為足以代表我們的在地文化。 (100 學測)

The night markets in Taiwan have long been considered _____ _____ _____ represent our local culture.

2. 根據最近的研究，12 歲以下的孩童通常還沒成熟到能辨識風險與處理危險的情況。

According to recent research, children under the age of 12 are generally not _____

_____ _____ recognize risk and deal with dangerous situations. (101 學測)

3. 它們 (蜘蛛絲) 通常很堅韌，能夠維持一天。 (100 指考)

They (The silk threads) are usually _____

_____

4. 英語學習者必須閱讀夠多才能提升能力。

_____

8-3

$$\left.\begin{array}{l}\text{What}\\\text{All (that)}\end{array}\right\} + S\ (+\ aux.)\ +\ do\ +\ be\ +\ (to)\ V$$

句型範例

- **All** the exhausted man wants to do **is** take a hot bath.

  這個很疲憊的男人想做的事情就是洗個熱水澡。

- **What** the nervous student could do **was** get prepared for the mid-term exam.

  這個焦慮的學生能做的事就是準備期中考。

用法詳解

1. 本句型意為「某人所…的就是…」，以 All 或 What 為主詞。兩者不同處為：

   a. 以 All 當主詞時，其後以 that 引導關係子句修飾，在關係子句中，因 that 是受詞，所以常被省略。

   b. 以 What 當主詞時，What 為複合關係代名詞，等於「先行詞＋關代」(The thing *which/that*)，故其後不需再接關係代名詞。

2. 以 All 或 What 為主詞時，視為單數，因此主要動詞使用單數形 is 或 was。

   - **All** (**that**) the newly elected president has to do **is** (to) lower unemployment rates. 這新上任的總統必須做的就是降低失業率。

   - **What** the boy needed to do before his mother got home **was** (to) tidy up his room. 這男孩在他母親回家前必須做的事情就是清理房間。

3. 本句型的主詞補語為不定詞 (to V) 形式，to 常被省略，故可用**原形動詞**。

   - **All** these scientists want to do **is** (to) find cure for AIDS.

     這些科學家們想做的事就是找到愛滋病的療法。

   - What these refugees expect **is** (to) settle down in a safe place.

     這些難民期待的是在安全的地方定居下來。

句型練習

一、選擇

(　) 1. Before the teacher announces the exam results, ＿＿＿＿ the students can do is wait.

　　(A) all which　　　(B) which　　　(C) all that　　　(D) what that

( ) 2. What the mother asks her children to do _____ brush their teeth before they go to bed.

(A) are   (B) is   (C) be   (D) has

( ) 3. As soon as the guests arrive at the hotel, what they have to do is _____.

(A) presented their ID cards   (B) making phone calls to their family

(C) to putting away their luggage   (D) check in

二、翻譯

1. 這位演員必須做的事情就是在幾小時內背好他的台詞。

_____ the actor must do _____ _____ his lines in a few hours.

2. 新來的學生想做的事情就是很快適應新班級。

_____ that the new student wants to do _____

_____

3. 警察所能為這迷路的孩子做的就是幫他找到父母。

_____

8-4

S + have + *something/nothing/much/little* + to do with + N

句型範例

- One man's success **has much to do with** his attitude toward life.

  一個人的成功和他的人生態度很有關係。

- The suspect claimed that he **had nothing to with** the murder.

  這個嫌疑犯聲稱他跟這件謀殺案沒有關係。

 ☆ Note, however, that rarity **has little to do with** the age of a coin. (102 學測)

然而，要注意的是，稀有性與錢幣的年份沒有有太大的關聯。

用法詳解

1. 本句型以「have . . . to do with」表示「和…有關係」，可以用 something、nothing、much、little 等字表示程度：

have something to do with	和…有些關係
have nothing to do with	和…沒有關係
have *much/a lot* to do with	和…很有關係
have little to do with	和…幾乎沒關係

- The doctor thinks that Tommy's illness **has something to do with** his living habits. 醫生認為 Tommy 的病和他的生活習慣有關係。

- The success of this movie **has little to do with** the beauty of the leading actress. 這部片成功的原因和女主角的美貌沒有多大關聯。

2. 表示疑問意義時，可用 **anything**；表示否定意義時，除了 **nothing**，也可以代換成 **not . . . anything**。

- A: Does this teenager have **anything** to do with the robbery?

  這年輕人和搶案有關係嗎？

- B: No, he has **nothing** to do with it. (= he **doesn't** have **anything** to do with it.)

  不，沒有關係。

句型練習

一、選擇

( ) 1. The fall of the kingdom is said to have _____ to do with this king's pride.

(A) many　　(B) much　　(C) a lot of　　(D) lot

( ) 2. The delay of the flight has _____ to do with the terrible weather condition.

    (A) few   (B) little   (C) less   (D) least

( ) 3. The fierce fight between Jennifer and her husband had _____ to do with misunderstanding.

    (A) never   (B) not   (C) no   (D) nothing

( ) 4. We firmly believe that this honest man doesn't have _____ to do with the scandal.

    (A) anything   (B) nothing   (C) little   (D) a thing

二、翻譯

1. Jeffrey 的腳傷和車禍沒有關係。事實上，是因為他在濕地板上滑倒。

Jeffrey's leg injury _____ _____ _____ _____ _____ any car accident. In fact, he slipped on the wet floor.

2. Susanne 對 Frank 迷戀的原因和他的外表幾乎沒關係。

The reason why Susanne has a crush on Frank _____

_____

3. 這個科學家的傑出成就和她致力於研究很有關係嗎？

Does the scientist's outstanding achievement _____

_____

4. 這些學生對英文的興趣和老師的鼓勵很有關係。

_____

8-5

$$S + V \ldots, + \begin{Bmatrix} \text{not to mention} \\ \text{not to speak of} \\ \text{to say nothing of} \end{Bmatrix} + \begin{Bmatrix} \text{N} \\ \text{V-ing} \end{Bmatrix}$$

句型範例

- The wealthy man owns almost everything, **not to mention** mansions and sports cars. 這富翁幾乎擁有一切，更不用說別墅和跑車。

- My brother can drive, **not to speak of** riding bicycles.
  我哥哥會開車，更不用說會騎單車。

用法詳解

　　本單元句型 not to mention、not to speak of、to say nothing of 表示「更不用說…；遑論…」，用於對前面所提的事情再做補充。

用法如下：(1) 其後接名詞或動名詞 (V-ing)。

　　　　　　(2) 可用於肯定句與否定句。

- Nick can speak several foreign languages, **not to mention** English.
  Nick 會說多種外語，英語就更不用說了。

- The seriously injured man can't walk, **not to speak of** running.
  這受重傷的男人無法走路，更不用說是跑步。

- Global warming has a negative influence on human beings, **to say nothing of** animals. 全球暖化對人類有負面影響，遑論對動物的影響。

學習補給站

與本單元句型同義的尚有 **let alone** 與 **much less**，注意分辨用法。

a. 兩者均有連接詞功能，其後接與前面對等詞性的字詞，常為名詞或動詞。

b. 用於**否定意義**的句子，表示其後提的事情更不可能。

- The beggar has neither food nor money, **let alone** any shelter.
  這乞丐沒食物也沒錢，更不用說任何棲身之地。

  ① shelter 與 food、money 對等，均為名詞。

- Unfortunately, shoes are not always readily available for people living in poverty, **let alone** shoes that are the right size. 不幸的是，對貧民來說，鞋子並不總是唾手可得，更別提尺寸剛好的鞋子。 (106 學測)

- Nora can't cook, **let alone** make cookies.

  Nora 不會做飯，更不用說做餅乾。① make 與 cook 對等，均為原形動詞。

- The illiterate man can't read, **much less** write.

  這目不識丁的人不識字，遑論書寫。

句型練習

一、選擇

( ) 1. The hungry boy ate everything on the table, _____ such a small hamburger.

    (A) let alone   (B) not to mention   (C) much less   (D) not to say of

( ) 2. The poor man can't afford a car, _____ buying a house.

    (A) let alone   (B) much less   (C) including   (D) not to mention

( ) 3. My aunt is a merciful lady. She would not hurt any animals, _____ kill an ant.

    (A) not to mention   (B) not to speak of   (C) let alone   (D) to say nothing of

( ) 4. The stingy student wouldn't share his stationery, _____.

    (A) not to mention his electronic dictionary

    (B) not to speak his smartphone

    (C) much less lending his video games

    (D) let alone sharing his tablet

二、翻譯

1. 很多家庭主婦喜歡看肥皂劇，綜藝節目就更不用說了。

    Many housewives like to watch soap operas, _____ _____ _____ variety shows.

2. Amy 吃素，她不吃任何乳製品，更不用說任何肉類。

    Amy is a vegetarian, who doesn't eat dairy products, _____ _____ any meat.

3. 這位受歡迎的部落客主持了好幾個電視節目，更不用說寫了好幾本書。

    This popular blogger has hosted several TV programs, _____

    _____

4. Frank 是膽小的男孩，他不敢一個人待在家，更不用說獨自走路回家。

    Frank is a timid boy, who dare not stay home alone, _____

    _____

8-6

To begin with/To sum up/To be sure/To be precise/etc., S + V . . .

句型範例

● **To be frank,** this dress doesn't suit you. 坦白說，這件洋裝不適合你。

● I think this idea is impractical, **to be honest**. 坦白說，我認為這個想法不切實際。

 ☆ **To begin with,** football is a quicker, more physical sport, and football fans enjoy the emotional involvement they feel while watching. (95 學測)

首先，足球是種較快且較需運用肢體的運動，而球迷也愛在看球賽時投入情感。

用法詳解

1. 獨立不定詞片語為不定詞與固定的字串組成，用於修飾整句，通常置於句首，也可放在句中、句尾，使用時必須以逗號與句子部分隔開。

   ● **To sum up,** in order to improve your English speaking skill, you must practice often.

   ➡ In order to improve your English speaking skill, you must practice often, **to sum up**. 總之，為了改善你的英語口語能力，你必須要多練習。

2. 常用的獨立不定詞片語有：

to begin with	首先
to sum up	總之
to be frank (with you)、to be honest、to tell the truth	坦白說；老實說
to be plain with you	坦白說
to put it simply、to be brief	簡言之
to make matters worse	更糟的是
to *cut/make* a long story short	長話短說
to be precise	確切地說
to do sb justice	公平評斷某人
strange to say	奇怪的是

   ● A motorcyclist got injured in a car accident. **To make matters worse,** the ambulance broke down on the way to the hospital.

   有個機車騎士在車禍中受傷。更糟的是，救護車在去醫院的途中故障了。

• Jessica was in trouble. **To cut a long story short,** she misplaced an important document and couldn't find it.

Jessica 有麻煩了。長話短說,她誤置重要的文件,而且找不到它。

句型練習

一、選擇

(　　) 1. That woman standing beside Mike isn't his mother. ＿＿＿＿＿, she's his wife.
(A) Telling the truth (B) To tell the truth
(C) Told the truth (D) Having told the truth

(　　) 2. To pass the mid-term exam is not difficult at all. ＿＿＿＿＿, you need to concentrate on your studies.
(A) To be precise (B) To do you justice
(C) To make matters worse (D) To begin with

(　　) 3. ＿＿＿＿＿, some people never seem to get bored of watching football games a whole day.
(A) Strangely saying (B) Strange to say (C) Strangely said (D) To strangely say

二、文意選填 (請做適當的變化)

to put it simply	strange to say	to do sb justice
to be precise	to make matters worse	

1. Anthony is getting heavier and heavier. He has put on 10kg, ＿＿＿＿＿＿＿＿＿＿＿＿

＿＿＿＿＿＿＿＿＿＿＿＿＿＿＿＿＿ .

2. The Internet has greatly changed people's lives. ＿＿＿＿＿＿＿＿＿＿＿＿＿＿

＿＿＿＿＿＿＿＿＿＿＿＿＿, it enables people to search information quickly and it also connects people around the world.

3. Alice is not to blame for this mistake. She, ＿＿＿＿＿＿＿＿＿＿＿＿＿＿＿＿

＿＿＿＿＿＿＿＿＿＿＿＿, is a very careful person.

三、翻譯

1. 坦白說,你的作文寫得不好。你最好修改一下。

＿＿＿＿＿＿＿＿＿＿＿＿＿＿＿＿＿＿＿＿＿＿＿＿＿, your composition is not well-written. You had better revise it.

2. Wright 太太收集很多帽子。確切地說,她擁有超過 200 頂帽子。

＿＿＿＿＿＿＿＿＿＿＿＿＿＿＿＿＿＿＿＿＿＿＿＿＿＿＿＿＿＿＿

9-1

V-ing/p.p. + N

句型範例

- The **falling** rain made much noise, which had awakened the **sleeping** baby.
  持續下的雨造成許多噪音,把睡著的嬰兒吵醒了。

- To these treasure hunters' disappointment, they found nothing except a **sunken** ship. 讓這些尋寶者失望的是,他們除了一艘沈船外,什麼也沒找到。

☆ The weta is a newly **discovered** insect species. (99 學測)
  紐西蘭蟋蟀是一種新發現的昆蟲物種。

☆ **Learning** style means a person's natural, habitual, and **preferred** way(s) of learning. 學習型態意指一個人天生、習慣與偏好的學習方式。 (93 學測)

用法詳解

1. 本單元介紹由動詞轉化而來的分詞置於名詞前做**形容詞**的用法。

   a. 現在分詞 (V-ing):表示主動或進行的意義。

   b. 過去分詞 (p.p):表示被動或完成的意義。

   - The African Bush Elephant is said to be the largest **living** land animal.
     據說草原象是現存最大的陸上動物。 ① 表示主動。

   - The lifeguard is trying to save the **drowning** child in the swimming pool.
     救生員正試圖救在游池中溺水的小孩。 ① 表示進行中。

   - The boy's finger was cut by the **broken** glass.
     這男孩的手指被碎玻璃割到。① 表示被動。

   - It is healthier to eat **cooked** food than raw food. 吃熟食比生食健康。
     ① 表示完成。

2. 表示情緒的動詞可以衍生出分詞,作為形容詞。

   a. 現在分詞 (V-ing):用於形容某人或某物,解為「令人覺得…」,如 interesting。

   b. 過去分詞 (p.p):用於形容某人自己的感受,解為「某人感覺…」,如 interested。

   c. 此時,分詞常會搭配特定的介系詞再接名詞,必須特別背誦。常見的用法有:

情緒動詞	意思	V-ing (令人覺得…)	p.p. (某人感覺…)	搭配的介系詞
interest	使有興趣	interesting	interested	in
excite	使興奮	exciting	excited	about

bore	使無聊	boring	bored	with
surprise	使驚訝	surprising	surprised	at
tire	使疲累	tiring	tired	of
confuse	使困惑	confusing	confused	about
embarrass	使困窘	embarrassing	embarrassed	*about/at*
disappoint	使失望	disappointing	disappointed	*at/with/about*
satisfy	使滿意	satisfying	satisfied	with
worry	使擔心	worrying	worried	about

● Lucy is **interested** in backpacking because she can meet many **interesting** people and visit **interesting** places during her trips.

Lucy 對自助旅行很有興趣，因為在旅行中，她能遇見有趣的人和參觀有趣的地方。

句型練習

一、選擇

(　) 1. According to government regulations, if employees are unable to work because of a serious illness, they are entitled to take an _____ sick leave. (104 指考)

　　(A) extended　　(B) extending　　(C) extensive　　(D) extension

(　) 2. With _____ oil prices, there is an increasing tendency for people to ride bicycles to work.

　　(A) arisen　　(B) raising　　(C) risen　　(D) rising (98 學測)

(　) 3. The _____ water is too hot to drink; I'd better get some _____ water.

　　(A) boiled; bottled　　(B) boiling; bottling　　(C) boiling; bottled　　(D) boiled; bottling

(　) 4. I was _____ about my first overseas trip, but my father assured me that he would help plan the trip so that nothing would go wrong. (105 學測)

　　(A) worrying　　(B) worried　　(C) exciting　　(D) excited

二、翻譯

1. 大多數人可能不會同情這些瀕臨絕種的生物，但是牠們真的需要保護。 (99 學測)

Most people probably don't feel sympathy for these _____ _____ , but they do need protecting.

2. 營養不良已經在食物有限的開發中國家造成數百萬人死亡。 (101 指考)

Poor nutrition has caused millions of deaths in _____ _____ where there is only a _____ amount of food.

3. 讓人失望的是，被埋在倒塌的建築物底下的人全都沒有生還。

It is _____ that _____

9-2

S + sense verb (*feel*/*see*/*hear*/*etc*.) + O + *V*/*V-ing*/*p.p.*

句型範例

● The visitors to the zoo were surprised to **see** a lion escape from the cage.
動物園的遊客看見獅子從籠子逃出很驚訝。

● Last night, Anna **noticed** a couple fighting near her house.
昨天晚上，Anna 注意到有一對夫妻在她家附近打架。

● Mrs. Robinson was happy to **hear** her son praised by his teacher.
Robinson 太太很高興聽到她兒子被老師稱讚。

☆ Relatives of the deceased want to **see** their beloved family members live comfortably in the next world.
過世者的家屬希望見到摯愛的家人在來生能過得舒適。　(103 指考)

☆ The tradition of men wearing it (the red dot) has faded in recent times, so nowadays we **see** a lot more women than men wearing one. 近年來男人點紅痣的傳統已逐漸消失，所以現在會看到點紅痣的女性多於男性。　(102 學測)

用法詳解

1. 本句型為感官動詞的用法。常見的感官動詞有：see、watch、look at、hear、listen to、overhear (偷聽)、feel、observe、notice。

2. 感官動詞 + 受詞 (O) 之後接續的動詞依不同意義使用原形 **V** 或分詞 (***V-ing***/***p.p.***)。

   a. 感官動詞 + O + V：用於受詞與受詞補語為主動關係時並表示事實或規律的事情。

   ● The coach **watches** the athletes practice every day.
   教練每天看著這些運動員練習。

   ● I **hear** my neighbor play the drums every evening.
   每天傍晚我都聽見鄰居打鼓。

   b. 感官動詞 + O + V-ing：用於受詞與受詞補語為主動關係時並強調動作正在進行。

   ● Many people **listened to** the news reporter reporting on the flooding.
   當時許多人在聽新聞記者報導水災。

   ● Victoria **heard** her colleagues complaining about their stress from work.
   Victoria 聽見她的同事抱怨工作壓力。

   c. 感官動詞 + O + p.p.：用於受詞與受詞補語為被動關係時。

● When the earthquake happened, we **saw** many people <u>frightened</u> and <u>injured</u>.

當地震發生時，我們看到很多人受到驚嚇與受傷。

● After the brothers fought, their parents **noticed** the window <u>broken</u>.

在這對兄弟打架過後，他們的父母注意到窗戶被打破。

學習補給站

感官動詞在改成被動語態時，用法為：be *seen/heard* + *V-ing/to V*。

● James **was overheard** <u>talking</u> with his girlfriend on the phone.

James 被偷聽到和女朋友講電話。① 強調動作正在進行。

● Sandra **was seen** <u>to have</u> a candle-lit dinner with a handsome young man.

我們看見 Sandra 和一個英俊的年輕人吃燭光晚餐。① 強調事實。

句型練習

一、選擇

(   ) 1. He saw Saint Nicholas ＿＿＿ out gifts from his baskets for a crowd of happy children. (102 指考)

　　(A) to pull 　　　　(B) pulled 　　　　(C) pulling 　　　　(D) pulls

(   ) 2. Some truffle merchants dig for their prizes themselves when they ＿＿＿ truffle flies ＿＿＿ around the base of a tree. (100 指考)

　　(A) watch; hovered 　　　　　　　(B) feel; to hover

　　(C) notice; will hover 　　　　　　(D) see; hovering

二、句子改寫

1. Before the nervous girl made the speech, her legs were shaking, and she felt it.

　＿＿＿＿＿＿＿＿＿＿＿＿＿＿＿＿＿＿＿＿＿＿＿＿＿＿＿＿＿＿＿＿＿

2. Justin's car was towed away by the police, and he saw it.

　＿＿＿＿＿＿＿＿＿＿＿＿＿＿＿＿＿＿＿＿＿＿＿＿＿＿＿＿＿＿＿＿＿

三、翻譯

1. 孩子們很高興看到小丑出現在舞台上，所以他們大笑、尖叫並開心地鼓掌。 (100 學測)

　The children were so delighted to ＿＿＿ the clown ＿＿＿ on stage that they laughed, screamed, and clapped their hands happily.

2. Helena 的男友被看見親吻一個迷人的女孩。當她聽到朋友們談論這件事時，她氣炸了。

　Helena's boyfriend ＿＿＿＿＿＿＿＿＿＿＿＿＿＿＿＿＿＿＿＿＿＿＿

　When she ＿＿＿＿＿＿＿＿＿＿＿＿＿＿＿＿＿＿＿＿＿＿＿＿＿ , she exploded with anger.

9–3

S + *find/keep/leave* + O + OC (*V-ing/p.p.*)

句型範例

- The mother **found** her son entering the house without taking off his shoes.
  這個媽媽發現她的兒子進門沒有脫鞋子。
- This popular actor was surprised to **find** himself spied on and his computer hacked.
  這個當紅的演員很驚訝發現自己被窺探而且電腦也被駭。

 ☆ We can **keep** the spirit going by communicating often and consciously.
我們可以藉由經常而自覺地與人交流來讓這個精神傳遞下去。 (101 學測)

用法詳解

1. 有些及物動詞需要受詞補語 (OC) 來補充說明受詞 (O) 的動作或狀態，讓受詞的意思更完整。這類動詞常見的有：find、keep、leave 等。

2. 受詞補語 (OC) 可用**現在分詞** (表示受詞與受詞補語之間是主動關係) 與**過去分詞** (表示受詞與受詞補語之間是被動關係) 來補充說明受詞。此外還可用**形容詞**與**介系詞片語**。

   - Dennis **found** his cat lying under the table. Dennis 發現他的貓躺在餐桌下。
     ① cat 與 lie 是主動關係，故用 lying。

   - Keri went downstairs to get the mails, so she **left** the door unlocked.
     Keri 下樓去拿信，所以沒把門上鎖。① the door 與 unlock 是被動關係，故用 unlocked。

   ☆ Packaging helps to **keep** food fresh. (95 指考) 包裝幫助保持食物的新鮮。

   ☆ Walking home from rehearsal at age 29, she was caught in the midst of a random shooting that **left** her paralyzed from the waist down. (101 學測)
   她 29 歲時，在排演完回家的路上，遭受街上突發的槍戰波及，讓她下半身癱瘓。

   - Without enough time to move, the woman **left** much clothing in her old apartment. 沒有足夠的時間搬家，這個女人留下很多衣物在舊公寓裡。

3. 注意下列特殊的分詞用法：

   a. 與自然界 (如 water、fire、wind) 有關之物，因無法被控制，與 OC 間常視為主動關係，故 OC 用 V-ing。
      - It is very dangerous to **leave** the fire **burning** in the fireplace after you go to bed. 在你就寢後，讓火繼續在壁爐裡燃燒很危險。

   b. 與人的四肢或五官有關的動作，搭配 close、cross、fold 等動詞時，與 OC 間常視為被動用關係，故 OC 用 p.p.。

● The nervous girl **kept** her fingers **crossed** before the final exam.

在期末考前，那個焦慮的女孩將手指交叉以祈求好運。

學習補給站

catch 也屬於這類動詞，表示「撞見…，逮到…」，受詞補語使用 V-ing，表示看到事情發生的當下。

● The clerk **caught** the man **stealing** some products in the mall.

店員逮到這男人偷了賣場的一些商品。

句型練習

一、選擇

( ) 1. Grass found himself _____ two opposing political parties. (99 指考)

    (A) fighting   (B) fought   (C) to fight   (D) being fought

( ) 2. With the help of modern technology, some supermarkets are now able to keep customers _____ about what others are buying. (96 指考)

    (A) to inform   (B) inform   (C) informing   (D) informed

( ) 3. As a consequence, it is not uncommon nowadays to find women _____ outside their homes and _____ very concerned about their careers and personal lives. (95 指考)

    (A) work; are   (B) working; being   (C) worked; were   (D) working; were

( ) 4. The girl found herself _____ by her father, so she tried hard to explain.

    (A) to misunderstand   (B) misunderstand

    (C) misunderstanding   (D) misunderstood

二、翻譯

1. 太空人穿太空衣讓自己保暖。 (95 學測)

The astronauts _____ in a space suit.

2. 在看完這部感人的電影後，Belle 發現她的淚水從臉頰滑落。

After watching this touching movie, _____

_____

3. Kauffman 夫婦沒時間清理房子，所以讓傢俱蓋滿了灰塵。

_____

4. 交通警察抓到這個酒醉司機闖紅燈。

_____

9-4
S + V + with + O + OC (*V-ing/p.p.*)

句型範例

● The wealthy man is having dinner **with** <u>a violinist</u> **playing** the violin for him.
　這個富翁正在吃晚餐，一個小提琴家為他彈奏小提琴。

● These workers were working hard **with** <u>their sleeves</u> **rolled** up.
　這些工人正在努力工作，他們的袖子捲起來。

 ☆ The success of J.K. Rowling is legendary, **with** <u>her Harry Potter series</u> **making** her a multi-millionaire in just a few years. (105 指考)
　J.K. 羅琳的成功很具傳奇性，《哈利波特》系列讓她在幾年內成為大富豪。

用法詳解

1. 本句型是以 with + O + OC 的句型表示「附帶」的動作或狀態。

2. 受詞補語 (OC) 可用**現在分詞** (表示受詞與受詞補語之間是主動關係) 與**過去分詞** (表示受詞與受詞補語之間是被動關係) 來補充說明受詞。此外還可用**形容詞**與**介系詞片語**。

　● Mrs. Brightman is talking to her neighbor **with** <u>her dog</u> **running** around.
　　Brightman 太太正在和鄰居聊天，她的狗到處跑。① her dog 與 run 是主動關係。

　● The girl was riding a bike **with** <u>her hair</u> **blowing** in the wind.
　　這女孩騎著腳踏車，她的頭髮在風中飄。① her hair 與 blow (飄動) 是主動關係。

　● The old man went to bed **with** <u>all the windows</u> **locked**.
　　這老人上床睡覺，窗戶全都鎖起來了。① windows 與 lock 是被動關係。

　● Mr. Bond felt embarrassed **with** <u>his wig</u> **blown** away.
　　Bond 先生覺得很尷尬，因為他的假髮被吹走了。① his wig 與 blow (吹走) 是被動關係。

　● The tired man fell asleep on the sofa **with** <u>his mouth</u> wide **open**.
　　這個疲憊的男人在沙發上睡著，他的嘴張得大大的。

　● All the guests attended the masquerade **with** <u>masks</u> **on their faces**.
　　所有的賓客臉上戴著面具參加化妝舞會。

3. 注意下列慣用的分詞用法：

　a. 與自然界有關的物質與 OC 間常視為主動關係，故使用 V-ing。

　　● The careless woman left the bathroom **with** <u>the water</u> **running**.
　　　這個粗心的婦人離開浴室，讓水一直流著。

b. 與人的四肢或五官有關的動作，搭配 close、fold 等動詞時，與 OC 間常視為被動關係，故 OC 使用 p.p.。

- The angry mother is shouting at her son **with** her arms **crossed**.
  那個生氣的母親正對著兒子吼叫，她的手交叉在胸前。

句型練習

一、選擇

(　) 1. The IQ is the ratio of "mental age" to chronological age times 100, with 100 _____ the average. (102 學測)

　(A) is 　　　　(B) are 　　　　(C) been 　　　　(D) being

(　) 2. Buddhism is the dominant religion in Thailand, with 90% of the total population _____ as Buddhists. (100 學測)

　(A) identifies 　　(B) identifying 　　(C) to identify 　　(D) identified

(　) 3. After the 1960s, and especially since the 1980s, the high school prom in many areas has become a serious exercise in excessive consumption, with boys _____ expensive tuxedos and girls _____ designer gowns. (99 學測)

　(A) to rent; to wear 　(B) rented; wore 　(C) renting; wearing 　(D) rented; worn

(　) 4. Justin is listening to classical music attentively with his eyes _____.

　(A) closed 　　　(B) closing 　　　(C) close 　　　(D) to close

二、句子改寫

1. The poor sick man passed away, and nothing was left to his children.

_____

2. The teacher was explaining a grammar rule, and a student dozed off in class.

_____

三、翻譯

1. 我們大部分的人都只對持續幾秒的目光接觸感到輕鬆自在。 (100 學測)

Most of us are comfortable _____ eye contact _____ a few seconds.

2. 這個十八歲跑者赤腳流著血全力衝刺到 12 英里賽程的終點。 (99 學測)

This 18-year-old sprinted to the finish of a 12-mile run _____

_____

3. Brooke 把長頭髮綁起來開始洗碗。

_____

4. 童子軍們 (scouts) 圍成一個圓圈玩遊戲，營火 (campfire) 一邊燃燒著。

_____

9–5

$S + V_1$, and $+ S + V_2 \rightarrow S + V_1, V_2$-ing

句型範例

- The singer cleared his throat, **starting** to sing.
  這歌手清清喉嚨，開始唱歌。
- The man sat by the heater, **rubbing** his hands together to stay warm.
  這男人坐在暖氣邊，搓著手來保暖。

- ☆ Lost and scared, the little dog wandered along the streets, **looking** for its master. 這隻小狗迷路又受到驚嚇，牠在街上徘徊，尋找主人。 (103 學測)
- ☆ Those college students work at the orphanage on a voluntary basis, **helping** the children with their studies without receiving any pay. (99 學測)
  那些大學生自願到孤兒院工作，幫助孩子課業而不收任何報酬。

用法詳解

1. 以對等連接詞 and 連接二個動詞片語或對等子句時，可以形成省略 and 的分詞構句。步驟如下：

   (1) 省略 and。若兩個主詞相同，省略第二個主詞。

   (2) 加上逗號。

   (3) 將第二個動詞 (V_2) 改為現在分詞 (V_2-ing)。

   - The old man climbed up the stairs **and** gasped for air.
   - ➡ The old man climbed up the stairs, **gasping** for air.
     這個老人很困難地爬上樓梯，氣喘吁吁。
   - The exhausted worker fell asleep quickly **and** snored loudly.
   - ➡ The exhausted worker fell asleep quickly, **snoring** loudly.
     這個疲憊的工人很快地睡著，大聲地打呼。
   - The student handed in his assignment at the last minute, **and** he gave a sigh of relief.
   - ➡ The student handed in his assignment at the last minute, **giving** a sigh of relief. 這學生在最後一分鐘交出作業，鬆了一口氣。

2. 含有分詞的否定用法以 **not + V-ing** 表示。

   - Hank lost his beloved wife last month, **and** he didn't know how to get over it.

➡ Hank lost his beloved wife last month, **not knowing** how to get over it.

Hank 的妻子上個月過世了，他不知道該如何度過哀傷。

句型練習

一、選擇

( ) 1. Typhoon Morakot claimed more than six hundred lives in early August of 2009, _____ it the most serious natural disaster in Taiwan in recent decades. (99 學測)

    (A) made   (B) makes   (C) and making   (D) making

( ) 2. As long as the children are willing to sing, I will always be there for them, _____ with them and _____ them to experience the meaning of the ballads. (104 學測)

    (A) sing; lead   (B) singing; leading   (C) sing; leading   (D) singing; lead

( ) 3. Karen heard a hilarious joke, _____.

    (A) couldn't help laughing   (B) she couldn't help laughing

    (C) and she couldn't help laughing   (D) not able to help laughing

( ) 4. The mountaineers got lost in the mountains, _____ which way to go.

    (A) not knowing   (B) knowing not   (C) no knowing   (D) knowing no

二、句子合併與改寫

1. { Lillian worked day and night.

   { She hoped to pay off the mortgage as early as possible.

_____

2. The tornado struck this city and caused many deaths and injuries.

_____

三、翻譯

1. 警察和目擊者談話，試著要找出謀殺案的線索。

The police talked to the witness, _____ _____ find some clues to solve the murder case.

2. 研究顯示，有外向特質的人往往較樂觀，常期待好事會發生。 (101 學測)

Research suggests that people with outgoing personalities tend to be more optimistic, often _____

3. Judy 站在學校前，等著她的媽媽來接她。

Judy stood in front of the school _____

4. 這個工作狂 (workaholic) 在半夜還繼續想著他的工作，無法入睡。

_____

9–6

. . . N + *V-ing/p.p.* . . .

句型範例

- The dog **barking** at strangers at midnight is Mr. Braun's.
  那隻在半夜對著陌生人吠叫的是 Braun 先生的狗。
- The roofer is repairing the roof **damaged** by a fallen tree branch.
  屋頂工正在修理被掉落樹枝砸毀的屋頂。

 ☆ People often avoid eye contact with someone **standing** close to them.
人們通常避免和站得靠近自己的人有眼神接觸。 (105 指考)

☆ Jeanie decided to make a stool **attached** to the bathroom cabinet door under the sink.
Jeanie 決定做一張板凳固定在水槽下的浴室櫥櫃門上。 (105 學測)

用法詳解

1. 當關係代名詞是關係子句的主詞時，其引導的形容詞子句可以簡化成分詞片語，置於名詞後做修飾。簡化步驟為：(1) 省略關係代名詞。(2) 關係子句中若有 be 動詞通常省略。(3) 關係子句的動詞改為分詞。當關係子句是主動語態時，使用**現在分詞 (V-ing)**；當關係子句是被動語態時，用**過去分詞 (p.p.)**，be 動詞通常省略，若要保留須改成 being。若關係子句的動詞為完成式，則將 have + p.p. 改為 having + p.p.。

- The street performer who is playing the saxophone amazes all the audience.
- ➡ The street performer **playing** the saxophone amazes all the audience.
  這位吹薩克斯風的街頭藝人驚艷全場。① 因動詞為主動語態，保留現在分詞 playing。
- The art museum is having an exhibition of sculptures which were made by female sculptors.
- ➡ The art museum is having an exhibition of sculptures **made** by female sculptors. 那間藝術博物館正在展出女性雕刻家的作品。
  ① (1) 省略關代 which；(2) 省略 be 動詞 were；(3) 因動詞為被動語態，保留過去分詞 made。
- The poster that had sparked controversy was taken down yesterday.
- ➡ The poster **having sparked** controversy was taken down yesterday.
  那張引起爭議的海報昨天被拆了。
  ① 動詞為完成式，改為 having + p.p.，即 having sparked。

2. 非限定用法的關係子句也可簡化，但必須保留**逗號**。此結構也被視為分詞構句的一種。

☆ Historical interpreters, **dressed** in period garb, give tours to the *Susan Constant, Godspeed,* and *Discovery.* (105 指考)

穿著古裝的歷史解說員提供導覽帶遊客參觀蘇珊‧康斯坦號、神佑號及發現號。

句型練習

一、選擇

(　) 1. An international team of researchers focused on a population of yellow-bellied sea snakes ＿＿＿ near Costa Rica. (105 學測)
　　(A) lived　　　　　(B) which living　　(C) living　　　　(D) have lived

(　) 2. Personal space involves certain invisible forces ＿＿＿ on you through all the senses. (105 指考)
　　(A) to impose　　　(B) that imposed　　(C) imposing　　　(D) imposed

(　) 3. If the number ＿＿＿ is in the same area as the number making the call, an area code usually doesn't need to be dialed. (102 學測)
　　(A) calling　　　　(B) being called　　(C) having called　(D) has been calling

(　) 4. Studies reveal that negative emotions are seated in an area of the brain ＿＿＿ the amygdala. (96 學測)
　　(A) call　　　　　(B) to call　　　　(C) calling　　　　(D) called

二、句子改寫

1. The letter which was torn to pieces was written by Kelly's boyfriend.

_____

2. The elegant lady who wears a grey dress is an experienced programmer.

_____

三、翻譯

1. 這些彩蛋主要由貴金屬或漆上 (coat) 漂亮色彩的礦石組成，並以珍貴珠寶點綴。
The eggs were made of valuable metals or stones _____

_____ and _____

_____ (104 指考)

2. 大部分在這家餐廳用過餐的人都很滿意他們的好服務和美味的食物。

_____

3. 令我們驚訝的是，這個聰明男子的大腦就像裝滿資料和知識的電腦。

_____

9-7

(Subordinating conjunction +) V₁-ing/p.p.₁, S + be/V₂...

$$(\text{Subordinating conjunction } +) \ V_1\text{-}ing/p.p._1, \ S + be/V_2 \ ...$$

句型範例

● **Noticing** a stranger stalking her, the young lady felt frightened.

注意到有陌生人跟蹤她,這位年輕女士感到很害怕。

● **Fascinated** by Egyptian culture, Simon wants to major in history in college.

被埃及的文化所吸引,Simon 想在大學中主修歷史。

☆ **Smiling**, the man answered, "I come from Argos, and there the people are all friendly, generous, and warm-hearted." (103 學測)

這男人笑答:「我來自阿哥斯,那裡的人都很友善、慷慨、而且很熱心。」

☆ **Given** the opportunity, they may retreat to a corner, putting distance between themselves and strangers. (105 指考)

若有機會,他們會退縮到角落,讓自己和陌生人保持距離。

用法詳解

1. 本單元介紹由**省略從屬連接詞**簡化而來的**分詞構句**。從屬連接詞用來引導副詞子句,表示「時間」、「原因」、「讓步」、「條件」等。常用的從屬連接詞有:when、while、before、after、as、because、since、although、though、if 等。

2. 形成分詞構句的步驟如下:

   (1) 省略主詞:若二個子句主詞相同,可以省略從屬子句的主詞。

   (2) 省略連接詞:若二個子句的關係明確,可以省略從屬連接詞。反之,則保留。但 because 通常會省略。

   (3) 將動詞改為分詞:若從屬子句的 S 與 V 間為主動關係,將動詞改為**現在分詞 (V-ing)**。若從屬子句的 S 與 V 間為被動關係,將動詞改為**過去分詞 (p.p.)**。

   (4) 分詞構句中的 **being** 與 **having been** 可以省略。在 Being + adj., S + V/be ... 的結構中,可將 being 省略,成為形容詞在句首的分詞構句:Adj., S + V/be ...。

   ● When Alice heard the phone ring, she rushed to answer it.

   ➡ (When) **Hearing** the phone ring, Alice rushed to answer it.

   　 Alice 聽到電話響時就跑去接。① 從屬連接詞可保留或省略。

   ● Because Robert was rejected by the attractive girl, he felt extremely frustrated.

   ➡ **(Being) Rejected** by the attractive girl, Robert felt extremely frustrated.

因為被那個迷人的女孩拒絕，Robert 覺得非常挫折。① Being 可省略。

- Although **(having been) hurt**, the man helped many people escape.

  雖然這男人受傷，他還是幫助許多人逃脫。① having been 通常被省略。

- **(Being) Nervous** about the upcoming exam, Ruth doesn't have a good appetite.

  對於考試感到很焦慮，Ruth 胃口不好。① 省略 Being 後成為 Adj. 在句首的結構。

3. 分詞構句的否定是在分詞的前面加上 **not**，成為 **not + V-ing/p.p.** 的結構。

- **Not feeling** well, Amy took a sick leave to rest at home.

  覺得不舒服，Amy 請病假在家休息。

句型練習

一、選擇

( ) 1. After ＿＿＿＿ from college, Morrison started to work as a teacher and got married in 1958. (103 學測)

　　(A) graduate　　　(B) graduating　　　(C) graduated　　　(D) she graduating

( ) 2. ＿＿＿＿ in 1992, with some 28,000 listings, this company bills itself as the world's largest home exchange club. (99 學測)

　　(A) Finding　　　(B) Founding　　　(C) Found　　　(D) Founded

( ) 3. ＿＿＿＿ the annual membership fee, William is not allowed to enter the gym.

　　(A) Paid never　　(B) Not paying　　(C) Not having paid　　(D) Never pays

( ) 4. Although ＿＿＿＿ close to the equator, Rwanda's "thousand hills," ranging from 1,500 m to 2,500 m in height, ensure that the temperature is pleasant all year around. (96 學測)

　　(A) situating　　　(B) sits　　　(C) located　　　(D) stand

二、句子改寫

1. Because the boy is wearing a sweater on such a hot day, he is sweating profusely.

　＿＿＿＿＿＿＿＿＿＿＿＿＿＿＿＿＿＿＿＿＿＿＿＿＿＿＿＿＿＿＿＿＿＿＿

2. Since Amy has been inspired by Raphael's works, she shows an interest in painting.

　＿＿＿＿＿＿＿＿＿＿＿＿＿＿＿＿＿＿＿＿＿＿＿＿＿＿＿＿＿＿＿＿＿＿＿

三、翻譯

1. 因為不同的人在說謊時會有不同的行為，所以測謊並非完美的設計。 (105 學測)

Because different people behave differently ＿＿＿＿ ＿＿＿＿, a polygraph test is by no means perfect.

2. 相較於他們父母的世代，現今年輕人享受較多的自由和繁榮。 (105 學測)

　＿＿＿＿＿＿＿＿＿＿＿＿＿＿＿＿＿＿＿＿＿＿＿＿＿＿＿＿＿＿＿＿＿＿＿

9-8

$$S_1 + V_1\text{-}ing/p.p._1 , S_2 + be/V_2 \ldots$$
$$S_1 + be/V_1 \ldots , S_2 + V_2\text{-}ing/p.p._2$$

句型範例

- It **being** raining, we have no choice but to stay home.
  因為下雨，我們別無選擇，只能待在家裡。

- The motorcyclist's legs **(being) injured** seriously in the car accident, he was sent
  to the hospital. 這個機車騎士在車禍中有嚴重腿傷，所以被送去醫院。

 ☆ And Rwanda **being** a tiny country, everything in Rwanda is within reach in
a few hours and the interesting spots can be explored comfortably in a
couple of weeks. 盧安達是小國家，每個地方都在幾小時內就能到達，而有趣
的景點能在幾星期內很舒適地探訪完。 (96 學測)

用法詳解

1. 先前的單元中提到，對等子句或從屬子句與主要子句的主詞相同時，可以將其簡化成分
   詞構句。但是，若對等子句或從屬子句與主要子句的主詞不同時，需保留各別主詞形成
   獨立分詞構句。

2. 步驟為：(1) 刪除連接詞；(2) 保留二個主詞；(3) 將對等子句或從屬子句的動詞改為分詞。

   - When dusk fell, these Scouts started to pitch their tents.
   - ➡ Dusk **falling**, these Scouts started to pitch their tents.
     天黑時，這些童子軍開始搭起帳棚。

   - Because the flight is seriously delayed, the airline has to compensate the
     passengers.
   - ➡ The flight **(being)** seriously **delayed**, the airline has to compensate the
     passengers. 因為班機嚴重誤點，航空公司必須賠償乘客。

   - Jessica is reading a letter from her boyfriend, and tears rolled down her cheeks.
   - ➡ Jessica is reading a letter from her boyfriend, tears **rolling** down her cheeks.
     Jessica 讀著她男友的信，淚水滑落臉頰。

   - The man was fixing the leaky faucet, and his shirt was unbuttoned.
   - ➡ The man was fixing the leaky faucet, his shirt **unbuttoned**.
     這男人在修理漏水的龍頭，襯衫的扣子沒扣上。

句型練習

一、選擇

( ) 1. The wind _____ hard, the lady turned up the collar of her coat.

    (A) blowing   (B) blew   (C) being blown   (D) was blowing

( ) 2. The show _____ over, the actors and actresses took bows.

    (A) has been   (B) is   (C) being   (D) was

( ) 3. His homework _____ , Keith played video games.

    (A) having done   (B) had done   (C) was done   (D) done

( ) 4. There _____ no bus, the students had to walk home.

    (A) was   (B) being   (C) having   (D) had

( ) 5. The kids went to bed, their toys _____ all over the floor.

    (A) were scattered   (B) were scattering   (C) scattered   (D) had scattered

二、句子合併與改寫

1. { Tanya broke several national records in a track meet.
   { Her family held a party in celebration of her achievement.

   _____, her family held a

   party in celebration of her achievement.

2. { The result of the exam had been announced.
   { Oliver gave a sigh of relief.

   _____, Oliver gave a sigh

   of relief.

3. After the bell had rung, many students ran to the playground.

   _____

4. Because Victoria's glasses were broken, she could not see clearly.

   _____

9–9

Generally speaking、Speaking of、Given that-clause、etc. . . .

句型範例

- **Frankly speaking**, this shirt doesn't fit Ian. 坦白說，這件襯衫不適合 Ian。
- **Speaking of** English radio stations, ICRT is my favorite.

  說到英語廣播電臺，我最喜歡 ICRT。

 ☆ **Generally speaking**, our biological clock is slightly disturbed if we just move into the next time zone. (94 學測)

一般而言，如果我們到了下一個時區，生理時鐘會輕微地受到干擾。

用法詳解

本單元介紹分詞的慣用語，亦稱無人稱獨立分詞構句。有些獨立分詞構句的主詞為泛指的對象，通常將其省略而成為慣用語。常用的慣用語與用法如下：

Generally speaking	一般而言	Judging from + N	由…判斷
Frankly/Honestly speaking	坦白說 / 老實說	Considering *N/that*-clause	考慮到…
Roughly speaking	概略地說	Supposing that-clause	假如；倘若
Strictly speaking	嚴格說來	Provided that-clause	
Speaking of + *N/V-ing*	說到…	Given *N/that-clause*	考慮…，鑒於…

- **Judging from** the coach's facial expression, he must be satisfied with the team's performance. 從教練的臉部表情來看，他一定很滿意團隊的表現。
- **Given that** our French friend can't get used to Chinese food, we took him to a French restaurant. 考慮到我們的法國朋友不習慣中餐，我們帶他去法國餐廳。

句型練習

一、選擇

( ) 1. _____, fried food is popular among young people.

    (A) Strict speaking   (B) Frankly speak

    (C) Roughly spoken   (D) Generally speaking

( ) 2. _____ his limited budget, Hugh chose the cheapest watch.

    (A) Judging   (B) Supposed   (C) Considering   (D) Provided

( ) 3. _____ that this project is finished on time, the boss will give you a bonus.

    (A) Judging   (B) Provided   (C) Speaking   (D) Considered

二、翻譯

1. 老實說，Adam 的言談和舉止讓他的父母感到尷尬。

_____ _____, Adam's words and behavior embarrassed his parents.

2. 說到網際網路，隱私是使用者應該注意到的事情。

_____ _____ the Internet, privacy is one thing that users should pay attention to.

3. 考慮這老人的年紀，他走得算很快了。

_____, he walks fast.

4. 假如你無法準時到機場，你會怎麼辦？

5. 從 Emily 奇怪的行為來看，她一定有事情瞞著我們。

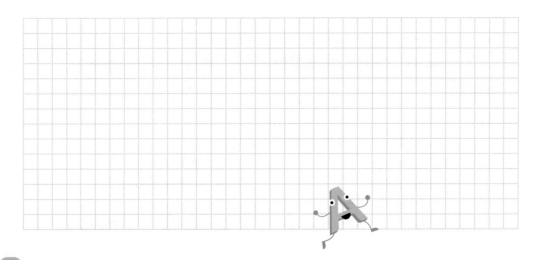

10–1

If + S₁ + were/V₁-ed . . . , S₂ + would/could/might + be/V₂ . . .

句型範例

- If Jennifer **were** trustworthy, we **would** believe what she says.
  如果 Jennifer 值得信任，我們就會相信她說的話。

- If I **knew** the answer to the question, I **could** tell you.
  如果我知道這問題的答案，我就可以告訴你。

☆ If we **were surrounded** by an unending abundance of diamonds, we probably **wouldn't value** them very much. (100 學測)
如果我們被源源不斷供應的鑽石圍繞，我們大概就不會很珍惜它們。

☆ If we **used** more of this source of heat and light, it **could supply** all the power needed throughout the world. (99 指考)
如果我們多利用這個熱能和光能的來源，它可以提供全世界所需的電力。

用法詳解

1. 表達「與現在事實相反的事情」或「不符合事實的願望」時，必須使用**與現在事實相反**的假設語氣。

2. 在「與現在事實相反」的假設語氣中，使用過去式的動詞或助動詞。注意，若 if 子句中的動詞為 **be 動詞**，不論主詞的人稱為何，一律使用 **were**。

   - If the sky **were** clear, we **could see** many twinkling stars.
     如果現在天空無雲，我們就能夠看到很多閃爍的星星。① 事實上，天空有雲，所以我們看不到很多閃爍的星星。與現在事實相反，故使用 were 與過去式助動詞 could。

   - If Irene **sang** well enough, she **would sign up** for a televised singing contest.
     如果 Irene 唱得夠好，她就會報名電視歌唱比賽。
     ① 事實上，Irene 唱得不好，所以她不會報名電視歌唱比賽。

   - If Jason **could** speak many foreign languages, he **would apply** for a job in a trading company. 如果 Jason 會說多國外語，他就會到貿易公司求職。
     ① 事實上，Jason 不會說多國外語，所以他沒去貿易公司上班。

3. 若 if 子句有一般動詞，以 **didn't** 形成否定的假設語氣。

   - If Emily **didn't** have to share a room with her sister, she **could enjoy** more privacy. 如果 Emily 不需要和她的姊姊共用房間，她可以享有更多隱私。

4. 若 if 子句有 **there be**，形成假設語氣時，不論其後接續名詞的單複數，一律使用 **there were**。

- If **there were** no electricity, what **would** our life **be** like?

  如果沒有電，我們的生活會是什麼樣子？

句型練習

一、選擇

( ) 1. If Brenda _____ a bit thinner, this dress would fit her like a glove.

    (A) is   (B) was   (C) were   (D) had been

( ) 2. If I _____ enough money, I would donate part of it to charitable causes.

    (A) have had   (B) will have   (C) have   (D) had

( ) 3. If the child _____ taller, he _____ the shelf. But in fact, the child is too short to reach the shelf.

    (A) is; can reach   (B) were; could reach

    (C) was; could reach   (D) had been; could have reached

( ) 4. Mrs. Boyle could live an extravagant life if she _____ a lot of debts to pay.

    (A) doesn't have   (B) didn't have   (C) hasn't   (D) hadn't

( ) 5. If _____ time machines in the world, we could return to the past.

    (A) there were   (B) there is   (C) there are   (D) there had been

二、句子改寫

1. The air-conditioning in this restaurant is out of order, so the customers can't dine comfortably.

_____

2. Leopards have powerful hind legs, so they can run very fast.

_____

三、翻譯

1. 如果這些水災災民有足夠的支援和金錢，他們就能夠重建家園。

_____, they could reconstruct their homes.

2. 如果我有足夠時間，我可能會到動物保護中心當志工。

_____

10-2

If + S$_1$ + had + *been/p.p.*$_1$ . . . ,
S$_2$ + *would/could/might/should* + have + *been/p.p.*$_2$ . . .

句型範例

- If I **had brought** an umbrella yesterday, I **would not have got** caught in the rain.
  如果我昨天有帶雨傘，我就不會被困在雨中。

- If Selina **had arrived** at the airport earlier, she **could have caught** the plane.
  如果 Selina 早點到達機場，她就可以趕上飛機。

 ☆ If I **had known** the fact, I **would have taken** action right away. (92 學測)
如果我之前知道事實，我就會馬上採取行動。

用法詳解

1. 要表達**與過去事實相反的事情**時，必須使用「與過去事實相反」的假設語氣。

2. 在「與過去事實相反」的假設語氣裡，if 子句中使用**過去完成式** (had + p.p.)，主要子句中使用**過去式助動詞 + have p.p.**。

   - If the patient **had taken** the doctor's advice, he **could have recovered** from his illness earlier. 如果這病人當初有接受醫生的建議，他本來可以早點從疾病中痊癒。
     ① 事實上，病人當初沒接受醫生建議，所以沒早點痊癒，屬於「與過去事實相反」的假設。

   - If the student **had not cheated** in the exam, he **would not have been punished**.
     如果這個學生考試沒作弊，他就不會被處罰。
     ① 事實上，這學生考試作弊，所以他被處罰，屬於「與過去事實相反」的假設。

3. 若 if 子句含有 there be，在與過去事實相反的假設法中必須使用 there had been。

   - If **there had been** enough food for the villagers, many of them **would not have died** of famine. 如果當時有足夠的食物可以給村民，很多人不會死於饑荒。

4. 依據句意的需求，與現在事實相反和與過去事實相反的假設語氣可以同時存在。

   - If the boy **had taken** medicine this morning, he **might feel** better now.
     如果這男孩今早有吃藥，他現在可能會覺得舒坦多了。① 第一句的時間點為 this morning，用過去假設 had taken；第二句的時間點為 now，用現在假設 might feel。

學習補給站

在由事實句轉換為假設句時，記得將肯定敘述改為否定敘述，將否定敘述改為肯定敘述。

- [事實] 肯 + 否 The laptop **is** expensive, so the student **can not afford** it.

➡ [假設] 否 + 肯 If the laptop **were not** expensive, the student **could afford** it.
如果筆記型電腦不是這麼貴，這學生就買得起。

● [事實] 肯 + 肯 The news **was reported**, so people **knew** it.

➡ [假設] 否 + 否 If the news **had not been reported**, people **would not have known** it.
如果這新聞沒被報導，人們就不會知道。

句型練習

一、選擇

( ) 1. If the driver _____ his seat belt, he might not have been killed in the car crash.
    (A) fastened   (B) has fastened   (C) had fastened   (D) didn't fasten

( ) 2. If our car hadn't broken down on the way, we _____ before evening.
    (A) can get home   (B) could have got home
    (C) couldn't get home   (D) couldn't have got home

( ) 3. Egyptian culture _____ so well-known if the museums _____ Egyptian mummies on show. (93 學測)
    (A) will become; didn't put   (B) will not become; had put
    (C) would not have become; had not put (D) may not become; has not put

( ) 4. If _____ airplanes thousands of years ago, ancient people could have traveled to a distant place in a short time.
    (A) there are   (B) there were   (C) there have been (D) there had been

二、句子改寫

1. Eva didn't bring her camera, so she couldn't take pictures on her trip to the national park.

    _____

2. These boys had a street fight, so they were taken to the police station.

    _____

三、翻譯

1. 如果這母親先前有足夠的耐心與兒子溝通，他們可能不會有代溝。
    If the mother _____ _____ enough patience to communicate with her son, they
    _____ _____ _____ a generation gap.

2. 如果昨天下雨過後出現太陽，我們也許能看見彩虹。

    _____

3. 如果我早上有吃早餐，我現在就不會這麼餓了。

    _____

10-3

$$\text{If} + S_1 + \text{were to} + V_1, S_2 + \textit{would/could/might/should} + V_2$$
$$\text{If} + S_1 + \text{should (+ happen to)} + V_1, S_2 + \text{aux.} + V_2$$

句型範例

- If the stars **were to** stop twinkling in the sky, I **would change** my mind.
  如果星星在天空中停止閃爍，我就會改變心意。
- If the severe typhoon **should** hit Taiwan next week, we **might have** a day off.
  萬一這強烈颱風下週侵襲台灣，我們可能會放一天假。

用法詳解

與未來事實相反的假設語氣可以用來表示「與未來事實相反的事情」與「萬一」之意。

a. 句型：If + S_1 + were to + V_1, S_2 + *would/could/might/should* + V_2

與未來事實相反：表示**未來絕對不可能發生**或者**發生的可能性極低**的事情。if 子句中使用 **were to + V**，主要子句中使用**過去式助動詞 + V**。

- If oxygen **were to** disappear, all the living animals on the Earth **would die**.
  如果氧氣消失，所有地球上的動物都會死去。
  ⓘ 事實上，氧氣不太可能消失，所以地球上的動物仍活著。
- If the Earth **were to** stop spinning, what **would happen** to human beings?
  如果地球停止轉動，人類會發生什麼事？ⓘ 事實上，地球不會停止轉動。

b. 句型：If + S_1 + should (+ happen to) + V_1, S_2 + aux. + V_2

萬一：表示**未來有可能發生的事情**，發生的可能性比 were to 高。if 子句中使用 **should + V**，主要子句中使用**過去式助動詞**或**現在式助動詞 + V**。使用過去式助動詞時表示可能性較不高，使用現在式助動詞時表示可能性較高。

- If the student **should** hand in the final project late, he **might fail** this subject.
  萬一這個學生遲交期末作業，他這科可能會被當。
- If George **should** be caught in the traffic jam, he **may call** us.
  萬一 George 遇到塞車，他可能會打電話給我們。

句型練習

一、選擇

( ) 1. If all the trees in the world _____ cut down, our ecosystem would be seriously affected.

    (A) were to be   (B) were   (C) have been   (D) could

( ) 2. If the rainbow ＿＿＿＿ forever, Selina ＿＿＿＿ Ken's proposal.

    (A) will last; will accept   (B) were to last; would accept

    (C) lasts; may accept   (D) should last; may accept

( ) 3. It is raining heavily now. If the open-air concert ＿＿＿＿ be cancelled tonight, we can go to a movie instead.

    (A) could   (B) should have   (C) were to   (D) should

( ) 4. Leon will take a taxi to the office if he ＿＿＿＿ miss the bus.

    (A) will   (B) was to   (C) should   (D) were to

( ) 5. If the flight ＿＿＿＿ cancelled, we ＿＿＿＿ change our travel plan.

    (A) will be; will have to   (B) were; might have to

    (C) should be; will have to   (D) were to be; will have to

二、句子改寫

1. It is impossible that time can be turned back, so we can't change the past.

    If ＿＿＿＿＿＿＿＿＿＿＿＿＿＿＿＿＿＿＿＿＿＿＿＿＿＿＿＿＿＿＿＿＿＿

2. It is likely that the plane will be delayed, so the passengers may have to wait.

    If ＿＿＿＿＿＿＿＿＿＿＿＿＿＿＿＿＿＿＿＿＿＿＿＿＿＿＿＿＿＿＿＿＿＿

三、翻譯

1. 如果 Janet 的頭髮在一夜中多長 20 公分，她明天就可以把頭髮綁起來了。

    Janet ＿＿＿＿ tie her hair tomorrow, if it ＿＿＿＿ ＿＿＿＿ grow 20 centimeters longer in one night.

2. 如果恐龍再次出現在地球上，很多生物會滅絕。

    ＿＿＿＿＿＿＿＿＿＿＿＿＿＿＿＿＿＿＿＿＿＿＿＿＿＿, many living things would die out.

3. 萬一 Nora 忘記把冷凍食品加熱，我們可能就沒有晚餐吃。

    ＿＿＿＿＿＿＿＿＿＿＿＿＿＿＿＿＿＿＿＿＿＿＿＿＿＿＿＿＿＿＿＿＿＿

10-4

Were + S + . . . , S + *would/could/might/should* + V
Had + S + p.p. , S + *would/could/might/should* + have + p.p.
Should + S + V, S + *would/could/might/should* + V

句型範例

- **Were** the weather sunny now, we **would go** bike riding.
  如果現在是晴天，我們會去騎自行車。

- **Had** Ray **been** confident enough, he **could have won** the speech contest.
  如果 Ray 夠有信心，他本來可以在演講比賽得名。

- **Should** any accident **happen**, customers **could escape** from this emergency exit.
  萬一意外發生，顧客可以由逃生門脫逃。

用法詳解

在含有 **were**、**had**、**should** 的「與現在事實相反」、「與過去事實相反」和「與未來事實相反」的假設法中，可以**將 if 省略**，並將 were、had、should 移至主詞前，形成**倒裝句**。

a. 與現在事實相反：Were + S + . . . , S + *would/could/might/should* + V

- **Were** this stingy man generous, he **might have** more friends.
  如果這個吝嗇的人慷慨些，他可能會有更多朋友。

b. 與過去事實相反：Had + S + p.p. , S + *would/could/might/should* + have + p.p.

- **Had** this company **promoted** their products, they **should have had** better sales.
  如果這公司有推銷產品，他們應該會有較好的銷售量。

c. 與未來事實相反：Should + S + V, S + *would/could/might/should* + V

- **Should** the boy **tell** any lie again, no one **would believe** him any longer.
  如果這個男孩再說一次謊，再也沒有人會相信他了。

句型練習

一、選擇

(　) 1. _____ in such a dangerous situation, what _____ you do?
    (A) You were; have   (B) Had you; could
    (C) Were you; would   (D) Should you; might

(　) 2. _____ controlled her diet, she _____ so much weight.
    (A) Were the girl; will not gain   (B) If the girl; would have gained
    (C) If the girl should have; will not gain   (D) Had the girl; would not have gained

( ) 3. _____ the library _____ tomorrow, I might go to the bookstore instead.
    (A) Had; been closed   (B) Should; be closed
    (C) Were; to be closed   (D) If; had been closed

二、句子改寫

1. If Kenny were very good at tennis, he could participate in the tennis tournament.

_____

2. If Carol had booked her flight earlier, she could have received a discount on airfare.

_____

3. If our car should break down on the way, we would have to walk home.

_____

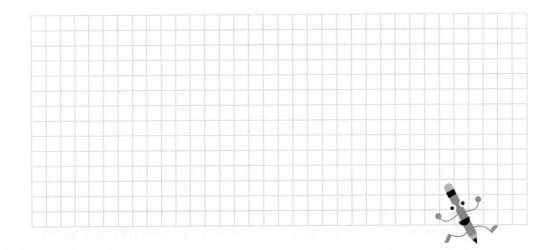

10–5

If it were/Were it not for + N, S + *would/could/might/ should + be/V* . . .
If it had/Had it not been for + N, S + *would/could/might* + have + p.p.

句型範例

● **If it were not for** the spice, the soup **would be** tasteless.
要不是有調味料，湯會嚐起來毫無味道。

● **If it had not been for** the traffic light, these cars **would have bumped** into one another. 要不是有交通號誌，這些車就會撞在一起。

用法詳解

1. 在假設法中，要表示「要不是…的話」或「若沒有…的話」時，會使用下列兩種句型：

  a. 與現在事實相反：If it were not for + N, S + *would/could/might/should + be/V* . . .

  ● **If it were not for** the cell phone, I **could** not **call** my friends anytime and anywhere. 要不是有手機，我就不能隨時隨地聯絡朋友。

  ● **If it were not for** water, no mammals **could survive**.
  要不是有水，沒有哺乳動物可以存活。

  b. 與過去事實相反：If it had not been for + N, S + *would/could/might* + have + p.p.

  ● **If it had not been for** his brother's ride, Jason **could** not **have arrived** at school on time. 要不是有哥哥載他，Jason 本來無法準時到校。

  ● **If it had not been for** her parents' financial support, Karen **could** not **have gone** abroad for further education.
  若非有她父母的經濟支持，Karen 無法出國留學。

2. 本句型可以**省略 if**，將 were 與 had 移至主詞前，形成倒裝句。

  a. 與現在事實相反：Were it not for + N, S + *would/could/might/should + be/V* . . .

  ● **Were it not for** the hair dryer, I **could** not **dry** my hair quickly.
  要不是有吹風機，我就無法很快吹乾頭髮。

  b. 與過去事實相反：Had it not been for + N, S + *would/could/might* + have + p.p.

  ● **Had it not been for** the spacecraft, astronauts **could** not **have landed** on the moon. 要不是有太空船，太空人就無法登陸月球。

3. 也可用 but for 或 without 改寫，請注意主要句的動詞使用。

a. 與現在事實相反：*But for/Without + N, S + would/could/might/should + be/V*
- **But for/Without** the alarm clock, Morris **could** not **get up** on time every day.
  要不是有鬧鐘，Morris 每天無法準時起床。

b. 與過去事實相反：*But for/Without + N, S + would/could/might/should* + have + p.p.
- **But for/Without** the tour guide, we **might have got lost** in this foreign country. 要不是有導遊，我們可能會在這個國家迷路。

句型練習

一、選擇

( ) 1. If it _____ for the reflectors, it would be very dangerous to drive on the road.
- (A) were not
- (B) was not
- (C) is not
- (D) had not been

( ) 2. This baseball team might have lost the game if it _____ for their coach's tactics.
- (A) is not
- (B) had not been
- (C) were not
- (D) would not have been

( ) 3. _____ airplanes, it would be impossible to travel to faraway places in a short time.
- (A) Were there not for
- (B) If there are no
- (C) Had it not been for
- (D) Were it not for

( ) 4. _____ the ambulance, this badly injured man would have died on the way to the hospital.
- (A) If it was not for
- (B) Were it not for
- (C) Had it not been for
- (D) Had there not been for

二、句子改寫

1. The human body has a nervous system, so human beings can feel pain and avoid it.
   If it _____

2. If it were not for the pension, many elderly people could not live in comfort after retirement.
   But for _____

三、翻譯

1. 要不是有火，我們就無法煮熟食物。
   _____ _____ _____ _____ fire, we _____ not cook food.

2. 若非有規律的飲食，這個老婦人早就生病了。
   _____ _____ _____ _____ _____ her regular diet, this old lady _____ _____ _____ sick.

10–6

S + *would/could/might/should* + have + p.p.

句型範例

● This marathon runner **could have won** the gold medal in the race, but he fell halfway. 這個馬拉松跑者本來能夠在比賽中贏得金牌，但是他跌倒了。

● The sleepy man **should have drunk** some coffee before he began his work. 這個想睡的人本來應該在開始工作前喝些咖啡。

用法詳解

1. 本單元句型用來描述「過去會、能夠、可能、應該發生，但實際上卻未發生的事」，解為「本來…」。

   ● I **could have lent** you my iPad; unfortunately, something was wrong with it. 我本來可以借你我的 iPad；可惜它有點故障。

   ● The construction of this multi-use stadium **should have been completed** several years ago. 這座多用途的體育館早該在幾年前就蓋好。

2. 本句型的否定形在助動詞後加上 **not**，表示「過去不會、不能夠、不可能、不應該發生，但事實上卻發生的事情」，帶有懊悔或遺憾之意。

   ● Titanic **would not have sunk**, but it hit a giant iceberg and sank in the end. 鐵達尼號本來不會沈船，但是它撞上了大冰山，最後沉沒。

   ● You **should not have talked** back to your parents; their feelings were deeply hurt. 你本來不應該對父母回嘴的；他們受到很深的傷害。

學習補給站

should + have + p.p. 可等於 ought to + have + p.p.，否定形為 ought + not + to + have + p.p.。

● Owen **ought to have got** up at 6 o'clock, but his alarm clock didn't go off. Owen 本來應該六點就起床，但是他的鬧鐘沒響。

● My friend **ought not to have called** after 10 pm; the ring disturbed my parents' sleep. 我的朋友不應該在 10 點後打電話來；鈴聲打擾到我父母的睡眠。

句型練習

一、選擇

( ) 1. A case of museum feet makes one feel like saying: "This is boring. I _____ the painting myself. When can we sit down? What time is it?" (95 指考)

(A) will do   (B) may not do   (C) could have done (D) had done

( ) 2. Helen _____ her personal information on the social networking website; it could be used by someone with bad intentions.

(A) didn't reveal   (B) had not revealed

(C) should not have revealed   (D) must not reveal

( ) 3. Fortunately, the skiers had a narrow escape. They _____ in the avalanche.

(A) had been killed   (B) would be killed

(C) can have been killed   (D) could have been killed

二、句子改寫

1. Ben didn't attend the field trip yesterday, as he had a high fever.

(以 . . . could . . . 改寫)

_____ , but he had a high fever.

2. Patricia didn't get up early, so she missed the first bus.

(以 should . . . ; . . . would . . . 改寫)

Patricia _____ , and then

she _____

三、翻譯

1. 當時服務生應該早點讓我們點餐的。我們等了半小時。

The waiter _____ _____ our order earlier. We had waited for half an hour.

2. 這個年輕演員原本不會被提名最佳演員獎，但他在這部片的傑出表現讓評審們印象深刻。

_____ Best Actor, but his

excellent performance in this film impressed the judges.

3. 火車本來可以準時離開，但是有些石頭被發現在鐵軌上。

_____

4. 在有效的溝通前，你本來不應該和朋友開始吵架。

_____

10–7

$$S + wish\ (+ that) + S + \begin{cases} \textit{were/V-ed/would/could} \\ \text{had} + \text{p.p.} \end{cases}$$

句型範例

- I wish (that) I **were** a bird. 但願我是一隻鳥。
- I wish (that) I **had** wings. 但願我有翅膀。
- I wish (that) I **could** fly. 但願我會飛。
- I wish (that) I **had taken** my parents' advice. 但願我之前有接受爸媽的建議。

用法詳解

本單元句型表示「不可能實現的願望」，因為已經跟現實相違，故使用假設語氣，解為「但願…」。在本句型裡，需注意：(1)主要子句中的 wish 代表說話者許願時的時態，不影響其後 that 子句的時態。that 子句中的時態代表願望本身，必須用假設語氣表示與事實相反的敘述。(2) that 可省略。(3) wish 後使用 be 動詞時，使用 were 較為正式。在口語上，第一人稱單數或第三人稱單數也可以使用 was。

a. 與現在事實相反的願望：S + wish + (that) + S + *were/V-ed/would/could*

- I **wish** (that) I **were** a millionaire. 但願我是百萬富翁。

    ⓘ 願望與現在事實相反，故動詞用過去式 were。

- We **wish** (that) we **had** a day off. 我們但願今天放假。

    ⓘ 願望與現在事實相反，故動詞用過去式 had。

- The disabled man **wishes** (that) he **could** walk on his own feet again.

    這位身障人士但願他能再以雙腳走路。ⓘ 願望與現在事實相反，故動詞用過去式 could。

- I **wish** I **knew** how to solve this tricky problem.

    但願我知道該如何解決這棘手的問題。ⓘ wish 的時態不影響 that 子句的時態。

b. 與過去事實相反的願望：S + wish + (that) + S + had + p.p.

- David **wishes** (that) he **had asked** the lady for her phone number.

    David 但願他之前有向這女士要電話。

    ⓘ David 現在表達過去的願望。願望與過去事實相反，故動詞用過去完成式 had asked。

- The bankrupt man **wishes** (that) he **hadn't gambled**. 這破產的人但願他以前沒賭博。

    ⓘ 這破產的人現在表達過去的願望。願望與過去事實相反，故動詞用過去完成式 hadn't gambled。

- The catcher **wishes** he **had caught** the last ball. 捕手但願他有接到最後一球。

- The student **wished** he **had done** spelling check before he submitted his English composition. 這學生但願他在繳交英文作文前有檢查拼字。

學習補給站

表示但願的句型尚有:「If only + 假設語氣」。

● If only my lost necklace **were** here! 但願我遺失的項鍊在這裡!

句型練習

一、選擇

( ) 1. The scenery is spectacular. I wish I _____ a camera now!

(A) had　　　　(B) have　　　　(C) have had　　　　(D) had had

( ) 2. Stella needs her parents' help. She wishes they _____ here with her.

(A) are　　　　(B) had been　　　　(C) were　　　　(D) must be

( ) 3. Nick feels like throwing up. He wishes he _____ that much this morning.

(A) shouldn't eat　　(B) didn't eat　　(C) hasn't eaten　　(D) hadn't eaten

( ) 4. Olivia wished _____.

(A) she went to the dentist yesterday

(B) her husband had not lost their wedding ring

(C) her daughter didn't say such offensive words to her

(D) the weather was fine today

二、句子改寫

1. The child is too short to reach the bathroom sink.

The child wishes that _____

to reach the bathroom sink.

2. Terry's grandfather had never been to Italy. It was his favorite country.

Terry's grandfather wished that _____

_____ , which was his favorite country.

三、翻譯

1. 這年輕人但願他是有錢人。

The young man _____ that he _____ a wealthy man.

2. Frank 但願他昨天沒抱怨老闆。

Frank wishes that he _____

yesterday.

3. 我的手機電池電力很低。但願我昨晚有充電。

_____

4. 去年 Nancy 但願她在紐約慶祝耶誕節,但是今年她但願能在倫敦渡過這節日。

10–8

$$S_1 + V_1 + \text{as if} + S_2 + were/V_2\text{-ed}/had\ p.p._2 \dots$$

句型範例

- The charming lady walks **as if** she **is** a model. 這迷人的女士走起路來好像模特兒。
- The conceited man talks **as if** he **were** a scholar. 這自負的人說起話來彷彿是學者。
- The stranger acts **as if** she **knew** me. 這個陌生人表現得彷彿認識我。
- The frightened man looks **as if** he **had seen** a ghost. 這受驚嚇的男人彷彿剛看到鬼。

☆ Cartier-Bresson later joked that due to his parents' frugal ways, it often seemed **as though** his family **was** poor. (104 學測)

Cartier-Bresson 笑說因為他父母過得很節儉，他的家庭彷彿讓人以為很貧窮。

☆ The tip of your nose feels numb—almost **as though** it **were** frozen.

你的鼻尖會變得麻木——感覺似乎結凍了。 (102 指考)

用法詳解

1. as if 為連接詞，引導副詞子句，意為「彷彿」，也可代換為 as though。

注意語氣上的判斷：

a. 若表示「可能發生的事情」，as if 引導的子句用直說法。

- The pale-faced man walks **as if** he **is** sick.

  這臉色蒼白的人走起路來彷彿生病了。

  ① 說話者認為這人很可能生病了，而這人也可能真的病了，故用直說法。

b. 若表示「不可能發生的事情」，as if 引導的子句用假設語氣。

- The child behaves **as if** he **were** an adult. 這小孩舉止彷彿他是大人。

  ① 小孩不是大人，故用與現在事實相反的假設語氣。

2. 注意本句型的動詞形態：

a. 主要子句與 as if 引導的子句為**同一時間點**發生的事情：$S_1 + V_1 + \text{as if} + S + were/V_2\text{-ed}$。

- The lady dresses **as if** she **were** a queen. 這女士打扮的樣子彷彿她是女王。
- Eric nodded **as if** he fully **understood** what the professor was talking about.

  那時 Eric 點頭，彷彿他完全懂得教授說的事情。

b. as if 引導的子句比主要子句**早發生**或持續一段時間：$S_1 + V_1 + \text{as if} + S + had + p.p._2$。

- The driver smells **as if** he **had drunk** some wine.

  這司機聞起來彷彿之前喝了酒。

● The woman ate the hamburger hungrily **as if** she **had** not **eaten** anything for a week. 這女人飢餓地吃漢堡，彷彿已經一週沒吃東西了。

句型練習

一、選擇

( ) 1. Falling in love is always magical. It feels eternal as if love _____ forever. (94 學測)

    (A) must last   (B) had lasted   (C) will last   (D) will have last

( ) 2. The host and hostess of this B&B are hospitable. They treat us as if we _____ their family.

    (A) were   (B) are   (C) have been   (D) had been

( ) 3. The naughty students talked loudly as if the teacher _____ absent at that time.

    (A) is   (B) were   (C) had been   (D) would be

( ) 4. The man talks as if he _____ in another country before, but actually he has never traveled outside his city.

    (A) had been living   (B) has lived   (C) had lived   (D) lived

二、翻譯

1. 這男人大聲講手機，彷彿戲院沒有其他人。

The man talked loudly on his cell phone _____ _____ nobody else _____ in the theater.

2. Nora 剛與男友分手，但是她表現出彷彿一切都很好的樣子。

Nora just broke up with her boyfriend, _____

_____

3. 在演講比賽中，這自信的學生說起話來彷彿觀眾都是他粉絲似的。

_____

4. 這滿身是汗的男孩聞起來好像十天沒洗澡似的。

_____

5. 這口渴的旅客將一瓶汽水一飲而盡，彷彿她已經一星期滴水未沾。

_____

10–9

It is time (+ that) + S + *were/V-ed* . . .
(= It is time + for + S + to V)

句型範例

- **It is time that** you **focused** your mind on your studies. 該是你專心於學業的時候了。
- **It is time for** the players **to** learn how to cooperate with one another.
  該是選手們學習互相合作的時候了。

☆ I think **it is time for** you **to** learn how to live without my help.
我認為該是你學習如何不依賴我的幫助過生活的時候了。 (95 學測)

☆ Finally, I thought **it was time to** get rid of the animal. (92 指考)
終於，我認為該是擺脫這隻動物的時候了。

用法詳解

1. 本句型用於表示「該做某事了」，其後可接 for sb + to V 或 that 子句。注意，使用 that
子句時，因含有「早就該做某事，但未做」之意，屬於「與現在事實相反」的假設法概
念，故 that 子句中的動詞用 were 或 V-ed。

- **It is time for** the child to brush his teeth. 這孩子該刷牙了。
- **It is time for** you to practice the piano. 該是你練習鋼琴的時候了。
- **It is time that** Gina got rid of her bad habits. 該是 Gina 戒除壞習慣的時候了。
- **It is time that** we washed the dishes. 該是我們洗碗的時候了。

2. 如果要強調語氣，可在 time 前面加上 **high** 或 **about**。

- It is **high** time that Rick turned off the computer and went to bed.
  該是 Rick 關電腦睡覺的時候了。
- It is **about** time that the government paid attention to food safety and hygiene
  issues. 該是政府注意食品安全和衛生議題的時候了。

句型練習

一、選擇

( ) 1. Last autumn, when nights got too cold to sleep in the park, Soapy realized it was
time _____ arrangements for his annual winter trip. (91 指考)
　(A) to make　　　(B) making　　　(C) makes　　　(D) made

( ) 2. It is time that the children _____ away their toys and _____ lunch.

    (A) put; have   (B) putting; having   (C) to put; to have   (D) put; had

( ) 3. It is _____ time for the girls _____ home.

    (A) that; go   (B) just; going   (C) about; went   (D) high; to go

( ) 4. It is time that the overweight man _____ down on his consumption of fat and sugar.

    (A) cuts   (B) cut   (C) will cut   (D) cutting

二、句子改寫

1. These people should face the music. (以 It is time for . . . 改寫)

    _____

2. It is time for the teacher to announce the test result. (以 It is time that . . . 改寫)

    _____

3. The chronic procrastinator should learn to manage his time. (以 It is time that . . . 改寫)

    _____

4. Michael should do the laundry now. (分別以 It is time for . . . 及 It is time that . . . 改寫)

    _____

    _____

三、翻譯

1. 當該是上大學的時候到來，Whitney 感到很緊張。 (98 指考)

    When _____ _____ _____ _____ _____ to college, Whitney was quite nervous.

2. 該是評審們做最後決定的時候了。

    _____

11-1

S + have + p.p. + since . . .

句型範例

- The best-selling novelist **has been writing since** her adolescent years.
  這個暢銷小說家自從青少年時就開始寫作。
- The new smartphones **have won** many people's favor **since** they were launched.
  自從這款新智慧型手機上市後，就受到許多人喜愛。

☆ Although Maggie **has been** physically **confined** to her wheelchair **since** the car accident, she does not limit herself to indoor activities. (105 學測)
雖然 Maggie 自從車禍後就離不開輪椅，但她不限制自己只從事室內活動。

☆ **Since** the early 1990s, the lithium-ion battery **has been** the most suitable battery for portable electronic equipment. (104 指考)
自 1990 年代初期以來，鋰離子電池就是最適合可攜式電子裝置的電池。

用法詳解

1. 本句型表示「從過去某時或某事發生開始，另一事就一直維持至今」的意思，故 since 之後接**過去的時間**或使用**過去式動詞的子句**，而**主要子句必須使用完成式**。
   - Kevin **has been** interested in science **since** his childhood.
     Kevin 自從童年時期就一直對科學有興趣。
   - We **have not heard** from the Lins **since** they moved to the US.
     自從林家人搬到美國後，我們就沒他們的消息了。

2. 若主要子句有「被動」之意時，用完成被動式 (have been p.p.)；有「持續某個狀態」之意時，用完成進行式 (have been V-ing)。可以用 ever since 加強語氣。
   - Ever since the rescue team came to help, over 10 victims of the earthquake **have been saved**. 自從搜救隊來協助後，十多名地震災民已經被拯救出來。
   - The children **have been playing** video games since they came home.
     孩子們自從回家後就一直在打電動。

學習補給站

當 since 做「因為」與「既然」解釋時，不使用本句型用法。

☆ **Since** it hasn't rained for months, there is a water shortage in many parts of the country. 因為已經好幾個月沒下雨，這國家的許多地區都缺水。 (101 指考)

☆ **Since** you have not decided on the topic of your composition, it's still premature to talk about how to write your conclusion.

既然你還沒決定作文的題目,現在談論怎麼寫結論太早了。 (101 指考)

句型練習

一、選擇

( ) 1. I've always wanted to work for an insurance company ever since I _____ a little girl.

(A) am   (B) used to be   (C) have been   (D) was (98 學測)

( ) 2. Since then, over 12 million copies of the game _____ from Apple's App Store.

(A) are purchased   (B) will purchase

(C) have been purchased   (D) have purchased (101 指考)

( ) 3. The construction of a bridge over the East River _____ since the early 19th century. (103 指考)

(A) discussed   (B) had been discussed

(C) is discussed   (D) was discussed

( ) 4. _____, the Nobel Peace Center has been educating, inspiring and entertaining its visitors through exhibitions, activities, lectures, and cultural events. (101 指考)

(A) Since it opened   (B) As it was opened

(C) After it opens   (D) Since its opening

二、句子改寫

1. Olivia started to learn English when she entered kindergarten. She is still learning English now.

_____ since she entered kindergarten.

2. The manager went on vacation. The project has been left undone since then.

_____

三、翻譯

1. 自從那時起,美國每年的博士人數以倍數成長至六萬四千人。 (100 指考)

Since then, America's annual output of PhDs _____ _____, to 64,000.

2. 自從 1900 年代以來,某些地區會組織另類的舞會來符合特殊學生的需求。 (99 學測)

_____ the 1990s, alternative proms _____

_____ in some areas to meet the needs of particular students.

3. 自從數位相機被發明以來,它們在人們的生活中扮演了重要的角色。

_____

11-2

not (. . .) until . . .

句型範例

● The boys did **not** finish the game **until** sunset. 男孩們直到日落才完成比賽。

● Many people **don't** realize the importance of health **until** they lose it.
許多人直到失去健康才瞭解它的重要性。

 ☆ Forks were **not** widely adopted there **until** the 16th century.
直到 16 世紀叉子才在當地被廣泛使用。 (101 學測)

☆ We **won't** know **until** the outcome of the election is announced.
直到選舉的結果公布後，我們才會知道。 (100 學測)

用法詳解

1. 本句型用來描述「直到…才…」之意。

● Mom was busy, so we **didn't** eat dinner **until** 7 o'clock.
媽媽很忙碌，所以我們直到七點才吃晚餐。

● The old man **couldn't** read the newspaper **until** he put on his glasses.
這老人直到戴上眼鏡才能讀報紙。

2. 使用此句型做中譯英時，語序與中文相反。須先寫出「才…(be/aux. not . . .)」的部分，再寫出「直到…(until . . .)」。

● These flowers **won't** bloom **until** spring. 這些花直到春天才會開。
① (1) 先以 won't bloom 表示「才會開」。(2) 再以 until spring 寫出「直到春天」。

● The students **didn't** know how to solve the math problem **until** the teacher taught them. 直到老師指導，學生們才知道如何解這道數學問題。
① (1) 先以 didn't know how to solve the math problem 寫出「才知道如何解決這道數學問題」。
(2) 再以 until the teacher taught them 寫出「直到老師指導」。

學習補給站

not (. . .) until 尚可與其他句型結合：

1. 與倒裝句結合：Not until . . . + aux. + S + V (用法請見 15-4)

● Kevin **didn't** know the meaning of the word **until** he looked it up in the dictionary.

➡ **Not until** Kevin looked up the word in the dictionary did he know its meaning.
直到 Kevin 查字典才知道這個字的意思。

2. 與分裂句結合：It + be + not until . . . + that-clause。注意，因為否定字已經移到前

面，that 子句裡使用肯定句即可。

● The chain smoker **didn't** quit smoking **until** he got sick.

➡ **It was not until** the chain smoker got sick **that** he quit smoking.

這老煙槍直到生病才戒煙。

句型練習

一、選擇

( ) 1. The first Doctor of Philosophy degree was awarded in Paris in 1150, but the degree _____ its modern status until the early 19th century. (100 指考)

    (A) acquired   (B) would acquire   (C) did not acquire   (D) had acquired

( ) 2. Coffee beans _____ Kopi Lowak _____ they've been digested and come out in the body waste of the palm civet. (99 指考)

    (A) have not been; after   (B) will be; before

    (C) are; until   (D) aren't; until

( ) 3. Sandra claimed that she _____ that her downloads were illegal until she was contacted by authorities. (98 指考)

    (A) should know   (B) knew   (C) was aware   (D) was unaware

( ) 4. Not until Mr. Lin apologized _____.

    (A) did Mrs. Lin forgive him   (B) that Mrs. Lin forgave him

    (C) that Mrs. Lin would never forgive him (D) forgave Mrs. Lin to him

二、句子改寫

1. Lisa couldn't quench her thirst before she drank a bottle of water.

2. The obese man changed his diet. He didn't do so before he was diagnosed with cancer.

三、翻譯

1. 直到 1813 年，鳳梨才出現在那裡。 (98 學測)

  Pineapples _____ _____ _____ there until 1813.

2. 直到朋友告訴我，我才知道萬聖節的由來。

  I _____ _____ _____ the origin of Halloween _____ my friend told me.

3. 直到媽媽生氣後，Derek 才後悔對她頂嘴。

4. 直到這學生使用搜尋引擎，她才知道這個問題的答案。

11-3

As soon as/*The minute* + S + V$_1$, S + V$_2$
On/*Upon* + N/V$_1$-*ing*, S + V$_2$
S$_1$ + had + no sooner + p.p.$_1$ + than + S$_2$ + V$_2$-ed

句型範例

- **As soon as** the clown appeared, the children roared with laughter.

  小丑一出現，孩子們就哄堂大笑。

- **The minute** the sun set, the temperature in the mountain dropped.

  太陽一下山，山裡的溫度就下降。

- **Upon** arriving at Tokyo, Tina checked in on Facebook.

  Tina 一到達東京就在臉書上打卡。

- The baseball players had **no sooner** won the game **than** they leaped into the air with joy. 這些棒球選手一贏得比賽就高興地跳起來。

☆ **As soon as** the popping slows down, remove the pot from the stove.

當爆米花爆開的速度一減緩時，將鍋子從火爐上移開。 (100 學測)

☆ **The moment** the students felt the earthquake, they ran swiftly out of the classroom to an open area outside. (104 學測)

一感覺到地震，學生們就迅速跑出教室到戶外空曠處。

用法詳解

1. 本句型表示 「一…就…」。as soon as 與 the minute 為連接詞，引導副詞子句，the minute 可代換成 the moment、the instant。在此類句型中，前後二句的主詞可不同。

   - **As soon as** Ian finished the big meal, he burped. Ian 一吃完大餐就打嗝。
   - **The minute** the alarm clock went off, Jacob got up from bed.

     鬧鐘一響，Jacob 就起床。

2. 在 *on*/*upon* 引導的句型中，*on*/*upon* 為介系詞，其後接名詞或動名詞，且前後二句的主詞相同時，才適用本句型。

   - The hotel guests have to return room keys *on*/*upon* departure.

     飯店房客在離開時必須歸還房間鑰匙。

   - *On*/*Upon* feeling seasick, the man began to vomit. 一暈船，這男人就開始嘔吐。

3. 在 no sooner . . . than 的句型中，必須搭配過去完成式與過去式使用。「一…」的部分以 had no sooner + p.p. 表示，而「就…」的部分為 than + S + V-ed。

● Susan Boyle had **no sooner** sung in the talent show **than** she amazed all the audience. Susan Boyle 一在才藝節目中唱歌就驚艷全場。

學習補給站

1. 「no sooner . . . than」可代換成「*hardly/scarcely . . . when/before . . .*」。
   ● Ron had *hardly/scarcely* heard the news *when/before* he cheered.
   Ron 一聽到消息就歡呼。
2. 「no sooner . . . than」可使用倒裝句來加強語氣 (用法請見 15–5)。
   ● **No sooner** had Miranda seen a boy fall off the bike **than** she went up to help him. Miranda 一看見男孩從單車跌落就上前去幫忙。

句型練習

一、選擇

( ) 1. _____ Jim saw a car accident, he pulled his car over to the side of the road and offered help.

  (A) As soon as   (B) Upon   (C) No sooner   (D) Hardly

( ) 2. _____, many people opened their umbrellas.

  (A) The minute raining   (B) It had no sooner begun to rain

  (C) The moment it started to rain   (D) Upon raining

( ) 3. _____ seeing her child taking the first steps, the mother felt joyful.

  (A) No sooner   (B) On   (C) The instant   (D) As soon as

( ) 4. _____, it began to bleed.

  (A) Upon cutting her finger   (B) No sooner had Bella cut her finger

  (C) As soon as Bella cut her finger   (D) The moment cutting her finger

二、翻譯

1. 這魔術師完成表演的瞬間，觀眾就熱烈鼓掌。

  _____ _____ the magician finished his performance, the audience gave him a burst of applause.

2. 一聞到芳香的空氣，這緊張的女孩就感到鬆了一口氣。

  _____ _____ the scented air, the nervous girl felt relieved.

3. 鐘一敲十二點，灰姑娘就跑出舞會大廳。

  _____ than Cinderella ran out of the ballroom.

11-4

By the time + S$_1$ + V$_1$-ed, S$_2$ + had + p.p.
By the time + S$_1$ + V$_1$, S$_2$ + will + have + p.p.

句型範例

- **By the time** Jim earns a master's degree abroad, he will have spent 2 million dollars. 在 Jim 取得國外的碩士學位時，他將會花上二百萬元。
- **By the time** Lily and Jason celebrated their anniversary, they had been married for ten years. 在 Lily 和 Jason 慶祝週年慶時，他們已經結婚十年了。

 ☆ **By the time** he was 23, he had already come up with the idea of what would be the modern computer—the Turing machine. (105 指考)

在他 23 歲時，他就已經構想出會成為現代電腦的概念——圖靈機。

☆ **By the time** he died in 1919, he had given away 350 million dollars.

在 1919 年過世時，他就已經捐出三億五千萬元。 (96 指考)

用法詳解

1. by the time 為連接詞，引導副詞子句，句型表示「在某事發生時，另一事早已經發生」，故主要子句常用完成式。

2. 主要子句的時態必須視 by the time 所引導的副詞子句時間點決定。

   a. 描述未來：by the time + 現在式，主要子句 + 未來完成式 (will + have + p.p.)。

   - **By the time** we get to train station, the train will have departed.
     在我們到達車站時，火車將已經出發了。

   b. 描述過去：by the time + 過去式，主要子句 + 過去完成式 (had + p.p.)。

   - **By the time** the ballroom dancers felt exhausted, they had practiced for three hours. 這些國標舞者感到疲憊的時候，他們已經練習三小時了。

句型練習

一、選擇

( ) 1. By the time Karen receives my e-mail, I _____ on my way to Taichung.

    (A) will be   (B) will have been   (C) am   (D) have been

( ) 2. By the time the waiter served the dessert, we _____ to our hearts' content.

    (A) will eat   (B) will have eaten   (C) had eaten   (D) would eat

(　) 3. The students ＿＿＿＿ their exam by the time the bell ＿＿＿＿.

(A) finish; rings 　　　　　　　　(B) finished; rang

(C) finished; had rung 　　　　　　(D) will have finished; rings

二、翻譯

1. 在 Shannon 說完睡前故事的時候，她的孩子們將會睡著了。

＿＿＿＿ ＿＿＿＿ ＿＿＿＿ Shannon finishes the bedtime stories, her children ＿＿＿＿

＿＿＿＿ ＿＿＿＿ asleep.

2. 爸爸關電視時，這男孩已經看海綿寶寶卡通一小時了。

＿＿＿＿ ＿＿＿＿ ＿＿＿＿ the father turned off the TV, the boy ＿＿＿＿ ＿＿＿＿ the

cartoon Sponge Bob Square Pants for one hour.

3. Carl 的太太回到家時，他將會把晚餐煮好。

＿＿

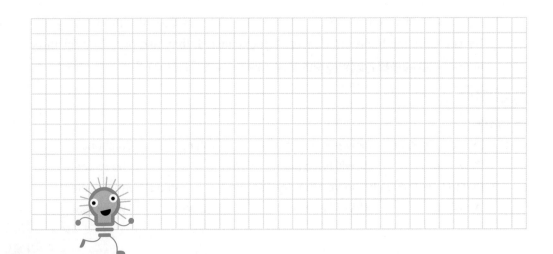

12–1

even if
even though

句型範例

● **Even if** you take a taxi, you will still miss the meeting.

即使你搭計程車還是會趕不上會議。

● **Even though** Simon's parents didn't support his dream, he never gave up.

即使 Simon 的父母不支持他的夢想，他從未放棄。

☆ **Even if** an advertisement claims to be purely informational, it still has persuasion at its core.

即使廣告宣稱是純粹傳遞資訊，它核心仍是要說服顧客。 (101 指考)

☆ Dr. Cizmar says that **even though** it is a few years away from practical use, the technology has huge potential for medical research. (102 指考) Cizmar 博士表示，儘管距離實際應用還需要幾年，這項技術在醫療研究上有極大潛力。

用法詳解

本句型屬於「讓步」的句型，意為「即使…」。even if 與 even though 為從屬連接詞，引導副詞子句。注意區別二者的用法：

	用法	備註
even if (即使；就算)	通常描述**尚未發生**的事情，或一般**可能會出現**的狀況。	有時帶有假設性，意思上等於 whether or not。
even though (即使；儘管)	通常描述**已經發生**或已經存在的狀況。	意思上等於 despite the fact that，語氣比 although 強烈。

● **Even if** the stingy man has much money, he won't spend a penny helping those in need. 即使這小氣鬼有很多錢，他也不會花一分一毫幫助窮困的人。

● **Even though** e-mail communication is very convenient, many people prefer to receive hand-written letters.

即使電子郵件通訊很方便，許多人比較喜歡收到手寫的信件。

● Henri Cartier-Bresson's family led frugal lives **even though** they were very wealthy. 儘管 Henri Cartier-Bresson 的家庭很富裕，他們過著勤儉的生活。

• Animal experimentation has taught humanity a great deal and saved countless lives. It needs to continue, **even if** that means animals sometimes suffer. (100 指考)
動物實驗讓人類有許多領悟且拯救了無數的生命。它必須繼續進行，就算那意味著動物有時會受苦。

句型練習

一、選擇

( ) 1. _____ they are still called "phones"—a word meaning "voice" in Greek—making voice calls may no longer be their primary function. (97 指考)

    (A) As long as   (B) Even if   (C) Just as   (D) Only when

( ) 2. _____ global warming has caused many problems, many people don't pay attention to environmental protection.

    (A) By the time   (B) The minute   (C) As soon as   (D) Even though

( ) 3. The manager verbally agreed to rent his apartment to me. _____ the agreement was not put in writing, I am sure he will keep his word. (105 指考)

    (A) Instead of   (B) Even if   (C) Even though   (D) No matter when

二、翻譯

1. 戰後，一座巨大的迴紋針雕像豎立在奧斯陸以紀念 Vaaler——儘管他的設計從未真正被大量製造過。 (104 學測)

After the war, a giant paperclip statue was erected in Oslo to honor Vaaler— _____ _____ his design was never actually manufactured.

2. 儘管 Danny 已經服了感冒藥，他仍然流鼻水。

_____ _____ Danny has taken the medicine for a cold, he has a runny nose.

3. Ted 是啃老族。就算有工作機會，他也不會接受。

Ted is a NEET. _____ , he won't take it.

4. 就算 Sarah 知道秘密也不會告訴我。

_____

12-2

despite/in spite of + $\begin{cases} \text{N/V-ing} \\ \text{the fact that-clause} \end{cases}$

句型範例

- **Despite** feeling exhausted and thirsty, the cyclist didn't stop pedaling.
  儘管感到又累又渴，這自行車手也不停歇。

- **In spite of** the fact that Beethoven lost his hearing, he had composed many great symphonies. 儘管貝多芬失去了聽力，他仍然譜出了許多偉大的交響樂。

☆ **Despite** their great variety, however, most domesticated apples can be traced back to a common ancestor, the wild apple of Central Asia. (104 學測)
儘管種類繁多，大多栽培的蘋果樹都能追溯至同個源頭——中亞的野蘋果樹。

☆ **Despite** its overall advantages, the lithium-ion battery has its drawbacks.
儘管擁有所有優點，鋰離子電池也有缺點。 (104 指考)

用法詳解

1. 本單元介紹利用 despite 與 in spite of 表示「讓步」的用法，意為「儘管…」。despite 是介系詞，in spite of 是介系詞片語，故其後需接名詞或動名詞。

- **Despite** his stomachache, the hungry boy ate four big hamburgers.
  儘管胃痛，這飢餓的男孩仍然吃了四個大漢堡。

- **Despite** having had some coffee, the man couldn't help feeling sleepy.
  儘管已經喝了些咖啡，這男人仍然無法感到想睡。

- **In spite of** the stormy weather, the fisherman set out for fishing.
  儘管有暴風雨，漁夫仍然出海捕魚。

2. despite 與 in spite of 之後亦可先接續受詞 the fact，再以 that 引導的名詞子句當 the fact 的同位語，寫成 *despite/in spite of* the fact that-clause。

- **Despite** the fact that Andy has lived in Spain for 3 years, he can't speak Spanish well. 儘管 Andy 已經住在西班牙三年了，他的西班牙文仍然說得不好。

- **In spite of** the fact that Mr. Stud didn't achieve success in his business, he led a happy life. 儘管 Stud 先生在事業上不成功，他過得很快樂。

學習補給站

本句型也可改寫成以 **although**、**even though** 引導的副詞子句。注意，although 與 even though 為連接詞,其後必須接子句,不可接名詞。

- **Although** the scientist has failed several times in his research, he never feels discouraged. 雖然這科學家在研究中遭受多次失敗,他從不覺得氣餒。
- **Even though** Arthur was grounded for breaking his curfew the other day, he hung out with his friends until 11:00 last night. 即使 Arthur 前幾天因為在外超過門禁時間被禁足,昨晚他仍然和朋友在外玩樂至 11 點。

句型練習

一、選擇

( ) 1. Her happy family life led to her excellent performance in school, _____ the atmosphere of racial discrimination in the society. (103 學測)

(A) so much as (B) as well as (C) despite (D) on behalf of

( ) 2. _____ these strong reactions from the pro-abortionists, the right of life takes precedence over a woman's right to choice. (95 指考)

(A) Although (B) In spite (C) Despite (D) Even though

( ) 3. Despite _____ , the little boy grew hair to donate to kids with cancer.

(A) he was teased (B) teasing (C) was teased (D) being teased

( ) 4. _____ the players practiced hard, they lost the game.

(A) Despite (B) In spite of

(C) Even though that (D) In spite of the fact that

二、句子改寫

1. Although the teacher explained the theory clearly, the students couldn't understand it.

Despite _____

2. Despite the girl's efforts, she failed to win the talent show.

(用 . . . the fact that . . . 改寫)

_____

三、翻譯

1. 儘管他的擔憂有道理,Sunny 航空公司的管理部仍向他施壓,要他在夜晚飛越汪洋。

_____ his valid concerns, Sunny Airlines' management pressured him to fly the airplane, over the ocean, at night. (101 指考)

2. 儘管 Mandy 道歉了,她的好友仍然無法原諒她所做的事情。

_____ , her best friend couldn't forgive her for what she had done.

3. 儘管已經得了許多獎,這發明家從未停止研究新發明。

_____

12-3

Adj./Adv./N + as + S$_1$ + *be/V*$_1$, S$_2$ + V$_2$

句型範例

● Hardworking **as** Mr. Pitt was, he didn't get a promotion.
  雖然 Pitt 先生努力工作，他沒獲得升遷。

● Carefully **as** the man drove, he bumped into a tree.
  雖然這男人小心開車，他仍然撞樹了。

● Child **as** Justin is, he talks like an adult.
  雖然 Justin 是個孩子，他說起話來像大人。

用法詳解

1. 本句型表示「雖然」之意，是讓步子句的倒裝結構，用來特別強調**形容詞**、**副詞**、**名詞**，故將強調的部分置於句首。

2. 特別注意本句型中的**名詞**須為**單數形且不加冠詞**。

   ● Exhausted **as** these dancers were, they practiced until sunset.
     雖然這些舞者很疲憊，他們仍然練習到日落。

   ● Fast **as** the boy ran, he didn't catch the bus.
     雖然這男孩跑得很快，他仍沒趕上公車。

   ● Chef **as** Hannah is, she dines out when she is on vacation.
     雖然 Hannah 是大廚，當她放假時仍在外用餐。

學習補給站

使用本句型時，注意**強調部分必須與主要動詞一致**。尤其以下幾種情況：

a. 主要動詞是**連綴動詞** (be、seem、look、sound . . . 等)，強調部分為**形容詞**。

b. 主要動詞是**一般動詞**，強調部分為**副詞**。

   ● **Smart** as the girl **is**, she fell for her friend's trick.
     雖然這女孩很聰明，她仍然上朋友的當。

   ● **Slowly** as the secretary **typed**, she made several mistakes.

   [誤] **Slow** as the secretary **typed**, she made several mistakes.
     雖然秘書慢慢打字，還是犯了幾個錯誤。

句型練習

一、選擇

( ) 1. _____ as Frank was, he took his father's advice.

 (A) A conservative man   (B) Stubborn

 (C) Carelessly   (D) Narrow mind

( ) 2. _____ as Mr. Wang is, he doesn't watch films often.

 (A) A director   (B) Moviegoers   (C) Actor   (D) Freely

( ) 3. _____ as the children enjoyed themselves, they felt exhausted after a full day at the theme park.

 (A) Happy   (B) Thrilled   (C) Excitedly   (D) Much

( ) 4. Hard as the employees _____, they are not paid well.

 (A) work   (B) are   (C) look   (D) seem

二、翻譯

1. 雖然 Lawrence 體重過重，他仍然不想節食。

_____ _____ Lawrence _____, he refuses to go on a diet.

2. 雖然 Green 太太是個愛好動物者，她並未養任何寵物。

_____, she doesn't keep any pets.

3. 雖然這個外國人努力試著要用中文表達，他無法讓大家了解他說的話。

_____

12–4

No matter *how-/what-/who-/when-/where-/which*-clause,
S + *be/V* . . .
Whoever/Whatever/Whichever/Wherever/Whenever/
However + S + *be/V* . . . , S + V

句型範例

● **No matter how** the mother tries to stop it, the child still bites his nails.

不論媽媽如何試著阻止，這孩子仍然會咬指甲。

● **Wherever** Kelly goes, she wears her lucky charm.

不論 Kelly 去哪裡，她都會戴著她的幸運物。

● The lady shows no interests in baseball games **however** exciting they may be.

這女士對棒球比賽沒興趣，不論它們多刺激。

☆ Jason always persists in finishing a task **no matter how** difficult it may be.

不論任務有多困難，Jason 總是堅持完成它。 (101 指考)

☆ **Whenever** he feels depressed, he returns to the warm, secure, and comfortable atmosphere of his home. (104 指考)

每當感到沮喪時，他就會回到家中溫暖、安全又舒適的氛圍。

用法詳解

1. 「no matter + 疑問詞」可等於「疑問詞 + -ever」，引導表示「讓步」的副詞子句，意為「不論…；無論…」。

no matter who	= whoever	不論誰	no matter when	= whenever	不論何時；每當
no matter what	= whatever	不論什麼	no matter where	= wherever	不論何處
no matter which	= whichever	不論哪個	no matter how	= however	不論如何

2. 分辨下列用法：

　　a. whoever、whatever、whichever 為複合關係代名詞，除了本單元所介紹，引導副詞子句的用法外，還可引導名詞子句 (表示「任何…」)，用法請見 6–5。

　　b. whenever、wherever、however 則為複合關係副詞，引導副詞子句。

3. 注意，「疑問詞 + -ever」當主詞時視為單數，後面接單數動詞。

4. 以 no matter + 疑問詞引導的副詞子句只可置於主要子句前，以疑問詞 + -ever 引導的副詞子句則置於主要子句前面或後面均可。

- **No matter who** calls, tell him or her that I am busy.

  不論誰打電話來，告訴他 / 她我在忙。① no matter 引導的副詞子句置主要子句前。

- **No matter how** cold the weather is, Stuart always wears a thin shirt.

  不論天氣有多冷，Stuart 總是穿薄襯衫。① no matter 引導的副詞子句置主要子句前。

- **Whatever** happens, Kate's parents will always support her.

  不論發生什麼事，Kate 的父母總是支持她。

  ① 疑問詞 + -ever 當主詞時後接單數動詞，其引導的副詞子句可置於主要子句前。

- Mr. Gibson's dog follows him **wherever** he goes.

  不論 Gibson 先生到哪裡，他的狗都跟著他。

  ① 疑問詞 + -ever 引導的副詞子句可置於主要子句後。

句型練習

一、選擇

( ) 1. Very few people, _____ intelligent or experienced, can take into account all the possibilities or outcomes of a policy or a course of action within just a short period of time. (103 學測)

　　(A) no matter what　(B) no matter how　(C) whenever　(D) wherever

( ) 2. _____ football is played, the players learn the rough-and-tumble lesson that only through the cooperation of each member can the team win. (99 學測)

　　(A) Wherever　(B) However　(C) Whatever　(D) Whichever

( ) 3. _____ I set foot on the soil of Rwanda, a country in east-central Africa, I feel as if I have entered paradise: green hills, red earth, sparkling rivers and mountain lakes. (96 學測)

　　(A) No matter how　(B) No matter which　(C) Whenever　(D) Whatever

( ) 4. _____ university you choose, your parents will support your decision.

　　(A) No matter where　(B) No matter which　(C) However　(D) Whoever

二、翻譯

1. 不論孩子吃什麼，餐後刷牙仍然是預防蛀牙的良方。 (96 學測)

   _____ _____ _____ a child eats, brushing after each meal is still the best way to fight cavities.

2. 每當你感到苦惱與沮喪時，試著唱唱歌。 (101 學測)

   Try to sing _____

3. 不論他們多努力嘗試，都無法改變 Johnny 的心意。

   _____

13-1

Because of + N, S + *be/V* . . .

Because + S$_1$ + *be/V$_1$* . . . , S$_2$ + *be/V$_2$* . . .

句型範例

- **Because of** high oil prices, many people choose to use public transportation.

  由於高油價，許多人選擇使用公共運輸工具。

- Many students got the flu **because of** the chilly weather.

  因為天氣寒冷，很多學生得了流感。

 ☆ **Because of** the engine problem in the new vans, the auto company decided to recall them from the market. (100 指考)

因為新車有引擎問題，這家汽車公司決定將它們從市場召回。

☆ He was discriminated against **because of** blood type. (105 學測)

他因為血型而受到歧視。

用法詳解

1. 要表示「因為」，除了可用 because 連接子句外，也可使用 because of + N 的句型。使用時，必須注意詞性的轉換。

2. because of 為介系詞片語，後接名詞或名詞片語，可置於句子前或後。

   - We had no choice but to cancel our plan for the picnic **because** the weather was bad.

   ➡ We had no choice but to cancel our plan for the picnic **because of** the bad weather. 由於天氣不好，我們別無選擇只好取消野餐的計畫。

   - **Because** black is often associated with death, it is seldom used for the Chinese New Year decorations.

   ➡ **Because of** its association with death, black is seldom used for the Chinese New Year decorations.

   因為黑色常令人聯想到死亡，它很少用在中國新年裝飾上。

學習補給站

與 because of 意義相同的尚有：owing to、due to、thanks to、as a result of、on account of、by virtue of，但 thanks to 後常接正面意義的字詞，若接負面意義的字詞，則表示諷刺語氣。

句型練習

一、選擇

( ) 1. The use of pigs is risky, though, _____ their natural tendency to eat any remotely edible thing. (100 指考)

(A) because   (B) because of   (C) on account   (D) as a result

( ) 2. According to government regulations, if employees are unable to work _____ a serious illness, they are entitled to take an extended sick leave. (104 指考)

(A) since   (B) thank to   (C) because of   (D) because

( ) 3. _____ global warming, a large amount of sea ice has melted and the sea level has risen.

(A) By virtue with   (B) Because   (C) Thanks for   (D) As a result of

二、翻譯

1. 臺北動物園的小貓熊圓仔因出生時受了輕傷而與媽媽分開。 她由管理員照顧了一段時間。 (103 學測)

The baby panda Yuan Zai at the Taipei Zoo was separated from her mother _____ _____ a minor injury that occurred during her birth. She was tended by zookeepers for a while.

2. 因為有機肥料，這個農場的作物和蔬菜都長得很好。

_____, the crops and vegetables on this farm grow very well.

3. 因為那位記者的無禮，這女演員拒絕回答他的問題。

_____

13-2

$$S_1 + V_1 + \textit{so that/in order that} + S_2 + \text{aux.} + V_2$$

$$S + V_1/be + \begin{cases} \textit{in order/so as to} + V_2 \\ \text{for the purpose of} + V_2\text{-ing} \end{cases}$$

句型範例

- Angel switched on the air-conditioner **so that** she could cool down her room.
  為了讓房間變涼，Angel 打開冷氣。

- The little boy made some noise **in order to** attract his mother's attention.
  為了吸引媽媽的注意，這小男孩製造一些噪音。

- Joshua created a Twitter account **for the purpose of** making more friends.
  為了交更多朋友，Joshua 在推特上註冊了一個帳號。

☆ Acquire a skill **so that** you can still be successful and famous. (101 學測)
去學習一項技能，以便你仍然能享有成功與聲望。

☆ All passengers riding in cars are required to fasten their seatbelts **in order to** reduce the risk of injury in case of an accident. (105 學測)
車上所有的乘客都被要求繫上安全帶，為了在車禍發生時能降低受傷的風險。

用法詳解

本單元介紹是表示「目的」的句型。主要有下列幾種用法：

a. $S_1 + V_1 + \textit{so that/in order that} + S_2 + \text{aux.} + V_2$。

- Tina highlighted the key words of this chapter *so that/in order that* she could learn more efficiently. 為了有效率地學習，Tina 標示出這章節的重點。

b. $S + V_1/be + \textit{in order/so as to} + V_2$：在此，to 為不定詞，之後接原形動詞。另外，in order to V 可置於句首，但 so as to V 不可置於句首。in order to 的否定形為 in order + not + to V，so as to 的否定形為 so as + not + to V。

- Inventors create products *in order/so as* to meet people's needs.
  發明家創造產品的目的是要符合人們的需求。

- The man walked across the room on tiptoe **in order not to** waken his children.
  為了不吵醒小孩，這男人踮著腳尖走過房間。

c. $S + V_1/be + \text{for the purpose of} + V_2\text{-ing}$。

- The manager held the meeting **for the purpose of** discussing the new project.
  經理舉行會議是為了討論新的計畫。

學習補給站

表示「為了…」的用法尚有：with a view to + V-ing、with an eye to + V-ing。

二者的 to 為介系詞，故之後接**名詞**或**動名詞**。

● Some measures have been taken **with a view to** <u>preventing</u> littering.

　採取某些措施的目的是為了預防亂丟垃圾。

句型練習

一、選擇

(　) 1. ＿＿＿＿ demolish a building safely, blasters must map out a careful plan ahead of time. (101 指考)

    (A) In order that　　　　　　(B) For the purpose of

    (C) In order to　　　　　　　(D) So as to

(　) 2. The student decided to study harder ＿＿＿＿ keep up with his peers academically.

    (A) so as not to　　　　　　　(B) for the purpose of

    (C) with a view to　　　　　　(D) so as to

(　) 3. In 1867, the New York State legislature passed an act incorporating the New York Bridge Company ＿＿＿＿ constructing and maintaining a bridge between Manhattan Island and Brooklyn. (103 指考)

    (A) in order to　　　　　　　(B) for the purpose of

    (C) so as that　　　　　　　　(D) so as to

(　) 4. I was worried about my first overseas trip, but my father assured me that he would help plan the trip ＿＿＿＿ nothing would go wrong. (104 學測)

    (A) in order to　　　　　　　(B) so that

    (C) so as to　　　　　　　　　(D) for the purpose of

二、翻譯

1. 醫生建議我們每年持續施打流感疫苗以常保健康。 (104 指考)

Doctors advise that we continue to get our annual flu shots ＿＿＿＿ ＿＿＿＿ ＿＿＿＿ stay healthy.

2. 下大雨時，為了避免車禍，你必須小心開車。 (98 指考)

When there is a heavy rain, you have to drive very cautiously ＿＿＿＿

＿＿＿＿＿＿＿＿

3. 為了不近視，這女孩從不花很多時間用電腦。

＿＿＿＿＿＿＿＿＿＿＿

13–3

$S_1 + V_1 + lest + S_2 (+ should) + V_2$
$S_1 + V_1 + for\ fear\ (that) + S_2 + aux. + V_2$
$S + V_1 + for\ fear\ of + N/V_2\text{-}ing$

句型範例

- Many people like to use Post-it notes **lest** they should forget what to do.
  很多人喜歡用便利貼，以免忘記該做的事。

- Angela hid her love letters **for fear that** her parents might find them.
  Angela 把情書藏起來，以免她的父母發現。

- The boy returned home before ten o'clock **for fear of** being grounded.
  這男孩在十點前回家，唯恐被禁足。

 ☆ The government is doing its best to preserve the cultures of the tribal people **for fear that** they may soon die out. (99 學測)
政府盡力保護部落文化，以免不久後會消失。

用法詳解

1. 本單元介紹表示「唯恐…，以免…」的句型，即做某事以避免另一事發生。

2. lest 後的子句必須使用助動詞 **should**，但可省略，故子句中的動詞常是原形動詞。

   - The student takes notes in class **lest** he (**should**) forget what the teacher has taught. 這學生在課堂上做筆記，以免忘記老師教的內容。

   - When going bird watching, you should keep your voice down **lest** birds be scared away. 賞鳥時，你應該要降低音量，以免鳥兒被嚇跑。

3. for fear 後可接 **that 子句**或 **of + N/V-ing**。

   a. 注意，接 that 子句時，句中常搭配助動詞 might、should 等，且不可省略。

   b. for fear of 的句型只適用於前後主詞相同時。

   - This famous actor wears a disguise whenever he goes out **for fear that** paparazzi might recognize him. 這位名演員出門時總會變裝，以免狗仔隊認出他來。

   - The singer doesn't speak before going on stage **for fear of** losing her voice during the performance. 這歌手上台前不說話，唯恐在表演中失聲。

4. 前後主詞相同時，本單元的句型亦可代換成 ***in order/so as* + not + to V**。

   - Never watch TV when you study **lest** you (**should**) get distracted.

➡ Never watch TV when you study **in order not to** get distracted.

讀書時絕對不要看電視，以免分心。

學習補給站

意義類似用法尚有：**in case + 子句**、**in case of + N**，表示「以免…，萬一…，如果…」。
in case 後方所接的子句，其動詞使用簡單式或 **should + V**。

● Hebe brought some water **in case** she felt thirsty. Hebe 帶了點水，以防口渴。

● Write down the contact number **in case** there should be a problem.

寫下聯絡電話，以防有問題。

● Take an umbrella with you **in case of** rain. 帶把傘吧，以防下雨。

句型練習

一、選擇

( ) 1. Make sure that the windows and doors are locked _____ a thief should break into the house.

(A) so that   (B) in order that   (C) for the purpose of   (D) lest

( ) 2. The employee stretched his arms from time to time lest he _____ fatigued.

(A) felt   (B) feel   (C) had felt   (D) might feel

( ) 3. Jay booked some tickets to the baseball game _____ they might be sold out.

(A) lest   (B) for fear that   (C) in order that   (D) so that

( ) 4. Andy took the initiative _____ losing the good chance to enter the trade company.

(A) for fear of   (B) lest   (C) so that   (D) in case

二、句子改寫

We should distinguish between facts and opinions in order not to be misled by mass media. (. . . lest . . .)

_____

三、翻譯

1. 不論總統在哪裡，都有護衛跟隨，以免有惡意人士會傷害他。

Wherever the President goes, he is surrounded by bodyguards, _____ anyone with bad intentions _____.

2. Teresa 不允許她兒子餐前吃甜點，以免破壞胃口。

Teresa doesn't allow her son to eat dessert before meals _____ his appetite

_____ _____.

3. Ivanov 夫婦從不責罵孩子，唯恐他們會失去自信。

13-4

$$S + \begin{Bmatrix} \text{be + so + adj.} \\ \text{V + so + adv.} \end{Bmatrix} + \text{that-clause}$$

$$S + be/V + \text{such} + N + \text{that-clause}$$

句型範例

- The automatic faucet is **so** <u>convenient</u> **that** it has changed people's lives.
  感應式水龍頭如此方便以致於它改變了人們的生活。

- Jack speaks English **so** <u>fluently</u> **that** he can communicate with foreigners without any difficulty. Jack 英文說得很流利,以致於他能和外國人毫無困難地溝通。

- Daisy is **such** <u>a patient teacher</u> **that** her students like her a lot.
  Daisy 是很有耐心的老師,以致於學生都很喜歡她。

 ☆ Most of the area is covered by woods, where bird species are **so** <u>numerous</u> **that** it is a paradise for birdwatchers. (105 學測)
這個地區擁有大片樹林,有多種鳥類於此棲息使其成為賞鳥客的天堂。

☆ It rained **so** <u>hard</u> yesterday **that** the baseball game had to be postponed until next Saturday. (102 學測) 昨天雨下得很大,以致於棒球賽得延到下週六。

☆ More than one-third are in **such** <u>bad shape</u> **that** they could die within ten years. (102 學測)
超過三分之一 (的珊瑚礁) 狀況非常糟,牠們十年內可能會死亡。

用法詳解

1. 本句型意為「如此…以致於…」,以 that 子句表示結果。

2. **so** 為副詞,其後接**形容詞**或**副詞**; **such** 為形容詞,其後接**名詞**。

- Niagara Falls is **so** <u>beautiful</u> **that** it has become a world famous tourist attraction. 尼加拉瀑布如此壯觀,以致於它已經成為世界有名的旅遊景點。

- The young man works **so** <u>hard</u> **that** he has saved enough money for future trips.
  這年輕人努力工作,以致於他已經存夠未來旅行的費用。

- Ben is **such** <u>an intelligent boy</u> **that** he can solve difficult math questions.
  Ben 是如此聰明的男孩,以致於他能解決困難的數學問題。

句型練習

一、選擇

( ) 1. A properly made kilt should not be _____ loose that the wearer can easily twist the kilt around the body. (101 學測)

(A) so   (B) such   (C) too   (D) much

( ) 2. It (MAMMA MIA!) has appealed to _____ many people that a film version was also made. (100 學測)

(A) very   (B) that   (C) such   (D) so

( ) 3. Empress Maria was so delighted by this gift _____ Alexander appointed Fabergé a "goldsmith by special appointment to the Imperial Crown." (104 指考)

(A) that   (B) such   (C) too   (D) much

( ) 4. Russian is _____ a difficult language that few foreigners can master it in a short time.

(A) so   (B) that   (C) such   (D) much

二、翻譯

1. 他 (Gunter Grass) 天生有太多項才華，以致於無法決定人生的方向。 (99 指考)

He (Gunter Grass) was born with _____ _____ talents _____ he couldn't choose a direction.

2. 這裡的土地極乾，一天要澆好幾次水。 (105 學測)

The land was so dry _____

3. *The Phantom of the Opera* 是如此受歡迎的音樂劇，以致於它已經上演超過二十年。

_____

13-5

As long as S + V, S + V . . .

句型範例

- **As long as** you have a positive attitude, you will lead a happy life.

  只要你抱持正面的態度，你會過快樂的生活。

- Edith surely can achieve her goal **as long as** she has confidence in herself.

  只要 Edith 有自信，她一定可以達成目標。

 ☆ **As long as** the children are willing to sing, I will always be there for them, singing with them and leading them to experience the meaning of the ballads. (104 學測) 只要孩子們願意唱，我就會一直陪伴他們，和他們一起唱，帶領他們體會古謠的意義。

用法詳解

as long as 為從屬連接詞，意為「只要…」，引導副詞子句。在 as long as 引導的副詞子句中，以現在式代替未來式。

- **As long as** drivers follow traffic rules, they won't be fined.

  只要駕駛人遵守交通規則，就不會被罰款。

  ① 在 as long as 引導的副詞子句中以現在式動詞 follow 代替未來式。

- **As long as** Hank finishes his project by the end of the month, he can get a promotion. 只要 Hank 月底前完成計畫，他就可以升職。

  ① 在 as long as 引導的副詞子句中以現在式動詞 finishes 代替未來式。

學習補給站

由於 as long as 也可依字面意思解為「像…一樣長」或譯成「長達…」，所以必須注意前後文以判別是何種用法。

- Sara's hair is **as long as** Amy's. Sara 的頭髮和 Amy 一樣長。

- ☆ They are very long-lived for insects, and some adult wetas can live **as long as** two years. (99 學測)

  就昆蟲而言，牠們很長壽，有些 weta 的成蟲可以活達二年之久。

句型練習

一、選擇

( ) 1. _____ Johnny stays focused on his homework, he can finish it in an hour.

(A) As well as　　　(B) As long as　　　(C) As soon as　　　(D) As far as

( ) 2. _____ you leave early, you won't be caught in the traffic jam.

(A) As much as　　　(B) As quickly as　　　(C) As short as　　　(D) As long as

( ) 3. The candidate will win the election as long as he _____ a bit more support.

(A) will get　　　(B) would have　　　(C) gets　　　(D) has had

二、翻譯

1. 只要男女二性能尊重與接受差別，愛情可能發展。　(94 學測)

_____ _____ _____ men and women are able to respect and accept their differences, love has a chance to blossom.

2. 只要我們少花時間在社群網路上，我們能有更多時間和家人在一起。

_____, we can have more time to be with our family.

3. 只要 Kevin 多使用批判性思考 (critical thinking) 的技巧，他就能提高 (boost) 解決問題的能力。

_____

13-6

now that + S + V . . .

句型範例

- **Now that** the law has been enforced, drunk drivers will face stiffer penalties.
  既然法律已經制定，酒醉駕駛會面臨更嚴厲的處罰。
- **Now that** Curiosity Rover has landed on Mars, we can know more about this planet. 既然好奇號已經登陸火星，我們可以更瞭解這個星球。

☆ **Now that** we all use pencils, doodling is on the increase, and the quality of pencilwomanship is impressive, as you can tell from my handwriting in this letter. (98 學測) 既然大家都使用鉛筆，塗鴉增加中，且筆跡的品質也給人強烈的印象，正如你能分辨出此封信中我的字跡。

☆ **Now that** women make up 46 percent of the U.S. workforce, girls can find role models in every occupational field. (98 指考) 既然女性佔美國勞動人口數的百分之四十六，女孩們可以在每個職業領域中找到模範。

用法詳解

1. now that 為連接詞，意為「既然」，引導副詞子句。在口語用法中可將 that 省略。
   - **Now (that)** you have read these books, you can return them to the library.
     既然你已經讀過這些書，可以將它們還給圖書館。
2. since 作「由於…，因為…」時，可與 now that 代換。
   - **Now that** the basketball player has seriously injured his back, he is forced to retire.
   - ➡ **Since** the basketball player has seriously injured his back, he is forced to retire.
     因為這位籃球選手嚴重傷到背部，他被迫退休。

句型練習

一、選擇

( ) 1. _____ the secretary has done the final check, she can print out the document.
  (A) No matter　　(B) As long as　　(C) Even if　　(D) Now that

( ) 2. _____ the singer's privacy had been invaded by the tabloid, he decided to take legal action against it.
  (A) As soon as　　(B) Now that　　(C) The minute　　(D) By the time

二、翻譯

1. 既然電梯壞掉了，我們只好爬樓梯。

    _____ _____ the elevator was out of order, we had to use the stairs instead.

2. 既然 Eric 已經完成高中學業，他可以利用空檔年參加志工計畫。

    _____, he can take a gap

    year to take part in volunteer programs.

3. 既然這病人已經動過手術，他很快會痊癒。

    _____

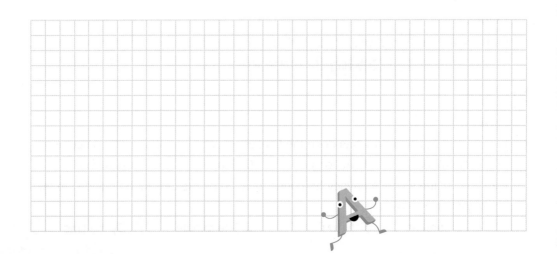

14-1

no/not . . . at all

句型範例

- My American-born Chinese friend has **no** difficulty using chopsticks **at all**.
  我朋友是在美國出生的華人，絲毫沒有使用筷子的困難。

- The boy who often lies is **not** trustworthy **at all**.
  這常說謊的男孩一點也不值得信任。

- The fruit salad on the blue plate **doesn't** look yummy **at all**.
  這放在藍色盤子的沙拉看起來一點也不美味。

☆ From that day, everything went wrong in Van Amsterdam's bakery. His bread rose too high or **not at all**. (102 指考) 從那天起，Van Amsterdam 麵包店的一切都不對勁。他的麵包不是過度發酵就是一點都不發酵。

用法詳解

1. 本句型以 no 或 not 形成否定意義，再加上 at all 來強調「一點也不」。
   - The demanding boss **isn't** satisfied with the project **at all**.
     這要求很高的老闆一點也不滿意這個計畫。
   - The mature teenager **doesn't** depend on his parents **at all**.
     這成熟的少年一點也不依賴父母。

2. 強調否定的其他用法有：be far from、anything but、not . . . by any means、by no means、not . . . in the least 等。
   - The student has to rewrite his composition because it **is far from** satisfactory.
     這學生必須重寫作文，因為它一點也不令人滿意。
   - The volleyball team lost the championship, and they were **not** happy about the result **by any means**.
     排球隊輸掉冠軍賽，這讓他們一點也不開心。
   - To Sheryl, making fun of people's mistake is **not** funny **in the least**.
     對 Sheryl 來說，取笑他人錯誤，這一點都不好笑。

句型練習

一、選擇

( ) 1. Europe _____ mice and rats as lab animals at all. (100 指考)

    (A) use   (B) does not use   (C) has used   (D) isn't used

( ) 2. Interestingly, the twin sisters _____ each other at all.

    (A) resemble   (B) resemble not   (C) don't resemble   (D) resemble no

( ) 3. The scientist was _____. The key to his success was diligence and perseverance.

    (A) a genius at all   (B) anything and a genius

    (C) nothing but a genius   (D) far from a genius

二、翻譯

1. 據說有機產品絲毫不含化學物質。

   It is said that organic products contain _____ chemical substances _____ _____.

2. 撞了好幾個行人的司機絕無企圖要傷害他們。他只是太疲憊了。

   The driver who had hit several pedestrians had _____ intention to hurt them _____ _____. He was just exhausted.

3. 讓大家驚訝的是，在好幾堂的訓練之後，這運動員一點也不覺得累。

   _____

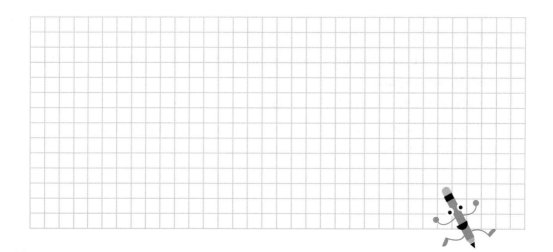

14-2

too + *adj./adv.* + to V

句型範例

- This gold bracelet is **too** expensive for me **to** buy. 這條金手鐲太昂貴了，我買不起。
- These visitors got up **too** late **to** watch the sunrise. 這些遊客太晚起床，看不到日出。

☆ This created a convenient, sturdy platform for any person **too** short **to** reach the sink. (105 學測)

這創造了一個方便、堅固的平台給任何身高太矮而搆不到水槽的人。

☆ The content of the book is very much technical and specialized; it is **too** difficult for a layman **to** understand. (104 指考)

這本書的內容很具技術性及專業性；對於一位門外漢來說太難理解。

用法詳解

1. 本單元介紹用 too + *adj./adv.* + to V 來表示「太…而不能…」，屬於否定用法的一種。

- Winning the tournament, the tennis player is **too** excited **to** say a word.
 贏了錦標賽，這個網球選手太興奮而說不出話。
- After a big dinner in a fancy restaurant, every one of us was **too** full **to** move.
 在高級餐廳吃過的豐盛晚餐後，我們每個人都吃太飽而動不了。

2. 若要表示「對某人而言」，可以在不定詞 (to V) 之前加上 for sb。

- Thai food is **too** spicy for some people **to** eat.
 對某些人而言，泰國食物太辣而無法下嚥。
- This grammar book is not **too** difficult for beginners **to** read.
 對初學者而言，這本文法書不會太難讀。

學習補給站

此用法可以代換為 so + *adj./adv.* + that + S + can't + V 或 such + N + that + S + can't + V。

- The crossword puzzle is **too** difficult for the students **to** solve.
➡ The crossword puzzle is **so** difficult **that** the students **can't** solve it.
➡ This is **such** a difficult crossword puzzle **that** the students **can't** solve it.
 這個字謎太難了，學生們無法解答。

句型練習

一、選擇

( ) 1. Microscopes are used in medical research labs for studying bacteria or germs that are _____ to be visible to the naked eye. (105 指考)

(A) very small   (B) to small   (C) too small   (D) so small

( ) 2. The scenery along the road is _____ beautiful for visitors _____ drive carefully. (97 學測)

(A) to; too   (B) too; to   (C) so; that   (D) such; that

( ) 3. The flood hit the gallery so quickly, and the staff had to give up the carvings and the paintings that were _____.

(A) very heavy for moving   (B) to heavy too move

(C) so heavy to move   (D) too heavy to move

( ) 4. The comedy show is _____.

(A) too funny that the audience can't help but laugh

(B) so interesting for the audience to laugh

(C) very entertaining for the audience to laugh

(D) so hilarious that the audience can't help laughing

二、句子合併

1. The job offer sounds so good that it can't be true.

_____

2. After the exciting game, the basketball player was very exhausted. He couldn't move his legs.

_____

三、翻譯

1. 「瑞士軍官刀」的德文對美國士兵來說似乎太難發音了,所以他們就叫它瑞士軍刀。

It seems that "Schweizer Offizier Messer" was _____ _____ for them (American soldiers) _____ _____, so they just called it the Swiss army knife. (102 學測)

2. 大部分的地震因規模太小而未被注意;它們只能被靈敏的儀器偵測到。 (100 指考)

Most earthquakes are _____ ;

they can only be detected by sensitive instruments.

3. 這個饑餓的年輕人吃太快而無法好好消化。

_____

4. 對現今很多有才能的人而言,成為明星的夢想並非太難而無法實現 (fulfill)。

14-3

否定字 . . . + without + *N/V-ing*

句型範例

- A trip to Hualien is **never** complete **without** a visit to Taroko National Park.
  太魯閣國家公園是到花蓮旅遊必訪之地。

- It is **impossible** to win the great prizes in life **without** running risks.
  不冒風險就不可能贏得人生中的種種精彩。—Theodore Roosevelt

- You **cannot** make an omelet **without** breaking eggs. 【諺】有失才有得。

☆ It is **impossible** to imagine Paris **without** its cafés. (97 指考)
想到巴黎一定會想到咖啡館。

用法詳解

1. 本句型以**雙重否定**表示「肯定」的用法 (可記為：負負得正)，意為「每…無不…」或「每…必定…」。前面先以否定字 never、impossible、cannot 等形成否定意思，後面再以 without + *N/V-ing* 構成另一個否定意思。

2. 在使用句型時，需注意字序。「每…」的部分以 never 等否定字表示，「無不…」或「必定…」的部分以 without + *N/V-ing* 表示。

   - David **never** meets us **without** making complaints about his boss.
           每…   必…
     David 每次和我們見面都抱怨老闆。

   - People **cannot** hurt others **without** hurting themselves. 傷人者必傷害到自己。
          每…   必…

   - It is **impossible** to watch the musical *Les Miserables* **without** being touched.
            每…   必…
     觀賞音樂劇悲慘世界的人一定會被感動。

3. 本句型可代換為 Whenever + S + V, S + V = Every time + S + V, S + V (每當…)。

   - I **never** hear the music **without** thinking of my favorite film.
   - ➡ **Whenever** I hear the music, I think of my favorite film.
   - ➡ **Every time** I hear the music, I think of my favorite film.
     每當我聽到這音樂，就想起我的最喜歡的電影。

學習補給站

其他表示「雙重否定」的用法有：否定詞 . . . + **but** (+ S) + V . . .。

● The boy **never** sees LEGO toys **but** he feels excited.

　　這男孩每次見到樂高玩具都很興奮。

● It **never** rains **but** it pours. 【諺】禍不單行。(不雨則已，一雨傾盆。)

● There is **no** mother **but** loves her own children. 沒有母親不愛孩子。

句型練習

一、選擇

( ) 1. This director is very talented. He ＿＿＿＿ shoots films without winning awards.

　　(A) unlikely　　　　(B) every time　　　(C) not　　　　　　(D) never

( ) 2. James never eats sashimi ＿＿＿＿ drinking beer.

　　(A) but　　　　　　(B) without　　　　　(C) and　　　　　　(D) or

( ) 3. The blind man ＿＿＿＿ goes out without his guide dog.

　　(A) not　　　　　　(B) impossible　　　　(C) never　　　　　(D) cannot

( ) 4. It is ＿＿＿＿ for most people to ride a roller coaster ＿＿＿＿ screaming.

　　(A) never; but　　　　　　　　　(B) unlikely; but

　　(C) possible; with　　　　　　　(D) impossible; without

二、句子改寫

1. Every time Angela's boyfriend visited her, he brought her flowers. (. . . never . . .)

　＿＿＿＿＿＿＿＿＿＿＿＿＿＿＿＿＿＿＿＿＿＿＿＿＿＿＿＿＿＿＿＿＿

2. Whenever Adam travels to France, he visits Notre–Dame Cathedral.

　(. . . impossible . . .)

　＿＿＿＿＿＿＿＿＿＿＿＿＿＿＿＿＿＿＿＿＿＿＿＿＿＿＿＿＿＿＿＿＿

三、翻譯

1. 到羅浮宮博物館一定要瞧瞧《蒙娜麗莎》。

　The visit to the Louvre Museum is ＿＿＿＿ ＿＿＿＿ ＿＿＿＿ taking a look at the Mona Lisa.

2. 每條規則必有例外。

　There is ＿＿＿＿ rule ＿＿＿＿ has exceptions.

3. Sandra 談到希臘神話必定會提到阿波羅。

　＿＿＿＿＿＿＿＿＿＿＿＿＿＿＿＿＿＿＿＿＿＿＿＿＿＿＿＿＿＿＿＿＿

14-4

$$S + \begin{cases} \text{cannot} \\ \text{can't} \\ \text{can never} \end{cases} + \begin{cases} be + too + adj./V + too + adv. \\ be + adj./V + adv. + \text{enough} \\ \text{over-V} \end{cases}$$

句型範例

- One is **never too** old to learn. 【諺】活到老，學到老。
- We **cannot** care **too** much about the protection of wild animals.
  我們再關懷野生動物的保育也不為過。

用法詳解

本單元介紹用來表示「再…也不為過」或「非常…」的用法。

- Students **can't** be **too** attentive in class. 學生們在課堂上再認真也不為過。
- Drivers **can't** be **too** careful when driving on slippery roads.
  司機在很滑的道路上開車再小心也不為過。
- The painter **cannot** thank her parents **too** much for supporting her dream.
  這個畫家非常感謝父母支持她的夢想。
- A leader **cannot** be rational **enough** in making important decisions.
  領導者在做重要決定時再理性也不為過。
- We **cannot overemphasize** the importance of traffic safety.
  我們再強調交通安全的重要性也不為過。

學習補貼站

1. S + can + *not/never* + V + *more/too much* 也表示「再…也不為過」或者「非常」。
   - Our teacher is right. I **can't** agree with him **more**.
     我們老師是對的。我非常同意他。
   - To win the championship, these golf players **can't** practice **too much**.
     為了贏得冠軍，這些高爾夫球選手再練習也不為過。
2. 注意，有時 *can't/cannot* . . . too 的結構單純表示「不能太…」，can't over-V 單純表示「不能過度…」，必須依文意判斷。
   - We **can't be too selfish** when dealing with others.
     和他人相處時，我們不能太自私。
   - People **can't overwork**; otherwise, they'll get sick.
     人不能工作過度，否則會生病。

句型練習

一、選擇

( ) 1. Parents _____ love their children too much.

    (A) cannot   (B) should   (C) must not   (D) will not

( ) 2. A successful businessman can't be _____ sensitive to customer needs.

    (A) enough   (B) more   (C) too   (D) so

( ) 3. Students can't be _____ in doing experiments in the laboratory.

    (A) much careful   (B) over careful   (C) very careful   (D) careful enough

( ) 4. Since English is the official language in many countries, _____.

    (A) people must not emphasize its importance

    (B) we cannot overemphasize the importance of learning it

    (C) no one can never spend too much time learning it

    (D) it is impossible for people to emphasize its importance

二、句子改寫

1. The athletic meeting is approaching. It is necessary for these young athletes to practice. (以 can't + V + too + adv. 的句型改寫)

    The athletic meeting is approaching, so _____

    _____

2. When starting one's own business, one should be hard-working.

    (以 can + never + be + too + adj. 改寫)

    When starting one's own business, _____

    _____

三、翻譯

1. 這有為的年輕人對於他的未來非常樂觀。

    The promising young man _____ be _____ optimistic about his future.

2. 一般人認為，護士們再有耐心也不為過。

    _____

3. Emily 對這個團隊的貢獻非常值得獎勵。

    _____

14-5

$$S + be + the\ last + N + \begin{cases} to\ V \\ that\text{-}clause \end{cases}$$

句型範例

- Alison is **the last** person **to** make such a silly mistake.
  Alison 是最不可能犯這種愚蠢錯誤的人。

- This dress is old-fashioned. It is **the last** dress **that** I would try on.
  這件連身裙過時了。這是我最不可能試穿的一件。

 ☆ Sea snakes will be **the last** creature (that are) affected by global warming.
海蛇是最不可能受全球暖化影響的生物。 (105 學測)

用法詳解

1. 本句型表示「⋯ 是最不可能 ⋯ 的」，the last N 的後面可以接**不定詞**或 **that** 引導的關係子句。

   - Catherine is **the last** person **to** cheat on the exam.
     Catherine 是最不可能在考試作弊的人。

   - Pig's blood cake is **the last** food **that** my British friend would try.
     豬血糕是我英國朋友最不可能嚐的食物。

2. 要表示「最不 ⋯」的意思時，可以使用 the least + *adj./adv.*。

   - The shy girl is **the least likely** person to win the speech contest.
     這個害羞的女孩是最不可能贏得演講比賽的人。

   - Among all the proposals, the committee chose the one that is **the least controversial**. 委員會從所有的提案中，選出最不受爭議的。

   - This movie is **the least interesting** one that I've ever seen.
     這部電影是我看過的電影中最不有趣 (最無聊) 的。

句型練習

一、選擇

( ) 1. The North Pole is the ＿＿＿＿＿ place that I would like to visit, because the temperature there is too low.

(A) late (B) last (C) least (D) latest

( ) 2. Tina never says what she means and means what she says. She is the last
person _____ our trust.
(A) be won　　　　(B) to win　　　　(C) to have won　　　(D) for winning

( ) 3. Staying up late is the last thing _____ my grandfather would do. He always
goes to bed early.
(A) that　　　　　(B) which　　　　　(C) who　　　　　(D) whose

( ) 4. School is the _____ place that these boys would like to go to.
(A) last like　　　　(B) last likely　　　　(C) least like　　　　(D) least likely

二、翻譯

1. 我的鄰居約翰是個老煙槍；他是最不可能戒煙的人。

My neighbor John is a chain smoker; he is _____ _____ _____ _____ give up
smoking.

2. 對我來說，數學太難了。它是我最不可能學好的科目。

Mathematics is too difficult for me. It is _____
_____ that I would learn well.

3. Johnson 是馬拉松紀錄保持者；他是最不可能輸掉這場比賽的跑者。

Johnson is the marathon record holder; _____

_____

4. 對這個小心的駕駛人來說，超速是他最不可能做的事情。

_____

14-6

Needless to say, S + V . . .
→ It goes without saying (that) + S + V . . .

句型範例

- **Needless to say**, water and air are indispensable to living things.
  不用說，水和空氣對生物是不可或缺的。
- **It goes without saying that** diligence is the key to success.
  不用說，勤勉是成功之鑰。

用法詳解

要表示「不用說⋯」或者「當然⋯」，用來描述顯而易見的事實，可以用 Needless to say 或以 It goes without saying that 引導子句的方式。

- **Needless to say**, people who eat nutritious foods are healthier than those who don't. 不用說，吃營養食物的人比沒吃的人健康。
- **It goes without saying that** necessity is the mother of invention.
  不用說，需要為發明之母。

句型練習

一、選擇

( ) 1. _____, optimistic people are much happier than those who are pessimistic.
  (A) It goes without saying   (B) It is needless to say
  (C) Needless to say   (D) It is needless

( ) 2. _____ that too much caffeine is harmful to our health.
  (A) Needless to say,   (B) It goes without saying
  (C) It is needless,   (D) Needless

二、翻譯

1. 不用說，101 大樓是台北最受歡迎的旅遊景點之一。

   _____ _____ _____, Taipei 101 Building is one of the most popular tourist attractions in Taipei.

2. 不用說，你越練習越能增進技巧。

   _____ _____ _____ _____ that the more you practice, the more you can improve your skills.

3. 不用說，減少污染有助於拯救環境。

_____, reducing pollution

can help save our environment.

4. 不用說，元宵節提燈籠是台灣的傳統之一。

_____

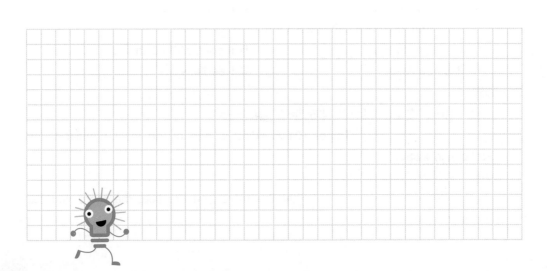

15-1

S + *be*/V + adverbial phrase
→ Adverbial phrase + *be*/V + S

句型範例

- **In the box** are some toys that Sarah bought for her son.

  箱子裡有一些 Sarah 買給兒子的玩具。

- **After a storm** comes a calm. 【諺】雨過天晴。

☆ **Just across the border**, in Canada, is the Waterton Lakes National Park.

穿越過邊界，就是加拿大的瓦特頓湖國家公園了。 (97 學測)

☆ In the Dutch colonial town later known as Albany, New York, **there** lived a baker, Van Amsterdam. 在紐約一個後來被稱作阿爾巴尼的荷蘭殖民小鎮裡，住著一位麵包師傅凡‧阿姆斯特丹。 (102 指考)

用法詳解

1. 為了加強語氣，可以將**表示地方與時間的副詞**移至句首，並將句子改為倒裝句，直接**將動詞移至主詞之前** (be/V + S)。

   - **In the city center** lives a generous billionaire.

     在市中心住著一位慷慨的億萬富翁。

   - **Before the rain** came the thunder. 下雨前先打雷了。

2. 除了表示地方或時間的副詞外，**表示方向的介副詞**，如 up、out、off、away 等也可以移到句首，後方句子同樣改為倒裝句。

   - **Away** ran the horse. 馬兒跑走了。

   - **Down** came the spider from the ceiling. 蜘蛛從天花板爬下來了。

3. 注意，主詞為**代名詞**時不需倒裝。本句型亦不用進行式的時態。

   - **Here** comes the bus. ➡ Here it comes. 公車來了。

   - **Under the table** lay a cat. ➡ Under the table it lay. 一隻貓躺在桌子下。

句型練習

一、選擇

( ) 1. The city is incredibly urbanized, but beneath its modern appearance _____ an unmistakable Thai-ness. (92 指考)

　　(A) has 　　　(B) are 　　　(C) lie 　　　(D) lies

( ) 2. In the middle of the park _____ several amateur rollerbladers.

    (A) have   (B) has   (C) is   (D) are

( ) 3. Near the lake _____ .

    (A) are some ducks walking   (B) lives an old lady

    (C) lives he   (D) has a cottage

( ) 4. As soon as the bell rang, out of the classrooms _____ .

    (A) the students rushed   (B) they rushed

    (C) were the boys running   (D) did they run

二、翻譯

1. 但讓皇后高興的是，釉蛋裏頭有個金蛋黃，蛋黃中有隻金色的母雞，母雞裡藏著鑽石迷你皇冠和很小的紅寶石蛋。 (104 指考)

But to the delight of the Empress, the egg opened to a golden yolk; within the yolk _____ a golden hen; and concealed within the hen _____ a diamond miniature of the royal crown and a tiny ruby egg.

2. 船開走了，而這女士的眼淚流下來了。

Off _____ the ship and down _____ the lady's tears.

3. 當我參觀朋友家時，我發現很多獎牌掛在牆上，而桌上有很多照片。

When I visited my friend's house, I found that on the wall of his room _____

_____ and on his desk _____

_____

15-2

Negative adv. (*seldom/hardly/never/etc.*) + $\begin{cases} \text{aux.} + \text{S} + \text{V} \\ \text{be} + \text{S} \end{cases}$

句型範例

- **Seldom** is Kate late to school. Kate 很少上學遲到。
- **Never** can the naughty boy learn how to behave himself.
  這頑皮的男孩永遠學不會守規矩。
- **No longer** does the employer need much workforce, so he will lay off some employees. 這雇主不再需要這麼多員工，所以他要裁員。

用法詳解

1. 為了加強語氣，可將否定詞移至句首，形成倒裝句。常用的否定詞有：seldom、rarely、never、little、hardly、no longer、by no means、under no circumstances、on no account、in no way 等。

2. 本單元的倒裝方式與 15-1 中直接將動詞移至主詞前的作法有些不同。否定詞置於句首的倒裝句結構類似**疑問句**：**be 動詞**或**助動詞**移至主詞之前。

   a. 主要動詞為 **be 動詞**時：將 be 動詞移至主詞之前。
   - The teacher is **seldom** impatient with her students.
   - ➡ **Seldom** is the teacher impatient with her students.
     這老師很少對學生感到不耐煩。
     ⓘ Seldom 在句首，須用倒裝句型，將 be 動詞 is 移至主詞 the teacher 之前。

   b. 句中有**情態助動詞** (*will/can/should/may* 等) 時：將情態助動詞移至主詞之前。
   - You should reveal your personal information to a stranger **under no circumstances**.
   - ➡ **Under no circumstances** should you reveal your personal information to a stranger. 在任何情況下你都不應該將個資洩漏給陌生人。
     ⓘ Under no circumstances 在句首，須用倒裝句型，將助動詞 should 移至主詞 you 之前。

   c. 主要動詞為**一般動詞**時：在主詞前加入 do、does、did。
   - We know **little** about other life forms in the universe.
   - ➡ **Little** do we know about other life forms in the universe.
     我們對宇宙中其他的生命體所知不多。
     ⓘ Little 在句首，須用倒裝句型，將助動詞 do 加到主詞 we 之前。

- Ben **no longer** trusted the salesman who had tricked him into buying a fake watch.

➡ **No longer** did Ben trust the salesman who had tricked him into buying a fake watch. Ben 再也無法信任那個騙他買假錶的推銷員。

① No longer 在句首，須用倒裝句型，將助動詞 did 加到主詞 Ben 之前。

學習補給站

除了 15−1「地方或時間副詞置於句首」的倒裝句是直接將 be 動詞與一般動詞移至主詞前，其他的倒裝句形成法都是與本單元相同，即改成**疑問句**結構。

句型練習

一、選擇

(   ) 1. _____ will the lazy student pass the exam.

　　(A) Someday 　　　(B) Never 　　　(C) Possibly 　　　(D) In the future

(   ) 2. Darren's appearance has changed so much that _____ him.

　　(A) hardly could I recognize 　　　(B) no longer I could recognize

　　(C) little recognized I 　　　(D) on no account I could recognized

(   ) 3. Seldom _____ late to the office. He often arrives at 8:00 in the morning.

　　(A) the manager will 　　　(B) the manager is

　　(C) is the manager 　　　(D) does the manager

(   ) 4. In no way _____ .

　　(A) should a person stopping learning 　　　(B) a person is stopping learning

　　(C) should a person stop learning 　　　(D) a person should stop learning

二、句子改寫

1. This telephone booth no longer served any useful purpose. (No longer . . .)

_____

2. The students in this poor country have never used tablets. (Never . . .)

_____

三、翻譯

1. 這本小說已經絕版好幾年了。現在已經買不到它了。

This novel has been out of print for several years. _____ _____ _____ its copies available.

2. 這男人在加入志工隊之前幾乎不瞭解互助的意義。(Little . . .)

_____

15–3

$$\text{Not only} + \begin{cases} \text{aux.} + S + V_1, \\ \text{be} + S \ldots, \end{cases} \text{but} + S \begin{cases} (+ \text{aux.}) + \text{also} + V_2 \\ + \text{be} + \text{also} \ldots \end{cases}$$

句型範例

- **Not only** was Charlie Chaplin a comedy actor, **but** he was (**also**) a filmmaker.
  卓別林不只是喜劇演員，他也是位影片製作人。

- **Not only** will the lottery winner donate money to the orphanage, **but** he will (**also**) help the poor. 這樂透得獎者不只將捐款給孤兒院，他也將會幫助窮人。

- **Not only** did these workers hope for a pay raise, **but** they (**also**) expected shorter working hours. 這些工人不只希望加薪，他們也要求較短的工時。

- ☆ **Not only** did he devote his whole self to his work, **but** he expected me to do the same. (97 指考)
  他不只將一生都奉獻給工作，他也期望我做一樣的事情。

- ☆ **Not only** will the summit lose its tourist attraction, **but** the disappearance of the snows will **also** cause major damage to the ecosystem on the dry African plains at its base. 這山峰不僅會失去觀光景點，積雪消失也將會對位於其底部乾燥非洲平原生態造成傷害。 (103 學測)

用法詳解

1. 本單元介紹由 not only A but also B (用法請見 3–1) 變化的倒裝，作為加強語氣用。

2. 將 not only 移至句首，形成否定詞在句首的倒裝句型，並將句子改成**疑問句結構**。注意，在本句型中，but (also) 引導的部分必須寫成 but + S . . . 形式。

   a. not only 所引導的句子，動詞為 **be 動詞**時：將 be 動詞移至主詞之前。

   - Harry **not only** is interested in writing **but** (also) enjoys reading.
   - ➡ **Not only** is Harry interested in writing, **but** he (also) enjoys reading.
     Harry 不只對寫作有興趣，他也喜歡閱讀。

   b. not only 所引導的句子，動詞含**情態助動詞** (*will/can/should/may* 等) 時：將情態助動詞移至主詞之前。

   - Susan can **not only** write computer programs **but** (also) fix computers.
   - ➡ **Not only** can Susan write computer programs, **but** she can (also) fix computers. Susan 不只會寫程式，她還會修電腦。

c. not only 所引導的句子，動詞為**一般動詞**時：在主詞前加入 do、does、did。

- The kind police officer **not only** gave the lost boy food and clothes **but also** helped him find his family.

➡ **Not only** did the kind police officer give the lost boy food and clothes, **but** she also helped him find his family.

這好心的警察不只提供這迷路的孩子食物和衣服，也幫他找到家人。

句型練習

一、選擇

( ) 1. _____ is the film touching, but it is also thought-provoking.

    (A) Not only   (B) Both   (C) Not until   (D) Either

( ) 2. Not only _____ a novelist and playwright, but he is also a renowned artist.

    (A) he is   (B) has he   (C) is he   (D) does he

( ) 3. To learn well, not only _____ stay focused in class, but we should also take notes.

    (A) are we   (B) we should   (C) should we   (D) do we

( ) 4. Not only _____ Mandarin fluently, but she can also write it well.

    (A) my Australian friend speaks   (B) my Australian friend can speak

    (C) speaks my Australian friend   (D) can my Australian friend speak

二、句子改寫

1. Apples are not only low in calories but also high in fiber.

_____

2. Bullying affects not only the bullied but his friends and classmates and the whole society. (100 指考)

_____

三、翻譯

1. 全球暖化不僅造成嚴重氣候變遷，還使得一些物種消失。

_____ global warming lead

to severe climate change, _____

some species extinct.

2. 這個俱樂部的貴賓會員不僅可以享用免費的下午茶，也可免費使用高爾夫球場。

_____, but they can also have free access to golf courses.

3. 為了慶祝結婚紀念日，Nick 不只買了 99 朵花給太太，也在餐廳預定好一桌席位。

15-4

Not until . . . + be/aux. + S + V

句型範例

- **Not until** Oliver turns 20 is he allowed to stay overnight with his friends.

  Oliver 直到 20 歲才被允許和朋友外宿。

- **Not until** dusk did the painter take a rest. 油漆工人直到黃昏才休息。

用法詳解

本單元介紹由 not (. . .) until . . . (用法請見 11–2) 的句型變化而來的用法，作為加強語氣，表示「直到…才 …」。用法為將 not until 移至句首，形成否定詞在句首的倒裝句型。

a. 主要動詞為 **be 動詞**時：將 be 動詞移至主詞之前。

- Patty was **not** aware of the mistake **until** her boss told her.

➡ **Not until** Patty's boss told her was she aware of the mistake.

直到老闆告訴她，Patty 才注意到這個錯誤。

b. 主要動詞含**情態助動詞** (*will/can/should/may* 等) 時：將情態助動詞移至主詞之前。

- These children can **not** eat their cupcakes **until** lunchtime.

➡ **Not until** lunchtime can these children eat their cupcakes.

這些孩子直到午餐時間才能吃杯子蛋糕。

c. 主要動詞為**一般動詞**時：在主詞前加入 do、does、did。

- The foreigner **didn't** like the taste of stinky tofu **until** he tried it several times.

➡ **Not until** the foreigner tried stinky tofu several times did he like its taste.

這個外國人直到嚐臭豆腐好幾次才喜歡上它的味道。

句型練習

一、選擇

( ) 1. _____ Peter bumped into his ex-girlfriend did he know that she got married.

　　(A) As soon as 　　(B) Not until 　　(C) No sooner 　　(D) Scarcely

( ) 2. Not until the animal rescue team arrived _____ this poor dog saved.

　　(A) was 　　(B) could 　　(C) did 　　(D) would

( ) 3. Not until the man felt pain _____ that his leg was bleeding.

　　(A) knew he 　　(B) did he know 　　(C) did know he 　　(D) he knew

( ) 4. In the tale, not until the fairy appeared _____ the princess know how to save the prince from the dragon that breathed fire.

(A) had   (B) would   (C) might   (D) did

二、翻譯

1. 直到我收到 Gabrielle 的簡訊才知道她不能參加我的生日派對。

_____ _____ I received Gabrielle's text message _____ _____ _____ that she could not attend my birthday party.

2. 直到耶誕夜，這些孩子們才被允許打開禮物。

_____ _____ _____ Christmas Eve _____ _____ _____ allowed to open their presents.

3. Jake 直到安裝防毒軟體才不需擔心電腦駭客。

_____

15–5

$$\text{No sooner had} + S_1 + \text{p.p.}_1 + \text{than} + S_2 + V_2\text{-ed}$$

$$\left.\begin{array}{l}\text{Hardly}\\\text{Scarcely}\end{array}\right\} + \text{had} + S_1 + \text{p.p.}_1 + \left\{\begin{array}{l}\text{when}\\\text{before}\end{array}\right\} + S_2 + V_2\text{-ed}$$

句型範例

- **No sooner** had the dog seen some strangers **than** it began to bark.
  這隻狗一看到陌生人就開始吠。
- **Hardly** had the child taken the bitter liquid medicine **when** he spat it out.
  這孩子一吃苦藥就吐出來。
- **Scarcely** had Aaron met the beautiful girl **before** he fell in love with her.
  Aaron 一看到那個美麗的女孩就愛上她了。

用法詳解

1. 在 11–3 單元中介紹過用來表示「一…就…」的用法：

   $S_1 + \text{had} + \text{no sooner} + \text{p.p.}_1 + \text{than} + S_2 + V_2\text{-ed}$

   $S_1 + \text{had} + \textit{hardly/scarcely} + \text{p.p.}_1 + \textit{when/before} + S_2 + V_2\text{-ed}$

   為了加強語氣，可將 no sooner、hardly、scarcely 置於句首並將後面句子改為倒裝句。

2. 倒裝句的改法：

   a. 將否定詞 no sooner、hardly 與 scarcely 移至句首。

   b. 將 had 移至主詞之前，形成 V + S 的倒裝句結構。

   - **No sooner** had the girl found someone stalking her **than** she called for help.
     這女孩一發現有人跟蹤，她就打電話求援。
   - **Hardly** had Jimmy's mother entered the room **when** he turned off his computer.
     Jimmy 的媽媽一進房間，他就關掉電腦。
   - **Scarcely** had we heard the thunder **before** the rain began to pour.
     我們一聽到雷聲，大雨就下了。

學習補給站

其它用來描述「一…就…」的句型有：*As soon as/The minute* + S + V₁, S + V₂ 及 *On/Upon* + *N/V₁-ing*, S + V₂。使用時，請注意各句型結構差別。

句型練習

一、選擇

( ) 1. _____ had Raymond seen the girl he had a crush on than his heart beat like drums.

(A) As soon as   (B) No sooner   (C) Scarcely   (D) Hardly

( ) 2. _____ had Amanda closed her eyes _____ she thought of her trip to France.

(A) No sooner; before   (B) The minute; than

(C) Hardly; when   (D) As soon as; when

( ) 3. _____ had the beggar seen the food _____ his mouth watered.

(A) Hardly; than   (B) Upon; than

(C) The moment; when   (D) Scarcely; before

( ) 4. No sooner _____ the alarm than they rushed out of the theater.

(A) had people heard   (B) people had heard

(C) did people hear   (D) people heard

二、翻譯

1. 水的溫度一到達攝氏 100 度就開始沸騰。

_____ _____ _____ the water temperature reached 100°C _____ the water began to boil.

2. 這男孩一被救出火場，他的父親就鬆了一口氣。

_____ when his father breathed a sigh of relief.

3. 這駕駛人一闖紅燈就被警察捉住。

No sooner _____ than

_____ by the police officer.

4. 這仁慈的婦人一見到流浪狗就流下眼淚。 (. . . when . . .)

_____

5. 這婦人一打開保險箱就發現她的結婚戒指不見了。

As soon as _____

Upon _____

Hardly _____

15-6

$S_1 + be/V \ldots$, and + so + $be/aux. + S_2$

$S_1 + \begin{cases} be + not \ldots, \\ aux. + not + V \ldots, \end{cases} + \begin{cases} and + neither + be/aux. + S_2 \\ nor + be/aux. + S_2 \end{cases}$

句型範例

● Adam is interested in extreme sports, **and so** are his friends.

Adam 對極限運動有興趣，他的朋友也是。

● Judy doesn't like horror movies, **and neither** do we.

Judy 不喜歡恐怖片，我們也不喜歡。

● Greg can't solve this crossword puzzle, **nor** can his classmates.

Greg 無法解出這字謎遊戲，他的同學也解不出。

☆ A properly made kilt should not be so loose that the wearer can easily twist the kilt around the body, **nor** should it be so tight that it causes bulging of the fabric where it is buckled. (101 學測) 裁製適當的蘇格蘭裙不應寬鬆到讓穿著者能輕易將蘇格蘭裙繞著身體轉動，也不該緊貼到讓扣環處的布料突起。

用法詳解

1. 以 so、neither、nor 表示「也…」或者「也不…」的**附和**意思時，其後的子句需使用**倒裝**結構，即改成**疑問句結構**。so 與 neither 為副詞，使用時必須加上 and 或分號，甚至用句號分開。美式用法常將 nor 視為連接詞，故不使用 and。注意，neither 與 nor 均已表達否定意義，後句的動詞不再加 not。請留意前後句的動詞須同為 be 動詞、同為助動詞或同為一般動詞。

2. 肯定附和：$S_1 + be/V/aux. \ldots$, and + so + $be/aux. + S_2$

否定附和：$S_1 + be + not/aux. + not + V \ldots$, and + neither + $be/aux. + S_2$

$S_1 + be + not/aux. + not + V \ldots$, nor + $be/aux. + S_2$

a. 動詞為 be 動詞、完成式 (have + p.p.) 或情態助動詞 (will/can/should/may 等) 時，直接將 **be 動詞**、**have** 或助動詞移至主詞之前。

● Kevin is a workaholic, **and so** is his wife. Kevin 是工作狂，他老婆也是。

● Mr. and Mrs. Jackson are not tall, **nor** is their son.

➡ Mr. and Mrs. Jackson are not tall, **and neither** is their son.

Jackson 夫婦不高，他們的兒子也不高。

① 前後動詞均為 be 動詞，後句動詞變化需與 S_2 一致。

● I have learned painting for five years; **so** has my brother.

　我學畫畫已經五年了，我弟弟也是。① 前後均為完成式，後句動詞變化與 S_2 一致。

● Mason will vote for that candidate, **and so** will his wife.

　Mason 會投票給那位候選人，他太太也會。① 前後動詞均為 will。

● Alexandra can't attend the prom, **and neither** can her boyfriend.

　Alexandra 無法參加舞會，她男友也無法。① 前後動詞均為 can。

b. 前句的動詞為一般動詞時：於後句中**在主詞前加入 do、does、did**。

● The professor buried himself in his research, **and so** did his assistants.

　教授埋首於研究，他的助理也是。

　① 前後動詞為一般動詞，使用 did，後句動詞變化與 S_2 一致。

● Ed didn't eat anything this morning. **Nor** did his brother.

　Ed 今早沒吃東西，他弟弟也是。

句型練習

一、選擇

( ) 1. The largest television network in America is not ABC, CBS, or Fox. Nor ＿＿＿＿＿ one of the cable networks such as CNN. (96 學測)

　(A) it is 　　　　(B) is it 　　　　(C) will it 　　　　(D) does it

( ) 2. Someone's biography is nonfiction; ＿＿＿＿＿ your autobiography. (91 指考)

　(A) so is 　　　　(B) and so is 　　　(C) nor is 　　　　(D) neither does

( ) 3. Smoking is not allowed in the library, ＿＿＿＿＿ drinking and eating.

　(A) and so is 　　(B) nor are 　　　(C) so are 　　　　(D) and neither is

( ) 4. Mr. and Mrs. Chen have never been to Switzerland, ＿＿＿＿＿ their son.

　(A) and so does 　(B) and nor does 　(C) and neither has 　(D) and so has

二、翻譯

1. 我在西班牙旅行時嚐過海鮮飯，我的旅伴也是。

　I tried paella during my trip to Spain, ＿＿＿＿＿ ＿＿＿＿＿ ＿＿＿＿＿ my travel companion.

2. 有外向特質的人經常不悲觀，他們也通常不憂鬱。(. . . nor . . .)

15-7

$$\text{only} \ldots + \begin{cases} \text{be} + \text{S} \\ \text{aux.} + \text{S} + \text{V} \end{cases}$$

句型範例

- **Only** then **was** the old lady aware that the man was a fraud.
  只有在那時這女士才意識到那男子是騙子。

- **Only** when Kelly volunteered in an orphanage **did** she realize the meaning of life.
  只有當 Kelly 在孤兒院當志工，她才理解到生命的意義。

- **Only** at night **can** nocturnal animals see clearly.
  只有在夜晚，夜行性動物才能看清楚。

☆ He realizes that **only** by cooperating **can** he do his share in making society what it should be. (99 學測)
他理解到只有藉著合作，他才能夠盡本分讓社會保有應有的樣貌。

用法詳解

當 only 後接**副詞**、**副詞子句**或**介系詞片語**時，可將其移至句首以加強語氣，並使用倒裝結構，即將子句改成疑問句結構。

a. 主要子句的動詞為 **be 動詞**或**情態助動詞**時：在主要子句中直接將其移至主詞之前。

- The wealthy man is safe only when his bodyguards are around.
- ➡ **Only** when his bodyguards are around **is** the wealthy man safe.
  只有當護衛隊在周圍時，總統才安全無虞。

- Jeremy will get his salary next week. He can buy new sports shoes only then.
- ➡ Jeremy will get his salary next week. **Only** then **can** he buy new sports shoes.
  Jeremy 下週會收到薪水。只有在那時他才能買新運動鞋。

b. 主要子句的動詞為**一般動詞**時：於主要子句的主詞前加入 do、does、did。

- People know the importance of health only when they lose it.
- ➡ **Only** when people lose health **do** they know its importance.
  只有在失去健康時，人們才知道其重要性。

- The student decided to study hard only after she failed the exam.
- ➡ **Only** after the student failed the exam **did** she decide to study hard.
  只有在被當後，這學生才決定要努力讀書。

句型練習

一、選擇

( ) 1. Only in the leading museums _____ fully appreciated by the world. (93 學測)
   (A) can the objects be
   (B) can be the objects
   (C) the objects can be
   (D) the objects are

( ) 2. Only when the students quieted down _____ the teacher announce the exam result.
   (A) will   (B) had   (C) did   (D) has

( ) 3. Only when the boy finishes his homework _____ to play online games.
   (A) does he allow   (B) allows he   (C) is he allowed   (D) he is allowed

( ) 4. Only in the northern woods of Wisconsin, Minnesota, and Michigan _____.
   (A) people heard the howl of native gray wolves
   (B) heard people the howl of native gray wolves
   (C) the howl of native gray wolves could be heard
   (D) could the howl of native gray wolves be heard
   (95 指考)

二、句子改寫

1. Wetas are nocturnal creatures; they come out of their caves and holes only after dark. (99 學測)
   Wetas are nocturnal creatures; only after dark _____

   _____

2. Jimmy knew the battle among the three goddesses only after he read the story of the Trojan War.
   Only _____

三、翻譯

1. 只有當這病人開始規律運動時，他才改善健康狀況。
   _____ _____ the patient began to take regular exercise _____ _____ improve his health condition.

2. 在還清貸款後，Katrina 才感覺不那麼焦慮。
   Only after Katrina paid off the loan _____

3. 只有搭計程車你才能及時到達機場。
   Only by taking a taxi _____

4. 這些人只有在失去言論自由後才會體會到它的價值。
   _____

15–8

$$\text{So} + \begin{cases} \text{adj.} + \text{be} + \text{S} \\ \text{adv.} + \text{aux.} + \text{S} + \text{V} \end{cases} + \text{that-clasue}$$

$$\text{Such} + \text{be} + \text{N(P)} + \text{S} + \text{that-clasue}$$

句型範例

● **Such** is Ang Lee's talent in directing **that** he has won many international awards.
李安很有導戲的天分，以致於他已經贏得許多國際大獎。

● **So** expensive is this pearl necklace **that** only few people can afford it.
這珍珠項鍊如此昂貴，以致於只有少數人能買得起。

● **So** well did Chaplin act **that** he is regarded as one of the most influential comedians. 卓別林演戲演得非常好，以致於他被視為最有影響力的喜劇演員之一。

用法詳解

在表示「如此…以致於…」的句型中，為了加強語氣可將 so + *adj./adv.* 或 such 移至句首，此時必須使用倒裝句型，將 so 或 such 引導的部分改成**疑問句結構**，that-clause 則不需倒裝。

a. 含 so 與 such 的句子裡，動詞為 **be 動詞**時：將 be 動詞移至主詞之前。

● The temperature was **so** low **that** the lake was frozen.

➡ **So** low **was** the temperature **that** the lake was frozen.
溫度如此低，以致於湖結冰了。

● The boy's fright was **such that** he closed his eyes.

➡ **Such was** the boy's fright **that** he closed his eyes.
這男孩如此害怕，以致於他閉上眼睛。

b. 含 so 的句子裡，動詞為**一般動詞**時：在主詞前加入 do、does、did。

● Kobe Bryant plays basketball **so** well **that** he is widely considered one of the greatest basketball players in history.

➡ **So** well **does** Kobe Bryant play basketball **that** he is widely considered one of the greatest basketball players in history.
Kobe Bryant 的籃球打得如此好，所以他被公認為史上最偉大的籃球員之一。

● This ballet dancer danced **so** elegantly **that** he received a thunderous applause.

➡ **So** elegantly **did** this ballet dancer dance **that** he received a thunderous applause. 這芭蕾舞者跳得如此優雅，以致於他贏得如雷的掌聲。

句型練習

一、選擇

( ) 1. So addicted _____ to online games that he has difficulty walking away from his computer once he begins to play.

　　(A) Justin is　　　　(B) is Justin　　　　(C) does Justin　　　　(D) Justin gets

( ) 2. Such _____ in her ankle that she had no choice but to give up the tennis game.

　　(A) does the tennis player's pain　　　(B) had the tennis player's pain

　　(C) the tennis player's pain was　　　(D) was the tennis player's pain

( ) 3. So little _____ eaten during these weeks that they suffered from malnutrition.

　　(A) did the children　　　　　　　(B) had the children

　　(C) the children would　　　　　　(D) the children have

二、翻譯

1. 林先生如此有幽默感，以致於他演講中觀眾不時哄堂大笑。

Such _____ Mr. Lin's sense of humor _____ during his speech the audience burst into laughter from time to time

2. 抗生素如此有效，以致於很多疾病都被治癒了。 (So . . .)

_____

3. Vicky 如此欣賞 Ann Frank 的勇敢，以致於將她的日記讀了好幾遍。 (So . . .)

_____

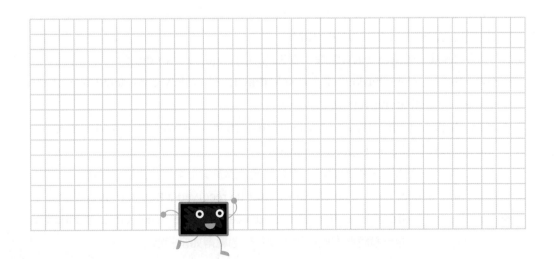

16-1

$$S + \begin{cases} let/have/make + O + V \\ get + O + to\ V \end{cases}$$

$$S + \begin{cases} let + O + be + p.p. \\ have/make/get + O + p.p. \end{cases}$$

句型範例

- Ms. Franco always **lets** her spoiled daughter do whatever she likes.
  Franco 太太總是讓她被寵壞的女兒做她想做的事。

- After a second thought, Eric finally decided to **have** his room painted blue.
  經過再三考慮，Eric 終於決定讓房間漆成藍色。

☆ The science teacher always demonstrates the use of the laboratory equipment before she **lets** her students use it on their own. (105 學測)
理化老師總會在讓學生自行操作實驗器材之前先做示範。

☆ In 1905 he developed a test in which he **had** children do tasks. (102 學測)
在 1950 年時，他研發了一種測試，讓孩童們執行任務。

☆ This behavior is likely to **make** the interviewer feel very uncomfortable.
這個行為可能會讓面試官感覺不舒服。 (100 學測)

用法詳解

本單元介紹使役動詞的用法。使役動詞後面常接受詞 (O) 與受詞補語 (OC)，受詞補語使用主動或被動語態會視其與受詞之間的關係來決定。請見下表：

V	O		OC	說明
let	O	主動	V	1. let 有「允許、同意」之意。 2. O 與 OC 為主動關係時，OC 用原形 V；若為被動關係用 be + p.p.。
		被動	be + p.p.	● Sonia **let** her good friend read the letter from her boyfriend. Sonia 讓好友讀她男友的信。 ● The kind king **let** the captives be treated mercifully. 仁慈的國王讓俘虜被寬容地對待。
have	O	主動	V	1. have 有「讓、使」之意。 2. O 與 OC 為主動關係時，OC 用原形 V；若為被動關係則用 p.p.。
		被動	p.p.	● The teacher **had** the students recite the poem in class.

			老師讓學生在課堂上朗誦這首詩。 ● The old man **had** the lawn mowed. 這老人找人來割草。
make O	主動	V	1. make 也有「讓、使」之意，但較具強迫意義。 2. O 與 OC 為主動關係時，OC 用原形 V；為被動關係用 p.p.。 ● The speaker's humorous speech **made** the audience roar with laughter. 這講者幽默的演說讓觀眾哄堂大笑。 ● Felix can **make** himself understood in Japanese. 　 Felix 可以用日文讓自己被理解。(表示他的日文流利。)
	被動	p.p.	3. 使役動詞中，只有 make 可改成被動語態，其後接不定詞， 　 形成 be made to V(被迫)。 ● Keith was **made** to quit smoking for the sake of health. 　 因健康緣故，Keith 被迫戒煙。
get O	主動	to V	1. get 有「讓、使」之意。 2. O 與 OC 為主動關係時， OC 用 to V；若為被動關係則用 　 p.p.。 ● The teacher **got** the students to recite the poem in class. 　 老師讓學生在課堂上朗誦這首詩。
	被動	p.p.	● To meet the boss' requirement, the employees must **get** the work done today. 　 為了符合老闆的要求，員工們必須今天做完工作。

句型練習

一、選擇

(　) 1. How much money does a band have to raise via MMC to have their music _____ ? (102 指考)
　　　(A) records　　　(B) recording　　　(C) recorded　　　(D) record

(　) 2. The ad informs the consumers with one purpose: to _____ the consumer _____ the brand. (101 指考)
　　　(A) make; liked　　(B) let; be gained　　(C) have; to buy　　(D) get; to like

(　) 3. The computer is not working. Dad promises to get it _____ by next Friday.
　　　(A) fix　　　(B) fixed　　　(C) be repaired　　　(D) to repair

二、翻譯

1. 過去的事就讓它過去吧。

　　_____ bygones _____ bygones.

2. 嚴重的火車誤點讓乘客們抱怨鐵路公司。

16-2

$$S + taste/smell/feel/look/sound/etc. + \begin{cases} adj. \\ like + N \end{cases}$$

句型範例

- The idea that Sheila came up with **sounds** ridiculous.
  Sheila 想到的主意聽起來很荒謬。

- Emma is not good at cooking. The soup she makes **tastes** like dishwater.
  Emma 不擅於烹飪。她煮的湯嚐起來像洗碗水。

 ☆ The graphic novel **looks** like a comic book, but it is longer, more sophisticated. (100 指考)
圖像小說看起來像是漫畫書，但篇幅較長也更加精緻。

用法詳解

1. look (看起來)、taste (嚐起來)、smell (聞起來)、sound (聽起來)、feel (感覺) 屬於連綴動詞，用於連接主詞與主詞補語，其後常接**形容詞**當主詞補語。

- After reaching the finishing line, the swimmer **looked** exhausted.
  游到終點線後，這游泳選手看起來累壞了。

- The leftovers **smell** disgusting. You'd better throw them away as soon as possible. 廚餘聞起來很噁心。你最好盡快丟掉。

2. 連綴動詞之後需接名詞時，必須使用 **like + 名詞**當主詞補語。

- The proposal that Gina made **sounds** like a good plan.
  Gina 的提案聽起來是個好計畫。

- The man who carries a backpack and talks to a group of people **looks** like a tour guide. 背著背包並跟一群人講話的男子看起來像是導遊。

句型練習

一、選擇

(　) 1. Though Kevin failed in last year's singing contest, he did not feel _____.
　　(A) frustrates　　(B) frustration　　(C) frustrated　　(D) frustrating (102 學測)

(　) 2. The tip of your nose _____ —almost as though it were frozen. (102 指考)
　　(A) feels numb　　　　　　　　(B) feels like numb
　　(C) feels numbly　　　　　　　(D) is feeling like numbness

(   ) 3. Jack is very proud of his fancy new motorcycle. He has been boasting to all his friends about how _____ and how fast it runs. (101 學測)

(A) coolly it looks   (B) cool it looks

(C) cool it looks like   (D) coolly it looks like

二、翻譯

1. 每當你感覺心煩而沮喪時，試著唱唱歌。 (101 學測)

    Try to sing whenever you _____ _____ and _____ .

2. 這款香水聞起來如此甜，所以它受到許多年輕女孩的歡迎。

_____

3. 這孩子把飲料吐出來，因為它嚐起來像藥水。

_____

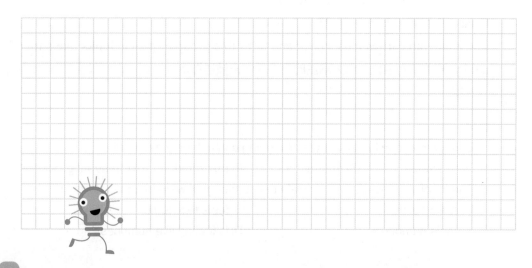

16-3

see/regard/think of/look upon/refer to/etc. + A + as + B
consider + A (+ to be) + B

句型範例

- Westerners **regard** the number 13 **as** a very unlucky number.
  西方人把 13 視為非常不吉祥的數字。
- Many people **look upon** Thomas Elva Edison **as** the greatest inventor of all time.
  許多人認為愛迪生是有史以來最偉大的發明家。
- People **consider** Martin Luther King Jr. (**to be**) the leader of the US civil rights
  movement. 人們認為馬丁路德 • 金恩是美國民權運動的領導人。

☆ He **viewed** the kidnapping **as** a wonderful camping trip. (105 學測)
他將這起綁架案視為一趟精彩的露營旅遊。

☆ Many scholars **consider** him the father of modern computer science.
許多學者將他視為現代電腦科學之父。 (105 指考)

用法詳解

1. 本單元介紹表示「把 A 視為 B」的用法，在動詞 see、take、view、regard、hail、
   think of、look upon、refer to 後加上 A + as + B。as 表「作為」之意，B 可為**名詞**或
   形容詞。

   - My mother *views/thinks of* breakfast **as** the most important meal in a day.
     我媽媽將早餐視為一天當中最重要的一餐。
   - Most committee members **regarded** this proposal **as** unrealistic.
     大部分的委員認為這項提議不切實際。

2. consider + A (+ to be) + B 亦可表示「把 A 視為 B」，B 可為**名詞**或**形容詞**，to be 可
   省略。

   - Tina is not a careful person. The manager doesn't **consider** her (to be) a good
     candidate for the job. Tina 不是細心的人。經理不認為她是這工作的好人選。
   - It is widely known that Indians **consider** cattle (to be) sacred.
     人們普遍知道印度人視牛為神聖的。

3. 注意本句型的被動語態用法：

   a. *think of/look upon/refer to* + A + as + B 改為被動語態時，句型為：A + be +
   thought of/looked upon/referred to + as + B。**as 不可被遺漏**。

● English **is *thought of/looked upon/referred to* as** an international language.

英文被視為國際語言。

b. consider + A (+ to be) + B 改為被動語態時，句型為 A + be considered (+ to be) + B。

● Confucius **is considered (to be)** China's first thinker and teacher.

孔子被認為是中國第一位思想家與老師。

4. consider 的句型也可以與虛受詞 it 連用，後方可接形容詞或名詞。

● The young actor **considers** it (to be) a great honor to be nominated as Best Actor. 這位年輕演員認為被提名角逐最佳演員是莫大的光榮。

① 虛受詞 it 指的是不定詞 to be nominated as Best Actor。

句型練習

一、選擇

( ) 1. Some people call it a traveling museum. Others _____ it as a living or open-air museum. (105 指考)

    (A) look at   (B) refer to   (C) think   (D) are regarded

( ) 2. In society, the former player does not _____ himself _____ a lone wolf who has the right to remain isolated from the society and go his own way. (99 學測)

    (A) consider; like   (B) think of; to be   (C) refer; as   (D) look upon; as

( ) 3. Today, the term "Fabergé eggs" has become a synonym of luxury and the eggs _____ masterpieces of the jeweler's art. (104 指考)

    (A) are referred to   (B) are regarded as (C) are thought of   (D) are looked upon

( ) 4. Smiling _____ a universal language that conveys warmth and happiness.

    (A) considered as   (B) referred to as   (C) is thought of as (D) is looked upon

( ) 5. Instead of _____ one of the crucial figures in defeating the Nazis, Turing was convicted of "gross indecency." (105 指考)

    (A) being thought of (B) viewing as   (C) being hailed as (D) considering to be

二、翻譯

1. 雖然那被認為是她們婚姻狀態的指標，但這項習俗主要是和印度教有關。 (102 學測)

While it is generally _____ _____ an indicator of their marital status, the practice is primarily related to the Hindu religion.

2. 很有幽默感的人通常被認為是快樂且具社交自信的人。 (101 指考)

16-4

what + N(P) + S + *be/V*!

how + $\begin{cases} \text{adj. + S + be!} \\ \text{adv. + S + V!} \end{cases}$

句型範例

- **What** a useful invention the selfie stick is! 自拍棒是多麼有用的發明啊！
- **How** exciting bungee jumping is! 高空彈跳多麼刺激啊！
- **How** hard Larry works to make ends meet! Larry 多麼認真工作要讓收支平衡！

用法詳解

1. 本單元介紹感嘆句。感嘆句用於表達對某事或某對象的讚嘆或驚訝之意。以 what 或 how 引導句子，句末通常加驚嘆號。

2. **what** 帶有形容詞性質，其後需接**名詞** (組) 做修飾，名詞 (組) 前可加形容詞。若不需指示修飾對象時，可以省略 S、V。

   - **What** a patient doctor Mr. Wang is! 王醫師是個多麼有耐心的醫生啊！
   - **What** a wonderful world (it is)! 世界真美好！ ⓘ 可省略 S + V。
   - **What** graceful dancers they are!
     她們真是優雅的舞者啊！ ⓘ What 後可接複數名詞。
   - **What** nice weather it is! 今天天氣真好！ ⓘ What 之後可接不可數名詞。

3. **how** 帶有副詞性質，其後需接**形容詞**或**副詞**做修飾。

   - **How** stunning the bike stunts are! 這單車特技多麼驚人啊！
   - **How** attentively the students listened to the lecture! 學生們聽課多專心啊！

句型練習

一、選擇

( ) 1. _____ a bustling city London is!

    (A) How   (B) That   (C) What   (D) Which

( ) 2. _____ delicious the roast snails are!

    (A) What   (B) How   (C) So   (D) These

( ) 3. _____ productive the writer is! Averagely, she writes two novels a year.

    (A) What   (B) How   (C) Such   (D) Which

( ) 4. _____ the girls ran on the sand!

    (A) What joyful   (B) How joyful   (C) What joyfully   (D) How joyfully

二、翻譯

1. 爺爺剛剛講的故事真誇張！

   _____ a _____ _____ Grandfather had just told!

2. 泰姬陵 (the Taj Mahal) 是多麼宏偉的建築啊！

   _____

3. 這部電影多感人啊！

   _____

4. 這些男孩多麼熱切地回答老師的問題啊！

   _____

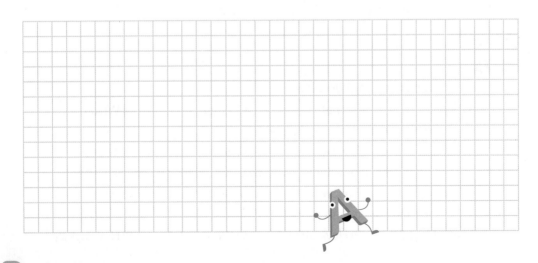

句型練習參考解答

1　介系詞、名詞與代名詞

1–1

一、1. C　2. C　3. B

二、1. The students have learned lessons of great value from Aesop's Fables.

2. The basketball coach taught the players with much patience.

三、1. of; responsibility　2. with; ease

3. is; of; great; importance

4. The dish is very hot, so the waiter has to serve it with great care/very carefully.

1–2

一、1. C　2. B　3. B

二、1. from; culture; to; culture

2. Indians may tilt their heads from side to side

3. The contagious disease may spread from person to person in a short time.

1–3

一、1. D　2. B　3. C

二、1. To everyone's sorrow/grief

2. To the director's satisfaction/To the satisfaction of the director

3. Much to the bride's disappointment/To the bride's great disappointment, her bosom/best friend was not able to attend her wedding ceremony.

1–4

一、1. B　2. D　3. C　4. A

二、1. Some; people; Others

2. Some; of; them; the; others

3. Some of them are from tropical areas, and the others are from subtropical areas.

2　It 和 There 相關

2–1

一、1. B　2. D

二、1. It; that

2. It is both legally and morally wrong

3. Is it possible that the world's food shortages will be solved in ten years?

2–2

一、1. A　2. D　3. B　4. C　5. D

二、1. It; is; for

2. it; is; for; to; wear

3. It was selfish of the boy

4. It is kind of the student to yield his seat to a pregnant woman on the MRT.

2–3

一、1. C　2. A　3. B　4. D

二、1. Shannon thinks it romantic to dine by candlelight.

2. Victor considers it unbelievable that some people eat hot pot on scorching hot days.

三、1. it; difficult; to; judge

2. made; it; possible; to; flow

3. Allen considers/thinks it a waste of time to play online games.

4. Some of my foreign friends consider/think it weird to eat millennium eggs.

2–4

一、1. D　2. A　3. C

二、1. It; seems; that　2. seems; to; have

3. It seems that Daniel bought three tablet computers on an impulse last week./Daniel seems to have bought three tablet computers on an impulse last week.

2–5

一、1. B　2. B　3. C

二、1. is; believed; to

2. Greek gods and goddesses are believed to look like humans and have human emotions./It is believed/People believe that Greek gods and goddesses look like humans and have human emotions.

2–6

一、1. B　2. D　3. D　4. A

二、1. It occurred to Phoebe to charge the cell phone battery.

2. It struck my father that we had run out of salt.

三、1. It; occurred; to; me

2. It struck/occurred to Mr. Cunningham

3. It has never occurred to Claire to make a shopping list before she goes shopping./It has never occurred to/struck Claire that she should make a shopping list before going shopping.

2–7

一、1. C　2. A　3. C　4. B

二、1. It is on Halloween that children go trick-or-treating.

2. It is coffee that Elaine usually drinks in the morning.

三、1. It; was; that　2. It; is; not; that

3. It is Hakka that Iris usually uses to talk with her grandmother.

2–8
一、1. B　2. D　3. C
二、1. It; is; useless; to
2. It/There; is; no; use
3. is no use feeling
4. It is useless to regret/It is no use regretting/There is no use regretting what has happened.

2–9
一、1. B　2. C　3. B　4. A
二、1. There's; no; denying
2. There's no arguing that
3. There's no telling/knowing what magic tricks this talented magician will present to the audience.

2–10
一、1. A　2. D　3. B　4. D　5. C
二、1. There is an annoying man talking loudly on the phone in the movie theater.
2. There is a new design school situated in the city center.
三、1. There; was; held　2. There; are; posted
3. There will be more than 400 million people playing
4. In the masquerade, there are many dancers wearing/dressed in strange costumes.

3　連接詞

3–1
一、1. A　2. C　3. B　4. C　5. D
二、1. not; only; but; also
2. not only a physical but also a mental
3. Not only the actors but also the special effects in this movie attract the audience.

3–2
一、1. D　2. A　3. C　4. B
二、1. Edith will either take a long vacation or quit her job to study abroad.
2. Mike will either buy an iPad or a smartphone for his wife.
三、1. either combine volunteer work; or make service work
2. Students should neither doze off nor use their cell phones/smartphones in class.

3–3
一、1. B　2. A　3. C　4. D　5. D
二、1. The protagonist in this popular TV series is not heroic but timid.
2. What this old man needs is not money but

care and company.
三、1. not; by; but; by
2. was not made of wood but stone.
3. Teresa decided to study overseas not because she wanted to improve her language skills but because she wanted to broaden her horizons.

3–4
一、1. D　2. B　3. C
二、1. Whether it is sunny or rainy, the newspaper boy has to deliver newspapers.
2. Whether people like it or not, the government will raise fuel prices.

3–5
一、1. C　2. D　3. A
二、1. Put; and　2. Keep; or
3. Drink some salty water, and you can ease your sore throat.

4　助動詞

4–1
1. A　2. B　3. B　4. C　5. C

4–2
一、1. C　2. B　3. A　4. D
二、1. The patient had better take the doctor's advice
2. The woman had better not eat any seafood
三、1. had; better; dry　2. had; better; hadn't he
3. we had better not forget to tip waiters.
4. You had better not believe what Julia says, because she always tells lies.

4–3
一、1. C　2. B　3. D　4. A
二、1. Did Nicky use to take delight in reading science fictions?
2. My brother didn't use to be allergic to nuts and pollen.
三、1. used; to
2. used to attract worldwide attention.
3. he used to have a miserable childhood.

4–4
一、1. D　2. C　3. A　4. B
二、Hank would rather stay up to do the report than miss the deadline.
三、1. would; rather; than
2. would rather get punished than do his assignment
3. That young man would rather quit his job

than lose his dream

4–5

一、 1. C　2. B　3. D　4. B

二、 1. advise; continue　2. recommend; discuss

3. suggested that she undergo a heart surgery.

4. The customer requested that the shop owner (should) give her some discounts.

4–6

一、 1. C　2. A　3. C　4. D

二、 1. It is essential that people infected with H1N1 flu (should) wear masks.

2. It is advisable that Karl (should) have his broken battered car fixed.

三、 1. It; is; natural; turn

2. It; is; urgent; be; delivered/sent

3. It is important that a class leader be responsible/have a sense of responsibility.

5 比較級

5–1

一、 1. C　2. A　3. D

二、 1. is as expensive as a three-story house.

2. has read as many novels as Hugh (has).

三、 1. be; as; as

2. As far as I am concerned/To me, learning English is as interesting as playing games.

3. Your coat is as expensive as hers, and mine is not so/as expensive as yours.

5–2

一、 1. D　2. C　3. A

二、 1. More; and; more　2. higher; and; higher

3. As it got darker and darker

4. Due to the entertainment agency's successful training program, this rock band performs better and better.

5. The patient refused any medical treatment, so his health condition got/became worse and worse.

5–3

一、 1. C　2. D　3. C

二、 1. sales promotions a mall has, the more customers it will attract.

2. The longer the man waited, the less patient he got.

三、 1. The; rarer; the; more

2. The less; the more difficult it is for them

3. The more often these basketball players

practice, the better they play.

5–4

一、 1. B　2. A　3. D　4. C

二、 1. is twice as expensive as the T-shirt.

2. is eight times older than she (is).

三、 1. four; times; larger; than

2. twice as much (money) as

3. Our English teacher is three times older than we/as old as we/the age of us.

4. This elderly writer's works are five times more than that young writer's.

5–5

一、 1. D　2. C　3. B　4. C　5. A

二、 1. as; hard; as; possible

2. as fast as she could/as possible

3. Jessica keeps her diet as balanced as possible/as she can to stay healthy.

4. You should practice speaking English as often as you can/possible so that you can speak English fluently.

5–6

一、 1. B　2. D　3. A　4. C　5. B

二、 1. no; other; drink; as; as

2. no; other; more; important; than

3. no other thing/nothing is as important as/more important than playing the piano.

4. no other boy in Luke's class is better than he.

5. Nothing in the world travels faster than light.

6 關係詞

6–1

一、 1. B　2. B　3. C　4. A

二、 1. that happen every day.

2. , who are farmers,

3. Luckily, the man and his dog that were trapped by heavy snow were rescued.

4. Sheila failed the GEPT test, which upset her completely.

6–2

一、 1. D　2. C　3. D　4. B　5. A

二、 1. people; who; are　2. People; who; use

3. those who are in need.

4. A person/Anyone/He/One who exercises regularly is more likely to look young.

5. Those/People who dump their garbage at will are going to/will be fined.

6-3

一、 1. C　2. D　3. B　4. D

二、 1. Sheila invited twenty friends to her birthday party, many of whom brought partners.

2. The pupils see a lot of animals in the zoo, some of which are herbivores.

三、 1. some; of; which　2. all of which were

3. Our math teacher asked us ten questions, half of which were very difficult.

4. My neighbor keeps two dogs, both of which bark at strangers.

6-4

一、 1. B　2. B　3. D　4. C

二、 1. Wyatt told me the reason why he quit his job.

2. These football players will always remember the day when they won the World Cup.

三、 1. when; it; is; delivered

2. where/in which I spent my happy childhood.

3. The locations where/in which these films were shot have become popular tourist attractions/sports.

6-5

一、 1. A　2. B　3. A　4. D

二、 1. Fashion is what these models always talk about.

2. What was written in the tabloid about the superstar proved true.

三、 1. what; it; should; be　2. what; leads; to

3. what was wrong with the plane.

4. Paul doesn't know for sure what he is going to do this weekend.

6-6

一、 1. C　2. D　3. C　4. B　5. C

二、 1. The demanding mother always seems dissatisfied with whatever her son does.

2. Legend has it that whoever gazed directly upon Medusa would be turned into stone.

三、 1. whatever

2. Whoever/Anyone who runs through the red light

3. The narrow-minded woman always complains about whomever/anyone whom she works with.

7　動名詞

7-1

一、 1. C　2. D　3. B　4. A

二、 1. Parrots have no difficulty imitating human sounds.

2. The young lady has a hard time getting rid of her bad habits.

三、 1. had; problems; reaching

2. has problems in adjusting

3. These boy scouts are beginner, so they have trouble building/making a fire.

7-2

一、 1. A　2. B　3. B　4. D

二、 1. These teenagers just finished practicing skateboarding for their upcoming game.

2. Many people enjoy communicating with their friends through social networking websites.

三、 1. keep; moving　2. avoid catching a cold.

3. Many foreigners who enjoy living in Taiwan have considered settling down here.

4. Those who want to enjoy good health should avoid staying up and quit eating high-fat foods.

7-3

一、 1. B　2. A　3. C　4. D

二、 1. worth; reading

2. is well worth/worthy of the government's attention.

3. Without a doubt, our freedom of speech is worth fighting for.

4. The controversial issue of welfare reform is worth debating/worthy of debates.

7-4

一、 1. A　2. B　3. A　4. D

二、 1. Irene couldn't help drinking up two bottles of juice.

2. Keith couldn't help but give a sigh of relief.

三、 1. can't; help; falling

2. the students can't help feeling nervous.

3. he had no choice but to call the police for help.

4. The speaker can't help coughing/can't but cough/can't help but cough to clear his throat.

7–5

一、 1. A　2. C　3. D　4. B

二、 1. are; devoted; to; helping
2. is addicted to; gets/is used to checking his smartphone hourly/every hour.
3. In addition to chatting with her old friends happily

7–6

一、 1. D　2. C　3. D　4. B

二、 1. The woman applies cream to her face every day to prevent her face from getting wrinkled.
2. The boy walked slowly on the wet floor to keep himself from slipping.

三、 1. protects; from
2. save; from; going; bankrupt
3. how to prevent eyeglasses from freezing.
4. If you want to keep your computer from being attacked by new viruses, you need to constantly renew and update your anti-virus software.

7–7

一、 1. C　2. A　3. D

二、 1. The student decided to take a gap year rather than finish his studies first.
2. altering my father's inability to express his feelings, I must accept myself.

三、 1. Instead; of
2. instead, he used his money to help others help themselves.

8　不定詞

8–1

一、 1. A　2. D　3. C

二、 1. The shy boy doesn't know what to talk about with girls.
2. The earthquake victims wonder whether to leave or to stay in their village.

三、 1. what; to; wear; how; to; behave
2. how to use tablets
3. how to warm up; how to prevent
4. When we get lost, compasses can show us which way to choose.

8–2

一、 1. A　2. D　3. B　4. B

二、 1. The ambulance ran fast enough to send the injured man to the hospital in time.
2. The engineer was smart enough to solve the complicated problem in 10 minutes.

三、 1. qualified; enough; to
2. mature; enough; to
3. strong enough to last for a day.
4. English learners must read much enough to increase their proficiency/skills.

8–3

一、 1. C　2. B　3. D

二、 1. What; is; memorize/remember
2. All; is (to) adapt himself/herself to his/her new class soon.
3. What/All (that) the police officer can do for the lost child is find his parents.

8–4

一、 1. B　2. B　3. D　4. A

二、 1. has; nothing; to; do; with
2. has little to do with his appearance.
3. have much/a lot to do with her devotion to research?
4. These students' interest in English has much/a lot to do with their/the teacher's encouragement.

8–5

一、 1. B　2. D　3. C　4. A

二、 1. not; to; mention　2. let; alone
3. not to mention/not to speak of/to say nothing of having written several books.
4. not to mention/not to speak of/to say nothing of walking home by himself

8–6

一、 1. B　2. D　3. B

二、 1. to be precise　2. To put it simply
3. to do her justice

三、 1. To be plain/frank with you
2. Mrs. Wright has a large collection of hats. She has more than 200 hats, to be precise.

9　分詞

9–1

一、 1. A　2. D　3. C　4. B

二、 1. endangered; creatures
2. developing; countries; limited
3. disappointing; people buried under the collapsed buildings were all found dead

9–2

一、 1. C　2. D

二、 1. Before the nervous girl made the speech, she felt her legs shaking.
2. Justin saw his car towed away by the police.

三、 1. see; appear
2. was seen to kiss an attractive girl.; heard her friends talking about this

9-3

一、 1. A 2. D 3. B 4. D

二、 1. keep themselves warm
2. Belle found tears rolling down her cheeks.
3. Mr. and Mrs. Kauffman have no time to clean their house, which left the furniture covered with dust.
4. The traffic police caught the drunk driver running through the red light.

9-4

一、 1. D 2. D 3. C 4. A

二、 1. The poor sick man passed away with nothing left to his children.
2. The teacher was explaining a grammar rule with a student dozing off in class.

三、 1. with; lasting
2. with his bare feet bleeding.
3. Brooke started to do the dishes with her long hair put/tied up.
4. The scouts formed a circle to play games with the campfire burning.

9-5

一、 1. D 2. B 3. C 4. A

二、 1. Lillian worked day and night, hoping to pay off the mortgage as early as possible.
2. The tornado struck this city, causing many deaths and injuries.

三、 1. trying; to
2. expecting that good things will happen.
3. , waiting for her mom to pick her up.
4. The workaholic kept thinking about his work at midnight, not being able to sleep.

9-6

一、 1. C 2. D 3. B 4. D

二、 1. The letter torn to pieces was written by Kelly's boyfriend.
2. The elegant lady wearing a grey dress is an experienced programmer.

三、 1. coated with beautiful colors; decorated with precious jewels.
2. Most people having dined in this restaurant are contented with their good service and delicious food.
3. To our surprise, this intelligent man's brain is like a computer filled with much data and knowledge.

9-7

一、 1. B 2. D 3. C 4. C

二、 1. Wearing a sweater on such a hot day, the boy is sweating profusely.
2. (Having been) Inspired by Raphael's works, Amy shows an interest in painting.

三、 1. when; lying
2. Compared with their parents' generation, young people nowadays enjoy more freedom and prosperity.

9-8

一、 1. A 2. C 3. D 4. B 5. C

二、 1. Tanya breaking several national records in a track meet
2. The result of the exam having been announced
3. The bell having rung, many students ran to the playground.
4. Her glasses (being) broken, Victoria could not see clearly.

9-9

一、 1. D 2. C 3. B

二、 1. Honestly/Frankly; speaking
2. Speaking; of
3. Considering/Given the old man's age
4. Supposing/Provided that you can't get to the airport on time, what will you do?
5. Judging from Emily's strange behavior, she must have hidden something from us.

10 假設語氣

10-1

一、 1. C 2. D 3. B 4. B 5. A

二、 1. If the air-conditioning in this restaurant were not out of order, the customers could dine comfortably.
2. If leopards didn't have powerful hind legs, they could not run very fast.

三、 1. If these flood victims had enough support and money
2. If I had enough time, I might volunteer in an animal protection center.

10-2

一、 1. C 2. B 3. C 4. D

二、 1. If Eva had brought her camera, she could have taken pictures on her trip to the national park.
2. If these boys hadn't had a street fight, they wouldn't have been taken to the police station.

三、 1. had; had; might; not; have; had
   2. If the sun had appeared after the rain yesterday, we might have been able to see the rainbow.
   3. If I had had/eaten breakfast this morning, I would not feel so hungry now.

10–3

一、 1. A 2. B 3. D 4. C 5. C
二、 1. time were to be turned back, we could change the past.
   2. the plane should be delayed, the passengers may have to wait.
三、 1. could; were; to
   2. If dinosaurs were to appear in the world again
   3. If Nora should forget to heat the frozen food, we may have nothing to eat for dinner.

10–4

一、 1. C 2. D 3. B
二、 1. Were Kenny very good at tennis, he could participate in the tennis tournament.
   2. Had Carol booked her flight earlier, she could have received a discount on airfare.
   3. Should our car break down on the way, we would have to walk home.

10–5

一、 1. A 2. B 3. D 4. C
二、 1. were not for the nervous system, human beings could not feel pain and avoid it.
   2. the pension, many elderly people could not live in comfort after retirement.
三、 1. If; it; were; not; for; could
   2. If; it; had; not; been; for; might/could; have; got/been

10–6

一、 1. C 2. C 3. D
二、 1. Ben could have attended the field trip yesterday
   2. should have got up early; wouldn't have missed the first bus.
三、 1. should; have; taken
   2. This young actor would not have been nominated for
   3. The train could have departed punctually/on time, but there were some stones found on the railway.
   4. Before effective communication, you should not/ought not to have begun a quarrel with your friend.

10–7

一、 1. A 2. C 3. D 4. B
二、 1. he were taller/tall enough
   2. he had been to Italy
三、 1. wishes; were
   2. had not complained about his boss
   3. My cell phone's battery is low. I wish I had charged it last night.
   4. Last year Nancy wished she had celebrated Christmas in New York, but this year she wishes she could spend this holiday in London.

10–8

一、 1. C 2. A 3. B 4. C
二、 1. as; if/though; were
   2. but she acted as if/though everything were fine.
   3. In the speech contest, the self-confident student spoke as if/though the audience were all his fans.
   4. The sweaty boy smells as if/though he had not showered for 10 days.
   5. The thirsty traveler gulped down a bottle of soda as if/though she had not drunk anything for a week.

10–9

一、 1. A 2. D 3. D 4. B
二、 1. It is time for these people to face the music.
   2. It is time that the teacher announced the test result.
   3. It is time that the chronic procrastinator learned to manage his time.
   4. It is time for Michael to do the laundry.; It is time that Michael did the laundry.
三、 1. it; was; time; to; go
   2. It is time for the judges to make the final decision./It is time that the judges made the final decision.

11　副詞子句 I

11–1

一、 1. D 2. C 3. B 4. D
二、 1. Olivia has been learning English
   2. The project has been left undone since the manager went on vacation.
三、 1. has; doubled
   2. Since; have been organized

3. Since digital cameras were invented, they have played an important role in people's lives.

11–2

一、 1. C 2. D 3. D 4. A

二、 1. Lisa couldn't quench her thirst until she drank a bottle of water.

2. The obese man didn't change his diet until he was diagnosed with cancer.

三、 1. did; not; appear

2. did; not; know; until

3. Derek didn't regret/feel regretful about talking back to his mother until she got mad.

4. The student didn't know the answer to the question until she used the search engine.

11–3

一、 1. A 2. C 3. B 4. C

二、 1. The; moment/minute/instant

2. On/Upon; smelling

3. The clock had no sooner struck twelve

11–4

一、 1. B 2. C 3. D

二、 1. By; the; time; will; have; fallen

2. By; the; time; had; watched

3. Carl will have finished cooking dinner by the time his wife comes home.

---

12 副詞子句 II

12–1

一、 1. B 2. D 3. C

二、 1. even; though

2. Even; though

3. Even if he has a job offer

4. Even if Sarah knows the secret, she won't tell me about it.

12–2

一、 1. C 2. C 3. D 4. D

二、 1. the teacher's clear explanation of the theory, the students couldn't understand it.

2. In spite of/Despite the fact that the girl made efforts, she failed to win the talent show.

三、 1. Despite

2. Despite/In spite of the fact that Mandy apologized

3. Despite/In spite of having won many prizes, this inventor never stops working on his new inventions.

12–3

一、 1. B 2. C 3. D 4. A

二、 1. Overweight; as; is

2. Animal lover as Mrs. Green is

3. Hard as the foreigner tried to express himself in Chinese, he couldn't make himself understood.

12–4

一、 1. B 2. A 3. C 4. B

二、 1. No; matter; what

2. whenever you feel upset and depressed.

3. However hard/No matter how hard they tried, they couldn't change Johnny's mind.

---

13 副詞子句 III

13–1

一、 1. B 2. C 3. D

二、 1. because; of

2. Because of organic fertilizers

3. The actress refused to answer the journalist's questions because of his rudeness.

13–2

一、 1. C 2. D 3. B 4. B

二、 1. in; order; to

2. so as to avoid traffic accidents/so that you can avoid traffic accidents.

3. In order not to get nearsighted, the girl never spends much time using the computer.

13–3

一、 1. D 2. B 3. B 4. A

二、We should distinguish between facts and opinions lest we (should) be misled by mass media.

三、 1. lest; should; hurt; him

2. lest; be; ruined

3. Mr. and Mrs. Ivanov never scold their children for fear that they might/lest they should lose self-confidence.

13–4

一、 1. A 2. D 3. A 4. C

二、 1. so; many; that

2. that it had to be watered several times a day.

3. The Phantom of the Opera is such a popular musical that it has been performed for over twenty years.

13–5

一、 1. B　2. D　3. C

二、 1. As; long; as

2. As long as we spend less time on social networking websites

3. As long as Kevin uses critical thinking skills more often, he can boost his ability of solving problems.

13–6

一、 1. D　2. B

二、 1. Now; that

2. Now that Eric has finished high school

3. Now that this patient has undergone an operation, he will recover soon.

14　否定句

14–1

一、 1. B　2. C　3. D

二、 1. no; at; all

2. no; at; all

3. To everyone's surprise, after several training sessions, the athlete does not feel tired at all/by any means/in the least.

14–2

一、 1. C　2. B　3. D　4. D

二、 1. The job offer sounds too good to be true.

2. After the exciting game, the basketball player was too exhausted to move his legs.

三、 1. too; difficult; to; say

2. too small to be noticed

3. This hungry young man ate too quickly to digest well.

4. To many talented people nowadays, it is not too difficult to fulfill their dreams of becoming stars.

14–3

一、 1. D　2. B　3. C　4. D

二、 1. Angela's boyfriend never visited her without bringing her flowers.

2. It is impossible for Adam to travel to France without visiting Notre-Dame Cathedral.

三、 1. never; complete; without

2. no; but

3. Sandra never talks about Greek mythology without mentioning Apollo.

14–4

一、 1. A　2. C　3. D　4. B

二、 1. these young athletes can't practice too much.

2. one can never be too hard-working.

三、 1. can't; too

2. It is believed that nurses cannot be too patient.

3. The effort Emily made to this team cannot be overpraised.

14–5

一、 1. B　2. B　3. A　4. D

二、 1. the; last; person; to

2. the last/least likely subject

3. he is the last/least likely runner to lose this race

4. As far as this careful driver is concerned/ For this careful driver, speeding is the last/least likely thing that he would do.

14–6

一、 1. C　2. B

二、 1. Needless; to; say

2. It; goes; without; saying

3. Needless to say

4. Needless to say,/It goes without saying that lifting lanterns on the Lantern Festival is one of Taiwan's traditions.

15　倒裝句

15–1

一、 1. D　2. D　3. B　4. B

二、 1. was; was

2. sailed; came

3. hung many medals; were many pictures.

15–2

一、 1. B　2. A　3. C　4. C

二、 1. No longer did this telephone booth serve any useful purpose.

2. Never have the students in this poor country used tablets.

三、 1. No; longer; are

2. Little did the man realize the meaning of mutual help before he joined a volunteer team.

15–3

一、 1. A　2. C　3. C　4. D

二、 1. Not only are apples low in calories, but they are (also) high in fiber.

2. Not only does bullying affect the bullied, but it also affects his friends and classmates and the whole society.

三、 1. Not only does; but it also makes
2. Not only can VIP members of this club enjoy free afternoon teas
3. To celebrate their anniversary, not only did Nick buy 99 flowers for his wife but he also reserved a table at a restaurant.

15-4
一、 1. B 2. A 3. B 4. D
二、 1. Not; until; did; I; know
2. Not; until; are; these; kids
3. Not until Jake installed antivirus software need he not worry about computer hacking.

15-5
一、 1. B 2. C 3. D 4. A
二、 1. No; sooner; had; than
2. Hardly had the boy been saved/rescued from fire
3. had the driver run through the red light; he was caught
4. Scarcely/Hardly had the kind-hearted woman seen the stray dog when tears rolled down her cheeks.
5. the woman opened her safe, she found her wedding ring gone.; opening her safe, the woman found her wedding ring gone.; had the woman opened her safe when/before she found her wedding ring gone.

15-6
一、 1. B 2. A 3. B 4. C
二、 1. and; so; did
2. People with an outgoing personality are often not pessimistic, nor are they usually depressed.

15-7
一、 1. A 2. C 3. C 4. D
二、 1. do they come out of their caves and holes.
2. after Jimmy read the story of the Trojan War did he know the battle among the three goddesses.
三、 1. Only; when; did; he
2. did she feel less stressful.
3. can you get to/arrive at the airport in time.
4. Only when these people lose the freedom of speech will they realize the value of it.

15-8
一、 1. B 2. D 3. B
二、 1. was; that
2. So effective are antibiotics that many diseases are cured.
3. So much does Vicky admire Ann Frank for her bravery/Ann Frank's bravery that she has read her diary again and again/several times.

16 其他句型

16-1
一、 1. C 2. D 3. B
二、 1. Let; be
2. The serious delay of the trains made the passengers complain about the railway company.

16-2
一、 1. C 2. A 3. B
二、 1. feel; upset; depressed
2. This perfume smells so sweet that it is popular with many young girls.
3. The child spat the drink out because it tasted like liquid medicine.

16-3
一、 1. B 2. D 3. B 4. C 5. C
二、 1. taken; as
2. A person who has a great sense of humor is often considered to be happy and socially confident.

16-4
一、 1. C 2. B 3. B 4. D
二、 1. What; ridiculous; story
2. What a magnificent structure the Taj Mahal is!
3. How heart-touching the movie is!
4. How enthusiastically these boys responded to the teacher's questions!

本書圖片來源：Shutterstock

英文寫作測驗：句子合併&克漏式翻譯
Writing Test: Sentence Combination & Guided Translation

王隆興　編著

句型 & 翻譯一次入手，
造就超強大考翻譯實力！

「句子合併」

統整 200 個關鍵連接詞與常見片語用法，教你寫出正確的合併句子。
融入關鍵連接詞、轉折語及各式重要句型的概念，帶你打下紮實的基本功。

「克漏式翻譯」

設計 40 篇短文閱讀結合克漏式翻譯題型，教你翻出最流暢的英文句子。
提示重要詞彙片語，引導你學習理解文意，循序漸進培養寫作能力。

大考翻譯實戰題本

王隆興　編著

1. 全新編排五大主題架構，串聯三十回三百句練習，爆量刷題練手感。
2. 融入時事及新課綱議題，取材多元豐富又生活化，命題趨勢一把抓。
3. 彙整大考熱門翻譯句型，提供建議寫法參考字詞，循序漸進好容易。
4. 解析本收錄單字補充包，有效擴增翻譯寫作用字，翻譯技能點到滿。

20分鐘稱霸大考英文作文

王靖賢　編著

- 共 16 回作文練習，涵蓋大考作文 3 大題型：看圖寫作、主題寫作、信函寫作。根據近年大考趨勢精心出題，題型多元且擬真度高。
- 每回作文練習皆有為考生精選的英文名言佳句，增強考生備考戰力。
- 附方便攜帶的解析本，針對每回作文題目提供寫作架構圖，讓寫作脈絡一目了然，並提供範文、寫作要點、寫作撇步及好用詞彙，一本在手即可增強英文作文能力。

神拿滿級分——英文學測總複習

孫至娟 編著

新型學測總複習必備！
十回十足準備，滿級分手到擒來！

重點搭配練習：雙效合一有感複習，讓你應試力UP！
議題式心智圖：補充時事議題單字，讓你單字力UP！
文章主題多元：符合學測多元取材，讓你閱讀力UP！
混合題最素養：多樣混合題型訓練，讓你理解力UP！
獨立作文頁面：作答空間超好運用，讓你寫作力UP！
詳盡解析考點：見題拆題精闢解析，讓你解題力UP！

隨堂評量

大考英文句型 GO

呂香瑩 編著

三民書局

大考英文句型 GO 隨堂評量 目次

TEST 1
1-1～1-4

一、選擇

( ) 1. On Halloween, children in costumes usually go _____ to ask for candy.
  (A) from a door to a door (B) from house to house
  (C) from one home to the other (D) from houses to houses

( ) 2. Dining habits and traditions differ _____, so it is important that we have basic knowledge of them before traveling to a foreign country.
  (A) from countries to countries (B) from a country to the other
  (C) from one culture to some cultures (D) from one culture to another

( ) 3. Having beaten his closest rival, this tennis player burst _____ excitement.
  (A) for (B) of (C) with (D) about

( ) 4. Finding that her favorite vase was broken, Clara shouted _____.
  (A) of rage (B) at rage (C) about anger (D) in anger

( ) 5. _____, the magician made the great statue disappear.
  (A) It made everyone surprised (B) Much to everyone's amazement
  (C) Everyone felt astonished (D) Great to people's relief

( ) 6. Choose the correct statement.
  (A) Mr. Ross, who is in charge of the project, is a man of responsibility.
  (B) Thank you for lending me your electronic dictionary, which is with great help.
  (C) We elected Wendy as our representative, for she is a person with intelligence.
  (D) The skilled mechanic fixed the broken machine of ease.

二、填空題 (根據文意，在空格中填入 some、some of them、other、others 或 the others)

7. _____ people believe in aliens, while _____ don't.

8. Teddy bought a dozen eggs. He stumbled on his way home, so _____ were broken, but, fortunately, _____ weren't.

9. Nora received many birthday gifts. _____ are from her friends; _____ are from her family.

10. _____ people call it a traveling museum. _____ refer to it as a living or open-air

museum. (105 指考)

11. Sometimes, the brilliant rays of light spread upward in the shape of a fan. At _____ times, they flash here and there like giant searchlights. (96 指考)

三、句子改寫 (根據提示改寫下列各句)

12. There's no denying that Mozart was a talented musician.

(以 . . . N + prep. + N 改寫)

➡ There's no denying that Mozart was _____ .

13. The surgeon performed the delicate operation very carefully.

(以 . . . N + prep. + N 改寫)

➡ _____

14. Joshua was relieved that his lost laptop was sent to the lost-and-found.

(以 To one's N 改寫)

➡ _____

15. Everyone was very disappointed that the two presidential candidates severely criticize each other. (以 to one's N 改寫)

➡ _____

四、翻譯

16. 別打擾他們。他們正在討論一個非常重要的事情。

Don't bother them. They are talking about something _____

_____ .

17. 當你感到疲憊時，喝點冰茶對消除疲勞很有幫助。

When you feel exhausted, _____

_____ for you to get refreshed.

18. 孔子是中國偉大的老師與思想家，他留下許多讓人們學習的至理名言。

Confucius was a great Chinese teacher and philosopher, who had left _____

_____ for people to learn.

19. 為了推銷新產品，這位售貨員必須到處旅行。

To promote the new product, _____ .

20. 讓許多顧客很滿意的是，這間公司提供良好的售後服務。

_____ , this company provides good after-sales service.

T E S T 2

2–1～2–5

一、選擇

( ) 1. _____ is true that having dessert before meals ruins appetite.

    (A) That   (B) It   (C) What   (D) All

( ) 2. It is kind _____ these volunteers to help with the reconstruction of this earthquake-stricken village.

    (A) of   (B) for   (C) that   (D) with

( ) 3. Today's worldwide transportation makes _____ even harder to control an epidemic.

    (A) that   (B) this   (C) it   (D) them

( ) 4. However, without the sense of sight, _____ lacking one of the keenest abilities that life forms use to react to their environment. (93 指考)

    (A) it seemed that their toys   (B) it seems that their toys

    (C) their toys seemed to be   (D) their toys seemed

( ) 5. This kind of medicine _____ date from the 4th century BC. (92 學測)

    (A) estimates   (B) was said   (C) is rumored that   (D) is believed to

二、句子合併與改寫

6. ⎰ The doctor's patients follow his prescriptions.
   ⎱ The doctor thinks it important.   (以虛受詞 it 合併)

➡ _____

7. That parents should not leave their children alone at home is important.

  (以虛主詞 it 改寫)

➡ _____

8. The old man seems to need a hearing aid. (以 It seems that . . . 改寫)

➡ _____

9. It seems that the singer's marriage has received extensive media coverage.

  (以 . . . seem to . . . 改寫)

➡ _____

10. Salt water helps cure a sore throat.

➡ _____ (以 It is said . . . 改寫)

➡ _____ (以 People . . . 改寫)

➡ _____ (以 Salt water . . . 改寫)

三、填空題 (根據文意，在空格中填入 for、of、to 或 it)

11. _____ is reported that hip-hop fashion alone generates $750 million to $1 billion annually. (92 學測)

12. It is convenient _____ people living in Taipei to commute by the MRT.

13. Our teacher suggests that we should make _____ a habit to memorize new words every day.

14. It is honest _____ the young man to send the money he found on the street to the police station.

15. Patrick seems _____ be interested in joining the school basketball team.

四、翻譯

16. 要控制冰的大小和形狀是很困難的。 (97 學測)

_____ the size and shape of the ice.

17. 平均上男人在十多歲時似乎比女人稍微快樂些。 (96 指考)

_____ on average than women in their teens.

18. Zoe 認為訪客進入她家之前應先脫鞋。

Zoe thinks it necessary _____

___ before entering her house.

19. 例如，希特勒被認為在童年時期曾是霸凌的受害者。 (100 指考)

Hitler, for example, is claimed to _____

_____ in his childhood.

20. 據說日本人深信一個人的血型會決定他或她的性格。

_____ that a person's personality is affected by his or her blood type.

TEST 3

2–6～2–10

一、選擇

( ) 1. It is on New Year's Eve _____ all my family members come home for a reunion.
    (A) which   (B) who   (C) where   (D) that

( ) 2. Tiffany is a credit card abuser. _____ to tell her to control her spending.
    (A) It is useless   (B) It is no use   (C) It is of no use   (D) There is no use

( ) 3. _____ that time and tide wait for no man.
    (A) It is impossible denying   (B) There's no denying
    (C) It is out of the question denying   (D) There is no possibility to deny

( ) 4. At dawn, in this park there are many people _____ Tai Chi and Qigong in groups.
    (A) practice   (B) practicing   (C) who practicing   (D) to practice

( ) 5. Choose the WRONG sentence.
    (A) A brilliant idea flashed through the salesman's mind.
    (B) A terrible thought came into the woman's mind.
    (C) A good idea came up with the businessman.
    (D) An interesting thought occurred to the boy.

二、句子合併與改寫

6. { Something occurred to the tourist.
   He should buy some souvenirs before he left this country.
  (以 It occurred to . . . that 合併)

➡ _____

7. { Something struck the clerk.
   The sports shoes were out of stock.   (以 It struck . . . that 合併)

➡ _____

8. { There are many tall trees in the mountain.
   These trees are covered in snow.   (以 There be + N . . . 合併)

➡ _____

9. The dog's barking disturbed Joseph's sleep last night.

   (以分裂句強調 the dog's barking)

➡ _____

三、配合題

(　　) 10. There is a police car . . .

(　　) 11. It is better working conditions . . .

(　　) 12. Stephanie is a shopaholic. It is of no use . . .

(　　) 13. There's no . . .

(　　) 14. It struck Aidan . . .

   (A) knowing what will happen in the future.

   (B) dissuading her from buying unnecessary things.

   (C) that these railway workers ask for.

   (D) that he could make some cupcakes for the party.

   (E) chasing the bank robbers on the street.

四、翻譯

15. 你曾經想過要環遊世界嗎？

   _____ to travel around the

   world?

16. 這頑皮的小孩突然有狡猾的計畫。

   A tricky plan _____ .

17. 很明顯地，是唱片業想要對抗盜版。 (91 指考)

   Obviously, _____ wants

   to fight piracy.

18. 在 1492 年發現美洲的人就是哥倫布。

   _____

19. 抱怨這家餐廳的服務是沒有用的。

   There's _____ .

20. Janet 的作文中有一些拼字錯誤被老師標示出來。

   There are _____ .

TEST 4

3-1～3-5

一、選擇

( ) 1. A recent study suggests the marine mammals _____ produce their own unique "signature whistles," but they also recognize and mimic whistles of other dolphins they are close to and want to see again. (104 指考)
  (A) not (B) either (C) both (D) not only

( ) 2. Not only the clown's body language but also his facial expressions _____ people laugh.
  (A) makes (B) make (C) will make (D) has made

( ) 3. Neither Adam nor his sisters _____ afraid of dogs.
  (A) are (B) is (C) feels (D) be

( ) 4. Miranda was fined because she didn't park her car in the parking lot _____ on the pavement.
  (A) and (B) or (C) but (D) nor

( ) 5. The boy has to run errands for his mother, _____ he likes it or not.
  (A) no matter (B) whatever (C) however (D) whether

( ) 6. Recent studies show that people spend an average of 64 hours a week sitting, _____ they exercise 150 minutes a week as recommended by World Health Organization (WHO). (104 學測)
  (A) whether (B) whether or not (C) if (D) no matter how

( ) 7. Turn off the light, _____ the baby will fall asleep soon.
  (A) otherwise (B) or (C) and (D) as if

( ) 8. Debby plans to either take her foreign friends to the night market _____.
  (A) and cook a big meal for them
  (B) but take them to visit National Palace Museum
  (C) or invite them to a famous restaurant
  (D) nor go to the zoo with them

二、句子合併與改寫

9. { Tommy is good at roller-skating.
   { Tommy plays tennis well.　(以 not only . . . but also . . . 合併)

➡ _____

10. { Wendy didn't eat toast and butter for breakfast.
     She didn't eat cereal for breakfast, either.   (以 neither . . . nor 合併)

➡ _____

11. { Customers in this shopping mall can pay by credit card.
     Customers in this shopping mall can also pay in cash.   (以 either . . . or 合併)

➡ _____

12. The policemen didn't discover the evidence of the crime. Instead, the detective discovered it.

➡ Not _____ .

三、句子重組

13. Anne Frank/courage/we can learn/not only/is/What/from/optimism/but also

_____

14. scripts/actors/follow/Whether/they/have to/like it or not

_____

四、翻譯

15. 在一項動物科學家所進行的實驗中,他們讓大象聞乾淨的衣物,或者聞由馬賽族人或坎巴族人穿過五天的衣物。 (100 學測)

In an experiment conducted by animal scientists, elephants were first presented with clean clothing or clothing that had been worn for five days by _____ a Maasai _____ a Kamba man.

16. 這橄欖球隊員午餐不僅吃漢堡也吃了披薩。

This football player ate _____ .

17. Brendan 不是步行就是騎自行車上學。

Brendan goes to school _____ .

18. 人們所欣賞的不是你擁有的一切,而是你的為人。

What people admire is _____ .

19. 早起,那麼你就能搭到第一班公車。

_____

20. 不論她的父母是否贊成,Penelope 將會嫁給她的男友。

_____

TEST 5

4–1～4–6

一、選擇

( ) 1. Chloe's eyes are red; she _____ .
    (A) cannot have been sad   (B) may be hurt
    (C) must not have felt blue   (D) must have cried

( ) 2. Sheila had better _____ her books before they are due.
    (A) returned   (B) return   (C) to return   (D) returning

( ) 3. The bad-tempered man would rather _____ quarrels with his wife than _____ with her.
    (A) have; communicate   (B) having; communicating
    (C) to have; to communicate   (D) having; to communicate

( ) 4. The lady _____ yoga lessons before she sprained her ankle.
    (A) used to taking   (B) used to take
    (C) was used to taking   (D) was used to take

( ) 5. The victim's family asked that this murder case _____ investigated at once.
    (A) was   (B) would be   (C) be   (D) must be

( ) 6. Choose the WRONG sentence.
    (A) The hairdresser suggested that Lily perm her hair.
    (B) It is advisable that people should recycle used batteries.
    (C) It is natural for people to get raged when their opinions are ignored.
    (D) It is urgent that the storm-damaged tree is removed from the sidewalk.

二、句子合併與改寫

7. ⎰ The little girl brushes her teeth before going to bed every day.
  ⎱ Her mother asks her to do it.   (以 ask that . . . 合併)
➡ The little girl's mother _____ .

8. ⎰ The weak patient took medicine three times a day.
  ⎱ This is necessary.   (以 It is + adj. + that . . . 合併)
➡ _____

9. There was a tall tree standing in front of my house, but it's no longer there.

(以 used to 改寫)

➡ _____, but it's no longer there.

10. If the tired bus driver doesn't take a rest, an accident may happen.

(以 had better 改寫)

➡ _____; otherwise, an accident may happen.

三、填空題 (將括弧中的動詞改為正確形式，並填入空格中)

11. The man looked anxious. He must _____ (be looking) for something.

12. Most students are not used to _____ (solve) problems on their own; they always expect their teachers to give standard answers. (98 學測)

13. The police demanded that the diver _____ (present) his driver's license.

14. Keith prefers _____ (watch) baseball games to _____ (play) online games.

四、翻譯

15. 每個蟻巢以前只有一個蟻后，但是現在許多土堆被發現有多個蟻后同住。 (94 學測)

Each nest _____ but one queen, but now many mounds are often found with multiple queens.

16. Owen 總是考得很好。他一定有很好的讀書計畫。

Owen always does well on his exams. He _____

_____.

17. 那個超重的男人最好不要吃太多食物，不是嗎？

That overweight man _____?

18. 這個認真的學生寧願在圖書館讀書，也不要在家上網。

This diligent student would rather _____

_____.

19. 如果孩子們真的喜歡糖果，牙醫建議他們吃巧克力替代。 (96 學測)

If children really love candy, _____

_____.

20. 行人與汽車駕駛都應該遵守交通規則。 (. . . essential . . .)

_____

TEST 6

5-1～5-6

一、選擇

( ) 1. Government authorities usually undertake aggressive emergency control measures _____ an outbreak is detected. (93 指考)

(A) as far as　　(B) as short as　　(C) as well as　　(D) as soon as

( ) 2. Nowadays, people become _____ willing to give money to street beggars as there are _____ fake ones.

(A) little and little; many and many　　(B) fewer and fewer; less and less

(C) fewer and fewer; less and less　　(D) less and less; more and more

( ) 3. There is a long-held belief that when meeting someone, the more eye contact we have with the person, _____ . (100 學測)

(A) it is better　　(B) it is the better　　(C) the better　　(D) it is good

( ) 4. Jason collected _____ Gerald.

(A) half stamps as many as　　(B) more twice stamps than

(C) six times as many stamps as　　(D) three times more stamps as

( ) 5. Since the toilet has been leaking for a few days, Mom asks that Dad repair it _____ .

(A) as soon as possible　　(B) as quick as he can

(C) as fast as possibly　　(D) as early as is possible

( ) 6. In my opinion, _____ is as great as *the Miserables*.

(A) many other musicals　　(B) no other musical

(C) all the other musicals　　(D) every musical

二、句子合併與改寫

7. ｛ Iris solved this difficult math problem in a minute.
　　Rebecca also solved this math problem in a minute.　　(以 as + adv. + as 合併)

➡ Iris _____ .

8. If Bell spends little money on clothing, she can save much money.

(以 The . . . , the . . . 改寫)

➡ _____

9. As it snowed more heavily, it was more difficult for drivers to see clearly.
   (以 The . . . , the . . . 改寫)

➡ _____

10. The white box is 3kg, and the black box is 15kg. (以 the + N + of 改寫)

➡ The black box _____ the

white box.

11. Ian ate four bagels, and his brother ate one bagel. (以 as + adj. + N + as 改寫)

➡ Ian _____ his brother.

三、文意選填 (依照句意將正確字詞填入空格中，並做適當變化)

more and more   **so fast as**   **as much as**   **more interesting than**

12. The best-selling author travels _____ he could to seek inspiration for his fictions.

13. To Monica, no other museum is _____ the British Museum.

14. When a person suffers from disconnect anxiety, he or she may become _____
    uncomfortable once being unable to access the online world.

15. Apparently, a turtle doesn't swim _____ a shark.

四、翻譯

16. 有時候這可能像碰觸到聖人而立刻被治癒一樣簡單。 (92 學測)
    Sometimes this may be _____
    touching the holy man and being immediately healed.

17. 這些綠色短襪是那些紅色長襪的一半長。
    These green socks _____
    those red stockings.

18. 小說可能很接近現實，以致於它似乎像是今早發生在你身上的事情一樣真實。
    (91 指考)
    It (Fiction) can be so close to the truth that _____
    _____ that happened to you this morning.

19. 這貪婪的人擁有的越多，就渴望得越多。

_____

20. 台北 101 是那棟百貨的十倍高。

_____

TEST 7

6–1～6–6

一、選擇

( ) 1. This program is aimed at people _____ goal is to obtains skills certificates.

　　(A) who 　　　(B) whose 　　　(C) which 　　　(D) that

( ) 2. _____ take pride in being decisive often try their best to consider all the factors beforehand. (103 學測)

　　(A) One who 　　(B) He who 　　(C) Those who 　　(D) Whoever

( ) 3. Elaine has a large collection of stamps, _____.

　　(A) part of which are rare and valuable　(B) one of them costs a fortune

　　(C) and most of which are foreign ones　(D) all of which was issued in Taiwan

( ) 4. The House of Fabergé made approximately 50 Imperial Easter Eggs for Tsar Alexander III and his son Nicholas II until 1917 _____ the Russian revolution broke out. (104 指考)

　　(A) which 　　(B) that 　　(C) when 　　(D) , when

( ) 5. Please teach me _____ in your heart that makes you so generous. (97 學測)

　　(A) you need what 　　　　(B) what you have

　　(C) what that you need 　　　(D) what do you have

( ) 6. Whatever Jeff does for his girlfriend _____ not appreciated.

　　(A) are 　　　(B) is 　　　(C) have been 　　　(D) were

二、句子合併與改寫

7. ⎰ Mr. Bowell wonders if he should travel with his only son.
　 ⎱ His only son is a toddler. (以關係代名詞合併)

➡ _____

8. ⎰ Grandfather told us five stories last night.
　 ⎱ All of them were very interesting. (以關係代名詞合併)

➡ _____

9. ⎰ The superstar's die-hard fans gathered in front of the hotel.
　 ⎱ The superstar lived in the hotel. (以關係副詞合併)

➡ _____

10. The forgetful man always forgets the things which he has done.
    (以 . . . what . . . 改寫)

    ➡ _____

11. All of the pictures in this book are interesting. I am sure any one of them that you choose will interest the kids. (以複合關係代名詞 wh- + ever 改寫)

➡ All of the pictures in this book are interesting. I am sure _____

    _____ .

三、文意選填 (根據文意將正確字詞填入空格中，並做適當變化)

what   **whoever**   **which**   **whatever**   **where**

12. Adam bought many souvenirs, most of _____ were for his girlfriend.

13. _____ our teachers teach us can be applied to our daily lives.

14. The couple will dine in a restaurant _____ they can enjoy a romantic dinner.

15. _____ can't afford his or her tuition can apply for a scholarship offered by this charitable organization.

16. The spoiled child always gets _____ he wants.

四、翻譯

17. 這個金髮美女吸引了很多追求者，其中有許多是名人。

    This beautiful blonde attracts many suitors, _____

    _____ .

18. 雖然你的計畫看起來很好，你必須要實際些，並且考慮你確實能做的事。 (97 學測)

    Although your plans look good, you have to be realistic and consider _____

    _____ .

19. 想體驗在極地酷寒中過夜 (an overnight stay) 的人可以嘗試冰旅館——即是用冰蓋成的建築。 (102 指考)

    _____ in arctic-like cold

    may try the ice hotel—a building of frozen water.

20. 感恩節是美國人和家人團聚的假日。

    _____

TEST 8

7–1～7–7

一、選擇

( ) 1. It is not unusual to hear friends and family members talk about the _____ they have _____ the stress of everyday life and the efforts they make to control the events that cause stress. (92 學測)
    (A) hard times; with managing   (B) problem; for managing
    (C) difficulty; in managing   (D) troubles; on managing

( ) 2. While one person _____ playing seventy-two holes of golf a week, another would rather play three sweaty, competitive games of tennis. (95 學測)
    (A) expects   (B) enjoys   (C) decides   (D) needs

( ) 3. Many historic sites in this small town are _____.
    (A) worth being visited   (B) worthwhile to visit
    (C) worthy of visiting   (D) worth visiting

( ) 4. Lauren misses her grandmother so much that she looks forward to _____ her.
    (A) visit   (B) visiting   (C) visited   (D) visits

( ) 5. The keepers at the sanctuary use recorded howls to prevent the howler monkeys _____ getting homesick. (97 學測)
    (A) from   (B) for   (C) about   (D) by

( ) 6. With the worsening of global economic conditions, it seems wiser and more sensible to keep cash in the bank _____ to invest in the stock market. (98 學測)
    (A) as far as   (B) as long as   (C) instead of   (D) rather than

( ) 7. The humorous speaker's speech was so funny that everyone _____.
    (A) couldn't help nod his or her head
    (B) couldn't but showing approval
    (C) couldn't help laughing out loud
    (D) had no choice but show his or her agreement

二、句子合併與改寫

8. { Driving after drinking alcohol is dangerous.
    Everyone should avoid it. (以 avoid . . . 合併)

➡ _____ because it is dangerous.

9. It is difficult for the heavy smoker to quit smoking. (以 have problems 改寫)

➡ _____

10. The mother sheep looked around carefully so that her baby lambs wouldn't be attacked by lions. (以 protect . . . from 合併)

➡ _____

11. Elaine didn't get impatient. Instead, she explained the complicated theory to her students again. (以 Instead of . . . 改寫)

➡ _____

三、配合題

(　　) 12. Some people have trouble . . .

(　　) 13. I can't imagine . . .

(　　) 14. The customer service that this company provides is worthy . . .

(　　) 15. My grandfather, who lives in the country, is used to . . .

　　　(A) living in a world without electricity.

　　　(B) controlling their tempers.

　　　(C) getting up early.

　　　(D) of praise.

四、翻譯

16. 他們通常不經意說出不當的言論或是難以在對話中與人輪流 (take turns) 發言。

(96 指考)

They often blurt out inappropriate comments or _____

_____ turns in conversation.

17. 這投手的教練建議絕對不要過度練習而傷害手臂。

The coach of this pitcher suggests _____

_____ so much as to hurt his arm.

18. 降落傘必須被打開，因為它可以阻止太空梭下墜。(95 學測)

A parachute needs to be opened because _____

_____ .

19. 發現家裡有蟑螂，Miranda 忍不住大聲尖叫。

Finding a cockroach in her house, _____ .

20. 為什麼我們不要以改變計畫取代抱怨呢？

_____

TEST 9

8–1~8–6

一、選擇

( ) 1. Having witnessed a car accident, the frightened boy didn't know _____.

    (A) how to do   (B) what to do

    (C) whether should he dial 911   (D) what should he say

( ) 2. In the story, the soldiers fought _____ the battle.

    (A) too bravely to win   (B) enough bravely to win

    (C) bravely enough to win   (D) so bravely to win

( ) 3. What Kelly has to do before the mid-term exam is _____ all the lessons.

    (A) reviewing   (B) reviewed

    (C) having reviewed   (D) review

( ) 4. The bankruptcy of this businessman _____ with his extravagance.

    (A) is something to do   (B) has some to do

    (C) has something to do   (D) is a thing to do

( ) 5. Leon is so shy that he dare not speak to strangers, let alone _____ a girl out.

    (A) asking   (B) ask   (C) to ask   (D) asked

( ) 6. The mechanic can fix anything, _____.

    (A) not to speak of this broken bike

    (B) let alone this broken computer

    (C) much less repairing this broken machine

    (D) not to mention repair this broken chair

二、句子改寫

7. I wonder where I can find a post office nearby. (以 wh– + to V 改寫)

➡ _____

8. Emma worked very diligently. She got a promotion last week.

   (以 enough + to V 改寫)

➡ _____

9. The audience of this boring speech can do nothing but try to stay awake.

   (以 All . . . + is +V 改寫)

➡ _____

10. It is said that lung cancer is strongly related to heavy smoking.

(以 have . . . to do with 改寫)

➡ _____

三、文意選填 (根據文意將正確字詞填入空格中，並做適當變化)

to begin with   **strange to say**   **to be precise**   **to make matters worse**

11. Jason got up late this morning. _____, the bus he took bumped into a tree.

12. My brother heard some noise in the yard. _____, I didn't hear anything at all.

13. _____, we should take everyone's idea into consideration so that we can draw up a good plan.

四、翻譯

14. 直到同事教她怎麼做之後，新來的秘書才知道到怎麼印出文件。

The new secretary couldn't figure out _____

_____ until her colleague showed it to her.

15. William 不知道是否該向那位女士要電話。

William wonders _____ .

16. 這孩子希望他長大後夠富有，能幫父母蓋間豪宅。

The child hopes that when he grows up _____

_____ for his parents.

17. 一般人相信，產品的銷售和廣告很有關係。

It is generally believed that the sales of products _____

_____ .

18. Brad 正在追求 Angelina。他寫了好幾封情書給她，更不用說電子郵件。

Brad is chasing Angelina. He has written her several love letters, _____

_____ .

19. Tina 剛寄出履歷表到一家公司。所有她能做的事情就是等待面試的電話通知。

Tina just sent her resume to a company. _____

_____ an interview call.

20. 所有這個褓母必須做的事就是照顧好這對二歲的雙胞胎。

_____

TEST 10

9–1～9–5

一、選擇

( ) 1. I went to a nightclub in New York and watched the stage lights _____ up. (101 學測)

    (A) went   (B) go   (C) gone   (D) to go

( ) 2. Mrs. Smith was angry to _____ .

    (A) find her expensive vase breaks

    (B) find that her son left the water run in the bathroom

    (C) catch some students cheating on the exam

    (D) see that her husband kept his eyes close when she talked to him

( ) 3. _____ 1:42 minutes left in the game, Deborah's team led by one point. (100 學測)

    (A) By   (B) With   (C) For   (D) In

( ) 4. With more than 13 million children already _____ from classrooms by conflict, it is no exaggeration to say that the educational prospects of a generation of children are in the balance. (105 學測)

    (A) driven   (B) driving   (C) to drive   (D) drove

( ) 5. Kids learn through repetition, so it's not _____ that they are never _____ with the same stories.

    (A) disappointed; confusing   (B) disappointed; confused

    (C) surprised; boring   (D) surprising; bored

( ) 6. The student turned off the radio, _____ to do his English assignment.

    (A) he started   (B) starting   (C) and he starts   (D) and starting

二、句子合併與改寫

7. { Yellow leaves fall from trees in autumn.   (以 watch + O + OC 合併)
     I like to watch it.

➡ _____

8. { When Derek saw the charming girl, his heart beat fast.   (以 find + O + OC 合併)
     Derek found it.

➡ When Derek saw the charming girl, he _____

  _____ .

9. { Teddy does the same work every day.
   { This makes him feel tired.   (以 feel + adj. + prep 合併)

➡ _____

10. The frightened witness didn't tell many details to the police.
    (以 leave + O + OC 改寫)

➡ _____

11. Phil took a hot spring bath and he released the tension from work.
    (省略 and 與主詞)

➡ _____

三、填空題 (將括弧中的動詞改為正確的分詞形式，並填入空格中)

12. This _____ (trouble) adolescent boy feels _____ (confuse) about his future.

13. It (The area code) was created in the format of XYX, with X _____ (be) any number between 2–9 and Y _____ (be) either 1 or 0. (102 學測)

14. Instead of coming to help the injured man, these people looked on with their arms _____ (fold).

15. Kevin had been standing on a ladder _____ (try) to reach for a book on the top shelf when he lost his balance and fell to the ground. (103 學測)

四、翻譯

16. 這部關於抗癌鬥士的感人電影讓許多人都感動得流淚了。
    This _____ about a brave cancer patient's struggle moved many people to tears.

17. 孩子們和父母的飲食偏好一致，而且如果他們看見父母吃某種食物，他們比較可能嘗試。 (98 學測)
    Kids are tuned into their parents' eating preferences and are far more likely to try foods if they _____ .

18. Matilda 因為讓男友等了一個小時而向他道歉。
    Matilda apologized to her boyfriend for _____

    _____ .

19. 一個奇怪的男人在公園裡遊蕩，他的臉用黑色的布包裹著。 (. . . with + O + OC)
    A strange man wandered through the park _____

    _____ .

20. 那些街舞舞者正來回地舞動，學習新的舞步。 (S + V, V-ing)

_____

TEST 11
9–6～9–9

一、選擇

( ) 1. Among his later works, the most outstanding is *The Old Man and the Sea* (1952), which became perhaps his most famous book _____ him the Pulitzer Prize he had long been denied. (104 指考)
- (A) finally won
- (B) which finally won
- (C) finally winning
- (D) , finally winning

( ) 2. Snakes _____ during the dry season contained significantly less body water than those scooped up in the rainy season. (105 學測)
- (A) captured
- (B) that captured
- (C) having captured
- (D) capturing

( ) 3. _____ much time carefully studying the patient's symptoms, the doctor finally made his diagnosis. (97 指考)
- (A) Being spent
- (B) The doctor spending
- (C) After he spending
- (D) After spending

( ) 4. _____ of the predator approaching, the flock of birds flew away.
- (A) Having aware
- (B) Awareness
- (C) Aware
- (D) Been unaware

( ) 5. This gardener is busy moving the plants to new locations, his sleeves _____ up.
- (A) were rolled
- (B) were rolling
- (C) rolled
- (D) rolling

( ) 6. _____ I get the invitation, I will attend the party.
- (A) Provided that
- (B) Considered that
- (C) Supposed that
- (D) Judged from that

二、句子合併

7. { The man was sent to the hospital by ambulance.
   { He was bitten by a poisonous snake.
   (以 N + 分詞片語合併)

➡ _____

8. { The walls will be torn down in a month.
   { The walls surround the park.
   (以 N + 分詞片語合併)

➡ _____

9. { Abate was forced to quit school in fifth grade after his father died.
   { Abate worked as a shoe-shine boy for years.

(以分詞構句合併)

➡ _____ , Abate worked as a shoe-shine boy for years. (99 學測)

10. { Eric was disappointed at the midterm exam result.
      He decided to spend more time studying.   (以分詞構句合併)

➡ _____ , Eric decided to spend more time studying.

三、填空題 (將括弧中的動詞改為正確的分詞形式，並填入空格中)

11. The lady _____ (dress) in pink is going to attend a wedding.

12. New York, _____ (be) the largest city in the United States, was assigned the 212 area code, _____ (follow) by Los Angeles at 213. (102 學測)

13. _____ (motivate) by such signs of success, thousands of kids from the villages _____ (surround) Bekoji have moved into town. (99 學測)

14. It _____ (snow) heavily, all the drivers had to drive with extra attention.

15. Generally _____ (speak), babies cry when they have hunger, pain or need help.

四、翻譯

16. 另一個使 (contribute to) 跑者邁向成功的重要因素就是一雙合適的跑鞋。 (104 指考)

    Another important factor _____

    _____ success is a suitable pair of running shoes.

17. 這二個名字被刪除均是因為以它們為名 (bear the names) 的颱風引起了嚴重災害。

    The deletion of both names was due to the severe damage _____ by the typhoons

    _____ the names. (101 學測)

18. 聽到她的兄弟在意外中沒受傷，Helen 鬆了一口氣。 (101 學測)

    Helen let out a sigh of relief after _____

    _____ .

19. Judy 正沿著河岸騎腳踏車，她的頭髮在風中飄。

    Judy is riding a bicycle along the bank, her hair _____

    _____ .

20. 大略地說，這位脫口秀主持人已經訪問過 50 位來賓。

    _____

TEST 12

10–1～10–4

一、選擇

( ) 1. The ancient civilizations would not be so deeply admired today if these ancient artifacts _____ not so widely available to an international public in major museums throughout Europe and America. (93 學測)

    (A) are   (B) were   (C) had   (D) had been

( ) 2. If Victor _____ to bed early, he would not have slept late this morning.

    (A) went   (B) had gone   (C) goes   (D) didn't go

( ) 3. If _____ trees, what would happen?

    (A) there are no   (B) there had been no

    (C) we didn't have   (D) we had had no

( ) 4. If Beth _____ so many lies before, she _____ our trust now.

    (A) didn't tell; may still have

    (B) shouldn't have told; might still have had

    (C) had not told; would still have

    (D) didn't tell; will still have

( ) 5. If the child _____ so many sweet things, his teeth _____.

    (A) hadn't eaten; wouldn't have been decayed

    (B) didn't eat; will not decay

    (C) had eaten; will not be decayed

    (D) hadn't eaten; would have been decayed

( ) 6. If the rain _____ for a week, the outdoor concert may have to be cancelled.

    (A) should continue   (B) were to continue

    (C) will continue   (D) has continued

( ) 7. _____ our order, we would not have got the wrong side dishes.

    (A) Were the waiter careful about   (B) Has the waiter had a good memory

    (C) Should the waiter verify   (D) Had the waiter written down

二、句子改寫 (以假設語氣的句型改寫下列各句)

8. There is Wi-Fi connection here in the library, so I can access the Internet.

➡ _____

9. Mom forgot to put the milk into the refrigerator, so it went sour.

➡ _____

10. Thomas Edison's mother educated him, so he became a great inventor.

➡ If _____.

11. It is impossible that the Earth will stop moving around the sun, so we have four seasons.

➡ If _____.

三、配合題

( ) 12. If Mr. and Mrs. Jefferson had children, . . .

( ) 13. If the athlete had done warm-up before the game, . . .

( ) 14. If your computer should be broken, . . .

( ) 15. Were this machine more user-friendly, . . .

    (A) they wouldn't feel lonely most of the time.

    (B) it would attract more customers.

    (C) you could use mine.

    (D) he would not have sprained his ankle.

四、翻譯

16. 萬一你需要任何更進一步的資訊，請別猶豫聯絡我。

_____ need any further information, please don't hesitate to contact me.

17. 如果長頸鹿沒有長脖子，牠們就不能吃到高高在樹上的葉子。

_____

18. 如果昨晚有月光，這些露營的人在夜晚就能有較好的視線。

_____

19. 如果老師沒有講解這個科學理論，這些學生就無法瞭解。

_____

20. 萬一棒球比賽的票售完了，Mike 將必須在電視上看比賽。

_____, Mike will have to watch the game on TV.

TEST 13

10–5～10–9

一、選擇

( ) 1. _____ the cat eye reflectors, many accidents might happen.
　　(A) If it is not for 　　　　　　(B) If there were not for
　　(C) Had it not been for 　　　　(D) Were it not for

( ) 2. Mr. Anderson _____ off; however, he worked hard and got promoted eventually.
　　(A) would be laid 　　　　　　(B) might have been laid
　　(C) could lay 　　　　　　　　(D) ought not to have been laid

( ) 3. The boy wishes he _____ tall enough to enter the school basketball team.
　　(A) were 　　　(B) was 　　　(C) is 　　　(D) would be

( ) 4. The lonely man wishes that his children _____ with him instead of moving to other cities.
　　(A) stay 　　　　　　　　　　(B) could stay
　　(C) will stay 　　　　　　　　(D) might have stayed

( ) 5. Larry talked as if he _____ the test results before the teacher's announcement.
　　(A) would have known 　　　　(B) has known
　　(C) knew 　　　　　　　　　　(D) had known

( ) 6. It is time that Alison _____ to think about her future.
　　(A) begins 　　(B) should start 　　(C) began 　　(D) will start

二、句子改寫 (根據提示改寫下列各句)

7. Chip drank some coffee, so he didn't fall asleep at work. (以假設語氣的句型改寫)
➡ If it _____.

8. The speaker couldn't finish his speech in time, because he was interrupted by several questions of the audience. (以 could + have p.p. 改寫)
➡ The speaker was interrupted by several questions of the audience; otherwise, _____
_____.

9. Debbie would like to start her own business, but she hasn't saved enough money.
➡ Debbie wishes that _____,
but she hasn't saved enough money.

10. It is time for the government to take action against poaching.

(以 It is time that . . . 改寫)

➡ _____

三、配合題

( ) 11. Had it not been for his determination and perseverance in learning dancing, . . .

( ) 12. Jenny should have left on Monday, but . . .

( ) 13. The hungry student wishes that . . .

( ) 14. The man walked . . .

    (A) as if he were drunk.

    (B) she deferred her departure for three days.

    (C) Lin Hwai-min might not have achieved such success.

    (D) he had eaten breakfast before the class.

四、翻譯

15. 若非有良好的時間管理，這個團隊本來無法完成這項計畫。

_____ good time management, this team _____ not _____

_____ the project.

= _____ good time management, this team _____ not _____

_____ the project.

16. Penelope 的歷史本來不會被當掉，但是她期中考的成績太差了。

Penelope _____ history,

but she did too poorly on her midterm exam.

17. 但願我瞭解我的寵物在想什麼。

_____ I _____ what is on my pet's mind.

18. 要不是有這些樹，城市裡的空氣品質會更糟。

_____, the air quality in

the city _____.

19. 這老婦人說起話來彷彿她年輕時曾去過歐洲。

_____ when she was

young.

20. 該是你改變讀書習慣的時候了。

_____

TEST 14

11-1~11-4

一、選擇

( ) 1. Since then, *World Hello Day*－November 21st of every year－＿＿＿＿ by people in 180 countries. (101 學測)
   (A) is observed   (B) has been observed
   (C) was observed   (D) had observed

( ) 2. The museum ＿＿＿＿ until the refurbishment is completed.
   (A) will reopen   (B) must reopen
   (C) won't reopen   (D) should have reopened

( ) 3. It was ＿＿＿＿ that the little girl started to feel sleepy.
   (A) her mother tucked her in   (B) not until her mother tucked her in
   (C) did her mother tuck her in   (D) until her mother tucked her in

( ) 4. ＿＿＿＿ Carter's parents saw his exam results, they smiled.
   (A) No sooner had   (B) One minute   (C) Upon   (D) As soon as

( ) 5. By the time Sion retires, he ＿＿＿＿ for this company for 20 years.
   (A) will have worked   (B) has worked
   (C) will be working   (D) has been working

二、句子改寫 (根據提示改寫下列各句)

6. Mr. Wang lost his job, so his family is living a poor life.
➡ Since Mr. Wang lost his job, ＿＿＿＿＿＿＿＿＿＿＿＿＿＿＿.

7. The poet didn't finish his poem until he drew inspiration from a walk in the woods.
➡ Not until ＿＿＿＿＿＿＿＿＿＿＿＿＿＿＿.

8. The moment the mountaineer reached the mountain top, he took a deep breath.
➡ Upon ＿＿＿＿＿＿＿＿＿＿＿＿＿＿＿.
➡ No sooner ＿＿＿＿＿＿＿＿＿＿＿＿＿＿＿.

9. When Grandmother heard the phone ring, she picked it up right away.
   (As soon as . . .)
➡ ＿＿＿＿＿＿＿＿＿＿＿＿＿＿＿

10. When the artist saw the beautiful scene, he immediately decided to paint it.
   (no sooner . . . than)

➡ _____

三、配合題

(   ) 11. Since my brother finished his homework, . . .

(   ) 12. It was not until the poor boy got financial aids from an anonymous man . . .

(   ) 13. The minute the teacher entered the classroom, . . .

(   ) 14. By the time Samantha hurried to the station, . . .

  (A) he has been watching TV.

  (B) the train had left.

  (C) that he could go on with his studies.

  (D) the students stopped talking.

四、翻譯

15. 疫情一被偵測到，政府當局通常會採取積極的控制措施。 (93 指考)

   Government authorities usually undertake aggressive emergency control measures
   _____ an outbreak is detected.

16. 直到 Jerry 聽 Mary 的自我介紹才認出她是他的小學同學。 (99 學測)

   Jerry _____ recognize his primary school classmate Mary _____ he listened to
   her self-introduction.

17. 這是她自從五歲起就一直懷抱的夢想。 (100 學測)

   It was something she _____ of _____ she was five.

18. 直到手術結束這病人才能吃喝東西。

   The patient _____ until
   his operation is finished.

19. 自從希臘羅馬時代開始， 松露 (truffles) 在歐洲就一直被使用作美食 ， 甚至是藥品。
   (100 指考)

   _____ the times of the Greeks and Romans, _____
   _____ .

20. 在音樂劇開始之前，所有的演員將已經排演好幾次了。

   _____

TEST 15

12–1～12–4

一、選擇

( ) 1. _____ the man retired on a generous pension, he spent it all within a year.

    (A) In spite of   (B) As soon as   (C) Even though   (D) Even if

( ) 2. _____ the terrible smell of durians, quite a few people like them.

    (A) Despite   (B) Through   (C) Besides   (D) Unlike

( ) 3. _____ you go, there are buildings in Romanic, Baroque, and Rococo styles that were popular hundreds of years ago. (97 學測)

    (A) Since   (B) Before   (C) Whatever   (D) Wherever

( ) 4. _____ as Teresa was, she couldn't help laughing when seeing her son making silly faces.

    (A) An angry mother   (B) Anger

    (C) Angrily   (D) Angry

二、句子改寫

5. Even though Ivy worked out regularly, she still gained some weight.

    (以 Despite . . . 改寫)

➡ _____

6. Although fuel costs are lower, airfares have been rising recently.

    (以 In spite of . . . 改寫)

➡ _____, airfares have been rising recently.

7. No matter how busy the teacher is, she is always patient with her students.

    (以 -ever . . . 改寫)

➡ _____

8. No matter which team wins the game, we will cheer for the players. (-ever . . .)

➡ _____

9. Whenever the dogs find this odor, they dig into the ground. (No matter . . .)

➡ _____

10. Although extreme sports are risky, many people enjoy them. (以 . . . as . . . 改寫)

➡ _____

三、句子重組

11. languages/Ian/major in/his interest/computer science/in/in spite of/decided to/in college

_____

12. nobody/said/believed/the strange man/him/whatever

_____

13. William/is/an unhappy childhood/had/he/comedian/as

_____

14. admit/the arrogant woman/a mistake/she/makes/won't/it/even if

_____

四、翻譯

15. 儘管有身體的缺陷，這年輕的盲人鋼琴家仍設法要克服所有的阻礙以贏得國際賽的冠軍。 (100 指考)

_____ her physical disability, the young blind pianist managed to overcome all obstacles to win the first prize in the international contest.

16. 雖然城市的生活比較方便，外婆仍然比較喜歡住在鄉下。

_____ the fact _____ living in the city is more convenient, Grandmother prefers living in the country.

17. 她每次感冒都必須住院三週。 (104 學測)

She had to be hospitalized for three weeks _____ she had a cold.

18. 即使我們已經將廣播的聲音轉小，我弟弟仍然無法專心唸書。

My brother can't concentrate on his studies _____

_____ .

19. 即使 Jimmy 清洗和仔細擦亮他的車，它也不會看起來像新的。

_____ , it won't look like a new one.

20. 不論他們多努力嘗試，都無法改變 Johnny 的心意。

_____

TEST 16

13–1～13–6

一、選擇

( ) 1. The airport was closed _____, and our departure for Paris had to be delayed until the following day. (104 學測)
   (A) because the bad weather　　　(B) because of the snowstorm
   (C) due to it snowed heavily　　　(D) owing to a typhoon approached

( ) 2. I was worried about my first overseas trip, but my father assured me that he would help plan the trip _____ nothing would go wrong. (104 學測)
   (A) in order to　　　　　　　(B) so that
   (C) so as to　　　　　　　　(D) for the purpose of

( ) 3. The marathon runner drank much water lest he _____ quickly.
   (A) dehydrate　　　　　　　(B) dehydrates
   (C) would have dehydrated　　(D) had dehydrated

( ) 4. The movie was _____ popular that many people came to the naive conclusion that it must be good; however, many professional critics thought otherwise. (104 指考)
   (A) that　　　(B) too　　　(C) very　　　(D) so

( ) 5. As long as Helena _____ the recipe, she can bake a delicious cake.
   (A) will follow　　(B) had followed　　(C) follow　　(D) follows

( ) 6. Jason is _____ an optimist that he always believes that good things will happen.
   (A) really　　　(B) so　　　(C) such　　　(D) what

二、句子改寫

7. The boy creates a study schedule so as not to fail the final exams.
   (以 . . . lest . . . 改寫)
   ➡ _____

8. Lucas was suspended from school because he was involved in street fights.
   (以 because of 改寫)
   ➡ _____

9. The vendor raised her voice in order to be heard. (以 . . . so that . . . 改寫)
   ➡ _____

10. It is such a hot day that I can't help drinking much ice water.

(以 so . . . that . . . 改寫)

➡ _____

三、文意選填 (依照句意將正確字詞填入空格中，並做適當變化)

for fear of	because of	in order to	as long as	now that

11. The student decided to study harder _____ keep up with his peers academically.

12. The secretary has checked the document several times _____ mistakes.

13. The street performances will continue _____ the weather is fine.

14. _____ the rain has stopped, we can go picnicking.

15. Many factories have been shut down _____ economic recession.

四、翻譯

16. 古時候，人們在戶外典禮中用大貝殼來擴大聲音，以便四面八方的部落居民都能聽到。

(104 指考)

In ancient times, people used large shells to amplify voices in open-air ceremonies _____ their tribal members near and far could hear what was said.

17. 由於管理不善，這家公司正面臨嚴重的財務危機。

_____, this company is facing serious financial crisis.

18. Jessica 在雨中小心開車，以免撞上大樹。

Jessica drove carefully in the rain _____

_____ .

19. 既然王氏夫婦已經退休，他們能夠盡可能到很多地方旅行。

_____, they can travel to as many places as they can.

20. Teddy 將信封黏好 (seal) 以免他的信被其他人讀到。

_____

TEST 17

14-1～14-6

一、選擇

( ) 1. The child is sleeping soundly. The noise _____ her at all.
  (A) bothered (B) has bothered (C) not bother (D) didn't bother

( ) 2. The world-famous magician never performs _____ making his audience amazed.
  (A) without (B) and (C) but (D) that

( ) 3. What you said sounds reasonable. I can't agree with you _____.
  (A) a lot (B) much (C) more (D) anymore

( ) 4. Adam is a reliable man. _____
  (A) He never makes a promise without breaking it.
  (B) You can't trust him too much.
  (C) It is impossible for us to believe what he says.
  (D) We can't trust him anymore.

( ) 5. Lydia is selfish. She is the _____ person to give us a hand.
  (A) latest (B) least (C) last (D) unlikely

( ) 6. _____, birds of a feather flock together.
  (A) There is no need to say (B) Needless to say
  (C) It goes without saying (D) It is needless to say

( ) 7. Stress is a state _____ to be kept under full control. (95 學測)
  (A) very complicated (B) too complicated
  (C) so complicated (D) really complicated

二、句子改寫

8. Every time Rita tells lies, she stutters. (以 never . . . without . . . 改寫)

➡ _____

9. The sick girl ran slowly. She couldn't keep up with her classmates.
  (以 too . . . to 改寫)

➡ _____

10. To attract young customers, it is important for the designer to be creative in designing his new products. (以 can't + be + too + adj. 的句型改寫)

➡ To attract young customers, _____ .

11. It is impossible for this shy girl to wear bikinis. (以 the last + N 改寫)

➡ _____

三、配合題

(   ) 12. These die-hard fans never . . .

(   ) 13. Oliver can't study too hard . . .

(   ) 14. The self-centered woman doesn't . . .

(   ) 15. Money is the last thing . . .

     (A) that this poor couple can offer.

     (B) see their idol without screaming excitedly.

     (C) in order to pass the exam.

     (D) care about others' feelings at all.

四、翻譯

16. 我每次遇到 Peter 都看見他在用手機。

   I never meet Peter _____ .

17. 為了創造出一個鉅作，這個建築師再專心於設計也不為過。

   In order to create a masterpiece, the architect _____ be _____ devoted to his design.

   = In order to create a masterpiece, the architect _____ be devoted _____ to his design.

18. 寫作業是這個小女孩最不想做的事。

   Doing homework is _____ .

19. 不用說，天助自助者。

   _____

20. 這正在等待工作面試的男人覺得太焦慮而無法吃下任何東西。

   _____

TEST 18

15–1～15–4

一、選擇

( ) 1. On the roof _____ several birds.

    (A) is   (B) have   (C) are   (D) are resting

( ) 2. Little _____ her ex-boyfriend, for she was once hurt deeply.

    (A) Karen thinks of   (B) Karen has written to

    (C) talks Karen about   (D) does Karen mention

( ) 3. My grandfather often exercises in the park. Not only _____ walks, but he also does some Tai-chi there.

    (A) he takes   (B) does he take   (C) takes he   (D) he does take

( ) 4. Not until this hungry woman felt full _____ eating.

    (A) she stopped   (B) that she stopped   (C) did she stop   (D) stopped she

二、句子改寫 (根據提示改寫下列各句)

5. Situated in a remote mountain area, this village is seldom visited by tourists.

➡ Because this village is situated in a remote mountain area, seldom _____

_____ .

6. The color red can not only draw people's attention but also make people feel warm.

➡ Not only _____ .

7. Numerous mysterious fairy circles lie in the desert of northwest Australia.

➡ In the desert of northwest Australia _____ .

8. Mr. Franklin didn't retire until he was 65.

➡ Not until _____ .

三、填空題 (根據文意與句型，在空格中填入 be 動詞或助動詞，並做適當變化)

9. Rarely _____ the diligent secretary complain about her work.

10. Not only _____ the audience give the conductor and the musicians thunderous applause, but they also stood up to show their respect.

11. On the road _____ a broken scooter and two injured pedestrians.

12. Not until the teacher reminded Nicole _____ she aware of her spelling mistakes.

13. Peter always treats his friends generously; by no means _____ he a stingy man.

四、翻譯

14. 在耶誕樹下有好多要給孩子們的禮物。

    Under the Christmas tree _____ for the children.

15. 玫瑰不只漂亮，也很香。

    _____ roses beautiful, but they are also fragrant.

16. 這款車不只便宜開起來又舒服。

    Not only _____.

17. 在任何情況下，政府官員都不應該收賄。

    Under no circumstances _____.

18. 直到這男人與我說話，我才注意到他的英國腔調。

    Not until _____.

19. 直到天黑我們才能看清楚月亮。

    Not until _____.

20. 這個決定對 Mandy 而言太困難了。她從未如此困惑過。 (. . . . Never . . .)

    _____

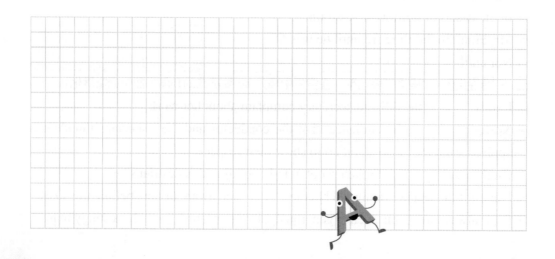

TEST 19

15–5～15–8

一、選擇

( ) 1. _____ the mother changed her baby's diaper than he stopped crying.

    (A) No sooner had   (B) As soon as   (C) Scarcely had   (D) Hardly had

( ) 2. My father enjoys taking a walk after dinner, _____ Lucy's.

    (A) and so enjoys   (B) nor has   (C) and neither does (D) and so does

( ) 3. Only by exercising your mind often _____ it sharp.

    (A) you can keep   (B) can you keep   (C) do you keep   (D) keep you

( ) 4. So hilarious _____ the story that we all burst into laughter.

    (A) did   (B) was   (C) sounded   (D) were

( ) 5. Such _____ Alexander's determination that nothing can stop him from realizing his dream.

    (A) did   (B) was   (C) is   (D) has

二、句子改寫 (根據提示改寫下列各句)

6. Owls catch their prey with their strong hooked bills, and hawks do, too.

   (以 . . . , and so . . . 改寫)

➡ _____

7. Nina can't speak English fluently, and her husband can't, either.

   (以 . . . nor . . . 改寫)

➡ _____

8. As soon as Hamlet found what his uncle had done, he decided to take revenge on him.

➡ Hardly had _____ .

9. Wisdom can be gained only through experience and challenges.

➡ Only _____ .

10. Miriam is so stubborn that no one wants to work with her.

➡ So _____ .

三、填空題 (根據文意與句型，在空格中填入 be 動詞或助動詞，並做適當變化)

11. Elephants are mammals, and so _____ whales.

12. You should not talk back to your parents, and neither _____ you shout at them.

13. No sooner _____ Lance smelled the odor of sweaty feet than he felt like

throwing up.

14. Only after the fierce earthquake happened _____ the villagers decide to move to a new place.

15. So thrilling _____ the roller coasters that many passengers cannot help screaming.

四、翻譯

16. 我的祖母沒去過日本，我祖父也沒去過。

My grandmother _____ been to Japan, and neither _____ my grandfather.

17. 健康不是你能買到的東西，也不是你快速就診就能重得的。 (95 學測)

Good health is not something you are able to buy, _____ can you get it back with a quick visit to a doctor.

18. 只有藉由毅力和堅強的決心，你才能達成目標。

Only with perseverance and strong determination _____

_____ .

19. 老闆一進到辦公室，他的手機就響了。 (No sooner . . .)

_____ than his cell phone rang.

20. Janet 很有條理 (organized)，以致於她總是能及時完成工作。 (So . . .)

_____

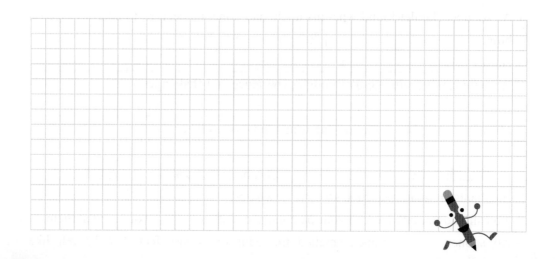

TEST 20

16-1～16-4

一、選擇

( ) 1. European politicians are trying to get the UK Government _____ cigarette companies _____ photos on the packets. (94 學測)

(A) make; printed　(B) to make ; print　(C) to have; to print　(D) have; printing

( ) 2. The Japanese _____ packaging a symbol of quality. (95 指考)

(A) view　　(B) take　　(C) consider　　(D) look upon

( ) 3. After 11 years of work, the final section of the road was completed in 1932. The road is _____ an engineering feat. (97 學測)

(A) considered　(B) taken　(C) looked as　(D) referred to

( ) 4. Jessica shares her itinerary with us. Her trip _____.

(A) looks interesting　　　　(B) sounds a tour

(C) sounds like fun　　　　(D) looks like bad

( ) 5. _____ a wonderful gift you have chosen for Zoe!

(A) How　　(B) Such　　(C) So　　(D) What

( ) 6. The girls _____ clean the mess they had made in the kitchen.

(A) were let to　(B) were made to　(C) were got to　(D) were had to

二、改錯 (挑出錯誤選項並改正，將答案寫於空格中。)

7. Kareem (A) got his forest grow (B) naturally, without (C) using fertilizers or insecticides. (105 學測)

8. Mom was (A) surprised (B) to find that the cake she baked tasted (C) brick.

9. This (A) monumental statue is often (B) regarded (C) a national symbol symbol of Egypt. (105 指考)

10. Sophia (A) has her daughter (B) to wash the dishes (C) three times a week.

11. (A) What dangerous (B) it is (C) to take selfies at the edge of a cliff!

7. ( ) _____　　8. ( ) _____　　9. ( ) _____　　10. ( ) _____　　11. ( ) _____

三、配合題

( ) 12. And how good a magic sword would feel in our hand . . . (91 學測)

( ) 13. Type-A people are generally considered . . . (105 學測)

( ) 14. The bullies are made . . .

(   ) 15. Father had our broken roof . . .

    (A) to apologize to all the victims.

    (B) as we go off to kill a dragon or win the hand of a beautiful princess.

    (C) sensitive perfectionists and good team players, but over-anxious.

    (D) fixed before the heavy rain.

四、翻譯

16. Brad 想到的主意多麼好啊！

_____ Brad has come up

with!

17. 這些學生多麼有創意啊！

_____

18. 在 1600 年中期，英國的有錢人認為用叉子用餐很時尚 (fashionable)。 (101 學測)

By the mid 1600s, eating with forks _____

_____ among the wealthy British.

19. Matilda 讓她兒子聽英文廣播以增進英文聽力技巧。 (. . . have . . .)

_____ to improve his

English listening skills.

20. 那個戴眼鏡拿著幾本書的男人看起來知識淵博 (knowledgeable)。

_____

TEST 1

一、選擇

1. B　2. D　3. C　4. D　5. B　6. A

二、填空題

7. Some; others　8. some of them; the others

9. Some of them; the others　10. Some; Others

11. other

三、句子改寫

12. a musician of talent

13. The surgeon performed the delicate operation with great care.

14. To Joshua's relief, his lost laptop was sent to the lost-and-found.

15. Much to everyone's disappointment, the two presidential candidates severely criticize each other.

四、翻譯

16. of great importance

17. drinking some ice tea is of much help

18. many words of wisdom

19. this salesperson has to travel from place to place

20. Much to many customers' satisfaction

TEST 2

一、選擇

1. B　2. A　3. C　4. C　5. D

二、句子合併與改寫

6. The doctor thinks it important for his patients to follow his prescriptions.

7. It is important that parents should not leave their children alone at home.

8. It seems that the old man needs a hearing aid.

9. The singer's marriage seems to have received extensive media coverage.

10. It is said that salt water helps cure a sore throat./People say that salt water helps cure a sore throat./Salt water is said to help cure a sore throat.

三、填空題

11. It　12. for　13. it　14. of　15. to

四、翻譯

16. It is hard to control

17. It seems that men are slightly happier

18. that her visitors should take off their shoes

19. have been a victim of bullying

20. It is said that the Japanese firmly believe

TEST 3

一、選擇

1. D　2. A　3. B　4. B　5. C

二、句子合併與改寫

6. It occurred to the tourist that he should buy some souvenirs before he left this country.

7. It struck the clerk that the sports shoes were out of stock.

8. There are many tall trees covered in snow in the mountain.

9. It was the dog's barking that disturbed Joseph's sleep last night.

三、配合題

10. E　11. C　12. B　13. A　14. D

四、翻譯

15. Has it ever occurred to/struck you

16. flashed through the naughty child's mind

17. it is the recording industry that

18. It was Columbus that discovered America in 1492.

19. no use complaining about the service in this restaurant.

20. some spelling mistakes in Janet's composition marked by the teacher.

TEST 4

一、選擇

1. D　2. B　3. A　4. C　5. D　6. B　7. C

8. C

二、句子合併與改寫

9. Tommy not only is good at roller-skating but also plays tennis well.

10. Wendy ate neither toast and butter nor cereal for breakfast.

11. Customers in this shopping mall can pay either by credit card or in cash.

12. the policemen but the detective discovered the evidence of the crime.

三、句子重組

13. What we can learn from Anne Frank is not only courage but also optimism.

14. Whether actors like it or not, they have to follow scripts.

四、翻譯

15. either; or

16. not only hamburgers but also pizza for lunch

17. either on foot or by bicycle

18. not what you have but what you are

19. Get up early, and you can catch the first bus.

20. Whether her parents approve of it or not, Penelope will marry her boyfriend.

TEST 5

一、選擇

1. D   2. B   3. A   4. B   5. C   6. D

二、句子合併與改寫

7. asks that she brush her teeth before going to bed every day

8. It is necessary that the patient (should) take medicine three times a day.

9. There used to be a tall tree standing in front of my house

10. The tired bus driver had better take a rest

三、填空題

11. have been looking

12. solving

13. present

14. watching; playing

四、翻譯

15. used to have

16. must have good study plans

17. had better not eat too much food, had he

18. study in the library than surf the Internet at home

19. dentists recommend that they (should) eat chocolate instead

20. It is essential that both pedestrians and motorists (should) follow traffic rules.

TEST 6

一、選擇

1. D   2. D   3. C   4. C   5. A   6. B

二、句子合併與改寫

7. solved this difficult math problem as quickly as Rebecca

8. The less (money) Bell spends on clothing, the more (money) she can save.

9. The more heavily it snowed, the more difficult it was for drivers to see clearly.

10. is five times the weight of

11. ate four times as many bagels as

三、文意選填

12. as much as

13. more interesting than

14. more and more

15. so fast as

四、翻譯

16. as simple as

17. are half the length of

18. it seems as real as something

19. The more this greedy man has, the more he desires.

20. Taipei 101 is ten times the height of/as tall as/taller than that department store.

TEST 7

一、選擇

1. B   2. C   3. A   4. D   5. B   6. B

二、句子合併與改寫

7. Mr. Bowell wonders if he should travel with his only son, who is a toddler.

8. Grandfather told us five stories last night, all of which were very interesting.

9. The superstar's die-hard fans gathered in front of the hotel where he/she lived.

10. The forgetful man always forgets what he has done.

11. whichever you choose will interest the kids

三、文意選填

12. which   13. What   14. where   15. Whoever

16. whatever

四、翻譯

17. many of whom are celebrities

18. what you can actually do

19. People who want to experience an overnight stay

20. Thanksgiving is a holiday when (= on which) Americans gather with their families.

TEST 8

一、選擇

1. C   2. B   3. D   4. B   5. A   6. D   7. C

二、句子合併與改寫

8. Everyone should avoid driving after drinking alcohol

9. The heavy smoker has problems quitting smoking.
10. The mother sheep looked around carefully to protect her baby lambs from being attacked by lions.
11. Instead of getting impatient, Elaine explained the complicated theory to her students again.

三、配合題
12. B   13. A   14. D   15. C

四、翻譯
16. have difficulty taking
17. never practicing
18. it can stop the shuttle from falling
19. Miranda couldn't help but scream/screaming loudly
20. Why don't we change our plans instead of complaining?

TEST 9

一、選擇
1. B   2. C   3. D   4. C   5. B   6. A

二、句子改寫
7. I wonder where to find a post office nearby.
8. Emma worked diligently enough to get a promotion last week.
9. All the audience of this boring speech can do is try to stay awake
10. It is said that lung cancer has much to do with heavy smoking.

三、文意選填
11. To make matters worse
12. Strange to say
13. To begin with

四、翻譯
14. how to print out the document
15. whether to ask for the lady's phone number
16. he can be wealthy enough to build a mansion
17. have much to do with advertising
18. not to mention/not to speak of/to say nothing of emails
19. All she can do is (to) wait for
20. All this babysitter has to do is (to) take good care of the 2–year-old twins.

TEST 10

一、選擇

1. B   2. C   3. B   4. A   5. D   6. B

二、句子合併與改寫
7. I like to watch yellow leaves fall from trees in autumn.
8. found his heart beating fast
9. Teddy feels tired of doing the same work every day.
10. The frightened witness left many details untold to the police.
11. Phil took a hot spring bath, releasing the tension from work.

三、填空題
12. troubled; confused
13. being; being
14. folded
15. trying

四、翻譯
16. touching movie
17. see their mother or father eating them
18. having kept him waiting for an hour
19. with his face covered in black cloth
20. Those street dancers are moving back and forth, learning new dance moves.

TEST 11

一、選擇
1. D   2. A   3. D   4. C   5. C   6. A

二、句子合併
7. The man bitten by a poisonous snake was sent to the hospital by ambulance.
8. The walls surrounding the park will be torn down in a month.
9. Forced to quit school in fifth grade after his father died
10. (Being) Disappointed at the midterm exam result

三、填空題
11. dressed
12. being; followed
13. Motivated; surrounding
14. snowing
15. speaking

四、翻譯
16. contributing to
17. caused; bearing
18. hearing that her brother was not injured in the

accident

19. blowing in the wind

20. Roughly speaking, the talk show host has interviewed 50 guests.

TEST 12

一、選擇

1. B   2. B   3. C   4. C   5. A   6. A   7. D

二、句子改寫

8. If there were no Wi-Fi connection here in the library, I could not access the Internet.

9. If Mom had not forgotten to put the milk into the refrigerator, it would not have gone sour.

10. Thomas Edison's mother hadn't educated him, he might not have become a great inventor

11. the Earth were to stop moving around the sun, we would not have four seasons

三、配合題

12. A   13. D   14. C   15. B

四、翻譯

16. Should you

17. If giraffes didn't have long necks, they couldn't reach leaves high in trees.

18. If there had been moonlight last night, these campers could have had better sight at night.

19. If the teacher hadn't explained this scientific theory, these students could not have understood it.

20. If the tickets to the baseball game should be sold out/Should the tickets to the baseball game be sold out

TEST 13

一、選擇

1. D   2. B   3. A   4. B   5. D   6. C

二、句子改寫

7. had not been for the coffee, Chip would have fallen asleep at work

8. he could have finished his speech in time

9. she could start her own business

10. It is time that the government took action against poaching.

三、配合題

11. C   12. B   13. D   14. A

四、翻譯

15. But for; could; have finished; Without; could;

have finished

16. would not have flunked

17. I wish/If only/Would that; knew

18. If it were not for these trees/Were it not for these trees; would be worse

19. The old lady talked as if she had been to Europe

20. It is time for you to change your study habits./It is time that you changed your study habits.

TEST 14

一、選擇

1. B   2. C   3. B   4. D   5. A

二、句子改寫

6. his family has been living a poor life

7. the poet drew inspiration from a walk in the woods did he finish his poem

8. reaching the mountain top, the mountaineer took a deep breath; had the mountaineer reached the mountain top than he took a deep breath

9. As soon as Grandmother heard the phone ring, she picked it up.

10. The artist had no sooner seen the beautiful scene than he decided to paint it.

三、配合題

11. A   12. C   13. D   14. B

四、翻譯

15. as soon as

16. didn't; until

17. had dreamed; since

18. can't eat nor drink

19. Since; truffles have been used in Europe as delicacies and even as medicines

20. By the time the musical begins, all the actors and actresses will have rehearsed several times.

TEST 15

一、選擇

1. C   2. A   3. D   4. D

二、句子改寫

5. Despite working out regularly, Ivy still gained some weight.

6. In spite of lower fuel costs

7. However busy the teacher is, she is always patient with her students.

8. Whichever team wins the game, we will cheer for the players.
9. No matter when the dogs find this odor, they dig into the ground.
10. Risky as extreme sports are, many people enjoy them.

三、句子重組

11. In spite of his interest in languages, Ian decided to major in computer science in college.
12. Whatever the strange man said, nobody believed him.
13. Comedian as William is, he had an unhappy childhood.
14. Even if the arrogant woman makes a mistake, she won't admit it.

四、翻譯

15. Despite
16. In spite of; that
17. whenever
18. even though we have turned down the radio
19. Even if Jimmy washes and polishes his car carefully
20. However hard/No matter how hard they tried, they couldn't change Johnny's mind.

TEST 16

一、選擇

1. B   2. B   3. A   4. D   5. D   6. C

二、句子改寫

7. The boy creates a study schedule lest he (should) fail the final exams.
8. Lucas was suspended from school because of his involvement in street fights.
9. The vendor raised her voice so that she could be heard.
10. It is so hot that I can't help drinking much ice water.

三、文意選填

11. in order to
12. for fear of
13. as long as
14. Now that
15. and

四、翻譯

16. so that
17. Because of poor management

18. lest she (should) bump into trees
19. Now that Mr. and Mrs. Wang have retired
20. Teddy sealed the envelope lest his letter be read by others.

TEST 17

一、選擇

1. D   2. A   3. C   4. B   5. C   6. B   7. B

二、句子改寫

8. Rita never tells lies without stuttering.
9. The sick girl ran too slowly to keep up with her classmates.
10. the designer can't be too creative in designing his new products
11. Bikinis are the last suit that this shy girl would wear.

三、配合題

12. B   13. C   14. D   15. A

四、翻譯

16. without seeing him using his smartphone
17. can't; too; can't; enough
18. the last thing that this little girl would like to do
19. It goes without saying that God helps those who help themselves.
20. The man who is waiting for a job interview feels too anxious to eat anything.

TEST 18

一、選擇

1. C   2. D   3. B   4. C

二、句子改寫

5. is it visited by tourists
6. can the color red draw people's attention, but it can (also) make people feel warm
7. lie numerous mysterious fairy circles
8. Mr. Franklin was 65 did he retire

三、填空題

9. does   10. did   11. were   12. was   13. is

四、翻譯

14. are many presents
15. Not only are
16. is the car cheap but it also feels good to drive
17. should government officials take bribes
18. this man talked to me did I notice his British accent
19. it got dark could we see the moon clearly

20. This decision is too difficult for Mandy to make. Never has she been so confused.

TEST 19

一、選擇
1. A 2. D 3. B 4. B 5. C

二、句子改寫

6. Owls catch their prey with their strong hooked bills, and so do hawks.
7. Nina can't speak English fluently, nor can her husband.
8. Hamlet found what his uncle had done when he decided to take revenge on him
9. through experience and challenges can wisdom be gained
10. stubborn is Miriam that no one wants to work with her

三、填空題

11. are 12. should 13. had 14. did 15. are

四、翻譯

16. hasn't; has
17. nor
18. can you achieve your goal
19. No sooner had the boss entered the office
20. So organized is Janet that she can always finish her work in time.

TEST 20

一、選擇
1. B 2. C 3. A 4. C 5. D 6. B

二、改錯

7. A; let
8. C; like brick
9. B; regarded as
10. B; wash
11. A; How

三、配合題

12. B 13. C 14. A 15. D

四、翻譯

16. What a brilliant idea
17. How creative these students are!
18. was considered fashionable
19. Matilda has her son listen to English radio programs
20. The man wearing glasses and holding several books looks knowledgeable.

FUN&LEARNING

✦ **完整20回：**
  按全書章節分類編排，複習句型一句不漏！

✦ **題型多元：**
  以各種題型反覆練習，文法概念穩扎穩打！

✦ **鑑往知來：**
  加入歷屆大考相關題，熟悉文法考題趨勢！